The Virginia Exiles

The Virginia Exiles
Second Edition with Foreword by Margaret Hope Bacon Printed in 2002

Printed in the United States of America
10 9 8 7 6 5 4 3 2 1

ISBN No. 0-941308-10-3

The Virginia Exiles

*The American Revolution tests Quaker principles
in this romantic novel by*

Elizabeth Gray Vining

PHILADELPHIA YEARLY MEETING OF THE RELIGIOUS SOCIETY OF FRIENDS

FOREWORD

FIRST PUBLISHED IN 1955, *The Virginia Exiles* by Elizabeth Gray Vining, is as fresh and as pertinent to our times as it was forty-six years ago. In the lively narrative prose she had perfected writing for young people, Elizabeth Vining tells the story of the seventeen Quakers who were exiled in 1777 to Winchester, Virginia for refusing to take a loyalty to oath to the newly created United States of America. To bolster their claim that the Quakers were disloyal, the Continental Congress used a manifestly forged document, the minutes of a non-existent Spanktown Yearly Meeting, which asked Friends to gather information to pass on to the British army. Given no hearing in which to defend themselves against the imputed charge of infidelity, without trial or the chance to consult lawyers—in violation of habeas corpus, the seventeen were treated roughly, forced to pay their own board and room, and housed in primitive conditions. Having been taken from their homes with no time to pack, they were not prepared for the rigors of a harsh winter. Two of their number died. Finally released after nine months of confinement, they were never given an opportunity to be heard in an open trial.

Elizabeth Vining has told this story with fidelity to the historic record. In order to make it a work of fiction she substituted one imaginary character, Caleb Middleton, for a real one. This enabled her to address the dilemmas which a young Friend of the period faced, his sympathy with the American cause against his allegiance to the peace testimony of Friends, his desire to please his iron-master father by following in his footsteps against his own clear leading toward a career in medicine, his need for action against the apparent passivity of standing aside. Through Caleb's eyes we see the variety within the Society of Friends of the period; from the wealthy Pembertons to poor cabinet

makers; from the nominal Friends to deeply committed ones such as
John Hunt, who died in Winchester.

Despite public suspicion, very few Friends were loyalists during
the American Revolution. Many of the Quaker merchants had supported the concept of boycotting British goods, a non-violent method
which might have in time caused the British to feel it was not worth-
while to hang on to the colonies, as they decided finally about India.
But some Friends, like Timothy Matlack, Nathaniel Greene and
Thomas Mifflin, left the Society at this time in order to fight under
General George Washington. Altogether only six Friends were disowned for joining the British forces, while between four and five hundred were expelled for fighting in the Revolutionary Army.

In the 1750s, Friends had begun to withdraw from the government
of Pennsylvania because they could no longer in good conscience support the British crown's demand for funds to support arms to fight the
French and the Indians. This crisis of conscience had awakened a re-
forming spirit within the Society of Friends, which began in the
American colonies and eventually spread to Great Britain. John
Woolman was one of a hundred or more ministers who took part in
this reformation. These traveling ministers urged Friends to adopt a
more withdrawn and spirit-directed life, as well as to rid themselves of
slave-owning, and to turn their attention to such reforms as better
prison conditions and better relations with the Native Americans.

Quakerism was therefore in flux at the time of the American Revolution. Elizabeth Vining manages to sketch in much of this back-
ground without losing her narrative thread. She has also drawn a
careful picture of Philadelphia at that period, its cobblestone streets,
its mansions along the waterfront, its coffee houses and public buildings, its bustling shambles and sedate Quaker meeting houses. One
cannot help but admire the careful research which went into the telling of this tale.

There is a sweet love story, as Caleb turns from his attraction to-
wards a flirtatious married woman, to a beautiful backwoods Quaker
maid with a talent for nursing. And there is mention—though not
quite as much, I think, as the story deserves—of the intervention of
four Philadelphia Quaker women, under the leadership of Elizabeth

Drinker, who traveled to Lancaster to lobby the Continental Congress for the release of the exiles.

Though *The Virginia Exiles* was very successful, Elizabeth Vining was never quite content with it, feeling the historical event had more profound consequences than a novel could convey. By 1977, at the two hundredth anniversary of the sending of the exiles to Virginia, she had reworked the story completely as a work not of fiction but of meticulously researched history. She spoke from this new version at the annual meeting of the Friends Historical Association. Unfortunately, her publisher, J. B. Lippincott, was in a state of flux at the time she submitted this manuscript and both the original and carbon copy were somehow lost in transition.

While historians mourn the loss of that second version, Philadelphia Yearly Meeting feels privileged to have the novel to reprint to bring the dilemmas of the time to the attention of another generation. In her autobiography, *A Quiet Pilgrimage*, Elizabeth Vining wrote that she decided to tell the story of the Virginia exiles at a time (1948–1954) when the United States was convulsed with what came to be called McCarthyism—teachers and government employees were being confronted with the necessity of taking loyalty oaths in order to prove themselves innocent of treachery. In that period, as in 1777, many Quakers decided that they should not comply. As a result they suffered unjust imprisonment or job loss, and some even decided that they must go into exile. Elizabeth Vining reminds us that the price of liberty is eternal vigilance.

MARGARET HOPE BACON
November 2001

PREFACE

THE LITTLE-KNOWN EPISODE in American history on which this novel is based is a matter of record. I have taken no liberties with the facts of the arrest, imprisonment, banishment, and return of the twenty Philadelphians. For the purposes of my story, however, I have removed one of the original exiles, Owen Jones, junior, and substituted an imaginary character, Caleb Middleton, junior. A list of the actual exiles is given below.

A note on the "plain language" of the Quakers may be helpful. At the time of the story a transition was taking place from the "thou" of the 17th century to the "thee" which is used by modern Quakers for all cases, subject or object. Even the grammatical older Friends, however, tended to slip into the use of the third person verb with the *thou* instead of the correct second person, e.g., Thou was, Thou said, Thou has.

THE EXILES

Thomas Affleck, cabinetmaker
Elijah Brown, merchant, father of Charles Brockden Brown,
   America's first novelist
Henry Drinker, merchant
Charles Eddy, ironmonger
Miers Fisher, lawyer
Samuel Fisher, merchant
Thomas Fisher, merchant
Thomas Gilpin, merchant
John Hunt, merchant
Charles Jervis, merchant
Owen Jones, junior, merchant

Israel Pemberton, merchant
James Pemberton, merchant
John Pemberton, concerned Friend, who lived on inherited income
    and devoted his life to the affairs of the Yearly Meeting
Edward Penington, merchant
Thomas Pike, fencing and dancing master
Samuel Pheasants, merchant
William Smith, broker
William Drewet Smith, apothecary
Thomas Wharton, merchant

I

THE TWO CALEB MIDDLETONS, father and son, walked together up the hill from the Phoebe Ann Furnace to the Big House. The heart of the son was hot with rebellion. He opened his mouth to protest once more.

"Not now, Caleb," his father anticipated him, raising his hand in the familiar, pompous gesture for silence. "Later, perhaps. But the decision is made. I have told the officer and he has gone. I have told our men."

"Does it make no difference at all what I think?" cried Caleb. "Or what I've heard in the city?"

He had ridden from Philadelphia that day in early August, 1777, full of the news that was pouring through the coffee houses and taverns like water through a sluice. Though he had sent his horse on to the stable by a boy, he was still in his dusty riding clothes, hot and tired, but conscious only of his feelings of outrage and revolt and his swollen thoughts.

"I told thee, I don't want to talk about it any further now. After supper. I have to save my breath to climb the hill, if thou doesn't. These things are not easy at my age."

The old appeal of age to the chivalry of youth! Caleb angrily brushed it aside. But I have had a great blow! he wanted to shout. This is a monstrous thing that has been done! I share in the work of the furnace, I should share in the decisions. I won't sit down under arbitrary pronouncements! The tyranny of the king and the tyranny of his father seemed to be two branches of the same smothering growth and he wanted to resist both. But the knowledge of the respect due to a father lay on him like the lid on a seething pot and kept him silent, scowling and slapping his boot with his riding crop.

He had known soon after he turned off the Great Road that the furnace was out of blast, for where normally he would have begun to hear its intermittent roar he had heard only the chatter of a yellowthroat in the undergrowth, the rustle of the wind in the tall trees overhead, and the other light sounds of the summer afternoon woods. He had been surprised and disappointed but not especially disturbed, since they sometimes had to shut down for a while in the summer when the water in the creek was low.

But when he had come out of the woods into the open valley where the village clustered around the furnace and the Big House on the hill brooded over all, he knew at once that something was wrong. The women who normally would have been off working in the fields at this time gathered around the doors of the tenant houses, talking, while the small children, sensing as children will the trouble of their elders, hung around their skirts instead of playing. Through the open doors of the wheelwright's shop and the smithy men could be seen with their heads together. The furnace at the end of the road was silent and deserted, no wagons hauling ore or charcoal up to the bank, no men running over the bridge to the tunnel-head with baskets and barrows, no voices from the casting shed, no roar from the cold stack.

At the square stone building across the road from the stack, Caleb had dismounted, hailed a passing boy and told him to take Ladybird up to the stable, and had gone inside to find out what had happened, expecting to hear of some serious accident to men or machinery. The store where the workmen and their families came to buy groceries and drygoods and other supplies was empty, but in the office beyond he had found his father and Jacob Heinzel, the iron founder. From them he had learned with shocking abruptness the thing that had been done.

The Phoebe Ann Furnace had been shut down for as long as the war should continue. No more iron would be made there until peace was restored. The forty-odd workmen—founders, keepers, fillers, gutterers, colliers, and the rest—would scatter. The Middletons, as soon as they could get off, would move into Philadelphia, to their house on Third Street. Caleb himself was to devote his time to the store and warehouse in the city and to the management of the real estate that had come into the family with Sarah Leigh Middleton, his stepmother. He had been away a little less than a week, on business for the furnace, and in his absence this high-handed and, to Caleb, unworthy action had been taken.

They climbed a shallow flight of stone steps from the driveway to the broad terrace in front of the house and paused automatically in the usual spot to look at the view. Caleb waited for his father to clear his throat and say, "A fair prospect, a very fair prospect." Although he braced himself for the well-worn words as if for a blow, made irritable by the turmoil within him, he was perversely disappointed when they did not come. His father only sighed and clasped his hands behind his broad back.

It was a fair prospect. Two towering buttonwood trees, left from the original forest, shaded the terrace. They were shedding now, their bark falling away in big flakes, leaving the surface of the upper trunks and limbs pale yellow and smooth as a peeled onion. Below the terrace was the garden which Caleb's own mother had made and loved, enclosed with English box and bright now with pinks and lilies. From the garden the ground fell away to the meadow below, where the creek cut its curves through rich grass, and rose again patterned with fields tawny with wheat stubble or green with corn to the line of plumy woods on the top of the southern hills. To the east, close under the knoll on which the Big House stood and partly hidden by trees, were the massed roofs of furnace and village. Up the hill behind the house and westward, the thousands of acres of woodland upon which the hungry furnace depended for its charcoal supply were a great shawl around the shoulders of the valley.

The Phoebe Ann Furnace, situated on Parson's Creek, a tributary of French Creek, was one of a number of ironworks hidden away among the hills behind the Schuylkill. Each plantation was a little world unto itself. It had its own mine hole and three or four miners to dig the ore out of the ground, its own share of the limestone that lay everywhere under the soil of this country; each had a small troop of woodcutters and colliers to provide the charcoal which was needed in enormous quantities. A furnace the size of the Phoebe Ann devoured the product of an acre or more of woods for every twenty-four hours that it was in blast. Each plantation had its farm and often its gristmill, its gardens and orchards, workshops, barns, store, and millpond. The men lived in the tenant houses in the village; their wives worked in the fields at seedtime and harvest, and in winter carded, spun, and wove the wool from the sheep. Overlooking all was the Big House on the hill, where the ironmaster lived, the feudal lord of his small community. The great wagons drawn by three mule teams that took the pig iron to the forges or over the rutted roads to Philadelphia and its wharves, brought back necessities for the workmen and luxuries for the ironmaster and his family, English china and silver, Turkish carpets, French silks, and Indian muslins.

Caleb had had other plans for himself than to succeed his father at the Phoebe Ann; but when, five years ago at seventeen, in obedience to Mr. Middleton's demand, he had put aside his desire to become a doctor, he had made a good second best of being an ironmaster. Though he had not chosen the furnace he had grown to love it and the drama of it: the fire against the sky at night, the pulsing roar, the fillers like ants crossing the bridge from the bank to the tunnel-head with their baskets of ore and limestone and charcoal and running back for more, the big water wheel turning slowly and the great bellows forcing the air into the crucible, the tension mounting till the moment came when the decision must be made to tap. Twice a day the climax came, yet it was ever new. A shrill blast on the horn brought the men running, the dam stone was pulled away and the molten iron came pouring forth in a fiery red flood, filling the sand molds of the casting bed, called the sow and pigs, or being ladled into the molds for hollow ware. He liked seeing the wagons go off loaded with pig iron for the forges in the vicinity, Mount Joy and Vincent and Warwick, where it would be reheated and hammered and refined. He liked riding over the wooded hills, inspecting the charcoal pits, deciding which stand of trees to cut next. Hickory made the best charcoal, but oak and chestnut were good too. He enjoyed his association with the men, Jacob Heinzel the chief founder and Mac Murchison his assistant, the Negro freedmen who worked as woodcutters, the Welsh miners, and the others. As Caleb had developed in experience and skill, his father had more and more withdrawn from active work into the office where, warmed on cold days by a tenplate stove cast on the place, he was busy with orders and accounts and the contents of the wall safe behind the chestnut paneling.

The news that the furnace was to be shut down permanently and that Caleb was to exchange his active life here for all the petty niggling details of a city countinghouse had come like a thunderclap. For the second time he saw the course in life on which he had set his feet threatened by the arbitrary decision of his father, and this time he did not intend to submit tamely.

"The men!" he burst out. "They'll only go to oilier furnaces, where they'll snap them up. If we let them go now, we'll never get them back. Or," he added pointedly, "they'll enlist in the militia."

His voice betrayed him. What was to have been a cool, ironic thrust came out like the growl of a sulky boy. Though he was almost twenty-three and a man in the eyes of the world, at home he was still a boy under his father's thumb. His smoldering anger tamed in upon himself.

"They must follow their own consciences," said Mr. Middleton calmly. "Jacob is a Mennonite—he feels as we do. He'll go back to his father's farm beyond Lancaster. The others will have to follow the light as God gives it to them—if they pay any attention, which I doubt, some of them at least. At any rate I must do what I think is right."

"But what about me?"

"Thou art a Friend, Caleb. Friends do not take part in war or in any work that is preparation for war."

Though his father used the plain language still, he was actually no longer a Friend. Four years ago his Monthly Meeting had disowned him for marrying out of union. Sarah Leigh was an Episcopalian. But still he spoke to his children in the Quaker way, still thought as a Quaker.

"Some Friends;" Caleb strove for a voice that should sound reasonable and mature, "have felt it right to resist tyranny." Almost all the other Pennsylvania ironmasters were making iron for the Continental army, and some of them were Quakers. Even if one could not conscientiously make cannon and cannon balls, pig iron was still in demand at the forges, which were turning out necessities for the army. Firebacks and cooking pots and stove plates might wait for the coming of peace, but salt pans were essential now. "Liberty, thee knows, is also an ancient testimony of Friends."

"There's a great deal of loose talk about tyranny and liberty going around. I told thee, Caleb, I don't want to discuss it now. Shall we go in? I think thy mother is waiting for us."

Caleb pulled a seed pod off a tall spire of dark red hollyhock that grew beside the door and pulled it apart with his thin, sinewy fingers—surgeon's fingers, he had thought once. Sarah Middleton was a good woman, but he would never call her mother.

"I'll be along in a little while," he said. "I want to see if Amos has rubbed down Ladybird properly."

For the first time since they had left the office and started up the hill he looked at his father squarely. His color was bad, almost gray, and the lines that went from his nostrils to the corners of his mouth were deeply etched; his cheeks sagged into his neck. He was sixty-four and he looked older.

"Thee feeling all right?" said Caleb, but the question, of its implications, was only an irritant, and they parted without further words.

As soon as he was inside the stableyard a kind of peace fell upon Caleb, the familiar soothing spell of the place, compounded of the smell of horses and manure, of trampled dirt in the sunshine and mossy stone walls in the shade, the sound of harness jingling, Amos' breathy whistle, the splashing of water into the trough or the whinny of a horse, and partly of the feeling of a safe enclosure that shut out irrelevancies and protected the busy concentrated life that went on within. Perhaps, he thought, as the cords within him loosened and his natural hopefulness asserted itself, perhaps it was too soon to give up. He and his father would talk again after supper, and a way would open. The men had not gone yet. The blowing-in of a furnace after it had been out of blast was tedious, but not much time would be lost.

A girl's laugh, shrill and taunting, cut across the peaceful sounds of the place, followed by a boy's enraged howl.

"I'll smash thy nose, Patty, thee skunk thee!"

From behind the cribhouse Caleb's sister Patty came running, and close behind her, red-faced and furious, his little brother Edward.

"Caleb, save me!" screamed Patty, flinging her arms around his waist and cowering behind him with a show of panic.

He scooped up Edward as he came by, and holding him, kicking and yelling, upside down under his arm, turned to look down at Patty. "What did thee do to him?" he asked.

"I didn't do *anything*! Did thee hear what he called me? And he said he'd smash my nose!"

"Thee's got a black smudge all across that noble organ. Thee'd better go and wash thy face."

She had their father's Roman nose, china blue eyes, slightly stupid, and an arrogant tilt to her tow-colored head. She was a tall, handsome girl, Caleb thought. She hadn't the kind of beauty that appealed to him, but she'd take some man in some day, and it was to be hoped for his sake that he wouldn't be the thin-skinned kind, for Patty walked where she pleased and she neither knew nor cared whose feelings she was stepping on. Not that that gave Edward license to call her a skunk.

He carried the wriggling small boy to the rain barrel, which was full, and with a swift movement reversed him quickly and dipped him in, giving his posterior a smart spank as he set him on his feet again. "That'll cool thee off—and warm thee up," he said, grinning, and turned to go into the stable.

Wiping his wet face with his sleeve and pushing his hair out of his eyes, Edward followed close on Caleb's heels, pleased on the whole by his big brother's attention.

Caroline Rutter, whom his father admired so much, thought Caleb, was just such another one as Patty, and he didn't like and never would like that fair, florid, Amazonish type, however subtly and persuasively she might be suggested to him. A very different little face, seldom far from his thoughts these days, swam into his mind, so vividly that he could almost see it dancing like the motes in the shaft of sunshine in the dim stable. It was a heart-shaped face, brown-eyed and piquant, with a patch at the corner of the red, moist mouth, calling attention to the pouting lower lip, and a powdered curl against the smooth white neck calling attention to the soft white hills of her bosom. Phyllis. "Phyllis is my only joy . . . Phyllis smiling and beguiling . . ." Phyllis—Pike. Mistress Thomas Pike, the wife of the dancing master.

Ladybird was in her box, eating the oats she had so fully earned. She tossed her head when she saw Caleb and snorted. He ran his hand over her neck. It was dry but he thought she ought to have the thin blanket.

"Amos! A-mos!"

He saw Edward there beside him. "Go find Amos and tell him to put a light blanket on Ladybird."

"Caleb, thee don't know what happened day before yesterday. Some soldiers came and took all the blankets for the army. They took all the ones in the chest, even the best blankets from England, and all the horse blankets."

"Where did they come from?"

"From Reading. How'll we keep warm next winter?"

"Oh, thee can't expect to keep warm. Thee'll have to stay up all night flapping thy arms around thee like the teamsters. There are some old blankets in the harness room. Tell Amos he's to find something."

Whistling the catchy song which had spread through the colonies, "By uniting we stand, by dividing we fall," Caleb crossed the stableyard and went on to the house. His progress as usual took on something of the air of a procession. Horace, the bound boy, ran ahead of him to his room with a brass can of hot water. Hettie, the broad-beamed cook, who had obviously been watching for him, emerged from the kitchen with offers of fresh buttermilk. In the back hall, which was cool and shady, he was met by Sarah Middleton.

She was a markedly homely woman, broad of frame and short of stature, with small eyes, heavy, plain features, and dark hairs on her upper lip and chin. Caleb, to whom beauty in a woman was not an adornment but the indispensable minimum, would have regarded her as a negligible element in the household, had he not been reminded a dozen times a day by the children's acceptance of her that she was the successor to his own lovely mother. That Sarah was strong and warmhearted, generous and quite without conceit, his mind acknowledged, but his heart, sore and jealous because the marriage had come so soon after his mother's death, still was closed against her.

"Caleb, I'm glad you're back," she said. "We've had such a time! I'm anxious about your father. He gets so excited over these people and it's not good for him. Be as soothing as you can, won't you? And Tacy fell down and scraped her knee. It ought to be dressed, but she won't let Sukie or me touch it. She insists you must do it for her."

Tacy, the small sister who had cost his mother her life, was his pet and his darling. He found her upstairs sitting on her nurse's lap, her round face streaked with tears, her brown eyes swimming, her wounded leg stuck out stiffly in front of her.

"Fix it," she commanded regally, with a hiccup.

He bent over and gravely examined the skinned and bloody knee, in which bits of gravel were buried. "It's all dirty," he said. "I'll wash it for thee and then I'll give thee a big bandage. How 'bout that?"

She nodded a little apprehensively, and he held out his arms to her. "Come on, let's go out into the hall."

He lifted her up, and she twined her arms tight around his neck, pressed her fat, damp cheek against his and gave him a wet kiss. Kissing the tip of her nose, he blinked his eyes quickly to tickle her face with his eyelashes in the special ritual that they had. She gave a sweet, delighted crow of laughter and he hugged her tight before he set her down carefully on the broad window sill, where the light was good.

The wide, second story hall, which ran the full depth of the house, was furnished with chairs and a sofa and the blanket chest. Between the two windows on the north was a big walnut secretary where stores of medicines were kept.

Mrs. Middleton brought the key and opened the door. On the shelves were jars of manna and senna and rhubarb preparations, opodeldoc and dried roseleaves, camomile and mint, bottles of laudanum and castor oil and Daffy's Elixir, bark both whole and ground, boxes of lint and tolls of old linen, little pots of deer suet and goose grease. Never a day passed on an iron plantation that someone did not come to the mistress for treatment.

It was an important occasion when Caleb officiated. Patty and Edward pressed close to watch, Patty ostentatiously holding her nose as Edward approached. Caleb took off his coat, handing it to Edward to hold, and rolled up his shirt sleeves; he washed his hands carefully in the basin held by Horace, then motioned for him to fill a bowl with fresh water.

"I saw thy nephew in Philadelphia," he told Tacy, dipping a wad of lint in the warm water and gently touching it to the dried blood and gravel on her knee. She whimpered. "Look at what comes off on the lint! He's a fine, big, saucy boy for his age, but he needs thee to teach him manners. Hold still, sweetie, if thee can. I know it stings. I thought it a little remiss of him not to inquire about his Aunt Tacy, but no doubt he will when—that's a good girl, just a little more—no doubt he will when he learns to speak."

For all her woe, this brought a brief flicker of a smile to Tacy's face, and he took advantage of the moment's distraction to swab a raw place that he had not yet dared touch. She shrieked and kicked.

"Shall I hold her?" offered Patty officiously.

They were all reminded of the harrowing time when Tacy had put part of a walnut shell up her nose and three people had had to pinion her while the doctor took it out with a silver hook. The suggestion was an unfortunate one. Tacy howled.

"Certainly not;" said Caleb. "Tacy is a brave girl. She'll hold herself." He removed Patty by planting an elbow in her stomach and pushing.

"Come on, Tace, just one more little bit and then I'll put some ointment on and a bandage and give thee the present I brought thee from Philadelphia. Can thee guess what it is?"

He worked swiftly, absorbed in what he was doing. Tall, broad-shouldered, narrow-hipped and muscular, he looked smart even in his travel-worn riding breeches, limp white cambric shirt and rolled-up sleeves. His hair, bright chestnut-brown with a natural wave, was brushed back from his forehead and tied in a fashion symbolic, to strict Quakers, of the society world. He had brown eyes, deep set and wide apart, a straight nose, flaring at the nostrils, a well-cut mouth, and a firm chin, delicately square. He was capable of great concentration, as now, when he was perhaps at his most attractive, capable also of hot rage and petulance, as well as humor and sudden bursts of gaiety.

"You're moody," his stepmother had said more than once. "It spoils you."

He knew that he never showed his best to her, though sometimes, he acknowledged reluctantly, she seemed to see more than she was shown.

"There!" he exclaimed, tucking in the end of an impressive bandage. "Thee's finished. And Sukie can fetch the package out of my saddlebag. . . . John goes to join his regiment next week," he said to Mrs. Middleton over his shoulder as he tidily folded linen and put away the jar of salve, "but first he's going to take Sue and little John to his parents in Lancaster. It seems to be generally expected that Howe will take Philadelphia and that Washington will not be able to prevent him."

She made no answer. They were alone in the hall now, for Edward and Patty had trailed along with Tacy to get the package out of Caleb's bag. "You ought to have been a doctor," she said impulsively. "It's still not too late. I could help you—if you want it."

She had come too close. They both knew it at once. He bowed slightly in the formal way he had picked up somewhere and said, "Thank you, ma'am. I am quite content with being an ironmaster."

"Well, never mind," she answered. "Thank you for tending to Tacy."

Frowning, he went into his own room and chased the children out.

"I will not have my son become a man-midwife," his father had declared, and in the end Caleb had yielded, after fruitlessly pointing to Dr. Shippen as an example of a distinguished physician who had saved the life of many an anguished woman without losing either his dignity or other people's respect.

Of the ten children Caleb's mother had borne, five had died in infancy—three little girls hopefully named for her, one after another, and two boys—and of the tenth, who came feet first, she herself had died, in torture. He picked up the miniature which Charlie Peale had painted when he first came back from England, and looked at it. Even then, at forty, a few months before her death, she had still been beautiful. The miniature caught something of the tenderness and humor in her brown eyes, but it was too stiff, too conventionally pretty, too limited by its paint and its ivory, even to suggest the luminous quality of her spirit, which had shone through her worn body as if it had been transparent.

II

AFTER SUPPER CALEB AND his father sat on the terrace in the twilight.
Mrs. Middleton hovered about protesting that the night vapors were
unhealthy and urging them to come into the parlor, but they remained
determinedly oblivious to her.

"I might be a fly for all the attention you pay to me," she complained.

She drew up a chair for herself, scraping its legs across the flagstones, and for a time she sat with them, slapping at mosquitoes and
inserting cheerful remarks into the conversation, until by an impatient twitch of the shoulder, a loud "harrumph!" and the pointed use
of short silences followed by some such phrase as, "I was about to say,"
or, "To go back to thy observation," her husband made it plain to her
that her presence was not required.

She retired in good order, with a mumbled exclamation that gave
them to understand she had recollected a duty elsewhere. Restored to
politeness once they had won their point, both rose punctiliously
when she left, and Caleb went to open the door for her. She mouthed a
silent message to him behind his father's back, "Don't keep him up
late!" The barrier between son and father thinned a little in the momentary warmth of masculine solidarity as they both felt the relief of
having routed the female intrusion.

Caleb knew that his father in his day had changed the direction of
his life in obedience to parental wish, and he wondered why the memory of it had not given him more understanding. Or had he accepted
long ago and never since examined the premise that the fact of father-
hood endowed a man with a supernatural knowledge of what was best
far his children?

Caleb's grandfather, youngest son of a yeoman in Northamptonshire, had come to Philadelphia just before 1700, had won himself a lucky foothold as a merchant, and prospered; he had become a Quaker and married the daughter of an elder in the Bank Meeting. When his third son, Caleb, was old enough, he had been apprenticed to his mother's brother, who had a small fleet of ships in the English trade. He had liked his work, tinged as it was with the drama of the sea; he had had one voyage to London and was looking forward to another, when his father become aware of the profits to be made from the iron industry developing in the Pennsylvania hills and bought a half interest in a furnace newly established on Parson's Creek. Following the fashion of giving women's names to iron furnaces, the owner, Richard Ross, had called it Phoebe for his wife and Ann for his daughter.

The satisfactory business relationship between Mr. Ross and Mr. Middleton resulted in the marriage of Caleb and Ann. Almost at once, in one of those small, sporadic but deadly epidemics of yellow fever, Caleb had lost his wife, his unborn child, and his father-in-law—and acquired the other half of the Phoebe Ann. He had intended to put a manager in to run the furnace which he and his father now owned jointly and to continue in the shipping business which he loved. Instead he found himself headed for the backwoods, with a new trade to master and a wholly new life to live. Whatever anguish of grief and loneliness he endured during those first years on Parson's Creek, he never spoke about it in later life.

He was thirty-seven when, strong, handsome, wearing the cloak of his ironmaster's authority, he went to Philadelphia to the bedside of his dying father and while in the city met Margaret Penington. The seventeen years between them had disappeared in the springing flame of their love, and when he returned to the Phoebe Ann he took his young wife with him. It had been a happy marriage, in spite of the recurrent toll of child-bearing and child-loss. Young Caleb could remember a golden time when there was laughter and tenderness in the house, and his father had seemed to him the embodiment of bravery, goodness, and wisdom.

Looking at his father now, while in the meadow below fireflies rose and gleamed in an endless slow ascension, Caleb felt a softening of his resentment, even as his determination not to be overborne stiffened.

"I've never seen the lightning bugs fly so high as they are doing this year," commented Mr. Middleton, apparently reluctant, even with Sarah safely in the house where she could not interrupt, to open the subject that lay before them.

"Washington was in Philadelphia while I was there," said Caleb. "I caught a glimpse of him going into Robert Morris's. They say he came to meet the young French marquis who is so enthusiastic. Nobody knows exactly where the British fleet is. Every day there's a different rumor. It was seen at the entrance to the Delaware Bay, but some say it went away again. Baltimore may be in danger, but most people think that Philadelphia is the real goal. Many people are evacuating. They are looking for just what we have here, a substantial house in the country off the main roads."

"Why are they all so eager to leave the city?"

"Most patriots don't want to be there when the British troops occupy it."

"I have nothing to fear from the British. On the other hand I have already experienced the depredations of the Continentals. Men who said they were from the Quartermaster General were here day before yesterday requisitioning blankets. They offered money—a ridiculous sum for imported English blankets. I refused to accept it. I'll not sell my blankets for purposes of war."

"So they took them anyhow."

"Yes, but not with my consent. Yesterday two officers came—in military uniform—also from the Quartermaster General. They brought an agreement for me to sign—so many cannons each month, so many balls, so many salt pans. Twenty-five tons a week. We've never cast more than twenty. But I'm to make a prodigious patriotic effort and produce twenty-five. He didn't say where we were to get the charcoal from. It would take six thousand cords of wood a year at that rate. But that's beside the point."

"Thee gave them a final refusal?"

"I did. They offered to argue, but I convinced them it was useless. But there will be more like them, now that they've found the way here and see what we have. That is why I determined to shut down altogether and clear out for the city."

"But, Father, isn't there a middle course? Thee and thy wife and the children go into Philadelphia, while I stay here and run the furnace. Then both of our consciences will be satisfied. I can't think it right to—"

"No, no, it's out of the question. I won't hear to it."

"I understand how thee feels about munitions of war. I don't agree in the circumstances, but if I honor thy scruples, if I make only pig iron and salt pans—no cannon—I think I can satisfy them with that much." He felt rather than saw the upraised hand in the dim light and rushed on. "I can't sit down tamely and do nothing, when the whole question of freedom and oppression is at stake! After all, it was thy wish that I should learn to make iron, and now thee'd prevent me from using that knowledge for my country's benefit."

"Be silent, Caleb. I want to talk to thee about the present commotions. Thou refers, doubtless, to the fact that thou wanted to enroll in the Medical College and I prevailed upon thee to do otherwise. Thou hast in mind, no doubt, whether thou knows it or not, that all fathers are oppressive and that England stands in a father's relation to America. But put aside thy private grievance and consider the facts in the public situation. I agree that the proceedings of the British ministry have been unjust. I am—and I have been—willing to join in peaceful legal resistance. But Friends—and in this I am still a Friend—have always been opposed to war and revolution. We cannot give allegiance to a revolutionary government any more than we could assist Britain in her unrighteous methods of conquering the rebellious provinces. I intend to maintain a position of strict neutrality. To supply the Continentals with material directly or indirectly used for war purposes would be to enlist on their side."

"Friends have taken literally Christ's injunction not to resist evil," said Caleb, borrowing an argument from William Penn's secretary a generation earlier, "but they seem to prefer to forget that he also said, Lay not up for yourselves treasures upon earth."

"That line of reasoning implies that if we disobey one of our Lord's commands we must disobey all. It is trivial and foolish, if not downright wicked. There is another, a very practical aspect. I have been to England, thou hast not. Thou hast not seen the might of England.

Thou sees Philadelphia, a large and prosperous city, but it is the only one of its proportions on this continent. How can thirteen scattered and feeble colonies, jealous of one another, prevail against the might and power of England?"

"But they *are* united—united in a common hatred of oppression, united by interest and faith, and if thee wants more concrete bonds, by a Continental Congress and a common army."

"My dear boy, Pennsylvania itself is not united. It is torn between the Quaker element in the east, with the Germans in their train, and the self-willed and militant Scotch-Irish frontiersmen in the west. Those violent men of the frontier would change the whole order of civilized life as we have known it—just as they have thrown out the good charter that William Penn gave us and have illegally set up their so-called Constitution with a Supreme Executive Council instead of a governor. But that's not all. They cannot possibly defeat Britain in an armed contest. We have no manufactures—"

"We have iron."

"A mere handful of forges and furnaces. We cannot make cloth for soldiers' uniforms or boots for their feet in quantity sufficient for an army of any size. We have no sea power. We are at the mercy of an army with a fleet that can move at will from Boston to New York to Philadelphia or to Charleston while Washington wonders helplessly where it will strike next."

He spoke as a man knowing life and the world to an ignorant boy. His tone, kindly in a condescending way, explanatory and slightly amused, galled Caleb into fury. With unsparing eyes, young and scornful and dear, he saw his father moved as much by the fear of being on the wrong side in a losing fight as by conscientious objection to munition-making. Despising caution as the meanest of motives, Caleb had moreover knowledge of the strength of the American cause that his father did not have, a knowledge that was part of his young bones and spirit, the product of the very air of the age in which he lived and to which his mind was open, derived not so much from what he heard his contemporaries say as what he saw and felt in men's gestures and faces and the tone of their voices, that revealed their purpose and their will and their vision.

"So now," he said bitterly, "we are to slink off to Philadelphia and leave the Phoebe Ann shut down behind us. Has thee thought it might be—probably will be—confiscated and that other men will make iron for the American cause if we don't?"

"Perhaps. But in the end, when this is all over, we shall recover it."

Caleb jumped to his feet. "But I shan't stay in Philadelphia," he cried, "because I can't agree to this—"

His father rose too. "Caleb, don't be overhasty—" His voice trailed off into silence.

For a moment he stood there as if bewildered, before he pitched forward, fuming as he fell, to lie stretched full length upon his back. Caleb's first thought as he leaped forward and knelt beside him, was relief that he had fallen on the grass instead of the flagstones. As he bent over his father's inert body, thrusting his hand into the bosom of his shirt in search of the heartbeat, he saw that the right side of the ashen face had slipped, so that it no longer matched the left. But even while his startled mind registered the fact and whispered to him the word "stroke," he saw the twisted features relax and consciousness slowly return. The pale, slightly bloodshot eyes opened and the blue lips moved.

"I'm all right," said his father with reassuring testiness. "Don't make a fuss. Help me up."

Caleb put his arm under his father's shoulders. Strong as he was, he had all he could do to pull the old man to his feet. Breathing hard, both of them, they stood together, swaying a little, at the edge of the terrace. Swiftly a squat figure emerged from the house and took Mr. Middleton's other arm.

"Lean on me, my dear," said Sarah. "Take it slowly. We'll put you to bed in the downstairs chamber."

She gave his son a long look of reproach. "Caleb, I warned you," she said.

III

IT TOOK THREE WEEKS to move the Middleton household from Parson's Creek to Philadelphia. It was a time of confusion, of nagging details, of endless decisions, many of them petty yet far-reaching in their results as they tied into the network of plans and arrangements in which the future of the family would be caught and held. Mr. Middleton's stroke, if it was a stroke, and the fear that a repetition of it might bring on paralysis or even death, hung over his wife and son like a threatening cloud, seldom mentioned but always there. Because of it, Caleb had promised his stepmother, in a long talk the morning after his father's fall, that he would help with the moving and that until his father was safely established in town be would make—or at least would announce—no drastic decisions of his own.

Mr. Middleton himself, who regarded his loss of consciousness that evening as a momentary upset caused by Caleb's willfulness, had no idea of being ill, now or later. He was, he said at intervals to anyone who would stop to listen to him, as good as ever, though when one was well launched into the sixties one naturally slowed up a little. All he required—and this, he implied, was a trifling matter manifestly due him—was that no one should cross him in any way. This assumption increased the pressure in the house, for he had to know all that was going on and they could never foresee when he would declare that a decision was too insignificant for him to be troubled about and that others should have taken it off his burdened shoulders, and when he would pounce upon some minor arrangement and complain that the disposal of it had been concealed from him with a view to circumventing his wishes.

In addition to all other difficulties, Mrs. Middleton was involved with the servant problem, which, always acute for those who were not willing to own slaves, arose at this moment in a most annoying form. Horace, the bound boy, ran off, and since it was reported that he had gone to offer himself to the army as a drummer boy it appeared useless to try to trace him and bring him back, though Caleb on his father's insistence did insert an advertisement in the *Pennsylvania Gazette*. Then the colored girl, Tess, the daughter of a freed slave, who had been left with the Middletons to be cared for and trained till she was twenty-one, dramatically revealed that she was pregnant. After much questioning and discussion it was decided which of the woodcutters was responsible and Tess was married, hopefully, to him; a disused cabin on the plantation was hastily repaired and furnished, and her husband, Mose, was employed to work under Ambrose Slack, the farmer. As the Middletons had suffered with Tess during the years when she broke everything she touched, nursing her through small-pox and several lesser illnesses and as she was only now at fifteen beginning to be of use to them, Mrs. Middleton was understandably exasperated.

Caleb rode to town twice to make arrangements for opening the house on Third Street and to superintend the wagonloads of supplies that were taken to it: firewood, fodder for the horses and the cow, ba-con and hams from the smokehouse and sacks of flour and baskets of apples and vegetables from the farm. Though he was outwardly self-controlled, efficient, and dutiful, inwardly his mind and heart were in a turmoil, caught in the double conflict between his desire to enlist in the cause of liberty, on the one hand, and the Quaker princi-ples in which he was brought up, on the other, between his determina-tion to assert his manhood and make his own decisions and his fear of being responsible for his father's serious illness if he should defy him openly.

While the Phoebe Ann had been running, Caleb had felt confident about the course before him. To make iron acutely needed by the new country in its birth struggle had seemed to him a useful and patriotic action and yet a possible one for a Quaker, since it was not fighting, not engaging in what from his earliest childhood he had heard called "carnal warfare." His knowledge of the Bible was less extensive, since he was a modern Friend with a classical education, than his knowledge of Tacitus or Horace, but there were certain texts that no Quaker child could escape and one of them was, "Put up thy sword into the sheath . . . . My kingdom is not of this world; if my kingdom were of this world, then would my servants fight."

With the Quaker scriptures, the words of Fox and Penn, he was even more familiar. He remembered summer afternoons when his mother, always expecting another baby, would sit sewing on the terrace, while he and Sue, warm from their play, would drop down beside her demanding a story. Even now as he thought of it the scene sprang vividly to his mind; he could see her eyes, warm and tender, feel the slight roughness of her forefinger where the needle had pricked it, hear her vibrant voice. She had a fund of stories, most of them from Quaker history, which was full of adventure: stories of persecutions bravely endured, of shipwrecks and pirates, of threatening Indians who became friendly, of the girl who died on the gallows on Boston Common, of young William Penn in the Tower of London declaring, "My prison shall be my grave before I will budge a jot, for I owe my conscience to no mortal man."

Perhaps oftenest she told the story of George Fox and the jailors at Derby. "They could see he had the build for a soldier," she would say, "for he was tall and broad and strong, and they knew he had courage. So they offered to let him out of prison and make him a captain in the army. And what did he say? He told them, 'I live in the virtue of that life and power that takes away the occasion of all wars.' "

With the Phoebe Ann shut down there were, Caleb thought, two possibilities open to him. He might offer his services to some other furnace. Mark Bird, of the Coventry, had raised a company of militia, equipped it at his own expense, and got a commission as a colonel; he might need a manager to leave behind him. Or he could enlist in the Philadelphia Light Horse. Samuel Morris, the captain of the troop, was a Friend, or had been before he was disowned. Caleb was not happy about either course; both represented a compromise between his desires and his principles.

Early in the morning, when the screech owl quavered through darkness just beginning to turn gray, he would wake up and tussle with his problem. Life, he told himself, thumping his hot pillow, was a matter of compromise at best. One had to decide at what point one would yield and at what point one must stand.

He thought of John Dickinson, who used to come sometimes to the Fourth Street Meeting when Caleb was a student in the College. With his *Letters from a Farmer* he had done more perhaps than anyone else except Sam Adams of Boston to arouse the colonies to resist the injustices of English taxation. He had been an influential member of the Continental Congress, believing firmly in remonstrance and redress by constitutional means. Yet when the Congress, despairing of ever bringing the English ministry to reason, decided to break away and form a new country, Dickinson could not join with them. He voted against the Declaration of Independence and refused to sign it. But after it was passed in spite of him, he felt free, though a Quaker, to fight for the new United States of America. As colonel of a Pennsylvania regiment he had been in action at Princeton and Trenton. The light as he saw it led him to fight for what he could not vote for, while Caleb found himself in the uncomfortable position of endorsing something with his mind and heart which he did not feel free to defend with his body.

At this point he would jump up and pull on breeches and shirt and tiptoe downstairs. Though it might grow hot later in the day the mornings were fresh, with the dew on the grass and the sun still so low that stones in the driveway cast a shadow. He would saddle Ladybird and ride through the orchard and up the wood road to the top of the ridge, to the place where a wide view opened out to the northeast across the valley of the Schuylkill to the hills beyond. There in the morning peace he would decide to go to Meeting the first Sunday they were in town and see whether, in the serenity of that quiet place, in the silence of many seeking hearts, he could find light that would reveal the path that should be uniquely his.

IV

THE MIDDLETONS REACHED PHILADELPHIA on August twenty-second, the day that General Howe with a large force had landed at the Head of Elk on Chesapeake Bay, fifty-five miles from the city. The first possible Sunday on which Caleb might have gone to Meeting was two days later, the twenty-fourth, but that was the day on which General Washington decided to march his brigades through Philadelphia on his way to meet the British, and Caleb went instead to see them pass. He decided that he could get the best view from the windows of Phyllis Pike's lodging.

He had first met Mrs. Pike the previous March, when he had been in town on some errand for the furnace. It had been a cold, glittery day with the merciless sunshine bright on wisps of paper blown against doorsteps and on stray bits of garbage frozen in alley gutters. The wind, flashing off the steely surface of the river, had whipped through bare tree branches and around street corners, carrying the flat city smell of wharf piles and river mud. Caleb had been glad after he had finished his business to turn toward the London Coffee House. He would have a cup of coffee to warm him, read the latest number of the *Pennsylvania Gazette*, and chat with whoever was there before he went to his Cousin Edward Penington's to spend the night.

As he walked up Front Street with his shoulders hunched against the wind at his back, he saw a vessel unloading at the public dock, and he paused for a moment to watch. She was a sloop from South Carolina, someone said, with a cargo evidently of pine products. He lingered idly for a moment, watching the men handling the big barrels with easy skill. He was about to go on again when he saw a little figure moving uncertainly in their midst, in danger of being jostled if not knocked down. It was a girl in a blue mantle with a smart hat perched

23

upon her powdered hair and an ostrich plume which rose and flapped in the wind like a flag on a staff. In her hand she carried a bird cage in which a small, bright bird hopped agitatedly from perch to floor to bar, and on her small, charming face was an expression of woe.

Caleb lost no time in going to her rescue.

"Watch yourself there, fellow," he said sternly to a man with a barrel, and then, in suaver tones, as he stood beside the little lady and looked down at her, "Can I help you?"

The wind swooped again at that moment and blew the end of her plume against his mouth. Having no hand free to take hold of her feather, she swung around, laughing a little, to let the wind blow it back, and the sharpness of the air brought tears to her eyes, which were brown and clear and set about with long, thick lashes. She was, he saw, extremely pretty and, though young, not in the least miss-ish.

"Lord, what a wind! I'm expecting my husband to meet me," she said in a voice plaintive yet vigorous. "I've come all the way from Charleston."

She handed him the bird cage and the bird became more hysterical than ever. "It's a nonpareil," she said, as if that explained everything.

By the act of handing Caleb the bird cage, she seemed to have handed him her whole problem, and by accepting it he felt he had made himself responsible for her. The transition was swift and easy. He seemed to expand under her confiding gaze. He was a man of the world, handsome, kind, capable, courtly. She was helpless, admiring, grateful, with the almost imperceptible yet comfortable gift of making him understand without words what he might do for her.

He ascertained her name and the address of her husband's lodging, took care of the formalities of arrival at the office of the ship's company near by on Front Street, he saw her modest luggage collected and obtained the services of a boy with a wheelbarrow. Then he suggested that he accompany her to her lodging, which was only three or four squares away, where she could rest and wait for her husband, who no doubt had been detained somewhere.

It was obviously a sensible suggestion, but both seemed reluctant to put it into effect at once. The boy with the wheelbarrow went ahead, with the bird cage perched on top of the boxes and instructions to wait when he reached the lodging house. Clouds had blown across the sun and the wind was raw now as well as sharp. The London Coffee House at the corner of Front and High Streets was near at hand. Caleb understood that Mrs. Pike would take heart from a cup of hot coffee and that, although it was a place that ladies seldom ventured into, she would not mind. He found an unoccupied box where they could be unobserved and he ordered two cups of mocha and some queen cakes.

Little Mrs. Pike pulled off her gloves and flexed her stiff fingers. "Cold!" she said, shivering prettily, and her voice, so warm and strong and yet somehow childish, sent pleasant impulses down Caleb's spine. "Feel!" She laid the back of her knuckles lightly against his cheek, and he felt it grow hot under her chilly touch. "This is a monstrous climate. The jessamine is blooming in Carolina now and the air is warm and fragrant."

The log fire blazing on the hearth was reflected on the coffee urn, and cast a glow on the rows of pewter plates and cups and the blue and white Delft ware on the shelves of polished wood. In the warmth and intimacy of the box Mrs. Pike told Caleb how she had romantically met and married Thomas, who was a dancing and fencing master, how he had left her in Charleston at the insistence of her family while he prepared a home for her in Philadelphia, how at last she could bear it no longer and had come to him. She did not say that she was the daughter of a great plantation, but her father, who appeared in her narrative as a towering figure, aristocratically strict and protective, could have belonged only to one of the large establishments, with slaves and gardens and pleasure boats on the river, which Phyllis described so vividly. "The Delaware is a shocking flat, dull stream, isn't it?" she threw in, and Caleb, startled because he had always understood it to be majestic, felt obliged to set her straight, and he ordered more coffee to occupy them while he explained.

Though the room had been almost empty when they entered, it now was beginning to fill up. The Congress and its committees, as well as the Pennsylvania Assembly, broke up about five, and the members liked to drop in at the coffee house afterward. The sound of footfalls and greetings, of waiters running with trays, increased, but at first Caleb was only vaguely aware of them. Presently, however, he realized that word had got around of a pretty woman in the far box, for men began to drift past casually, glancing in as they went. Two or three acquaintances nodded to him, and he saw in their faces either disapproval or an arch you-gay-dog-you look. The thought that Mrs. Pike might be made uncomfortable roused his anger, and he was casting about for some way of putting an end to the parade, when he caught the look on her face. Not in the least displeased, she might almost be said to bridle. Little sidelong glances, bright and soft, stole from her modestly lowered eyelids, and a conscious smile played around the corners of her warm red mouth.

For the first time it occurred to Caleb that she might be less childlike and even less—he hesitated—virtuous than he had thought her. Somewhat to his surprise he found that this realization did not repel him. On the contrary it made his pulses leap, and he leaned toward her across the table.

Mr. Pike had returned from Wilmington, where he had a regular engagement, just as Caleb delivered Phyllis to Mrs. Duncannon's boardinghouse, and Caleb, loaded down with their thanks, had left them to their reunion. Walking away, he wondered, as interested persons so regularly do, how the man had got the girl. He had recognized Mr. Pike the moment he saw him; he had often seen that conspicuous red coat and laced hat on the street. He was a thin man, with a thin, rather hatchety profile and light eyes set close together. His manner was too obliging.

It was only polite that before starting for home next morning, Caleb should stop in to inquire for Mrs. Pike, and that it should become habit whenever he was in town after that to pay his respects to her. It had not been difficult to arrange his business trips so that he was in Philadelphia on the days when Mr. Pike was in Wilmington.

On the Sunday morning of August twenty-fourth, Mr. Pike was at home. Not only was he there, in the second story parlor with the windows overlooking Front Street, but a captain and a major, whose brief terms in the militia had already expired, were on hand too, very jovial and, Caleb thought disapprovingly, very bumptious.

The day had begun badly, with a downpour at seven. Though the rain soon stopped, still the sky was overcast and the air was cool, damp, and lifeless. People gathered early along the sidewalks to watch the parade and every window on Front Street was filled with spectators. It was generally said that Washington intended to impress the Tories in the city and reassure the patriots by a show of the strength of his army, but the faces of people waiting looked indistinguishably anxious.

In Mrs. Pike's little parlor there was an uneasy air of bonhomie in which Caleb did not join. Mr. Pike, in has scarlet coat with a fresh set of ruffles, was offering wine to the company and proposing toasts to Liberty. The Captain and the Major drained their glasses and smacked their lips and sat down again, sprawling out their legs as if they had been in a tavern—where indeed one of them belonged, behind the bar. Caleb recognized the Major as the onetime barkeeper at the Indian Queen, and he guessed that the Captain, from his general manner and way of talking, had been the driver of a stagecoach. But they were officers now, and gentlemen, under the new dispensation.

Phyllis, charming in a flowered chintz gown with a gauze apron, her unpowdered brown curls escaping from her cap, was mourning the death of her bird and calling for expressions of sympathy.

"I can't be sorry," said Caleb flatly. "I don't like song birds in cages."

She widened her eyes at him reproachfully. "But that one," she said, "was my friend, and he brought me one of my dearest friends."

There was a message for him in her voice and glance as well as in her words, but Caleb's mood was heavy and he could not rise to it. He was put out by the presence of the military, he did not in any case like exchanging soft glances and speeches with double meanings under the hatchet nose of Mr. Pike, and he wished that the parade would hurry up and begin. When the Major, whose sibilants became blurred with his sixth glass of wine, offered to preshent Mistresh Pike with a bigger bird, a better bird, Caleb went to the window and stood looking out in morose silence.

The house was situated on Front Street near Vine, almost at the edge of the Northern Liberties, that region of row houses, shambles, empty lots, and military barracks, where on Saturday nights the butchers from Spring Garden warred wildly with the ship carpenters from Kensington. Beyond West's shipyards across the street the river could be seen, and beyond its pewter-colored breadth, the trees of the Jersey shore rose out of the mist. It was a broad, slow-moving, inexorable and, yes, a majestic river.

"Have you heard," said Phyllis in a low voice at his side, "there's a list circulating of about five hundred people who are to be arrested and banished from the city?"

"What for? What have they done?"

"Nobody seems to know exactly. Inimical to the American cause, or something of the kind. Thomas talked to someone who said he had seen it, but he couldn't find out any of the names from him, though they say they are some of the most respectable citizens."

"Don't worry," said Caleb. "There are certain to be all kinds of rumors with the British army so near."

He looked speculatively at Mr. Pike, who was loudly proposing another toast to Liberty and Down with Tyranny. The dancing master was commonly supposed to be a loyalist.

In the street below a ragged boy raised a shrill cry: "Yonder they come!" and a sharp rat-a-tat of drums almost at the same moment brought everyone in the parlor crowding to the windows.

In another moment the first column was there, and with the approach of marching feet on the brick-paved street began the steady rhythmic beat which was to continue till all of the army had passed before their eyes. The men carried arms, well burnished, and in each man's hat was pinned a sprig of fresh green. "For hope?" Caleb wondered.

From the wild burst of shouts and cheers he knew that Washington must be approaching. He had expected somehow that the general would come later as a climax to the show, but here he was at the head of his troops. Feeling the contagion of emotion, Caleb thrust his head and shoulders out of a window.

He saw, mounted on a fine, high-stepping horse, the tall, stately, grave yet cheerful, already almost legendary man who held in his steady hands the future of the little band of rebellious colonies. He was surrounded by his mounted aides and yet they might all have been invisible, so completely did Washington dominate the scene. As he came directly under the window Caleb's heart beat fast. He had with others complained that the mob made a demi-god of Washington, and yet, this morning, he himself felt an impression of an integrity, a dedication, a largeness of spirit that was superior to the ordinary run of men.

Behind General Washington and his aides came twelve gentlemen of the Philadelphia Light Horse led by Cornet John Dunlap, who in his daily life published the *Pennsylvania Packet*. The troop was well turned out in brown coats, white waistcoats and breeches, and high-topped black boots. Their long cavalrymen's swords, unsheathed, rested against their left arms, their carbines were at their backs, their pistols in brown holsters initialed in white hung at either side of the pommel. On their heads were the visored black hunting caps with a bucktail turned up over the top which they had borrowed from the Gloucester Fox-hunting Club, to which many of them had belonged before the City Troop was founded. Caleb had ridden to hounds with them several times, over the flat fields across the river. He knew that he would be welcomed if he should decide to join the troop. The members were all gentlemen; they armed and equipped themselves; based at Philadelphia, detachments of them went out from time to time on guard or escort duty. Some of them had been in actual fighting last winter in the victories at Trenton and Princeton, but they were not committed to following the army into distant winter quarters or to staying with it during the long frustrating intervals between actions.

The Virginia Cavalry followed, and then after a gap of a hundred yards or so a company of Pioneers in linen hunting shirts belted at the waist, with axes over their shoulders. After another space rode General Nathanael Greene, in whom Caleb felt a particular interest. A Quaker of Rhode Island, the son of a successful iron foundryman, he had applied for a commission in the Rhode Island Kentish Guards, but because he had a stiff knee he had been rejected. Whereupon he had promptly volunteered as a private—and now he was a major general and in people's estimation second only to Washington. The fringe on his gold epaulettes shook as he rode slowly past and his stars gleamed. Caleb looked to see if the struggle with his Quaker heritage had left any traces in his face, but he saw only a large, smooth countenance, open and pleasant, without any subtleties.

"Here comes the Parson," said the Major, digging his elbow into Caleb's ribs as if he had said something roguish.

"What Parson? Oh, Muhlenberg, you mean."

The story was well known, how Peter Muhlenberg, minister of a Lutheran church in a little town in Virginia, at the end of his sermon one Sunday had flung open his gown to reveal his blue and buff uniform beneath it, announcing that he was leaving at once to join General Washington. He was now a brigadier, with the men of his regiment marching twelve abreast behind him. They were not quite in step, but their heads were high and they wore their green sprigs at a confident angle.

Behind the artillery, which rumbled noisily over the bricks of the street, came massed drummers and fifers, and the roll of the drums, the shrill notes of a lively tune smartened the steps of the infantry following.

The gay tune faded out, the steady tramping steps came on, column after column, with almost hypnotic effect. Many of the uniforms were shabby, but all were clean and all the guns were polished. Though their hats were cocked at all angles, their faces were set straight ahead and wore a look of common purpose. Here and there one stood out from the rest: a tall, gawky redhead, probably a Scot; a short, slim, swarthy lad who might have been Portuguese; a man with the high cheekbones and reddish skin that revealed Indian blood; a boy so fair and young that he looked like a girl among the others. The Baltimore regiment was composed of farmers in hunting shirts; they had the farmer's weather-beaten features, his dogged mildness and comfortable walk—no nonsense about keeping step or carrying his head as if he wore a check-rein.

There was a flurry in the room when General Stirling rode past at the head of his division. Was he a lord or wasn't he?

"Certainly he's a lord," said Mr. Pike. "He went to court about it in England and won his case."

"Then why ain't he sitting in the House of Lords?" objected the Captain. "We got no use for lords in a republic."

Caleb was conscious of the light pressure of Phyllis's body against his as she leaned forward eagerly to see the lord. He clasped her slender shoulders with his two hands and moved her in front of him, where he could see over her head and smell the fragrance of her hair. "Silly face, hasn't he?" he murmured. "Look at that pretty mouth."

She turned to look at him in surprise, her face so close that he might have snatched a kiss without the others' knowing. "Why, I think he's right handsome," she protested.

"Too soft," said Caleb, amazed, not for the first time, at the kind of man a woman will think good-looking.

Behind the last company of infantry a cavalry troop brought up the rear. Caleb paid more attention to the horses than to the men. Most of them looked thin and hard used. He wondered where the supply wagons were, and tried to estimate the number it must take just to keep the beasts fed.

"That's all," said the Major.

Caleb looked at his watch in surprise. It had been two hours.

"That'll show them—" declared the Captain, "—the Tories and the folks that are afraid of the British. Did you see the Fourth Pennsylvania? They marched good. That was my regiment. After I get a bit of rest I think I'll enlist for another term."

"How long was your first one?"

"Five months, and then I signed on for the rest of the campaign, so it was almost nine altogether." In the pause that followed he must have felt an implied criticism, for he said with a pugnacious thrust of his jaw, "I gotta live, ain't I? I came back to move my family outa the city and make a little money."

Caleb thought of Washington, with an inkling of what it might be to fight a war depending on an army that dissolved under his fingers, against British regulars and Hessian mercenaries, who were disciplined and battle tested, and prevented, furthermore, by the whole width of the Atlantic Ocean from going home for the harvest or a lawsuit or a desire for a rest. The coarse and trifling character of the two specimens with whom he had shared the view from the windows increased his sympathy and heightened his admiration for that lonely and noble figure whose image was still vivid in his mind. He had not seen the British march, but he had a shrewd idea that in comparison with them this two-hour display would seem pathetic and homemade. Yet he found his ardor kindled, and he left the house filled with the idea of joining a regiment of the Continental line under General Washington himself.

Reaction came inevitably.

The next week Caleb spent in the outward activity of his father's business and an inward conflict both distressing and engrossing. The various compromises which he had contemplated between his Quaker principles and his desire to take part in America's struggle for independence now appeared unacceptable to him. Yet the deep tides of his early training and belief, his conviction that war was wrong, arose to check him when he thought of actually enlisting and taking a gun in his hands.

Temperamentally not given to introspection and self-analysis, he yet dimly knew himself capable of two extremes: of being a dedicated and concerned Friend, with none of the latitude which he now allowed himself, or of abandoning altogether the religion of his mother and going the way of many young Friends of his age, who were now captains and majors in the Continental army and whose names had been stricken from the records of their Meetings. The events of the last month had waked him out of his complacent slumber and he felt he must now choose one course or the other.

Moral questions of right and wrong, elements of his long-standing rebellion against his father's domination, the division of loyalty between his inbred conviction of religious truth and his fresh-springing belief in the ideal of a new liberty and justice in a new land, eagerness to take a brave and energetic part, to share the risks and dangers others faced: all this confusion and contradiction of thoughts and impulses, insights and desires, occupied his mind, waking and sleeping. There was no one whose advice he wanted to ask, since he felt that it was his own dilemma, for which he alone must take responsibility. He went to Meeting on Sunday, but the clamor of his own thoughts was so insistent that he could hear no voice from beyond, and the two or three Friends who spoke out of the silence quoted Old Testament texts that did not touch his need.

The week went by without action or decision.

V

LOUD POUNDING ON THE front door sounded through the house. Caleb looked up from the desk in the back parlor, where he was searching for a mislaid document that his father wanted, and listened. The urgency of the knocking made Caleb wonder apprehensively if his father, who, in spite of the muggy heat of the day, had gone to call on a sick friend, might again have collapsed. From the sound of footsteps overhead he knew that his stepmother, probably with the same thought, had gone to the top of the stairs to listen. It was much more probable, he told himself, that some news had come from the armies to the southwest of the city and that the citizens were being aroused, although so far there had been no sound of gunfire.

He heard voices at the front door, indistinguishable at first; then Amos's squeaky tones rose high. "Just a minute, gentlemen," Caleb heard him protest. "If you'll wait in here, please sit, I'll tell him—"

Peremptory footsteps drew near along the hall and the next moment three men strode into the room. Caleb rose, surprised.

He recognized Charles Peale at once. Slight, bright-eyed and handsome, he looked smart in the brown and green uniform of the Philadelphia company of which he was captain. Caleb had come to know him rather well in the days when the young artist, then almost unknown, was painting the miniature of his mother. A genuine pleasure in seeing him again washed out Caleb's momentary annoyance at the abruptness of his entrance.

"It's a long time since I've seen you, Charlie," he said cordially, and turned to the other two, who were strangers. "I believe I've not had the honor—"

Peale said unsmiling, "Mr. Heysham and Mr. Marsh are my associates in the cause of liberty. They accompany me on an errand which I assure you is disagreeable to me."

Stung by the unexpected rebuff, Caleb swept some papers off a chair and dropped them on the desk. "Pray be seated," he said stiffly.

Mr. Marsh, a youngish man, pleasant enough in his appearance, openly leaned over and craned his neck to look at the papers. They were memoranda of agreements, deeds of trust, some bills and personal letters, which had been brought down from the office at the Phoebe Ann. Flushing angrily at the man's rudeness, Caleb deliberately turned up the front of the desk, shutting all the papers inside.

"Hold on!" said Mr. Marsh.

Peale, who was evidently the spokesman, interposed quickly. "I regret very much, Mr. Middleton, the errand that brings me here. I am commanded by the Supreme Executive Council to secure your signature to this document."

Mr. Heysham, a rather short man with a square-jawed, monkey-like face, whipped a sheet of paper out of the portfolio which he carried and presented it to Caleb.

"If you will read that," said Peale, "I think it is self-explanatory."

Wondering, Caleb took the paper and began to read. Flies buzzed around and around the room under the ceiling. Outside in the garden below the window Tacy was playing with her dolls. Her sweet little childish pipe floated into the tense silence of the room. "Will thee have some sugar, my dear? Do have some more of this bohea. It's very fine."

"I—, do promise;" read Caleb, "not to depart from my dwelling house—" The first part was so preposterous that he went back and read it again. "—not to depart from my dwelling house and to be ready to appear on demand of the President and Council of Pennsylvania—"

Indignation followed upon bewilderment as he continued: "—and do engage to refrain from doing anything injurious to the United States of North America—" He read the final words aloud, slowly, " '—by speaking, writing, or otherwise, and from giving intelligence to the Commander of the British forces or any person whatsoever concerning public affairs.' This has nothing to do with me!" he exclaimed. "There must be some mistake!"

He turned to the three men standing there, Peale embarrassed but determined, Heysham and Marsh staring at him with bold, accusing eyes.

"I can't sign that," said Caleb, tossing it contemptuously onto the table.

"I advise you very strongly to comply," said Captain Peale. "That will relieve you of any further difficulty now, and in the course of time you can straighten yourself out with the Council."

The memory of Phyllis Pike standing by the window and saying that five hundred of the most respectable citizens were to be arrested and banished, returned to him. This visitation, then, must be part of a general gathering up of Tories. Conscious of his own clearness, he said with a smile, "You have the wrong man."

There was no answering smile on Peale's face as he consulted his list. "Caleb Middleton, junior?"

"At your service. But there is no reason for me to be on such a list. I have not the slightest intention of doing anything injurious to the United States of America. On the contrary—" He stopped. It occurred to him that they had confused him with his father. But even his father had done nothing beyond refusing for conscientious reasons to make iron for the army. He had indeed harbored secret doubts about the patriots' chances of success, but a man cannot be condemned to house arrest for his thoughts.

"Then you can have no valid objection to signing this parole," said Captain Peale smoothly.

"It is impossible for me to sign it. The word 'parole' itself implies an admission of guilt."

"In that case I shall have to conduct you to the Freemasons' Hall. Time is short, and I shall have to require you to come at once without further delay."

"On what authority?"

"By virtue of a Resolution of the Congress and by order of council."

"May I see your orders?"

"I am not permitted to show them to you, but I can tell you that the Congress on Thursday of last week passed a Resolution that the executive authorities of Pennsylvania be requested to cause all notoriously disaffected persons to be apprehended, disarmed, and secured. The Council yesterday determined that the parole which you have just read might be offered to certain ones on the list. I assure you, Mr. Middleton, I am making this as easy for you as possible. There are others who would use more rigor." He smiled almost coaxingly, and for a moment Caleb saw again the young artist whom he had as a boy so much admired.

"No one," said Caleb, "no one at all can say with any truth that I am a disaffected person."

"I am obliged also," said Peale, as if he had not heard, "to make a search for firearms and papers of a political nature."

He nodded, and Heysham stepped forward as if this was what he had been eagerly waiting for, and laid his hand on the desk.

"Those are purely personal and private papers," said Caleb. "They have to do with my father's business affairs. You may take my word for it."

Paying no attention at all, Heysham opened the desk and began to rummage through it, untying bundles of letters, leafing through ledgers, running his fingers deep into pigeonholes, pausing to read anything that interested him. The other man, Marsh, walked around the room looking in the corners and behind the door. Discovering no guns stacked against the walls, he went out into the hall, where he could be heard pulling things about in the closet under the stairs. Caleb stood silent, struggling to control his temper.

"No papers, sir;" reported Heysham, turning from a desk now so disordered that it would be a day's work to find anything. A few seconds later Marsh reappeared with the news that he had been unable to discover any firearms.

Sarah Middleton swept into the room after him, with Edward breathing hard in her wake.

"What is all this?" she demanded. "Have you a warrant for searching our house?"

"I have, madam."

"Then show it to me. It is my right to see it"

"I am acting by order of the Supreme Executive Council, madam," said Peale. "I assure you it is disagreeable to me to execute such orders and I do not do it by my own wish. Once more, Mr. Middleton, will you sign the parole?"

"I will not."

"Then I shall have to take you under arrest."

"For mercy's sake!" exclaimed Mrs. Middleton. "On what grounds?"

"On grounds of being suspected of being inimical to the American cause."

"This is a thoroughly arbitrary proceeding!" exclaimed Caleb. "You have no grounds for such a suspicion and no possible right to arrest me without a definite charge."

"You can tell all that to the Council," said Marsh roughly, "when you get to the Masons' Hall."

Caleb caught eagerly at the idea of an immediate hearing. The Freemasons' Hall was not a prison; if the Council were in session there, he would have little difficulty in clearing himself before it. These were, after all, the guardians of American liberty whom he was to meet, not the British oppressors. It occurred to him, furthermore, that it would be a good idea to get off before his father came in and said anything injudicious.

"Very well, then," he said evenly. "I am ready to go."

To his stepmother, whose broad face was twisted with distress, he said, "Don't worry. It's all a mistake and will soon be corrected." He rumpled Edward's hair affectionately, and took his hat from Amos's hands. Patty came flying down the front stairs, alight with curiosity, but before she had finished shrieking, "Where's Caleb going?" he was out in the street, preceded by Captain Peale and followed by Heysham and Marsh.

In spite of his consciousness of innocence and his confidence in the fairness of the Council, he felt keenly the indignity of being thus paraded publicly through the streets. People turned to look at him as he passed, and a small boy scrambling over a board fence screeched to another, "Hey, Pete, here's another Tory being taken up!"

At the corner, when they turned to go down Spruce Street, he looked back. Mrs. Middleton and Patty were standing on the steps, while Amos had come out onto the sidewalk and Edward had run halfway to the corner behind him. They all waved when they saw him turn, and Patty threw a kiss.

VI

THE FREEMASONS' HALL WAS a handsome building in the narrow street called Lodge Alley, which ran west from Second Street between Walnut and Chestnut. It was often used for public concerts and meetings, and the regular dancing assemblies had been held there until the war put an end to them.

As Caleb and his captors turned into the alley, which was lined with rows of posts on both sides to protect the footway, they had to clear a passage through the crowd that had gathered around the entrance to the hall. Among the anxious faces Caleb recognized Karl, the respectable, middle-aged German who was his cousin Edward Penington's devoted servant. The man's heavy face lit up when he saw Caleb, and he made his way through the crowd toward him.

"Is Cousin Edward in there, Karl?" said Caleb.

"*Ja,* Master Caleb. I can't get in to speak with him. Will you ask him, should I fetch his night things? *Ach, es ist schrecklich!* I can bring a pallet. I looked in the window before they drove me off and there's nothing but hard benches and wooden chairs."

"Stand aside there," barked Heysham.

"We'll be away from here before nightfall," said Caleb hastily.

"*Ja, ja,* but chust ask him to come to the window and nod—chust nod and I'll know to bring his things—"

Members of the uniformed City Guard pushed the crowd back as Captain Peale stopped to confer with their commanding officer, Colonel Nicola. Caleb waited, unpleasantly aware of many eyes fastened on him and of the whispering buzz, "Who's that? Who's he?"

Peale turned from Nicola to Heysham and Marsh. "Wait for me here," he said. "I will be with you in a few moments. Now, Mr. Middleton, if you will come this way—"

A guard opened the door of the Lodge and they stepped into the entrance hall, which ran across the front of the building, with a door to the auditorium in the center and stairs on one side leading to the upper floor. Captain Peale drew Caleb into the shadow of the staircase.

"I wanted to have a word with you privately. I have a message from Colonel Matlack. This will be understood to be confidential."

For a moment Caleb was at a loss to understand why Timothy Matlack should send a message to him, until he remembered that Mr. Matlack, apart from being a colonel of militia and a disowned Friend, was the Secretary of the Supreme Executive Council of Pennsylvania, the body responsible for Caleb's arrest. He nodded.

Captain Peale went on in a low voice. "Colonel Matlack is not unforgetful of kindness done to him by your father some years ago when he was in great difficulty. He is aware also that Mr. Middleton, senior, is elderly and infirm. Accordingly when he registered the names of the prisoners, he added 'junior' to that of Caleb Middleton. He trusts that will be satisfactory to both of you. If it is not, will you signify as much immediately through me, so that the mistake can be corrected before any question arises?"

Caleb caught his breath, speechless for a moment in his surprise; then he heard himself saying steadily, "It is entirely satisfactory to me, but I have no doubt that my father would object vigorously if he knew. Will you ask Colonel Matlack to add to his kindness by doing everything in his power to keep my father from finding out what has been done?"

"I will tell him."

"But I regret," said Caleb, unable to suppress the hot words that rose to his lips as the full meaning of Timothy Matlack's message became clear to him, "that a little more kindness did not lead him to omit the name altogether, since his conscience evidently did not prevent him from tampering with the document."

Captain Peale looked at him coldly. "I will tell him that too. Your servant, sir."

He turned on his heel so swiftly that the skirts of his brown and green coat flew out and his sword clanked. The guard opened the front door for him, and then motioned to Caleb to go into the auditorium.

It was a large room with benches down the sides, chairs stacked in the corners and a platform at the far end. Tall, dirty-paned windows, half-open along both sides of the room, let in flies as well as light and the sultry, lifeless air.

Caleb saw perhaps ten or a dozen men in the big room, gathered in little knots of two or three. He turned quickly to the guard. "Where is the Council?"

"Huh?"

"I said, where is the Council? Is it sitting in one of the upstairs rooms, or what?"

"I don't know nothing about no Council. This is where you're to stay."

The door closed behind him.

Caleb would have liked to call Captain Peale back now and unsay that last sarcastic speech of his. It was impolitic, to say the least, and might bring trouble for both Caleb and his father. But more than that, it was ungrateful. He was belatedly aware of Colonel Matlack's real intention of kindness. Though both Caleb and his father were innocent, yet the elder Caleb, having refused to make munitions for the Continental army, was more open to the suspicion of disaffection. Caleb had no doubt of being able to clear himself as soon as he got a hearing. Meanwhile, he could endure a few hours of waiting in the Freemasons' Hall more easily than his choleric parent.

He looked about for his cousin and found him sitting in a chair with his back to the room, reading.

Edward Penington was Caleb's mother's cousin. A prosperous merchant, a man with a dozen public interests and concerns, he achieved a delicate balance between the world and the Meeting. His clothes were "of the best sort, but plain," of the finest broadcloth and linen, the brown coat cut long and without pockets, the fine white shirt made without frills. His graying hair, which was receding at the temples, he wore clubbed at the back. His clean-shaven face had a look of humor and benevolence about the eyes, of stern, almost tight control about the thin, fine lips.

"Cousin Edward—"

Penington looked up, taken by surprise, then smiled. "Well, Caleb," he said, "thou too! I thought thou wert a zealous advocate of independency!"

"I thought so too," said Caleb ruefully.

"Bring up a chair, my boy, and sit down. Thou hast a long wait before thee. I've been here since ten o'clock this morning, and I still do not know either my crime or the sentence."

"Isn't the Council meeting here?"

"No. Why should thou suppose it was?"

"I was told—or at least I was given to understand—that I could talk to the Council here and clear myself."

"Of what? Hast thou been charged with anything?"

"Nothing definite. Something about being inimical to the American cause, which is absurd. Did they show thee their orders? Who brought thee here?"

"No less a person than William Bradford, with some young men who professed great attachment to the cause of liberty. No one is permitted to see their orders. So far as I can tell I am here for having been a friend of Joseph Galloway—who I believe is now with the Royal Army in New York—as if sedition were contagious like the pox. And doubtless also for the crime of being a rich Quaker."

Caleb saw on the other side of the room a slight, dejected figure sitting on the end of a bench with his elbows on his knees and his head in his hands.

"Isn't that Tom Affleck over there?" he said. "He's not a rich Quaker."

"No, poor Tom. He's fairly dazed by the blow. He has four small children all under six and his wife's poorly. They've nothing to live on but what he makes with his hands. Incidentally, he made this chair I'm sitting on, and it's a very good piece of work, too."

Caleb had known Tom Affleck from the time when, not long come from Aberdeen, he had made the coffin for Caleb's mother. He had used the best mahogany and put it together and polished it with care, as if it were to be on view for a lifetime instead of hidden away in the ground. He had worked all through one night to have it finished in time, and there had been a gentleness about his simple, honest manner that had lingered in Caleb's memory.

"I can't see any reason for arresting a man like him," he said slowly. "His sympathies may be with Britain. It would be natural enough if they were, he's not been here many years. But he's a quiet, hard-working craftsman with a family to support. He'd be a Friend still if he hadn't married out. He won't fight in any case."

His cousin raised an eyebrow. "If thou and others could contemplate fighting for the American cause, possibly other Friends might find it possible to bear arms for Britain—though certainly I have not heard of any who have. But that is their line of reasoning. They are taking the ground that he who is not for them is against them. Sit down, Caleb, sit down. Thou makes me nervous."

Caleb was too restless to sit down. "What's thy book?" He gave a little yelp of laughter when his cousin turned the title page toward him. "*Life of Mahomet* by Prideaux! I thought at least it was Law's *Serious Call to a Devout and Holy Life.*"

Penington looked a little apologetic. "I picked it up in a hurry," he admitted. "I've had it a long time and never read it. I find it very interesting. Mahommet was a more solid character than I realized. Caleb, has thou thought thou might have been taken by mistake for thy father?"

"What makes thee say that?"

"It's obvious. We're all rather weighty people—except Affleck, and he was Governor Penn's protege. They've escorted the Governor to Fredericksburg, I hear. But thee is young and—thee'll forgive my mentioning it—quite unimportant."

"Please don't express thy thought where any of these captains and majors can overhear thee, or they might take Father up too. He's done nothing, but he might talk rather unwisely. I can easily clear myself."

"If we have a hearing."

"But we must have a hearing! They can't keep us here without giving us a chance to speak in our own defense!" He remembered Karl at the door. "Oh, Karl asked me to find out if thee wants him to bring thy night things. Just go to the window and nod and he'll understand."

He saw James Pemberton standing with two of the sons of his father's friend, Joshua Fisher, and he went over to speak to them. James was the middle one of the three powerful and important Pemberton brothers. Though he habitually sat at the head of the facing-bench in the Great Meeting on High Street and was a very weighty Friend—in terms of spiritual rather than physical poundage—Caleb was less in awe of James than of Israel or John, partly because James was rather more human than the other two and partly because his son Phineas had gone to college with Caleb and the two were of the same age, to the day.

"Ah, Caleb," said James Pemberton without preliminary, "wast thou told the Council would hear thee in this place?"

Caleb tried to remember exactly what Marsh had said. "I certainly understood that it would," he said, "but I am not sure of the precise words."

"Thomas Affleck and Charles Eddy came with the same understanding. Charles declares that it was an actual promise. Wast thou on the Congress's list or on that made up by the Council?"

"Why, I don't know, Friend Pemberton. I haven't seen any list at all, and I didn't know there was a distinction."

"The fellow who brought me here showed me—on my insistence—a part of the Resolution of Congress, which spoke of 'apprehending and securing' the persons of certain Friends. I did not see the list, however. There was nothing at all about a hearing. It is my opinion that we are prisoners, and likely to continue so for an indefinite period."

"Prisoners." The word had a shocking sound. The room, which had had a restless, disorganized atmosphere, seemed suddenly to close in upon Caleb, as if this word were what it had been waiting for.

Thomas Fisher, a man about twelve years older than himself, whom he knew through his father's business dealings with the firm of Joshua Fisher and Sons, now turned to him. Caleb admired Thomas. Like his brothers, he had been sent abroad on coming of age to travel in Europe, but he had had the distinction of being captured at sea by a privateer and taken as a prisoner to Spain, whence he had escaped to England after a series of adventures and perils. He had married lively

Sarah Logan of Stenton, and their house on Second Street was one of the most elegant and popular in the city.

"Has thy father been taken up?" said Thomas.

"Not yet, at any rate. He went to see thy father this morning and he had not returned when I—left."

"Father is still in bed. He's been ill for several weeks. They came to him early this morning and he gave them a verbal promise not to go out of the house—since he is prevented by the doctor' s orders in any case. I left him before thy father got there. I do not understand on what basis people are being apprehended."

Caleb thought he could see why the Fishers might be under suspicion. On the outbreak of the war Joshua and his two older sons had refused to sell supplies to the Continental army, and when their warehouse had been broken into and the goods seized they had refused to accept the paper money issued by the Congress. Samuel, the second son, was outspoken in his loyalty to the English government and unnecessarily antagonistic, even belligerent, in his attitude toward those whose consciences led them to take a different course from his, a curious but not uncommon phenomenon in one who had dedicated his life to peace. Another brother, Jabez Maud, who was in England now, and Miers, the youngest, a lawyer, Caleb knew only by sight.

Assured that Thomas had no information he did not himself possess, Caleb drifted through the door into the hall, to look out from the front window into the alley. At the edge of the crowd that still filled the narrow street, he caught sight of his father in an argument with one of the guard. He could not hear the words, but from the thrust of his father's jaw and the periodic jerk of his head he knew that he was angry. Caleb flung open the window and leaned out.

"Father!" he shouted.

Mr. Middleton turned and in his face the anger cleared away as the sand of a beach is washed smooth by a wave, and his ragged features and his gray eyes in their fleshy hammocks were suffused with anxiety and tenderness.

"Wait there, Caleb," he called. "I'll come to thee."

He began to elbow his way through the milling crowd, which was made up of relatives and servants of the prisoners, mingled with curiosity seekers and the inevitable scuffling small boys and ragged girls. Before he could get near the window he was stopped by a guard, who was clearing a passage for a party approaching from Second Street.

Captain Peale, Caleb saw, was bringing in another captive. He stalked ahead, red faced and resolute, and behind him came Marsh and Heysham, one on each side of the prisoner, whom they held firmly by the arms in such a way as almost to carry him along. Behind, marching in step, came a squad of ten soldiers with muskets. After the soldiers, leaning on the arm of a broad-hatted, gray-clad Friend, was a slender, delicate-looking woman in a dove-colored dress with a white fichu.

A hush came over the crowd as they saw who it was that was being brought in with such a display of forte.

John Pemberton, the youngest of the three Pemberton brothers, was well known for his integrity and his kindness. It was still remembered among the poorer people of the city that on the day of his marriage ten years earlier he had ordered provisions sent to all the prisoners in Philadelphia. When he was a young man, no older than Caleb was now, he had withdrawn from the family business and had given himself to the service of religion. His life since then had been filled with preaching missions to England, Ireland, and Holland, arduous travels in the ministry through the backwoods of Pennsylvania and Virginia, tireless effort for friendly relations with the Indians and for the relief of freed slaves, and endless, patient work on the committees of the Yearly Meeting.

Peace was his great concern, peace with Britain, peace within one's own mind. As clerk of the Meeting for Sufferings he had signed—and probably had helped to compose—some "Advises" setting forth the traditional Quaker position against war, urging the young people of the Meeting to refrain from taking part in the present commotions.

Shocked, Caleb watched as John Pemberton was dragged in and taken upstairs. The guards made a motion to prevent his wife from following him, but Hannah Pemberton, still leaning on her companions arm, looked at them, as a mother quells a child with a long, mild, compelling look, and they stood aside awkwardly to let her pass.

Caleb heard Colonel Nicola say in an undertone to Captain Peale, "May as well let her in. In fact, I don't see any need to keep the families out now. They'll have to bring food and bedding."

Caleb went back to the window to signal to his father, but he had vanished.

In rapid succession more prisoners were brought in, several of whom signed the parole and were released at once; others, according to rumor, were transferred to the New Prison on Walnut Street. Among those who remained to join the group in the auditorium or the room upstairs, Caleb recognized Thomas Gilpin, the brother-in-law and partner of the Fishers, Miers, the lawyer brother, the Reverend Thomas Combe, who was the Rector of Christ Church, and Thomas Wharton, senior, of the firm of Wharton and James.

These were, as Phyllis Pike had said, the most respectable of Philadelphia's citizens. Thomas Wharton, indeed, was a cousin of the man with the same name who was President of the Supreme Executive Council and who was at least partly responsible for the orders that had brought them all here.

With the coming on of twilight the word got around that relatives were being permitted to come in and talk to the prisoners. It was evident now that they would have to spend the night there and that nothing would be done until the next day to clarify their position. A steady stream of wives, mothers, brothers, and servants came trickling in, bearing pillows and bedclothes and covered dishes. Little family groups gathered together in separate clusters over the big room, each one making a small enclosure for itself from chairs and benches. All looked troubled and they talked together in low tones. When candles were lit, mosquitoes and moths came swarming.

Caleb discovered that he was hungry and began to watch the door impatiently, expecting someone to come to his assistance; but the word evidently had not reached home that they would now be admitted. One or two others in the same plight sent to the City Tavern around the corner on Second Street to have supper brought in, but Caleb found that he had come off without any money in his pockets.

He was about to borrow some from his cousin when Karl arrived with a big basket containing a teapot wrapped in flannel to keep it hot and a generous supply of cold meat, biscuits, cheese, and pears. Edward and Caleb shared it, drinking in turns out of the one cap.

"Cousin Edward—" said Caleb suddenly, interrupting the older man's anxious account of his wife, Sally, who had taken the children to visit their grandparents in Germantown and who would be immeasurably distressed when she heard what had happened—"has thee ever heard of Father's doing a kindness to Timothy Matlack?"

"Yes, I remember something about it. It was ten or twelve years ago, when Timothy's beer-bottling business in Fourth Street failed. Thy father wrote off the debt owed to him. It didn't save Timothy from ruin, though. He threw in everything he had, poor fellow, and still he couldn't satisfy his creditors, many of whom were Friends. The Meeting disowned him."

"I thought he was disowned for taking part in war. He joined the militia quite early, didn't he, before he became Secretary of the Council?"

"Yes, but that was years after he was disowned. It wasn't only that he failed in business—though certainly Friends are not easy on people who cannot maintain their financial affairs in good order—but he was over fond of cockfighting and horse racing. Friends felt that the company he kept caused him to neglect his business. Besides, he was negligent in attending religious meetings. He was very resentful of censure, and the upshot of it was that he was disowned. He's never forgiven the Meeting, and I think myself that it was unnecessarily harsh. That may be one reason why such a large proportion of the prisoners here are Friends—but no, I don't believe he would be spiteful. Timothy is very hot tempered and he has a long memory for injuries—for favors, too, to do him justice—but I don't believe he is revengeful."

Tag ends of old stories came back to Caleb now, as he reached for another pear.

"He was in debtors' prison, wasn't he?"

"Yes, but not for very long. James Pemberton put up the money and got him released."

"James Pemberton is here. It's odd that Timothy Matlack didn't remember that, when he registered the names—I mean, if he has such a long memory for kindnesses."

"James was like a cow that gave a good bucket of milk and kicked it over. When Timothy first took up the cause of independency and began appearing in the street with his sword dangling by his side, Friends used to stop him and ask what he was doing with that thing. He would always answer grandly, 'I carry it to defend my property and my liberty!' One day he said it to James, and James replied, 'As to thy property, Timothy, thou knows very well thou hasn't any, and as to thy liberty, thou owes it to me.' "

Caleb whistled softly. "It would be hard for anybody to forget that."

"James didn't mean it unkindly. It's one of those flat-footed things Friends say sometimes. It's true, the Pembertons are a little arrogant, all but John, and even he never forgets that he is a Pemberton. They have many enemies besides Timothy. But I don't suppose Timothy had much to say about who was taken up and who wasn't. He is only the Secretary, after all, and chosen largely for his fine penmanship. He made the official copy of the Declaration of Independence."

They had barely finished eating when Sarah Middleton came with more food, accompanied by Amos carrying a lantern in his hand and a roll of bedding over his shoulder.

Sarah drew Caleb aside. "I've persuaded your father to rest," she said in a whisper. "He's almost beside himself. He thinks it's he they want because of the iron, not you, and I've had all I could do to keep him from giving himself up so that you can go free. But from what I hear, it's some paper the Friends issued advising their members to stay out of war that's behind it all. They say it's seditious. You're a Friend and he isn't. If he gives himself up they'll only keep the two of you. And I've told him he can do more to help you if he stays outside. He's going to see the Council tomorrow. I hear that President Wharton's own cousin is in here—is that true? So it's just for tonight, I think, Caleb. You can stand it for tonight, can't you?"

Reassured, she made up a bed for him on one of the benches, and promising to come in the morning with his breakfast she went off, with fresh lamentations when she learned that the minister of her own church was there among them.

From the front door, to which he accompanied her, Caleb watched her walk down the alley and disappear around the corner. The light of Amos's lantern, bobbing behind her, fell on the gunstock of a guard who stood motionless at the entrance to the alley. Disturbed, bewildered, indignant, but still confident that all would soon be set straight, Caleb turned back to the dim hall, where the prisoners were preparing for the night.

VII

IN THE MORNING BREAKFAST of a sort was brought in from a near-by ordinary. Since relatives and friends who gathered anxiously at the door were again shut out, Caleb carried on a highly unsatisfactory conversation with Patty through a window.

"I need money," he told her, "and some clean linen and my razor. We'll probably be out of here by afternoon, but I need those things this morning. Thee run home and send Amos back with them. Don't come thyself."

She was switching her yellow hair over her shoulders and gazing up at him with a die-away, self-conscious display of sisterly devotion in which, be saw with fury, there was not one iota of real attention. It was all for the benefit, no doubt, of some pipsqueak of a boy she had her mind on. He saw Josh Gilpin in the crowd, tall and weedy, with a pretty, babyish profile and a lazy, good humored assurance which made him irresistible to Patty and her like.

"Tell Mother," he repeated, unaware of using the word he had vowed never to use, "I need money and my razor."

"And some clean linen. I heard thee. It's coming, Mother's getting everything for thee. I didn't wait. I thought thee'd want to know we're all thinking about thee every minute:"

"Humph. How's Father?"

"He's very much agitated. But he did say now maybe thee'll learn something at first hand about liberty and tyranny."

"Thee go home!" roared Caleb.

His heated reflections on this ungrateful remark of his father's, which might or might not have been exactly as Patty reported it—though Caleb could too well imagine the wry chuckle that would accompany it—were diverted by an altercation that was taking place at the next window.

Two of the prisoners had been talking with two men outside and the guard had ordered them to stop. Even while they were reluctantly finishing their sentences, one of the soldiers cocked his gun, aimed it, and threatened to shoot. One prisoner withdrew hastily, but the other, who was Tom Affleck, stood his ground.

"Ye've no rrright to cock yon gun at me," he said, his voice thrilling with indignation and his Scotch r's. "Ah'm unarmed and ah'm brreaking no law. If ye shoot ye'll have murrrder on your conscience."

Although some bright boy outside called, "He's not that good a shot, Tommy!" there was a general buzz of protest from the people in the alley, and Colonel Nicola sharply ordered the guard away from the window.

The immediate result of the incident was a conference between the prisoners and Colonel Nicola, in which James Pemberton and Miers Fisher acted as spokesmen for the group while the rest stood about and listened. Nicola was a Frenchman, a surveyor and something of a scientist, who dealt in dry goods in a small way for his living and to whom the war had brought opportunities for breaking out of a restricting pattern and moving among men of affairs. With a good deal of originality and enterprise he had organized a corps of invalids, composed of eight companies of a hundred men each, who having been invalided home were still unfit to return to field service but were strong enough for garrison duty. This was the City Guard, of which he was colonel. They were honest, energetic patriots, willing to give of themselves beyond the ordinary call of duty; they loathed Tories and they thought of Quakers only as rich skinflints, Indian-lovers, and probable traitors.

"All I know about your imprisonment," said Colonel Nicola to James Pemberton, "is that the Council ordered me to furnish Colonel Bradford with a guard for the Freemasons' Hall and I have done as they commanded. I have nothing whatever to do with the arrests, and as far as I am concerned there is no reason why your friends should not come in and talk with you. That fellow with the gun was overzealous, and I have reprimanded him."

Having thus transferred his responsibility to William Bradford, Colonel Nicola took his departure, and shortly after that Henry Drinker was brought in.

A severe-looking man, with a heavy nose, long upper lip, firmly compressed, and a long sharp chin, reflected by a second, softer chin beneath it, Henry Drinker was one of the leading Quaker merchants of the city. He had a large brick house and grounds at the corner of Front Street and Drinker's Alley, his own dock on the river, and well-stocked warehouses. His coach was often seen on the road between the city and his country estate at Frankford. In addition, he owned considerable land on the Ohio, and he lent his support to forward movements in manufacturing; he was a member of the American Philosophical Society. Whatever he touched was sound, enlightened, and profitable. He was, in addition, a plain Friend, clerk of the Bank Meeting, and free from all temptations to levity.

In his wake came Charles Jervis, a lesser, lighter figure, and a distant cousin of Henry's charming wife, Elizabeth, whose parents had both been born in Ireland.

The prisoners gathered around the fresh arrivals, eager for news, but Drinker, like the rest, knew only that men had searched his desk for incriminating papers, proffered an unacceptable parole, and brought him here with no prospect of a hearing.

"It is entirely illegal and unprecedented," he said, "and we must make some kind of concerted protest. William Bradford seems to be in charge of the proceedings. He is thy tenant, isn't he, John? Hast thou no influence?"

It was well known that John Pemberton owned the building in which William Bradford conducted the London Coffee House, as well as his print shop next door. John Pemberton's scruples were responsible for the fact that no liquor or tobacco was sold in the Coffee House on Sunday. When Colonel Bradford passed down the alley a little later, it was John Pemberton who called him in and, as an opening, complained of the misbehavior of the guard.

"My dear Mr. Pemberton," said Bradford genially, "I have nothing to do with the guard, who are under the command of Colonel Nicola, and I have no charge over you."

"Then wilt thou be so good as to inform us," said Edward Penington acidly, "by what authority we are confined?"

"By authority of a warrant signed by Mr. George Bryan, Vice President of the Council, acting upon a recommendation of the Congress."

"We have heard of that warrant," said James Pemberton, "but we have none of us had so much as a glimpse of it."

"I'll read it to you," said Bradford. He took a paper from his inner pocket and unfolded it.

The circle of men waited, silent and intent. Caleb, the youngest, was possibly the only one who had slept well the night before, and even he looked fagged. The suddenness of the attack, the difficulty of getting definite information, the uncertainty as to the future, added a weight of tension to the burden of outrage and injustice that all felt.

There was little in what Colonel Bradford was reading so fast, skimming over the words, that was different from what Caleb had heard from Captain Peale the day before. The phrases rolled on. " 'All persons who have in their general conduct and conversation evinced a disposition inimical to the cause of America . . .' " But a disposition was not action. And why select these few among all the thousands who had thought the Declaration of Independence premature, or who believed that wrongs would be better corrected through remonstrance and discussion than through warfare? " 'Whereas it is necessary for the public safety at this time when a British army has landed in Maryland with a professed design of enslaving this free country and is now advancing toward this city as a principal object of hostility . . .' "

That was it, thought Caleb. That was what they all forgot, John Pemberton and Cousin Edward and Tom Afeck and even Caleb himself—the might of the British army less than fifty miles away and only Washington with his green-sprigged troops to stand between. And if the rebellion failed, not only would a free country be enslaved but its leaders would be hanged as traitors, and no doubt they saw the shadow of the ropes sometimes.

"William, all this is very surprising to us," said John Pemberton in a mild and reasonable tone. "Thou knows our testimony as Friends, and so does the Council, if the Congress does not, being composed mainly of men from other parts where there are few of our persuasion. But in all civilized countries, whatever be the government, men accused of crimes are considered entitled to an opportunity of being heard in their own defense. We should like to know when we shall have this opportunity, and we desire a copy of this warrant which thou hast just folded away so carefully."

"We demand it as our right," interpolated someone at the back of the group.

"If thou wilt leave it with us, we will take a copy and return the original to thee promptly."

"No, no," said Bradford. "I can't do that. But I will report your desire for a hearing to the Council and I will myself make a copy of the warrant for you."

He made his escape, with an air of relief.

Two hours later, when the fiery sun stood overhead and the day seemed already as long as three days together, he was back again. He had just come from the Council, he reported, and they had informed him that since they still had not arrested all the persons on the list, it would not be proper to give a copy of the warrant now. Council had nothing to say about the possibility of a hearing.

The guard was instructed to admit friends of the prisoners, and there was the relief of diversion as people poured in with food and other comforts. Sarah Middleton came herself with the things that Caleb had asked for. She had little news. His father had been out all morning, besieging everyone of influence whom he knew, but the doors of the Council and of the Congress had been closed to him. He had been to see Magistrate Paschall, however, and he had promised to look into the matter. Sarah had persuaded her husband to lie down for a little while after dinner, for his face was as red as a beet and she was afraid he would have an apoplexy.

"I'm surprised they haven't brought in Israel Pemberton" said Sarah. " 'The King of the Quakers!' They say John Adams can't abide the sight of him—says he is Jesuitical." She liked a bit of gossip; she found it distracting and relaxing even—or perhaps especially—in the midst of anxiety. "I saw Mrs. Miers Fisher—now she's a bright, amiable young woman, I wish we could find a wife like that for you. I think Caroline Rutter is a nice girl enough, but she's too open about wanting her own way, and you'd never be able to stand that. Anyhow, Mrs. Fisher told me the Congress had appointed a committee of Mr.

Adams and Mr. Dues and Mr. Lee to get up this fine Resolution of theirs, and Mr. Adams would never leave Israel Pemberton off any such list. Mrs. Fisher can't see why he included Miers, though. He—Mr. Adams—came to their house for dinner two-three years ago, and they all got along famously. Mr. Adams paid her many compliments about her hospitality. Oh, well, I mustn't rattle on. This is a tiring, comfortless place for you to be, Caleb, and the worst of it is we don't know how long."

After she had gone Caleb occupied himself with making a list of his fellow prisoners, trying to see some thread of reason in the selection. Sixteen were now confined in the Lodge. Of them, Miers Fisher was a lawyer, Thomas Combe a minister, Tom Affleck a cabinetmaker, Drewet Smith an apothecary, Charles Eddy an ironmonger, John Pemberton a Yearly Meeting Friend, Caleb himself an iron manufacturer; the rest were Quaker merchants. It was natural that the merchants should oppose war for more than religious reasons; their prosperity and indeed their livelihood were tied up with trade with England. Yet many of them had openly opposed British policy for years. Offhand he could count eight or nine who had signed the non-importation agreement and stuck to it, in spite of heavy losses, until merchants in Baltimore and New York had privately traded with England and undermined the whole movement. He had often heard it discussed, both at home and at the Peningtons'. Cousin Edward had been a member of the Committee of Correspondence which brought the first Continental Congress into being. Thomas Wharton was known to be a friend of Benjamin Franklin's—who was now in France—and he was on so many of the same committees as his cousin Thomas Wharton, the President of the Council, that people called them Senior and junior to distinguish them.

About three o'clock, Benjamin Paschall, Justice of the Peace, accompanied by Caleb's father, came walking into the big hall. He addressed himself to the man nearest the door, who happened to be William Smith, a wholesale and retail merchant who liked to call himself a broker.

"I am come as a magistrate of this city to know what you are confined here for."

His voice, a little prim and pedantic, sounded through the hot, languid room where flies buzzed in angular circles, and the bored and dispirited men who sat dozing or meditating, conversing in low voices or merely enduring the hot hours, sprang to attention, as if animated by new life.

"We are waiting to know that ourselves," replied William Smith firmly. "We were sent here and detained by a military force, in direct violation of civil procedures, and our cause is the cause of every free man in Pennsylvania!"

He was a Yorkshireman in his thirties, forthright, red-faced, and stoutly built. Caleb was surprised by his modest eloquence.

"Then who is confining you?"

James Pemberton stepped forward. "We do not know that either. But we have been told it is in pursuance of a recommendation of Congress and a resolve of the Council."

"Have you had a hearing?" persisted Mr. Paschall, and was answered by a chorus of "No!"

"Then if you do not know what you are confined for, it is my business as a magistrate to find out."

At this pronouncement several faces brightened. Caleb had a moment for a few words with his father before Mr. Middleton left with the magistrate.

"Don't lose heart, Caleb. It is an outrage, entirely without precedent, and Mr. Paschall is determined to get justice for you. I am going with him now to see these great men of the Council. Keep thy chin up!"

Mr. Middleton was in confident spirits when he used this homely phrase, with which he had been wont to exhort Caleb when he was a little boy. It came out now as an expression of tenderness, and Caleb understood it as such. A little cheered, in spite of his overwhelming ennui, he drifted over to his cousin Edward and sat down.

"I hope they may not be clouds without rain and wind without water," said Edward skeptically.

With the lengthening of the shadows a little breeze sprang up, bringing with it the sound of Christ Church bells ringing five, and as the last note died away Mr. Paschall returned with a heavy step. Failure rode on his sagging shoulders and downcast face.

The Council meeting had broken up before he got there and its members, of whom only five or six were still in town, had scattered. Vice-President Bryan was the only one he had been able to talk with.

"We learned from Mr. Bryan," said Paschall flatly, "that you are to be sent to Virginia, without a hearing."

The words fell in the room with the effect of an explosion. The angry, the bored, the hopeful, the reasonable, the scornful, the fearful, all heard and were stunned.

"Your father, Mr. Middleton," said Mr. Paschall aside to Caleb, "has gone in his chaise to Walnut Grove, where there is some reason to believe that President Wharton has retired. There is no possibility of moving Mr. Bryan. His mind is set, and I regret to say it, but I fear he is indelibly prejudiced against the Society of Friends."

"Bryan is Irish," said Edward Penington, who had a kindly tolerance for everyone, Indians, Negroes, Roman Catholics, Jews, Turks, and Bostonians—everyone but the Irish.

"Where in Virginia are we to be banished?" inquired Thomas Gilpin.

"Staunton was mentioned," replied Mr. Paschall unhappily.

"Staunton! But that is nearly three hundred miles away—in the backwoods!"

"Anywhere in Virginia is outside the jurisdiction of the Council of Pennsylvania," said James Pemberton.

"It is an extraordinary stretch of arbitrary power," said Miers Fisher, "and we must consider how best to meet it. There are legal recourses. Article Nine of the Pennsylvania Constitution guarantees the right to trial by jury, and Article Ten has to do with freedom from search or seizure."

"The public should be informed," suggested Henry Drinker. "It is an alarming precedent. The citizens for their own sakes, if not for ours, would take an interest if they knew what was happening."

They drew chairs into a circle and sat down, with Mr. Paschall in the center. He was doubtless, Caleb thought, a conscientious magistrate, careful about details, but his personality was narrowly intellectual, fussy, and weak. He heard each speaker sympathetically, agreed and tut-tutted, becoming visibly more shocked and burdened as each opinion was added, but be had no vigorous course of action to suggest.

It was decided that a written Remonstrance was the most effective protest open to them, and a committee was named to write a draft. Caleb, sitting on the periphery beside Tom Affleck, made no contribution to the discussion. He had moved away from his cousin Edward, whose mixture of irony and temper, usually amusing to him, now set his teeth on edge.

Caleb's easy assumption of his father's place on the list of prisoners had, he was beginning to realize, placed him in a far more serious position than he had foreseen. It was no longer a matter of a few days' imprisonment, with a hearing at the end of it and swift exoneration. It was now clearly possible, even probable, that he would be sent three hundred miles away, with a company of older men, to some backwoods stockade where the chances of being heard would be small indeed. He was thankful that he could spare his father an experience which would almost certainly bring on another stroke, but the event that called forth the substitution, the arrest on suspicion of sober and responsible citizens and their sentence without a chance to defend themselves, filled Caleb with a deep and smoldering anger. He could free himself, no doubt, by declaring his devotion to the cause of liberty and offering to enlist at once in a regiment of the Continental line, but he no longer wanted to enlist. This was not the kind of liberty for which he could think of sacrificing his Quaker principles.

VIII

TWO MORE PRISONERS WERE brought in before bedtime.

With surprise Caleb recognized Dr. Phineas Bond. The younger brother of Dr. Thomas Bond, the founder of the Pennsylvania Hospital, Phineas was the physician in whose office Caleb would have started his medical career, had he been permitted to have one. Dr. Bond's enchanting daughter, Nancy, was the first girl Caleb had loved. As he now, half incredulous, watched Nancy's father, spare and fastidious, enter the cluttered auditorium, Caleb's wound, which had been a deep one, reopened. He had lost Nancy twice, first by her preference for another man, and then by her death at nineteen.

The ever-present specter of illness and early death rose to confront him. The doctors bled and blistered and applied leeches, they prescribed purges and emetics and febrifuges, and still the bloody fluxes and the fevers and the coughs and putrid sore throats went on, the mothers and the babies died, and women who had lost two husbands married men who had had three wives before them. Even Dr. Bond with all his skill and knowledge had not been able to save his adored daughter. It was presumptuous of Caleb to think that he, given the training and opportunity, might be able to cure when other men could not, and yet, surely, the urge to learn and practice new ways of healing indicated at least a possibility of latent power.

He had yielded too easily. With the cooler perspective that five years had given him, he realized that his father might have thought him more influenced by love and grief than by a real vocation for medicine. He should have stood firm. Self-contempt, the bitter, hot, unsparing flame by which the young see their transient failures and weaknesses fused with their enduring selves, poured over him in a searing flood.

To escape the discomfort of his thoughts, he jumped to his feet and started toward Dr. Bond. Then he saw the second new prisoner.

Hesitating in the doorway, his powdered wig neatly curled in a roll over each ear, his tricorne under his arm, his narrow eyes darting here and there, his scarlet coat garish even in the half-light, stood Thomas Pike, the dancing master.

Amused at seeing him like a bright tropical bird among the sober sparrows and disposed to hear news of Phyllis, Caleb made his way down the hall to greet Mr. Pike.

"Who are these gentlemen?" said Pike. "I recognize Mr. Wharton and Mr. James Pemberton, but who is the tall gentleman in the corner?"

"My cousin, Edward Penington"

"Oh, indeed? I have heard of him. Isn't that Mr. Thomas Fisher—and Mr. Drinker? And who is the gentleman sitting with his eyes closed?"

"John Pemberton," said Caleb shortly. He sought for a way to introduce the subject of Phyllis. Where was she and what would she do while her husband was away?

"Is Mr. Israel Pemberton here too—King Wampum, as they say?"

"He is still at large."

"At any rate," said Mr. Pike, settling the ruffles at his wrists, "I am in very good company."

Caleb opened his mouth to speak and shut it quickly, biting off the scornful words that pressed against his lips. "It looks," he said mildly after a moment, "as if you would have plenty of time to enjoy it."

The next day, which was Thursday, September fourth, Israel Pemberton himself, disrespectfully known as the "King of the Quakers," joined the company at the Masons' Hall.

Israel, Samuel Pleasants, his son-in-law, and John Hunt, an English Friend who had married and settled in Germantown, came in a body. The three had been together in Israel's house when the soldiers first came for them on Tuesday, and they had acted in concert. Their refusal to budge without a copy of the warrant had been so convincing—or perhaps the amplitude of Israel's mansion on Chestnut Street and his formal gardens sloping down to Dock Creek had been so awe-inspiring—that the soldiers had returned to headquarters without them. During the two days that it took the Council to issue a special order for the arrest of the three, Israel Pemberton had summoned his lawyers to help him write a letter of protest to the President and Council. Thus fortified, the three friends went with their counsel to the State House and demanded a hearing. It availed them nothing, however, and they were marched to the Lodge by Colonel Nicola himself at the head of a squad of soldiers. They arrived in time to take part in the discussion of the Remonstrance which had been prepared by the committee appointed to draw up a draft.

The Remonstrance was addressed to the President and Council of Pennsylvania. Miers Fisher and Thomas Wharton had been among its authors, and their legal knowledge and mastery of the trenchant phrase were evident in its composition. The paper began by recapitulating the history of the arrest and imprisonment of the subscribers, and went on to claim "the liberties and privileges to which we are entitled, by the fundamental rules of justice, by our birthright and inheritance, by the laws of the land, and by the express provision of the present Constitution under which your board derives its power." It proceeded then to quote in full the pertinent articles of the Constitution and to demonstrate clause by clause how they had been violated: by the vagueness of the charge; the unprecedentedly general nature of the warrant; the authorization of the agents who made the arrests to break into and search private desks for papers indefinitely "political" in nature, without limiting the search to any particular houses; the appointment of unqualified men, who held no civil office, to make the arrests and the search; and the fact that no limit was named for the duration of the imprisonment and no provision made for a hearing.

Such a precedent, it was pointed out, other and more colorful pens now taking their turn at the writing, would establish a system of arbitrary power comparable only to the Inquisition or the despotic courts of the East. They reminded the members of the Council how bitterly they themselves had criticized the British Parliament for condemning the town of Boston unheard, and inquired pointedly how they reconciled their own present conduct with their former declarations in favor of liberty.

The essay closed by committing to the Righteous judge of all the earth the integrity of the prisoners' hearts and the unparalleled tyranny of the measures of the President and Council.

After some minor corrections and improvements, all the prisoners signed the document except Samuel Fisher, who, never having approved the new government of Pennsylvania, believing it to have been formed without sufficient legal basis after the Declaration of Independence, felt that to address a Remonstrance to it would be tantamount to recognizing it.

John Reynall, a prominent Quaker merchant, and Caleb Middleton, senior, both of whom happened to be visiting the Lodge at the moment, volunteered to take the Remonstrance to the Council, although Edward Pennington pointed out to them that they did so at some risk of being themselves arrested, since they were as open to suspicion as any of the men now confined.

The messengers returned safely, however, an hour later, with the report that the Council had already adjourned when they got there. They had been fortunate to find the President, Thomas Wharton, junior, still there; he had read the Remonstrance and had appeared to be somewhat affected by it.

"He blamed you, though," said Mr. Middleton, "for not having accepted the terms of the parole first and then remonstrating. But I think he is in error there. Your position would be very much less strong if you had made what would amount to an acknowledgment of guilt by accepting parole. At all events, he promised to lay it before Council, and thinks he can send you an answer by ten o'clock tomorrow."

The hopes aroused by this prospect were soon dashed by a visit from a Quaker teamster, who came to tell them that he had been ordered to procure wagons for their removal by next Saturday. As Thursday afternoon was already well along, this news threw the company into a fever of agitation.

"Friends!" cried Israel Pemberton, shouting above the babel of voices, "I have a suggestion to make!" A man of sixty-two, tall and still erect, his brown hair streaked with white, his blue eyes fading to gray, his chin sharpening as his lips folded over the gap left by the loss of his front teeth, he was an impressive figure still, a man accustomed to authority, strong-willed, kind and generous, impatient of opposition.

In the lull that followed he continued: "In the light of the unprecedented strides Council is making in the abolition of liberty, would it not be prudent for us to acquaint out fellow citizens with the hardships we are likely to suffer? Men will do things hastily and in the dark which they are ashamed or afraid to do with deliberation in the full daylight. I cannot believe that the people of Philadelphia would countenance this injustice if they knew about it."

The force of this suggestion was immediately felt. There was a murmur of agreement throughout the group.

Henry Drinker raised his voice. "I was saying exactly that last evening, Israel, before thee came. The public should be informed. The citizens would take an interest for their own sakes, if not for ours, if they knew about what is happening."

"How do you propose going about letting them know?" asked Dr. Bond. "Is there time to get an account of the whole affair into Saturday's *Packet*?"

"Would John Dunlop consent to publish such a statement?" queried Miers Fisher. "He is hand-in-glove with the more violent members of the Council."

"We have two papers already written containing both history and argument:" said Israel Pemberton, "the protest that John Hunt and Samuel Pleasants and I drew up, and this Remonstrance which we have all signed and sent to Council. My thought would be to publish both in a handbill and get our friends outside to distribute copies as widely as possible."

This procedure was agreed upon and, since the previous messengers had some time ago departed, full of satisfaction in their efforts and ignorant of the new blow, Edward Penington's Karl was dispatched to the printer's shop on Third Street to summon Robert Bell.

Bell was a Scotsman who had come to Philadelphia eleven years earlier. He had a well-stocked bookstore next to St. Paul's Church, and a print shop at the back where he reprinted a variety of books, from Blackstone's *Commentaries on English Law* to the latest romantic drama, as well as a stream of pamphlets, mostly republican in nature.

Bell came and agreed to get their Remonstrances out at once, on a single sheet printed on both sides, which would be cheap, quickly read, and easily distributed.

By that time it was past eight o'clock. All visitors had departed; the hall was dimly lit by tallow candles here and there. Most of the prisoners were ready to go to bed for lack of anything better to do, and the family groups congregated in little circles, like bobwhites in a November field. Israel Pemberton alone sat on the platform at a table on which a three-branched candlestick blazed with light, and wrote letter after letter dated "from the place of my unjust imprisonment."

The following day, Friday, Elijah Brown was slipped in almost as an afterthought. He was a gentle, reflective man in his early thirties, very much a father and full of talk about his little son, Charles Brockden, who had just got his first pair of breeches.

The prisoners now numbered twenty-two, of whom all but five were members of the Society of Friends.

IX

"FRIENDS, THE ANSWER TO our Remonstrance has come."

All day they had waited for this. The sun had gone down on their hopes deferred, their speculations, their frayed nerves. Now, gathered in one of the smaller rooms upstairs, they were discussing the draft of a proposed "Address to the Inhabitants of Pennsylvania" when a messenger came with a letter which he handed to James Pemberton, who was acting as clerk of the meeting.

Caleb, who had been slouching in a chair at the back of the room, dejected and irritable, sat up with a jerk and folded his arms across his chest. His confidence in the free new government of Pennsylvania, worn theadbare by four days in the Masons' Hall, renewed itself with a surge. The Remonstrance had been a strong one, and if the members of the Council gave any thought to it at all—and evidently they had, since they were answering it—tbere was but one possible outcome. Nothing further had been heard about their leaving on Saturday, tomorrow, and that in itself gave room for hope.

James Pemberton, having fumbled with his spectacles, opened the letter and held it close to the candle on the table. In the shadowy room, twenty-two men waited expectantly.

There was a long pause, while James Pemberton read the paper, turned it over, read it again.

"It is not addressed to us;" he said finally. Disappointment and dismay were written in all the drooping lines of his tired, kindly face. "It is a letter from Timothy Matlack, Secretary of the Council, to Colonel William Bradford, dated September 5, 1777—today, that is. I will read it in toto.

"Sir,

A remonstrance, signed by the gentlemen confined at the Masons' Lodge, having been presented to Council and read, the Council took the same into consideration, and asked the advice of Congress thereupon, which being received, Council thereupon passed the following resolve, which they beg the favor of you to communicate to the aforesaid gentlemen."

"They *asked the advice* of Congress!" interpolated Thomas Wharton indignantly. "What! Are unaccused citizens of Pennsylvania demanding their inherent rights to be delayed a hearing until Congress can be consulted! The Congress from the beginning has been engaged not to interfere in the internal affairs of the governments."

"Let us bear the rest of it," urged the dry voice of Henry Drinker.

"Resolved, That such of the persons now confined in the Lodge as shall take and subscribe the oath or affirmation required by law in this commonwealth, or that shall take and subscribe the following oath or affirmation, to wit:

" 'I do swear (or affirm) that I will be faithful and bear true allegiance to the Commonwealth of Pennsylvania as a free and independent state' shall be discharged."

James Pemberton paused for a moment, then, heavily, finished the letter. " 'I am respectfully, Your very humble servant, Timothy Matlack, Secretary.' "

There was a stunned, incredulous silence.

"Will the clerk please read it again?" said Dr. Combe.

"All of it?"

"Just the resolution of the Council will be enough."

It was read, and another silence ensued.

Samuel Pleasants rose. His eyes looked very large and dark in the candlelight, and the qualities of innocence and good nature that led his intimates to call him Sammy spoke in his slow, soft voice. "Since there is nothing in that letter about a hearing," he said, "I wonder if it *is* an answer to our Remonstrance, or just an independent communication, in which case we may look for an answer to our document at some future time?"

"The letter begins with a reference to our Remonstrance and to their consideration of it, so that I think we must regard this as their answer."

"In any case," said Israel Pemberton impatiently, with snapping eyes and jutting chin, "it is a very improper proposition to make to men in our situation. First they deprive us of our liberty, on one pretext, and then when they find they cannot justify that, they waive it and require, as a condition before setting us free, that we take this test oath. By taking it under these circumstances, we should confess ourselves to be suspicious characters."

Edward Penington and Charles Jervis stood up at the same moment and Charles Jervis hastily sat down again. "Friends," said Edward, "this is nothing new in history. We have all been brought up on stories of the sufferings of the early Friends. Probably there are few of us here who have not at least one ancestor who was dragged before a magistrate for refusing to take off his hat to someone in authority or for attending a meeting for worship in defiance of the Conventicle Act, and then afterward was offered a test oath which he could not conscientiously take as the only condition on which he could be set free. The pages of history in both old and new England are stained with such accounts. But I should not have expected that these examples would be followed by men professing to be reformers devoted to civil and religious liberty."

"*I* should not have expected," said Israel Pemberton, "that the haven which Friends established in Pennsylvania for the persecuted of all religions would ever become a place of danger to Friends themselves."

Caleb put his elbows on his knees and his head in his hands, moving his fingers through his hair, wishing that he could shut out the speeches that people were making. He had no objection to the substance of the oath or affirmation, but how could he take it when it was put to him in this way, at the point of a gun, so to speak, so that the taking of it would not be the act of a free man offering his loyalty but a prisoner's craven grasping at anything for release?

He heard the Scotch voice of Tom Affleck and raised his head to listen.

"If they think we are so dangerous that we must be sent three hundred miles away, out of their jurisdiction altogether, then what difference do they suppose an oath could make? Everybody knows that bad men will swear to anything."

Caleb grinned at him and lowered his head into his hands again. As one after another expressed himself to the same effect, Caleb sighed long, gusty sighs, flung himself back in his chair and stared up at the ceiling, slewed around in his seat with his arm over the back of it and watched a mosquito which had settled itself on his knuckle visibly swell. He felt no desire to add to the spate of words himself; it had all been said, six times over, and there was nothing to say anyhow. He would have given ten years of his life to be able to mount Ladybird and ride up over the hill behind the furnace. The crickets and the katydids would be singing, the air would be as soft as velvet, and the whole enormous star-studded sky would be wheeling slowly overhead.

"It is plainly the sense of the meeting," said James Pemberton, "that we should refuse this proposal. How do you wish to go about it?"

"I think we should draw up a statement refusing the test oath or affirmation, giving the reasons which have already been expressed here," said Thomas Fisher. "We should declare our innocence once more and repeat our demand to be informed of the cause of our commitment and to have a hearing by which we can be acquitted or condemned by our fellow men."

There was a murmur of approval: "I unite with that." "I hope that will be done."

"I should like to see a *small* committee appointed to draw up such a statement," suggested Henry Drinker, who had worked on the Remonstrance. "Six are too many."

"Would three be a suitable number?"

"Two would be still better. Enough has been said here tonight to give them all they need to work on."

Nobody objecting to that, the clerk called for two names.

"Miers Fisher."

"Thomas Wharton."

"If these Friends are willing to serve, I have no doubt they will be open to suggestions from others."

The meeting was winding itself up according to the usual ritual and would soon close "with a few moments of silence." Caleb groaned inwardly when his cousin Edward began to speak.

"The making of a fair copy of such a statement is a task in itself, and I think those who have the arduous labor of composition should not be burdened with copying. Caleb Middleton has a rapid and legible—though scarcely an elegant—hand, and I suggest that he be added to the committee as amanuensis."

Somebody obligingly hoped that would be done, James Pemberton looked at Caleb to see if he had any objections, and Caleb nodded a little self-consciously, pleased on the whole at the idea. It would at least be something to do.

X

AGAINST THE PROTESTS OF his wife, who was sure that he was overtiring himself, Mr. Middleton set forth on Sunday morning to visit his son in the Masons' Hall. Already the day was warm and oppressive, with the September sun magnified by the mist, and the leaves of trees, grown overlarge in the damp summer heat, acting as a roof to keep out any breeze there might be. A brooding air of impending crisis hung over the city, and the people whom he passed looked troubled and restless. Men in uniform were everywhere, and there was none of the usual cheerful Sunday atmosphere of churchgoing and roast chicken.

To his surprise the guard at the Masons' Hall refused to let him in.

"What's this?" he demanded. "Some new measure of the Council's?"

"No, Sir. It's the request of the prisoners themselves. They're having their religious services and they don't want to be disturbed."

He felt curiously rejected as he tramped away, leaning rather heavily on his stick. He might have known, he told himself, that they would be holding meeting for worship. That could be held anywhere; no church or altar was needed. If he had got there earlier, he might have joined them.

He had missed the Meeting comparatively little since his disownment, though occasionally, as now, he felt a sharp longing to he part of that waiting stillness. There was nothing to keep him, of course, from attending Meeting in Pine Street as he used to do. More than one disowned Friend continued placidly to appear at meetings for worship, even though he could no longer take part in meetings for business or other activities. But that would not be satisfactory to Mr. Middleton. He could not worship where he had been denied membership.

Sarah was always after him to go to church with her, but he was still too much of a Quaker to feel comfortable at Christ Church. He did not like all that restless jumping up and down, the singing, the repetition of formal prayers. For the most part, he stayed home quite contentedly and caught up with his reading. In the country they were too far away from either Church or Meeting to go often in any case.

He did not regret his marriage, he reflected, waiting for a chaise to pass before he crossed Third Street, even though it had cost him his membership in the Meeting and to same extent the confidence of his son. Sarah was a good woman and a comfort to him in every way. She had been a real mother to the younger children and they gave her the love they would have given their own mother. Her coming into the family had freed Sue to marry young Mercer instead of being sacrificed to the necessity of taking care of her younger brother and sisters, and the property that Sarah brought with her would not be amiss when it came to providing for the younger ones. Caleb of course would have his inheritance from his mother's father in another year or so.

Caleb alone had not welcomed his stepmother. It seemed as if the boy were determined to oppose his father in everything. All that fever to be a doctor, when he was needed at the furnace and a brilliant future lay before him there! If he had wanted to be a lawyer, Mr. Middleton reflected, it might have been different. But doctoring was a messy, morbid sort of business; it put one on too intimate terms with all kinds of people. "I'll not have a man-midwife in the family," he had declared firmly, and in the end the boy had come round. He had thrown himself into the manufacture of iron with a vim and capability that proved how right he, the father, had been. It hadn't taken young Caleb long to adopt the manner and style of an ironmaster, and he plainly enjoyed all the deference and attention that went with his position. Mr. Middleton smiled reminiscently. He had liked to see Caleb taking his proper place, had been proud of him.

It was strange—but just like Caleb's contrariness—that after making such a fuss about going into the iron business, he should be so hotly opposed to closing down the furnace when it was obviously the sensible thing to do. Well, he was getting a dose of "liberty" now—perhaps not a bad thing if it opened his eyes. But it had gone on too long already, and Mr. Middleton meant to get his son out of the Lodge if it was humanly possible.

He would have liked to get Caleb's approval of his plan of action, but since the boy wasn't available he would just have to go ahead with it anyhow. He did not like—turning down Fourth Street past the Meeting House and the school—to remind a man of past favors, and he would not. All that was over and done; it belonged to the past. He would not so much as hint at it. But it had been a considerable sum and he doubted if Timothy Matlack had entirely forgotten. Matlack had never been financially able to offer to repay it, but since he had embraced the cause of the colonies his political advancement had been noteworthy and he was in a position now to make a return in a different coin. That was one more thing Mr. Middleton had against the new government of Pennsylvania: the way people who could not stay solvent in business or were not received in the better houses could scramble up the political ladder to places of power and trust.

He came to the Matlack house, a modest brick dwelling in a row, and tapped briskly with the knocker.

The door was opened by Timothy's wife, Ellen, who looked disappointed for a moment but quickly rallied. "I thought it was Timothy come home," she explained. "It's Mr. Middleton, isn't it? Won't you come in, sir?"

"Timothy's not here?"

"No, he had to go back to the State House. The Council's meeting again this morning, even though it's Sunday. They had so much business yesterday they couldn't finish. He said he thought it wouldn't be long. Will you come in and wait for him?"

"No, thank you. I think I'll walk around to the State House and catch him there." He fished in his memory for the subject of a kind inquiry. "How are the little boys?" he found.

"They're not little any longer. Billy is a sergeant in Colonel Bradford's battalion and Mordecai has gone to sea as a midshipman. He seems young for it, though he's turned fourteen."

"Dear me, I'd no idea. You must miss them. Thank you, Madam, and good morning."

He went up Walnut Street to the new prison and crossed the State

House yard. The prison was a very fine, large, stone building and Philadelphia was proud of it. Mr. Middleton thought it was perhaps not a bad thing to have the gaol so clearly visible from the back windows of the State House—it might remind the legislators that they too were not above the law and its penalties.

The Congress, which on weekdays shared the building with the state bodies, was not meeting this morning, nor was the Pennsylvania Assembly. Only the Council was carrying on its business behind closed doors. The hallway had the upswept, hard-used, shabby look of public buildings, and Mr. Middleton dusted off a bench with his handkerchief before he sat down to wait for the Council meeting to break up.

He was glad to sit down, for the sudden exhaustion that came so quickly these days swept over him, bringing a hot wave of dizziness with it. He folded his hands over the ivory head of his stick and closed his eyes.

As the clock struck eleven a door opened upstairs, followed by the sound of voices and footsteps. Six men came down the stairs, President Wharton in front, talking with a Mr. Scott, whom Mr. Middleton knew only by sight. They were followed by three who were strangers to him, upcountry men probably, and then Timothy Matlack, the Secretary, brought up the rear.

President Wharton pretended to be so engrossed in his conversation that he did not see Mr. Middleton sitting there on the bench, and he whisked his companion out the back door before there was any chance of his being approached. The others went through the front door onto Chestnut Street. Matlack stopped to speak to the janitor, who had come up from the cellar.

"That's all for today, John. You can lock up now. Ah, good morning, Mr. Middleton. You were waiting for me?"

"Timothy, how are you? I'd like to have a word with you. It's rather a private matter. I thought we might just have a few minutes in one of the rooms here."

"Come to the Coach and Horses Inn with me across the street. There's seldom anybody there when the State House is closed, and I don't like to keep our janitor any longer than necessary."

The small, old, hip-roofed tavern, which at certain hours on week-days overflowed with politicians, was deserted now. The two men went in under the swinging sign with its somewhat faded picture of a coach and horses, and sitting down at a table in the far corner, ordered coffee.

"You are very busy, I know. I'll be brief."

"We are extremely busy. The Council was so much occupied yester-day with political affairs that there was no time to finish the most pressing military matter, the calling out of the entire Pennsylvania mi-litia to meet the emergency. We met this morning to complete the ar-rangements."

"Yes, yes." Mr. Middleton brushed aside the city's danger, eager to get on with his business before the other man could finish his coffee and escape. "Timothy, we are old friends. We have been through cer-tain difficulties. We have both been disowned by our Meetings. There is a certain bond between us. That is why I come to you now. Extricate my boy from this unreasonable imprisonment. They're talking about banishment now."

Colonel Matlack's brows drew together in a frown and there was an odd expression in his eyes, Mr. Middleton thought, as Timothy looked at him and then looked away, staring out through the small-paned window at the straggly asters in the vacant lot next to the tavern. The Colonel was a large man, not much over forty, with gray-ing hair, a big, egg-shaped face, a long, heavy nose, and rather small, thin-lipped mouth. It was not easy to read his face, except when it was contorted with anger, as it not infrequently was. But he was not angry now.

"Your boy can free himself quite easily," he said after a long silence, "simply by taking the oath of allegiance. He doesn't even need to swear, he can affirm."

"He won't do that. They won't any of them take an oath or affirma-tion of allegiance now. They say they were taken up on suspicion and given no chance to clear themselves. Now they're offered a test oath as the price of freedom. They won't take it. It isn't a question of loyalty, it's a matter of principle. Caleb's no traitor to the American cause. To say the truth, he's troubled me because he embraces it too uncriti-cally."

"Then why doesn't he join the militia? Both my sons are in the service of their country, and they are much younger than yours."

"Caleb is a Friend."

"So was I. So were Anthony and Sam Morris and about a fifth of all young men members of the Philadelphia Meetings. No, I'm sorry, Mr. Middleton, there's nothing I can do for your son unless he cares to do the simple and obvious thing for himself. Both the Congress and the Council spent hours on the case yesterday, and that in the midst of the most pressing and vital affairs. Do you realize that the British army is within fifty miles of Philadelphia on the west and that the British navy has been reported at the mouth of the Delaware heading for the city?"

"It would take no more than a few minutes to release a score of innocent gentlemen—if you haven't time to give them a hearing."

"How do you know they are all innocent? They are notoriously disaffected. The British army marches toward Philadelphia over country largely inhabited by Quaker farmers, who are likely to be very much influenced by those same innocent gentlemen in the Masons' Lodge. They won't oppose the British—and they may go over to them altogether. Any government has the right in an hour of crisis to attest and secure persons suspected of giving aid to the enemy or injuring the patriot cause. The crowd in the Masons' Hall can take the oath or affirmation of allegiance and go free. Or they can go to Staunton as prisoners. They have their choice. The Congress and the Council will not go back on that. And no argument and no handbills will move them now. I'm going to give you, Mr. Middleton, the same advice I have already given Mr. Reynell and Mr. Paschall. Stop running around with remonstrances and protests and appeals, and stay quietly in your homes. I mean it kindly."

"The prisoners are not all Quakers. Five are Church of England."

"They are separate cases. They can take the oath too, and they haven't the peculiarly tender consciences Friends have in such matters."

"On what basis have these men been taken up? Why my son, for instance, and not myself? Why Israel Pemberton and not John Reynell? Why Miers Fisher and not Nicholas Waln?"

Timothy gulped the last of his coffee and rose from the table. "I must leave you now," he said. "I cannot linger any longer." As he spoke a boy came in with a pile of newspapers and put them down on a table. Matlack picked one up and scanned it with interest. After a second's hesitation Mr. Middleton possessed himself of another.

It was a supplement to the weekly *Pennsylvania Packet* and it contained a series of "Papers Published by the Order of Congress." Mr. Middleton, as he took in their content, uttered a cry of outrage and reached out to seize the skirt of Matlack's coat to prevent him from leaving.

"Look at this!" he exclaimed. "What do you know about this? *Spanktown Yearly Meeting!*"

He passed over four or five statements issued by various Quaker bodies between 1775 and 1777, advising their members to hold fast to the ancient Quaker testimony against war and rebellion, and pointed to one headed, "Extract of a letter from General Sullivan to Congress, August 25, 1777."

"Among the baggage taken on Staten Island," the letter ran, "the 22nd instant, I find a number of important papers. A copy of three I enclose for the perusal of Congress. The one from the Yearly Meeting at Spanktown, held the 19th instant, I think worthy the attention of Congress."

Then came a list of eight questions concerning military matters, beginning with, "Where is Washington? What number of men or cannon?" and ending, "Be very particular about time and place."

Following that were the answers, described as "Information from Jersey," dated August nineteenth. "It is said Howe landed near the head of Chesapeake Bay but cannot learn the particular spot now, when Washington lays in Pennsylvania, about 12 miles from Coryell's ferry. Sullivan lays about 6 miles northwestward of Morristown, with about 2000 men. *Spanktown Yearly Meeting.*" Another, headed "Intelligence from Jersey July 28, 1777," dealt with troop movements near Morristown and was unsigned.

"You know very well," exclaimed Mr. Middleton, "that there is no Spanktown Yearly Meeting. Even if there were such a body, any official paper would be signed by the clerk for the Meeting. This is a patent forgery, designed to put the prisoners in the worst possible light!"

Colonel Matlack looked uneasy. "I myself have never heard of a Meeting at Spanktown—"

"The very name of Spanktown is an obvious fiction!"

"But the papers were published by the order of Congress, not of Council. The greater part of them are Philadelphia Yearly Meeting Epistles and Advices. They call on their members to be neutral at a time when there can be no neutrality. To us, anyone who is neutral is actually supporting the enemy. I must go, Mr. Middleton. But I'll tell you this—" he was angry now; his temples throbbed and his cheek twitched and two deep lines like exclamation marks had sprang up between his eyebrows—"the prisoners brought the publication of these papers on themselves. When they printed their Remonstrance and it became clear they meant to raise a ferment, then the Congress decided to give its account of this transaction to the public. The Congress has had these papers two weeks or more and would not have published them unless they had felt it to be necessary. I bid you good-day, sir."

Mr. Middleton plumped down again and ordered another cup of coffee. When it came, he was too much agitated to drink it, but sat swishing it round and round in the cup, staring at the table. Caleb would go, then, as a prisoner and unheard, to some remote spot on the Virginia frontier. In an undefinable yet disturbing way he felt responsible for this disaster that had come upon his son. His own decision to close the furnace was, he felt sure, behind it. They had taken the young man, caring nothing for the injustice of it, casting aside the old one as used up and negligible.

He felt a hand on his shoulder and lifted his eyes to see Dr. Hutchinson looking down at him in kindly concern.

"Thee looks tired, Friend Middleton. Ought thee to have come out this morning?"

He had seen the young Quaker physician often during the past few days, for he too had been busy carrying messages and running errands for the prisoners. Already portly at twenty-five, pink-cheeked, kind, and indefatigable, James Hutchinson was, though a birthright Friend and a nephew by marriage of Israel Pemberton, an outspoken republican who went further than many of the radicals in his opposition to wealth and privilege. Family loyalty and frank disapproval of what he called "Star-Chamber methods" had led him to take a conspicuous part in trying to obtain a hearing for the prisoners.

"So thee's seen the supplement to the *Packet*," said Dr. Hutchinson. "An unpleasant affair. I cannot see any justification whatever for printing that."

"Sit down, won't thee, James, and join me in a cup of coffee? Boy! Another cup of mocha. Thou'rt a Whig. Can thee explain to me why the members of the Congress would so lower themselves as to publish a palpable forgery like this—these '*Spanktown*' papers?"

"I find it difficult to understand. Perhaps those actually responsible for their publication believed them to be genuine. Friends' ways are totally incomprehensible to many non-Friends."

"Anyone who took the slightest trouble to compare the genuine Advices and Epistles with the Spanktown papers could see at a glance the difference in both content and form. These Spanktown papers were written by someone ignorant of the common usages of English grammar. Washington *lays*—Sullivan *lays*—as if they were hens! Did one of the members of Congress himself invent them? Who did it?"

"I think there is no doubt that they were taken from captured prisoners by officers of General Sullivan's army. My own conjecture would be that the papers were the work of a genuine spy—though not a very skillful one—and that someone hostile to Quakers, possibly one of the officers themselves, added the signature, 'Spanktown Yearly Meeting'; either as a joke or with the intention of discrediting the whole Society of Friends. General Sullivan himself obviously believed it to be genuine and so did some of the members of Congress though certainly not all of them."

"Thou'rt very calm about this disgraceful affair."

"I deplore it, I assure thee, and I regret very much that the Congress and Council have thought it necessary to arrest those now in the Lodge. It makes many of us in the patriot cause uneasy. But when a city is threatened with invasion by an approaching enemy, things are done that would not be done under ordinary circumstances. I still have a hope that reason will prevail. Our friends in the Lodge are en-

gaged in writing another Remonstrance to the Council and one to the
Congress, and I wish they may have an effect. If I may make a suggestion to thee, Friend Middleton, I think thee would be wise to go home
and go to bed. Thee has done all for thy son that thee can do at present,
and now thee ought to conserve thy strength."

Mr. Middleton struggled up from his seat at the table and the
high-backed settee behind him heaved with his efforts. "I had intended to return to the Lodge to see my son—their Meeting is surely
over by now—but perhaps thou'rt right." His breath came in little
gasps. "Perhaps I had better go home."

It was only a matter of six squares, but home seemed suddenly a
long distance away.

"I have my chaise outside. I had to make a call in the Northern Liberties earlier. I'll just drive thee home."

The young doctor's smooth, round, healthy face was full of kindness and sympathy as he helped Mr. Middleton into the shabby chaise
and went to unhitch his apathetic horse. It was a pity, thought Caleb
Middleton, that young Hutchinson had thrown himself so deeply
into the Continental cause, though certainly he was not following the
leaders blindly or uncritically. He was sound in his attitude to both the
Spanktown papers and the imprisonment of Caleb and the rest. No
doubt young Hutchinson was another of those who, like Timothy
Matlack, saw opportunities for advancement in a republican government that they would not have in a royal government. In spite of having married Israel Pemberton's niece, Hutchinson was still the son of
a stone mason and might find it more difficult in a settled society to
rise above his origin.

But he was showing courage in standing by Israel Pemberton now.
Mr. Middleton smoothed out the copy of the *Packet* which he still carried crumpled in his hand and folded it carefully, as they moved slowly
over the cobblestones on Chestnut Sheet past Israel Pemberton's big
mansion. Israel had enemies, social, religious, political, who no doubt
were rejoicing in his downfall.

"Fear and malice," he said aloud, as the chaise pulled up at the
cross-street to let a squad of men in uniform march past, "make a bad
combination."

XI

CALEB PUT DOWN HIS quill and pressed his flattened forefinger back into shape. It was midday on Monday and he had been writing all morning, copying the prisoners' answer to the offer of the Council to free those who would take the oath of affirmation of allegiance.

It was a long document, written by Thomas Wharton and Miers Fisher and incorporating suggestions made by others. The first draft had been much shorter, but while they were discussing it the afternoon before, a supplement to the *Pennsylvania Packet* had been brought in, containing papers purporting to be from Spanktown Yearly Meeting. Indignation had run high within the Masons' Lodge and there had been many useless speculations as to who had perpetrated this outrage. When they returned to the consideration of their answer to the Council, their attitude had hardened and their words became sharper and tinged with sarcasm.

They had been united in refusing to take the oath or affirmation of allegiance. The five members of the Church of England, although the papers in the Packet, directed wholly against Friends, did not incriminate them, stood firm with the test.

"We have none of us," said Mr. Combe, speaking for the five, "directly or indirectly communicated any intelligence to the British forces, and we would quite cheerfully engage not to hold any correspondence in future, if the demand had not been coupled with ignominious and illegal restrictions. Our consciousness of our own innocence forbids us to accede under the circumstances."

It would have been better, Caleb thought, to make the answer a brief and strong refusal to take the oath, without going over once more all the arguments dealing with their imprisonment, but he was much the youngest among them and his opinions were not solicited.

John Hunt, the oldest of the group, complained that the document was lacking in expressions of conciliating love, but Israel Pemberton declared himself satisfied that "We shall send them such a Remonstrance as they have not before read!" and it was decided to make no further changes in the draft, except for the addition of a pronouncement by Lord Halifax on the subject of test oaths after the Revolution of 1688. "As there is no real security to any state by oaths, so no private person, much less statesman, would ever order his affairs as relying on it; for no man would ever sleep with open doors or unlocked-up treasure, should all the town be sworn not to rob." This quotation was supplied by Elijah Brown, who kept a commonplace book from which apparently he was never separated.

Caleb had copied the Remonstrance in his best hand, and it now lay on the table ready for their twenty-two signatures. Even Samuel Fisher was now willing to concede that recognition did not necessarily signify approval and had promised to sign this protest. Dr. James Hutchinson offered to carry it to the Council.

"Thy father is remaining in bed today, on my advice," he told Caleb, "though he was very anxious to come and see thee. He sent his love to thee."

Caleb thanked him, rather relieved than otherwise that he would not have to hear the lamentations and fulminations of his aroused parent. He was feeling very low in spirits and almost intolerably irked by the fact of imprisonment. The enclosing walls, the dingy windows with their oblongs of cloudy sky, the pressure of other and older men's inescapable presence, the irregular and unappetizing meals, the endless conversations, rumors, speculations, denunciations, mingled with the admonitions of the more pious to avoid "murmuring" and to submit to the will of God, fretted his spirit as the rebellion of his young muscles and nerves against the enforced inactivity tortured his body. Despite his anger at the officials of the Congress and Council, he could still see that beyond the fears and suspicions and petty animosities of the stuffy rooms in the Stare House, there was taking place under the open sky a struggle for the freedom from which he was now debarred. He had no hope that their remonstrances and protests would avail them anything now. Congress would not have published the Spanktown forgery if it had not already made up its mind to banish the prisoners. The only prospect of change from the Masons' Hall that he saw ahead of him was some gaol in the depths of the Virginia mountains, where their voices could not be heard and where they might lie forgotten till they moldered away. Once they were out of sight and sound, who would remember them again, in the midst of a war to be fought against appalling odds?

The afternoon passed somehow. Dr. Hutchinson, round and perspiring in the muggy gray heat of the day, returned with a note from Timothy Matlack saying that the Remonstrance had been read in Council and their business referred to Congress. The prisoners sent him hurrying back to Colonel Matlack to request a copy of the minute of referral and to ask whose prisoners the Council considered them to be, the Council's or the Congress's.

It was late when he returned, without the minute but with the retort from Timothy Matlack that their question was "artful and insidious" and that he was not authorized to answer it.

Pouncing on this evasion like a cat on the tip of a tail disappearing into a mousehole, the prisoners early the next morning, which was Tuesday the ninth of September, sent the same request in writing to the President of the Council. They got no answer but they learned how awkward a question it was. Neither Council nor Congress, Dr. Hutchinson told them, wished to take responsibility for holding them.

"On Seventh Day last, the Congress advised the Council to give you a hearing," he said. "The Council answered that it had no time in the present alarming crisis and requested the Congress to dispose of you. Thomas Wharton, junior, told me he thought you should have a hearing, but others were opposed. They are still debating."

Since there was yet a faint chance that the Council might be moved by reason, the prisoners wrote another protest, their fourth. Caleb, copying it, thought it was the clearest and strongest of all.

"You condemn us to banishment unheard . . . . You determine matters concerning us which we could have disproved, had our right to a hearing been granted . . . . The charge against us of 'refusing to promise to *refrain* from corresponding with the enemy' insinuates that we have already held such correspondence, *which we utterly and solemnly deny.*"

Caleb had also to copy an "Address to the Inhabitants of Pennsylvania," which contained the entire history of their imprisonment, the general warrant for their arrest, all their remonstrances, a protest on their behalf signed by one hundred and thirteen Friends, and the various communications from the Council. This was to be printed in a pamphlet and distributed as widely as possible.

At half past four that afternoon the axe fell.

A messenger came from the Council with the Resolution that had ended the debate. It named the twenty-two "apprehended as persons who have uniformly manifested by their general conduct and conversation a disposition highly inimical to the cause of America," declared that they had renounced all the privileges of citizenship, and ordered that they be "without further delay removed to Staunton in Virginia, there to be treated according to their characters and stations as far as may be consistent with the security of their persons."

Some further delay there was, however—caused by the difficulty of procuring wagons at a time when every available vehicle was needed for carrying stores out of the threatened city, for transporting people who were fleeing before the British advance, and for the demands of Washington's army, now reported to be marching to intercept the British in the valley of the Brandywine.

All Wednesday agents of the Council combed the town for wagons, and those prisoners who had horses or chaises of their own were urged to use them. In the afternoon they were told that they might go home to make their final arrangements for departure on Thursday; if they wished, they might even stay overnight.

"It is the early Quakers all over again," said Edward Penington. "They imprison us unjustly, with every reason for us to feel morally justified in absconding, and then they trust us to go home for the night unattended. My own great-grandfather and others were allowed to transfer themselves from Bridewell to Newgate prison without a guard. It is our influence they fear, not our actions."

XII

BORED AND DISGUSTED THOUGH he was with life in the Masons' Hall, Caleb went home without pleasure. His brown eyes under the level brows were clouded, his lips set and his chin defiant as he walked along the dusty street, where buttonwood leaves, curled and dry, had already fallen. For the moment he was free under the blue September sky, but there was no lift in his heart. What he had seen bearing down upon him like a black storm cloud of a runaway horse was actually coming to pass. He would be sent to Virginia as a disaffected and dangerous person.

He was not looking forward to seeing his father. Too much lay unresolved between them. He could not master the resentment that rose from the conviction that if only they had stayed in the country as he himself had wished and kept the Phoebe Ann going, none of this would have happened. His father had made the decision without consulting him and then, by falling ill, had bound him to it. The report that Patty had brought of the parental humor—now perhaps he'll learn something at first hand about liberty and tyranny—rankled. Like an infection it spread to inflame the wound which his enthusiasm for the American cause had suffered. The consciousness of his sacrifice in taking his father's place as a prisoner brought him none of the consolations of virtue, since he had merely acquiesced in the substitution, not initiated it. Divided and torn within himself, he wanted to escape, not to go back to the place which he held responsible for his pain.

He would do his duty and no more. He would pay his respects to his father and Sarah, see the children, get his things for the journey, and he might as well have a decent meal, but he would not spend the night under his father's roof. He would give Amos instructions about bringing Ladybird to the Lodge next day. The one ray of light in the gloom was that he would be allowed to ride his own mare.

Tacy, playing on the doorstep, was the first to see him. She gave a shriek of joy and came running toward him with her arms spread wide. He stood still to meet the impact and she climbed up his legs like a monkey on a stick, till he caught her up in his arms and lifted her to his shoulders, where she rode in triumph, clutching his forehead with sticky hands. Edward was next, and Amos grinned broadly as he opened the door. Patty had gone to see a classmate, and Mrs. Middleton was upstairs with Caleb's father.

"He's not so good, Master Caleb," said Amos in a low voice. "Dr. Hutchinson's been twice. He say he'll git over it if he rest, but all this runnin' aroun' in the heat afussin' himself ain' done him any good."

The house was cool and elegant, with the shifting shadows of the trees on the pale, papered walls, the reflection of asters in a silver bowl on a polished table. He could look down the dim hall and see the door open upon the sunny garden beyond and smell the faint fragrance of beeswax and the spiced rose petals in the blue and white jars on the mantel.

His stepmother met him at the top of the stairs.

"I'm so thankful you could come, Caleb. I can hardly keep your father in bed. He's been determined to get up and go to meet you. He has overdone, that's all. He'll be all right if he stays quiet. All this running back and forth to the Council and the Congress, trying to see Mr. Hancock and Mr. Wharton and anybody else he thinks of has been almost too much for him. Be careful what you say and don't get him excited. He has really suffered over all this."

Caleb went into the front bedroom where his father lay propped against pillows in the big tester bed. He looked better than he had when Caleb last saw him, as people so often do in bed, surrounded by expanses of white linen, rested, and wearing an expression of welcome for the visitor.

"I brought thee a copy of our 'Address to the Inhabitants,' " said Caleb, wrenching a pamphlet out of his coat pocket. "It came from the printer at noon. We are each to have twenty-five copies to distribute. I thought I'd leave mine with thee. Amos can get them when he takes my things to the Lodge."

Mr. Middleton took the pamphlet in his hands and examined the title page.

"Printed by Robert Bell, I see. I thought he was on the other side of the fence. That clerk of his—what was his name?—Paine?—was a rabid republican, with his *Crisis*. Called the Quakers 'fallen, cringing, and Pemberton-ridden people,' I remember distinctly."

"A printer doesn't necessarily believe everything he prints," said Caleb. "Bell has courage. Benjamin Towne refused to print our Remonstrance. He said openly he was afraid of being taken up as a disaffected person and having his press stopped. William Sellers said he would consult a friend about it, but he hasn't been back since."

"This is well put," said Mr. Middleton, riffling through the pages: " 'Nor can any man think himself safe if a precedent of so extraordinary a nature be established by a tame acquiescence with the present wrong.' That's a very revolutionary statement—too revolutionary for even the new rebel government, I should think. Most governments prefer a tame acquiescence on the part of the governed."

Caleb tilted his chair back on two legs, clasped his hands behind his head and yawned. The words of the Address were almost meaningless to him now. He had heard them read and reread, the succeeding drafts discussed and corrected, a word substituted here, a phrase cut there; he had copied one after another six separate remonstrances and protests and the final "Address to the Inhabitants." He was unspeakably weary of what one of the documents called the "peaceable though firm assertion of the inalienable rights of free men," and his hands twitched for action, preferably violent.

"They are right," his father said, "to resist this outrage, even to banishment. But, Caleb, I don't want thee to do it. Thou'rt young. Thou'rt entangled in this through no fault or wish of thy own. Thy sympathies are all on the American side and have been. I saw Dr. Smith the other day. He told me he had been on their list. No, no, not the apothecary—Provost Smith. He was in town earlier, he's gone now to the Falls. He took the test oath, he said. He advised thee to."

Caleb had a good deal of respect for the President of the College of Philadelphia. He would have liked to talk with him about the whole question of oaths of allegiance, for he was conscious of painful confusions in his own mind, but he did not want Dr. Smith's opinions filtered through his father's commands. "No, I can't do it, Father. I won't even think about it."

The older man sighed.

Caleb let the front legs of his chair down to the floor with a thud, and buried his head in his hands. The new government of Pennsylvania, to which the oath or affirmation promised allegiance, had ceased to be for him a noble abstraction and had become instead a personal entity. Thomas Wharton, junior, self-righteous and evasive, George Bryan, the Irishman, who hated everything that was English and noisily identified himself with the people against the well-born, Timothy Matlack, born a Friend, knowing what Friends stood for, accepting as valid papers which he could not help knowing were forged: there they were, mouthing all the slogans about liberty, calling on men to die for it, and in their actions denying the first essentials of it. If he could promise allegiance to what General Washington stood for, that would be one thing, but to swear, or affirm, his faith in Messrs. Wharton, Bryan, Matlack and company, no thanks. Nor was he going to dance when his father pulled the strings.

"I hear that there has been no appropriation for your expenses," his father was saying.

"Council will pay our expenses on the road and then Congress will be applied to, to consider our support during our absence. We got that much from Nicola this morning. But they still won't say whose prisoners we are."

"Who will have custody of you when you get to Virginia?"

"The Governor of Virginia, according to Nicola. Who is the Governor of Virginia anyhow?"

"Mr. Henry, I believe. Give him liberty or give him death."

Caleb swore.

"No, no, Caleb, don't swear! That was too bad of me to say that! What I'm getting at, my boy, is that I have foreseen that thou wilt need funds. In the top drawer of the chest, in the righthand corner, there is a money-belt which I want thee to take. There are twenty gold half-joes in it, and I'll find a way to get more to thee if thou needs it. Thou'll have to change them for Continental bills, but get the best rate thou can."

Caleb took the belt, heavy with coins, and fastened it around his waist inside his shirt. He felt a kind of strength and even a sense of release coming to him from the touch and weight of that belt, which seemed to permeate his viscera directly without passing through his brain.

"I wonder what some of the others will do," he commented, after thanking his father. "Tom Affleck, for instance. He's nearly frantic about his wife and children. And Mr. Pike won't be giving any more lessons in dancing or fencing. If there's any sewing to be done in our house, I wish Mrs. Pike could be employed." She had been a seamstress in Charleston; her husband had let that out one evening. It made no difference to Caleb, but why had she concealed it?

"Speak to thy mother about it."

A faintness in his voice warned Caleb that his father was feeling the sudden devastating fatigue of his condition. He patted the old man's knee, which felt thin and knobby under the sheet, and went off to his own room, where he found his stepmother bent over an open portmanteau. It was the same one that he had used when he came to the city to college, boarding at Mrs. Graydon's until the family moved to town for the winter months; on its shabby lid were his initials in brass-headed tacks.

"I've put your greatcoat in, in case it turns cold in the mountains before you can get home, and your leather breeches, and your nankeen jacket and breeches, and two pairs of flannel drawers and two flannel shirts as well as cambric shirts and underwear. I put in half a dozen fine linen shirts and I hope there will be some way to get them properly laundered. Plenty of worsted and thread stockings. Now what I want to know is, should I put in one of your good suits and silk stockings? I suppose I'd better. You never know."

"I'm not making the grand tour of Europe. I'll need some salt. It's getting scarce, and the food from the tavern has been tasteless."

"Yes, that's another thing. I've got tea and chocolate and sugar, and a little bag of raisins, and coffee. And I put in four napkins and a table-cloth, too."

"I'm not going to set up housekeeping out there!"

"No, but you're used to having things nice, and it might make a difference. I put in the plum-colored damask morning-gown with the green baize lining, because that one is warmer than your others. You're a bit of a dandy, Caleb. I never saw such a collection of neckcloths. You go through them and decide which you want to take."

He opened the drawer of the chest and tossed out four or five at random, then carefully selected handkerchiefs, the blue and white silk, the dark green silk, the yellow silk, and a pile of linen ones.

"I'm putting in a quantity of writing paper and your brass ink pot. He sure to send us word as you can. Have they said anything about letters?"

Caleb made a wry face as he quoted, "Correspondence to be allowed by open letters through the hands of the Continental Secretary of War."

"Who is he?"

"Dick Peters."

"That smart, satirical young sprig! Well, be careful what you write."

"Oh, I don't suppose he'll read the letters personally."

"Somebody will. Just say if you are well, and tell us anything you need, and I'll find a way of sending it somehow."

"Leave some room for books." He took Tom Jones from the table by the window, and saw that the sash was propped up with a stick. The weights had been taken to make bullets.

Supper was delicious. The dining-room was in the extension of the house that can back into the yard, where a few late roses were blooming and a red apple fell now and then from the tree by the well. Sarah had remembered his favorite dishes and had provided cold beef and duck, Indian corn pudding, delicate hot biscuits with sweet butter and gooseberry jam, frothy syllabub, and clear strong coffee. Patty had come home full of the afternoon spent with her bosom friend, Betty Pleasants.

"Betty is the genteelest girl in town," she pronounced, "and no wonder, because her mother and father are exceedingly genteel. I should think it would do thee good, Caleb, to be associated with Mr. Pleasants. His manners are positively courtly, which can't be said of thine. He stood up when I came into the room. *He* isn't a wet Quaker, either."

"I stand up for ladies," replied Caleb blandly, and flicked a few drops of water with his teaspoon at Patty. "Furthermore, I'm not wet, only a little damp."

"Wet Quaker" was the slang term for those fashionable Friends who walked the top of the wall between the world and the Meeting, sometimes tumbling over the edge altogether and landing in the baptismal font at St. Peter's.

They had scarcely finished supper when a long succession of calls from sympathizing friends began, which lasted all evening. Caleb, senior, upstairs in bed began to feel neglected and rang his little bell furiously; Tacy had a nightmare and awoke screaming; Edward, having begged to stay up because it was Caleb's last night, fell asleep with his head heavy against his brother's arm. Finally the last caller left, and Caleb, having never consciously made the decision to stay all night, went thankfully to his own bed for the first time in nine days and the last for who could say how long?

XIII

IN THE MORNING AMOS trundled Caleb's portmanteau in a wheelbarrow to the Lodge and brought back word that the wagons would
not be ready till late afternoon. At three, when Caleb was saying
good-by to his family, Patty clinging to him with wet eyes in a sudden
belated realization, the sound of firing began. It came from the southwest, the ominous, angry thunder of canon. They knew without being
told that the battle for Philadelphia had started and that in any separa-
tion of families now, none could prophesy who would be the fortunate
ones or when they would be reunited.

As Caleb walked through the streets he found the city pulsing with
excitement. A man went ahead of him up Third Street clanging a
handbell and shouting, "Shut up your houses! All men who can carry
a gun are ordered to appear on the Commons!" The corporal of a
squad of militia matching up Spruce Street stopped Caleb and demanded to know why he was not with his regiment, but when he replied that he was on his way to the Masons' Hall under orders of
Council, they went on without further ado. Some wagons rumbled
past, piled high with household goods, obviously on their way out of
the city. Three carpenters under the direction of a colonel in uniform
were at work on St. Paul's Church taking down the bell. Women
peered with distraught white faces out of doorways and whisked inside again when anyone approached. Again and again the distant cannon boomed, now faint, now louder, as the light breeze rose or died
away. Once Caleb heard the crisp, sharp rattle of drums beating to
arms from a street corner, and his scalp prickled.

At the Lodge the first person he met was Miers Fisher.

"Ah, Caleb, I'm glad to see thee back. Dr. Combe last night gave his
parole. It is a great surprise to us, after all his protestations."

97

"Did he take the test oath?"

"No, it was some sort of patched-up arrangement, I understand. What he really wants, it seems, is to get to England, and I believe he is to be sent as a prisoner of war to the West Indies for exchange. And Dr. Bond has been in difficulties."

Dr. Bond, it developed, had attempted to give a parole of his own devising and thought at first that it would be accepted. When, however, he was offered only the same oath that he had refused before, he returned to the Lodge, determined to go on with the others. Colonel Nicola, by this time exasperated, declared that he had already struck the doctor off the list and that he would have to remain in Philadelphia under custody.

The prisoners now numbered twenty, seventeen of whom were Friends.

Miers Fisher had suggested the day before that writs of habeas corpus might be applied for, and after some discussion it had been decided that those who felt inclined to do so were free to proceed. Ten of them, including Caleb, now signed an application and it was taken away to be delivered to Chief Justice M'Kean.

Two members of the Philadelphia Light Horse, as well as a detachment of the City Guard, had been assigned to escort the prisoners as far as Reading. Both Alexander Nesbitt and Samuel Caldwell would have much preferred going with the rest of the troop to the assistance of Washington to escorting a number of their fathers' richest friends and acquaintances out of town in disgrace, and Sam Caldwell, who was in command, was in a towering bad temper.

So many citizens had taken flight that it had been difficult to procure enough vehicles for the prisoners and even to get horses for the members of the City Guard. The baggage wagons proved to be entirely inadequate for the number of portmanteaus and bales that the gentlemen thought necessary, and there was considerable altercation before a promise was extracted that more wagons would be found and sent after them.

The endless delays and adjustments and changes of mind involved in organizing such a cavalcade stretched out the time of departure until the tempers of all were at the snapping point. The large and sober crowd that gathered to bid the prisoners farewell or simply to watch their departure further impeded operations. They offered no resistance, but they got in the way, scores of silent, somber people, moving docilely when they were asked to, flattening themselves against the walls of the houses apposite, but still filling the sidewalks with their bodies, spilling over into the street, so that it was difficult to move a wagon when it was filled or to bring up another horse. They were a mixed group of people interested for one reason or another. Many of them were freed Negroes who had been helped to start their new life by John Pemberton, and they wept aloud when they saw their benefactor led out and boosted into a wagon with a backless bench for a seat.

John Hunt came next. Both he and John Pemberton took the extreme position that they could not co-operate with wrong even to the extent of climbing voluntarily into the wagon, but whereas John Pemberton admitted a symbol of force in the two men who assisted him, one at each elbow, John Hunt had to be lifted up bodily and carried. He did not resist, but he was a dead weight and it took three of the guards to do it. In going through the door they brushed his hat off and it rolled on its round brim to Caleb's feet. He followed and handed it up to John after he was seated, a quaint little figure, with his collarless coat, his gentle and serene countenance, his white hair.

"Thank thee, Caleb," said John, with a flicker of a smile that, like a door opened and quickly shut, revealed the glint of humor within.

"Would you mind stepping aside, Mr. Middleton?" said Caldwell, drawing with visible effort on his last stores of patience.

The wagons as they were filled passed out of the alley and lined up in Second Street. Those who were to ride their own horses or drive their own carriages would come next, and finally as much of the baggage as could be piled onto the two shaky wagons.

"Mr. Affleck, Mr. Brown," shouted Caldwell. "Mr. Pike—"

Caleb looked for Phyllis, but like most of the wives and mothers she had said her farewells in the privacy of home. He had written a note to her earlier and sent it by Amos. It was brief and he was not satisfied with it, but he had had no time to rewrite it. "I cannot leave without sending you a word," he had written. "I shall be thinking of you, alone and unprotected. If you are looking for sewing, please go to my mother. Don't be troubled about us who are in exile. I cannot think it will be for long. I am, Your most humble servant, C.M. Jr."

"Mr. Wharton!"

Thomas Wharton came slowly and ponderously forward and paused on the steps with a look of distaste directed equally at the wagon and the perspiring guard who stood ready to help him up. Something about his deliberation, his disdain, and his consciousness of his own worth irritated the guard beyond control.

"Get in there, you damned Tory!" he snarled, and put his hand on Wharton's shoulder to hustle him.

Out from the crowd of passive bystanders leaped a plain working man, a very angry man, who struck down the soldier's hand, drove him back against the wagon, and towered over him, threatening.

"Dare to abuse a prisoner," he roared, "and I'll thrust my hands down your throat and pull out your heart!"

A murmur of approval went through the crowd.

Thomas Wharton put his hand lightly on the man's arm. "Never mind, Murdoch," he said soothingly. "Thou'rt a good friend, but violence solves nothing. Give me thy hand and help me into this chariot."

The soldier wiped his forehead with his sleeve and signaled to the driver of the next wagon to move up.

After the wagons came Edward Penington's chaise, driven by Karl, and Charles Eddy driving his own sulky with James Pemberton on the seat beside him. Israel Pemberton's man Martin brought up his four-wheeled chaise, and Mr. Caldwell, very taut now and very brisk, read out, "Mr. I. Pemberton."

Israel, like most of the others, had been home the previous night and he showed the benefits of it. Freshly shaven, his hair dressed by a barber, he wore an immaculate gray suit and fresh white neckcloth, silk stockings and polished shoes with silver buckles. His thin, high-nosed aristocratic face expressed a calm self-control. He nodded to Martin, who had got out of the chaise to stand beside the step, the very embodiment of a well-trained, respectful English coachman ready to take his employer on some conventional outing.

"Friend Caldwell," said Israel, "before I get into the chaise I should like to see thy orders."

"Mr. Pemberton, you are holding up the line. There is no necessity for you to see my orders."

"If thou wilt not show them to me, I must ask that thou at least read them to me."

"No, sir, I will not. Please move along."

"It is plainly our right to have a certified copy of our commitment to the authorities in Virginia and of the orders accompanying it, so that we may know in what light we are being represented to them and in what manner we are to be treated."

Caleb, who was now behind Israel, could not see his face, but he heard his voice, calm and reasonable but commanding, and he saw Caldwell's eyes fall.

"Mr. Nesbitt and I, with some of the City Guards, will accompany you to Reading. From there on you will be in charge of the lieutenants of the counties through which you pass. That is all I can tell you. It is late. Make haste, sir."

His dignity unruffled, Mr. Pemberton stepped into his chaise and was driven out of Lodge Alley.

Amos brought up Ladybird, with a saddlebag in which Sarah Middleton had carefully packed necessities for the journey. Amos's honest face was eloquent with affection and distress as Caleb leaned down from the saddle to shake his hand in farewell.

"Did thee deliver the note? Directly into her hand?"

"Yes, sir"

"Any answer?"

Amos looked reproachful. "I'd have guv it right to you, Master Caleb."

The Fishers and Sammy Pleasants were riding too. Horses' hooves grated on the cobblestones as they moved at last, a little before six o'clock, out of the alley and into Second Street. Behind them came the two baggage wagons and six members of the City Guard mounted on a motley assortment of nags. Caldwell and Nesbitt, riding their own fine pacers, went to the head of the column, and the first of the wagons moved slowly forward. The crowd in the alley came surging after. From somewhere a fife and drum appeared, and the mocking strains of "Yankee Doodle" followed them up Second Street as far as Vine.

Out of the crowd, spreading to the guard in the rear and from the guard to the prisoners, like fire licking through a field of dry grass, came news.

"What is it?" said Caleb. "What's happened?"

"Something about a battle," said Sammy Pleasants. "Things are going badly and General Lafayette has been wounded."

XIV

IT WAS DARK WHEN they reached Palmer's Tavern at the Falls of Schuylkill and there was not room for all of them in that small and rather primitive inn. Word had gone out, however, of their coming, and hospitable friends in the neighborhood opened their homes to the overflow. A messenger from Dr. William Smith, Provost of the College of Philadelphia, was waiting with an invitation for Caleb and Edward Penington and Thomas and Miers Fisher. One of the guards rode with them up the steep hill to the Smith place and was accommodated in a humbler house near by.

The official residence of the Provost was situated in Fourth Street opposite the Friends' burying ground, but Dr. Smith had built himself a country retreat high above the Schuylkill with a superb view of the river. It was a simple enough stone house, plastered over and whitewashed, but its inaccessibility and the wildness of the surrounding woods had given rise to its name, "Smith's Folly." Here, after an excellent supper presided over by the provost's old-maid sister, Isabella, who remained with him after his wife and children had gone to his father-in-law at Moore Hall, the six men sat on the porch and talked late into the night.

The cordial and genial Dr. Smith, it was rather maliciously whispered, had long cherished hopes of a "pair of lawn sleeves" and people assumed that his "Letters of Cato" opposing independence had been written in the belief that a bishopric would come to him more surely from His Majesty's government than from any new republic; but of late he had expressed his support of the American cause and ten days ago had taken the oath of allegiance. Though he belonged to the Church of England party which opposed the Society of Friends at many points, he still had many friends among the Quakers, and he offered his hospitality tonight as if it were an ordinary social opportunity instead of a possibly incriminating act of kindness to people under a political cloud.

Conscious of being the youngest and least important, Caleb sat silent while the rest talked, looking out over the rough, steep lawn, the tops of the forest trees below, the dark, gunmetal coils of the river, watching the moon slowly fall down the sky toward the hills on the other side. The conversation ranged with jerks and silences over a variety of subjects, the career of Benjamin West, the Philadelphia artist now fashionable in London, whom both Edward Penington and Dr. Smith had assisted in his unknown, farm-boy youth, the inferior men lately elected to the Continental Congress, the probable outcome of today's battle reported to have been near the Brandywine, and came to rest on the question of oaths of allegiance.

"Granted," said Dr. Smith, "that there is no security in the oath of an unscrupulous man—what was it your own Penn said, something about the man that fears to tell untruth not needing to swear because he will not lie, while he that does not fear untruth, what is his oath worth?—granted all that, I am still at a loss to understand why Friends refuse an affirmation of loyalty where they honestly feel it—"

"It is partly because history has proved the uselessness of oaths," said Edward Penington. "Oaths have never yet prevented a revolution. The Long Parliament swore allegiance to Charles the First—and beheaded him. General Monk and his army took all the test oaths the Commonwealth imposed—and proceeded to restore Charles the Second to the throne. Oaths only oppress the virtuous element of the people."

Miers Fisher tapped his pipe against the sole of his shoe. Caleb could not see his square, keen, mobile face in the shadows, but he could imagine how it lit up as the young lawyer launched into the subject on which Caleb had already heard him several times hold forth with passionate conviction. Caleb admired and liked Miers more than any of his fellow prisoners. His quick intelligence, his knowledge of the law, his attractive personality and his faithfulness to Friends' principles combined to make him in Caleb's eyes an ideal combination of the Quaker and the man of the world.

"More than that," said Miers, "oaths are actually dangerous to the principle of liberty in a free government. Men who feel free and secure under a government will support it because it is to their interest to do so. You can get no surer safeguard for a government than that. But if the ruling party forces people to swear to whatever arbitrary laws it may enact, then civil liberty disappears and religious liberty with it."

"In a time of crisis," objected Dr. Smith, "when the very life of the state is threatened, then it seems to me the state must have some way of dealing with suspected persons, or all liberty may be lost."

"But some cause of suspicion should be proved against a man before he is publicly stigmatized by being singled out to take an oath which the unsuspected need not subscribe to. If proper legal process proves him disloyal, then suitable action can be taken against him."

"There is another aspect to it," said Thomas Fisher slowly. "I wish John Pemberton were here, for he can express the moral and religious implications better than I can, but it is this, as best I can put it. The body may be subject to compulsion, the mind is not. But if, to make life easier for the body, to avoid imprisonment, to keep one's employment, to win advancement, the mind assents to something it considers wrong, then it suffers a wound from which it does not easily recover. It loses strength for the next encounter, so that a test act in the end is subversive of the morality of the inhabitants."

Now he was invading, with a layman's vocabulary and a Quaker's assurance, the field in which William Smith, D.D., might be supposed to speak as a professional. Caleb turned from watching the round dark shape of a small animal—probably an opossum—crossing the grass at the edge of the trees, and looked at the theologian.

Dr. Smith made a slight soothing gesture with his hands, and spoke smoothly with something of the unction of his pulpit voice. "I wonder if that isn't taking it a little too seriously. Most people, I think, regard such an oath as a sort of formality, an open and forthright statement of where their loyalties are placed, a sign of a willingness to stand forth and be counted. I have always understood that it was Friends' policy to submit peaceably to all government and to effect change if necessary only by peaceful means and not by violence, so that I should think

THE VIRGINIA EXILES

Friends of all people could subscribe with a clear conscience to such an affirmation of loyalty. Then those who are disaffected or who subscribe dishonestly as a cover, can be easily apprehended by the government as perjurers."

"Thou'rt quite right, Friends are not revolutionaries, but on the other hand we do not acknowledge government as the highest authority. We must obey God rather than man, and where laws of men are at variance with the laws of God we must follow our conscience—as in refusing to take part in warfare. If I commit myself by an oath to act or think in a particular way in the future according to the dictates of a government, then where is my religious liberty? How can I then follow the leadings of the Spirit?"

Dr. Smith shook his head slightly. "I can understand your point and honor your sincerity, sitting here high above the turmoil and out of earshot of the guns. But I can also understand that a political group burdened with many decisions, carrying on war for its very existence in the face of present military defeat and invasion, might have difficulty in grasping your somewhat fine-spun theories."

"They do not have to understand our fine-spun theories," said Miers crisply. "They have only to stand by their own definitely enunciated principles in regard to certain fundamental rights of man, which are, not to be arrested without charge, to be heard in his own defense, and to be presumed innocent until proved guilty."

Caleb suppressed a yawn and wondered what time it was. He had wanted to talk with the Provost about oaths of allegiance, but he found in the conversation no clearing of his own confusions.

You did what you had to do, he thought, pushed by some voiceless force within you and pulled by outside circumstances beyond your control, and sometimes you did not know what your answer would be until you heard the "yes" or "no" emerging from your own throat. He yawned again, almost overcome with sleep, and lost the thread of what they were saying. Through his mind drifted fragmentary memories, no more than shadows and entirely disconnected: his father falling full length on the terrace at the Phoebe Ann, the two militia officers in Phyllis's sitting room the day that Washington rode past, John Hunt being lifted into the wagon in the alley, his father's face as he gave him the money-belt.

He and Miers shared a room that night. As they were undressing, Miers said suddenly in a voice so sharp with pain that Caleb scarcely recognized it, "Our little Tommy is only eleven months old, head-strong already and hard to handle, and there will be another child this winter. Sarah's not yet twenty-two. I ought to be there with her."

"There are still the writs of habeas corpus," said Caleb, to comfort him. "They'll reach us at Reading, at the latest."

XV

THE GROUP REASSEMBLED NEXT morning at Palmer's Tavern, some coming from the Vanderins' house and some from Joseph Warner's. The contingent from Dr. Smith's came hurrying up last of all, late, apologetic, but fortified with a most satisfactory breakfast. There was a change in the order of march, so that those who rode horseback went first, leaving the slower wagons to follow.

The road, after they passed through the ford at the Wissahickon Creek, was appallingly bad, full of stones and ruts, treacherous soft spots and gaping holes. Caleb was sorry for those in the springless wagons, who were tossed against one another continually by the jolting and lurching. Up they toiled to the ridge above the Schuylkill, through the little village of Barren Hill, past fields where the stumps of trees still marched in untidy ranks, past whitewashed taverns that catered to a trade of drovers and wagoners, through stretches of woodland where squirrels chattered.

Ladybird was fresh and lively, the morning was cool. Caleb was not unaware of the troubles and anxieties which weighed upon the spirits of his companions, but for himself, decision was past and out of his control and he was away from the Masons' Hall.

They stopped at Thompson's Tavern for a dinner of boiled mutton and kidney beans, for which they paid five shillings, and went on again without lingering. In the afternoon the wind veered around to the northwest and blew out as cold and raw as if it had been November. They expected to spend the night at Widow Lloyd's tavern, thirty miles from Philadelphia, but when they reached there at sunset they found if already crowded with refugees from the city.

"Washington has been routed," the word was passed down the line. "Birmingham Meetinghouse is filled with the wounded. Bands of soldiers are running leaderless about the countryside, dropping their blankets and muskets on the road."

Pottsgrove, seven miles farther on, was the next possible stop. Weary now and chilled through and through by the sharp wind, they pressed on.

Here again, as at the Falls, word of their coming had somehow preceded them, and when they reached the little tavern on the wide, grass-bordered street, they found friends waiting to welcome them to their homes. Pottsgrove, a settlement of perhaps twenty brick or stone houses, was the stronghold of the Potts family, a large and varied clan, most of whom were engaged in the manufacture of iron for the Continental army, though a few were Tories and a still smaller number were Quaker objectors to war. Old John Potts, who was dead now, had been a friend and adviser of Caleb's father when he was a young man, and so Caleb was not surprised to find himself invited to the Mansion, where the Widow Potts lived with her eldest son, Thomas, now a colonel in the Continental army, and her unmarried daughters.

The parlor in the great house was big and comfortable, with a fire blazing on the hearth, servants bringing hot drinks, and the pleasant sounds overhead of housewifely bustle with sheets and blankets. A lump of ore gleaming with iron pyrites on the mantelpiece, the elaborately decorated iron fireback, and the diagram of a furnace stack pinned to the wall made Caleb feel himself once more in an ironmaster's house, and he leaned back in his chair sipping his hot spiced cider with a feeling of deep content.

Presently Ruth Potts came into the room to say that the bedrooms were ready whenever the travelers wished to retire. The youngest daughter of John Potts and thirteenth child, Ruth was famous in a small way for having said out loud that she had no intention of marrying until she was too old to bear children. Caleb, who in his imagination had endowed her with the figure and features of his sister Patty, saw instead a slight, vivid, charming young thing with an air of elegance. Charles Eddy, who seemed to know her well, persuaded her to play for them, and she sat down at the spinet and in a fresh sweet voice sang a gay little French song. Her accent was pronounced by Caleb, without knowing very much about it, as truly Parisian.

The next day those prisoners whose baggage had been left behind
asked that the group be permitted to wait in Pottsgrove until the extra
wagons which had been promised should catch up with them. The
weather continued unseasonably cold and they were shivering in summer clothing; some of them had no clean shirts to put on. The gentlemen of the Light Horse assented.

Caleb, whose portmanteau, thanks to Amos's efforts, had got into
the first wagon, extracted from it his leather breeches and brown
homespun coat and some of the flannels, which he lent to Charles
Eddy, his roommate at the Mansion. Charles was a trader in iron,
whom Caleb had known through business dealings and also as a
member of the Pine Street Meeting. Why Charles should have been
arrested and his brother Thomas left free, nobody knew, but as
Charles was a bachelor it was less of a hardship for him. He was
older than Caleb by ten years at least, a plain, hearty man with a long
chin.

Caleb spent most of the day chatting with him, hoping to see Ruth
again, and watching the wagons, coaches and chaises that passed in a
steady stream along the road, all fleeing from the doomed city. Caleb
knew that his own family would stay where they were, confident of
good treatment from the British army, which his father apparently believed was composed entirely of gentlemen; but Caleb wondered,
since Americans had proved themselves so little able to discriminate
between friend and foe, if the English would be very much more dis-
cerning.

In the late afternoon in search of diversion he walked down the road
to the tavern. To his surprise he found it surrounded by armed men,
twenty or more of the local militia, all speaking German and sounding
angry and excited. He passed through them without being stopped,
nodded to the familiar guards at the door, and went inside. He found
the taproom crowded and the atmosphere tense. A number of his fellow prisoners stood massed together, listening with varying expressions of dismay and incredulity to the harangue of a pugnacious
young man wearing a captain's insignia.

"I know what is behind this," he was shouting. "I have been warned
of your perfidy! But you shall not succeed in it. If you will not come

peaceably, then you must come by force. My men are outside. I will give you half an hour to get ready."

James Pemberton spoke for the group. "Friend," he said quietly, "we are peaceable people. Thou needs no threats. But it is not possible for us to collect ourselves and our belongings in half an hour. It is now past four o'clock. Even if we leave here at five, it will be dark long before we could reach Reading. Consider what thou'rt asking. Thou knows the state of the roads. We should run the risk of lamed horses, broken wagons, possibly serious injuries to men old and unaccustomed to rough travel at night."

"You should have thought of that before you dug your heels in and refused to budge."

"We have remained here with the permission of our guard."

"Then you have deceived them. We have had reliable word that you expect to be rescued here by a British force. We intend to forestall that by removing you to Reading immediately. Is that clear?"

"Someone has misrepresented us!" cried Caleb. "There is not one of us who has had any communication with the British."

Nesbitt and Caldwell, who were housed at David Potts', now came in and made themselves known to the Captain, drawing him aside for a low-voiced consultation. Mr. Pike, conspicuous in his red coat, summoned the barkeeper, who had vanished during the shouting, and persuaded him to produce drinks for the military, while the prisoners took stock of their situation. The outlook was not encouraging.

The Germans who made up the greater part of the population hereabouts were not the gentle pietists from the Rhineland who had followed William Penn, but a harder, more aggressive people who came later for economic rather than religious reasons. They could hardly be expected to understand the Quaker position. "If the German translation of our 'Address to the Inhabitants' were only ready," said Israel Pemberton, "this is exactly the situation in which it would be useful."

The upshot of the conference between the gentlemen of the Light Horse and the captain of the militia was that the prisoners were permitted to stay that night in Pottsgrove but they must be ready, baggage or no baggage, to leave at seven the next morning.

They were all on hand even a little before the hour, but before they got under way a messenger, who had ridden most of the night, came with the ten writs of habeas corpus that had been applied for the day they left Philadelphia. They had been allowed by Chief Justice M'Kean and were in good order.

The ten promptly served their writs on Alexander Nesbitt and Samuel Caldwell, who without hesitation refused to touch them.

"We have orders to deliver you to Reading," said Caldwell. "After that we have no further responsibility. You can try your writs then on somebody else."

In spite of this refusal the very fact that the writs had been allowed was evidence that justice still lived, and the spirits of the prisoners rose accordingly. The ten who had not before applied for writs now decided to do so, and a young man who lived in Pottsgrove offered to ride to Philadelphia at once with the new applications.

All this delayed their departure and it was nine o'clock before the cavalcade set off once more. All their friends in Pottsgrove, including the pretty Ruth, were out to wave them off, and Caleb had a warm sense of the sympathy and even approbation of people who understood their position even though they might not share it.

At the edge of the village the company of militia fell in sullenly behind them.

During the ensuing hours Caleb was aware of those steadily tramping feet. In spite of the satisfaction of being able to ride Ladybird, in spite of the glow created by the Pottses' good will, and the relief which he felt from the possession of the writ of habeas corpus, he tasted, following the slow plodding pace of the wagons in front and hearing the militia behind, the peculiar bitterness of being a prisoner, of knowing himself to be an object of fear, hatred, and contempt.

One small incident lit up for him the temper of the people of the region, their ignorance and their passion.

The cavalcade had stopped to rest the horses, and Caleb, seeing behind a small, mean house a woman drawing water from a well, rode over to ask her for a drink. She was Irish, from the look of her, with bold blue eyes, white skin sown with freckles, and coarse dark hair springing off her forehead with a life of its own. She handed him a gourdful of water and stood waiting, her arms akimbo, for him to drink.

"What's the news from the camp?" she demanded.

"None that I know of. Which camp?"

"Where are those Tories that are to be banished?"

"Why, I suppose I am one of them."

"No, go on. You can't be. You're a gentleman."

"But I am—and you'll see the rest like me. Over there. Look for yourself."

"I don't believe you. If I thought you were telling the truth," she threw back her head and screeched fiercely, "I'd take a gun and shoot you through myself!"

Caleb laughed and handed back the gourd. "No, you wouldn't," he said. "You're too kind. Thanks for the water."

But he was sober as he rejoined the group.

It was a beautiful country through which they rode that bright, cold, windy Sunday morning. The road rose over rib-like hills and dipped to cross the sparkling brooks that cut little valleys to the river, turning as they went the mill-wheels, paper, saw, grist, oil, that ground out prosperity for all the region. Already leaves were beginning to scurry along the road and rustle at the feet of goldenrod and asters in the ditches; here and there a swamp maple flung a flaming branch against the predominant green, or a sweet gum spread out its five-fingered leaves touched with scarlet at the tips.

Now the hills on the other side of the river began to show blue in the distance, and at last the pointed, forest-clad hill called Mt. Penn loomed up ahead of them. A little after two they rode into Reading. It lay on a slight eminence half encircled by the winding Schuylkill, a comparatively new city, now in the throes of wartime activity. A repository for essential stores which had been moved out of Philadelphia, a center for refugees, a meeting place for Continental officers, it was the vital link, with Philadelphia as good as captured, between the northern and the southern states. Every house and inn was bulging. Most of the indigenous population were German and so ardently pro-American that they saw Tories everywhere, even among those who had fled from Philadelphia to get away from the British.

The streets were full of people returning from church, and the faces turned toward the prisoners as they entered the town were not friendly. Dark looks, shrugs, clenched fists, and a volley of flung stones and clods greeted them; a few men spat contemptuously.

The inn kept by the Widow Withington had been assigned to them. It was a large, bare building near the jail and offered few amenities. The sheriff of the county, Daniel Levan, who was there waiting for them, seemed to be a civil, decent sort of man, sober and short in his manner; but he, like the captain of the militia, believed that they had refused to leave Pottsgrove in the hope of armed intervention, and they soon saw that he was going to take no risk of their escaping. The guards who had come from Philadelphia were dismissed and German-speaking soldiers posted at all the doors of the inn. Friends who came to inquire or to offer their services were peremptorily ordered away.

In Reading, Caleb saw at once, there would be no pleasant hospitality, no pretty girls singing French songs in a firelit parlor of genial talk over a bountiful breakfast. With Charles Eddy, John Hunt, and Thomas Gilpin, he was assigned to a small room with two beds and a chair that was apparently attached to the wall by a cobweb. Leaving his saddlebag on the floor in a corner, Caleb went downstairs again to see what chance there was of getting something to eat.

The parlor was a plain room with a sanded floor, scarred pine tables and benches, some pewter mugs and wooden plates on shelves, and a fireplace black and sour with old smoke. He found Thomas Pike in the kitchen eloquently describing their hunger to the Widow Withington.

"I was told to provide beds for you," she said, "and beds you'll have. I did not engage to give you meals. It's Sunday and this is a God-fearing house. I've let my servants off. I'm not agoing to turn in and cook a meal for twenty Tories and that is all there is to that and you can put it in your pipe and smoke it."

She opened a door which gave onto a stairway, and slammed it behind her.

The fire on the big hearth had been banked, but a kettle on the crane still gave off a thin spiral of steam.

"I think, Mr. Middleton," said Pike, "we could at least make ourselves tea, if we could get at the wagons. There is cheese in one of them, too, and some bread."

A shadow passed across the window. It was one of the guards, matching back and forth with his musket over his shoulder. Caleb went to the back door and opened it. Another guard blocked his way.

"I only want to get some food out of one of the wagons."

The guard said something in German, of which all that Caleb could understand was "nicht."

"Essen," said Caleb. "Ich bin hungry. Let me go get some stuff out of the wagon. I won't run away. Essen. You ought to understand that. You look as if you did plenty of it. Come on, that's a good fellow."

The guard remained blank, unyielding.

Hearing shouts from the other side of the house, Caleb turned away, letting the door close behind him, and went to find out what was going on.

Through the big front door, which stood open, came the confused noise of a scuffle. Caleb got there in time to see a soldier lay rough hands on an old man, pull him back from the doorway, and fling him off with such force that he would have gone sprawling into the street if he had not fallen against a younger man behind him. There were shouts from a crowd that had gathered outside, and the next moment stones thudded against the side of the house. One crashed across the floor and Caleb moved just in time. A heavy stone struck the old man on the shoulder and another smaller one hit his cheek. With a little grunt of pain he put his hand up to his face, and looked at it with a dazed air when it came away covered with blood.

Sickened, Caleb recognized the old man as Isaac Zane, a venerable Friend of Philadelphia, John Pemberton's father-in-law. The younger man behind him he did not know by name, but he had seen him in the gallery of the Great Meetinghouse. The next moment a guard slammed the door in Caleb's face.

With the prisoners inside he crowded to a window. Old Isaac Zane, with his handkerchief pressed to his cheek, was being assisted down the street, while an urchin ran after him to fling a handful of gravel at his back. The shouting in the street grew louder, and the faces of the massed men and boys took on the evil and dangerous look of a crowd that is becoming a mob.

"Come away from the window," said the quiet voice of John Hunt. "They see us and we are only exciting them."

John Pemberton sat down heavily on the nearest bench.

"He came out of kindness to inquire for us," he said brokenly. "That such a thing could happen in Pennsylvania!"

XVI

THEY SPENT A WEEK in Reading.

The hostility that greeted them on their arrival was not again manifested in so sharp a form. The captain of the Light Horse, Samuel Morris, newly arrived from the battle at the Brandywine, sent in to them that first night a dinner complete with wine and decreed that they were to be allowed to see their friends freely. A birthright Quaker who had been disowned for taking part in war, he had family connections among the prisoners, which gave him an understanding of their point of view and a personal sympathy for them.

Although Isaac Zane returned to Philadelphia without making any further attempt to see them, a number of Friends of Reading and the nearby communities of Exeter and Maiden Creek visited the inn to offer their sympathy and to bring provisions. Some of them were refugees from Philadelphia, but most were country people, dressed in homespun, sober, forthright, plain, and deeply religious. Their respect for the prisoners was based not on outward marks of eminence, which they tended to distrust and disapprove, but upon the solid consideration of their courage and faith in resisting all temptations to compromise. This feeling was not expressed in open approbation, but it emerged in the times of "retirement" when the whole group would sit together in silence in the Quaker way, seeking to experience the presence of God. Out of the silence might come a prayer that the banished Friends be strengthened to endure and upheld in their service for Truth. That they were making a stand for civil and religious liberty and in so doing were tendering their country as definite a service as if they fought for it, was the conviction of the majority of the prisoners. The recognition by their fellow Quakers of the greatness of the issues and the degree of the sacrifice that might be required was as invigorating to the spirits of the prisoners as the fresh country butter and eggs and chickens which the visitors brought were comforting to their bodies.

Caleb, though he was too divided in his own mind, too torn by his private conflict, too restless, to sit through many of these periods of retirement, still saw their effect in the increased steadiness and peace of mind which was shown by the others. Through the indignity and injustice of their confinement, the delays, the discomforts, the anxiety about their families left behind, the exiled Quakers moved as men united in a high purpose and sustained by a sense of divine assistance.

Feeling sometimes a little set apart from the group by his youth, Caleb had a sympathy for the three who were not Friends and sought them out.

Thomas Pike was busy with the problems of catering, making himself a sort of major-domo for the company. He enlisted the services of Richard, Martin, and Karl, the servants of the Pembertons and Edward Penington, persuaded the Widow Withington to co-operate, found tactful ways of letting the visiting Friends know what was needed, and saw to it that Mr. Pemberton, Mr. Wharton, Mr. Drinker, and Mr. Penington got the kind of wine they liked before the supply ran out. Caleb, despising the snobbery that lay behind all this solicitude, still enjoyed talking with Friend Pike, as the grateful gentlemen called him, especially when he could steer the conversation around to Phyllis.

That she had been a seamstress he already knew. Now he learned that she had lived in a little house in a little court in Charleston, supporting a father who pretended to be a gentleman but who in his cups, as he usually was, revealed a knowledge of sleight of hand with cards and a familiarity with the interior arrangements of Newgate prison that were probably not unconnected. Phyllis's fingers had been rough with needle pricks, but she had known how to dance—how she could dance!—and Thomas and Phyllis had danced together for exhibition. The pupils had come crowding until, they said, why not make a partnership of it, and so they had married and Thomas had moved into the little house. But that had not been happy. The father had been difficult. Thomas had come to Philadelphia, where he taught fencing as well as dancing, and Phyllis later had followed him. The father? Mr. Pike was vague about the father. He was drunk most of the time. He scarcely knew what was happening.

Tom Affleck, in contrast to Mr. Pike, was unpretentious, plain, uncompromisingly independent. He was one of the small, dark Scots, quiet, intense, and gentle. He was also a very unhappy man, distraught with worry about his young wife, Isabella, left at home to fend for herself and the four small children.

"We have some good furniture she can sell. That will take care of them for a time. Then I'll just have to get back. They can't keep me away."

"You could have got out of this quite easily, you know," said Caleb, curious to see what he would answer, "if you'd only made a few promises."

"And so could everyone else that's here, including yourself. No, I couldna do it, and I think Isabella understands. I explained it to her this way: Suppose someone cam' to me and said, 'Noo, ye must promise to stop beating your wife.' I've never beat my wife and I never would, but what kind of a man would I be to make a promise put like that? I didna come to America to knuckle under to test oaths and such goings-on."

"I can't see why they took you up anyhow. You're not responsible for anything the Yearly Meeting says—even if you were still a Friend, and you're not. You were just going along quietly making furniture, so far as I can see. You haven't any particular British connections now, have you?"

"I was in and out of Governor Penn's house, making furniture for him before they sent him away. He brought me to this country in the first place. He's been kind to me, I'd never turn against him. I don't hold with overthrowing our lawful rulers any more than our Lord did—and He was a carpenter too. Render unto Caesar the things that are Caesar's and unto God the things that are God's. That's what our Lord said and that's what I believe. I never made a secret of it. Perhaps the Council didna like that. But it's a fine thing to put a man in prison for his thoughts, is it no'?"

With Drewet Smith, a slender, active man with an odd nervous trick of twisting and screwing his face as he talked, Caleb discussed horses and hunting. Smith, like Nesbitt and Caldwell, had been a member of the Gloucester Fox-hunting Club, though Caleb had never met him on those rare occasions when he rode with the club. They talked too of the drugs that Smith sold in his shop on Chestnut Street, and Smith was rather free in his comments on the doctors and their methods. He was himself practically as good as a doctor, he said, and he could bleed a patient more skillfully than most of them. He had his lancets with him, and he showed Caleb a neat little case with a new device called a thumb-lancet, that worked with a spring, so that the patient could not see the blade or know just when the cut would come.

When John Pemberton came down with a bad cold, a fever, and a pain in his chest, Smith rummaged in his baggage and brought out remedies. For a little while all of the group were worried about John, who seemed to be sinking and who himself took a serious enough view of his condition to declare his forgiveness of his persecutors (together with a not unnatural wish that they might be "humbled before the Lord"); but between Dr. Smith's doses of camomile tea and Peruvian bark and the tender care of Israel and James, who waited on their younger brother and nursed him as if he were a beloved child, he began, before the week was out, to mend.

The most oppressive element in the confinement at the Widow Withington was the lack of privacy. Four bedrooms and two small parlors were little space for twenty men. They had no place to go to escape the pressure of other personalities, the actual physical nearness of other bodies, the sound of voices in endless conversations, or, at night, of snores and coughs and sighs, the sight of little mannerisms, unnoticed in ordinary times, which became in this tense crowded atmosphere a painful cause of irritation. Caleb, who had never been unduly squeamish, now found his nerves rubbed raw by no more than a way of sitting down, of using a handkerchief, of scratching a head, of pursing the lips and blowing out the cheeks, and the knowledge that he too would one day be old and would blow his nose and creak his false teeth or mumble his sunken lips, smote him with such bitterness of disgust and depression that he longed for death tomorrow, or perhaps the next day. Certainly he would not willingly linger on into senility after his fortieth birthday.

The weather contributed its share to the dreariness of their situation. On the sixteenth the wind swung round to the northeast and the rain poured down, dashing against the windows in furious pelting gusts. Shutters banged, wet logs hissed in the fireplace and the fire sulked, damp spots appeared on the plastered walls, and a penetrating chill crept out of every crack.

On the evening of the seventeenth, the second day of restless wind and lashing rain, a messenger came from Philadelphia with letters for some of the prisoners. Caleb, having discovered that there was nothing for him, with the depressing conviction of being neglected and outcast that comes to those who are passed over when the mail comes, retreated to a bench against the wall, where he sat yawning and squirming, changing his position so often and so convulsively that one after another those who thought to share the bench with him got up and moved.

Among the letters was a printed bill. Israel Pemberton read it first through his small square spectacles, uttered a sharp exclamation, and handed it to his brother James. From James it went to Thomas Wharton, and then the heads of the three Fishers bent over it together.

"Oh my God," thought Caleb, "now we'll have some more remonstrances and protests."

The room was buzzing. Thomas Wharton raised his hand. "Friends, this concerns us all. Are we all here?"

John Pemberton was in bed above; two or three others were missing; the rest turned with an apprehensive expectancy toward Wharton, who held the paper at arms length to the light of a cluster of candles.

"It is a bill," he explained, "introduced into the House of Assembly on the fifteenth and passed on the sixteenth, that is, yesterday. It suspends the Habeas Corpus Act. Now we shall have no chance of a trial."

Edward Penington spoke from the shadows on the far side of the room. His voice was calm and reasoning with the familiar overtone of irony. "This may deprive future dangerous persons like ourselves of their rights, Thomas, but our writs were allowed well before the six-teenth."

"The intention to include us is clear. The bill mentions the taking up of several persons who have refused to take the oath of allegiance."

They argued late as to whether such an act could be made retroactive of not. In the morning the answer came. Samuel Morris arrived to inform them that orders had come that the writs of habeas corpus were to be disregarded and that they would be dispatched within a day or two to Winchester, Virginia.

Caleb, who had scarcely heard of a writ of habeas corpus before he himself applied for one, had fastened upon it then with a faith compounded partly of the urgency of his desire for freedom and partly of his respect for his own newly acquired legal knowledge. He turned his back on the room and stood by the window, looking out and scowling.

The storm had passed. The fresh sunny air had the new tang of fall in it. The stableyard was strewn with leaves and twigs; the horse trough and the puddles caught and held the deep blue of the sky.

Behind Caleb voices rose and fell in question, complaint, demand. The baggage wagons. Stores for the journey were on the way from Philadelphia. Clothing was on the way. They could not go till it came. The two baggage wagons that had come with them from Philadelphia had been taken away. Two of the traveling wagons had gone. The third was so dilapidated that it was all but useless. Four wagons they must have at least, four more wagons.

We lose our freedom, thought Caleb, we are driven out of Pennsylvania like cattle, and we clamor and whine about baggage wagons.

The words changed and with them the voices. Now a note of pleading entered. John Pemberton was ill. He was in no condition for a long and difficult journey. He was old. Several were old. They were infirm.

The legal voices took over. The writs of habeas corpus had been served before witnesses. They antedated the bill suspending the Habeas Corpus Act. The voices charged Samuel Morris and the lieutenant of Berks County on their peril to remove the prisoners from Reading; they must, the legal voices said, pay due regard to the writs.

Caleb turned from the window. Captain Morris looked harassed. His temper was rising.

"I have a new warrant," he said sharply, "dated the sixteenth. This supersedes all previous orders."

"Be so good as to read it to us."

" 'Whereas Israel Pemberton, James Pemberton, John Pemberton . . .' " began Morris promptly, and plowed through the whole list. Caleb heard his own name near the end, with the "junior" still firmly attached. What did they think he had done, the donkeys? " '. . . have been attested by the Supreme Executive Council of Pennsylvania as persons whose uniform conduct and conversation has evidenced that they are highly inimical to the thirteen United States of North America.' "

So there it was, hearsay and suspicion stated as certainty.

"Sam Morris, I've done nothing and I've said nothing inimical to the United States," shouted Caleb, tearing the charged but decorous silence into pieces.

"Mr. Middleton, you may free yourself at any time by taking the oath of allegiance," said Morris coldly.

John Hunt slipped around two or three and came to stand beside Caleb. He said nothing, but his eyes were bright with affection and his touch on Caleb's arm was light and quieting.

"Shall I continue?" said Captain Morris huffily.

There was nothing new in it, except the substitution of Winchester for Staunton as their destination.

Winchester was almost a hundred miles nearer to Philadelphia. There were Friends in Winchester. Isaac Zane, junior, who with his ironworks and his mills was in high favor with the Whigs, had his plantation only a few miles south of the town. Winchester was better, much better. For a time an actual cheerfulness prevailed.

The two missing baggage wagons rumbled into the yard that afternoon, laden with portmanteaus and bales, with stores of food sent by anxious families in Philadelphia. During the next three days while the final arrangements were made for their departure the prisoners wrote letters. Messengers dashed back and forth between Reading and Philadelphia. Israel Pemberton sent for his Bible and a book called *British Liberty*, his gloves, and his best plush breeches. John Pemberton wanted two pairs of hose and a Testament with larger print than the one he had brought. Miers Fisher, on behalf of them all, wrote a letter to Chief Justice M'Kean, thanking him for the futile writs and, "as thou hast done thy part," sending him the established fees for them, which amounted to seventeen pounds and ten shillings.

With the letters and messages came rumors from the armies which now prowled around the outskirts of Philadelphia, maneuvering for position, warily estimating each other's strength. For several days Washington, crossing and recrossing the Schuylkill, had moved between Howe's army and the city. Then they heard that in the torrents of rain during the storm, the cartridge boxes of the Americans had proved to be so badly made that their powder had got wet and tens of thousands of rounds of ammunition had been ruined. The Continental brigades, drawn up at a favorable spot to attack the marching red-coats, could not fire a shot. Later they heard that Howe was with his army at Swede's Ford with a clear road before him to Philadelphia if he cared to take it. The next day, so it was said, Reading was full of members of the Congress and of the Pennsylvania Assembly who had left Philadelphia in a great hurry. The report went around with a snicker that the delegate from New Hampshire had not even waited for his horse to be saddled but had galloped off bareback.

All through the week in Reading Caleb shared a bed with John Hunt.

"We are the oldest and the youngest," said John. "If we add our ages together and divide by two, we shall find that the mean age of our company is about forty-five, which appears old to thee, doubtless, but still rather young to me."

Caleb made a quick calculation and discovered John Hunt to be about sixty-six. Short and spate and quick, he moved almost with the ease of a young man; his white hair stood up around his face like a halo; his fine, transparent skin, flushed at the cheeks with a pattern of tiny veins, seemed to let out an inward shining; and his clear blue eyes as they looked at Caleb were lit with humor and even tenderness.

"Thee doesn't look so old as some of the others," said Caleb awkwardly, knowing that he was being awkward and that John Hunt knew it and still not feeling uncomfortable.

"I have less to carry than some of them," said John. He might have added that he still had his teeth.

At first Caleb tried so hard not to take more than his share of the bed that he balanced precariously on the extreme edge, but later he forgot.

"Thou rolled completely over on me last night," said John one morning, folding his arms behind his head and smiling benignly. "But I shoved thee back. I find I am able to hold my own even with such a powerful young giant as thou. It gives me some satisfaction."

Caleb turned his betraying face away, to hide his foolish pleasure in being called a powerful young giant.

Sometimes as they lay in bed waiting for the other two in the room to dress, since there was not space for all four to move about at once, John reminisced about his youth.

"I am a convinced Friend," he said once. "It is not the same as being a birthright Friend. A convinced Friend is often a little excessive, proving to himself and others that he has had good reasons for his choice, whereas a birthright Friend wears his Quakerism as natu-rally—and sometimes as thoughtlessly—as he wears his skin. I grew up in Ipswich and joined the Meeting there, mostly, I think, because of one man who lived his religion in every act of his daily life. I might have found such a man within the Church, but it just happened that I did not. I had seen too much of pulpit religion, of ritual that never went beyond the church door."

"When did thee first come to Pennsylvania?"

"Almost forty years ago, the first time. I had a leading, while I was riding home from a Meeting near London, to visit Friends in Amer-ica."

"Three years older than I am now."

"Yes. I don't know why they let me come. I am not sure, today, that I should be able to distinguish between a genuine leading in a young, convinced Friend, and a desire to see the world. But the Meeting heard me out, they gave me a traveling minute, and some of them helped me with funds. So I came. I thought I was led to minister to the Americans, and I uttered many safe, correct discourses, no doubt, but in reality it was they who ministered to me. It was on that trip I first met John Woolman. After knowing him I became converted as well as convinced."

"And the next time thee came, thee stayed?"

"No, not the next time. I made another visit in 1756, when there was all the trouble with the Indian war and the Meeting for Sufferings was established. I went back after that, and returned in sixty-nine. I met my dear Rachel, we were married, and I stayed."

"And then this war started. What does thee think will come out of it all?"

"I think America will win her independence. The British are fighting across three thousand miles of sea, and the French, who have never been averse to striking a blow when it suits, are a threat at their back. But whether the United States will destroy their own freedom by the means they use to win it, is another question. It is a time of great sifting and testing, Caleb."

XVII

ONCE AGAIN THEY SET off on a Sunday Morning. Israel Pemberton, having made a private arrangement, got into Charles Eddy's sulky, with a guard to drive it, and sped off before the rest were ready. Charles Eddy and John Pemberton rode in Israel's chaise. Edward Penington, having found his own chaise, which was a light one, miserably uncomfortable on the rough roads, sent it back to the city with Karl, and himself climbed into one of the wagons and sat down beside Thomas Wharton. He had wanted to send his man back anyhow, because he was anxious about his wife and children and would feel easier if the faithful Karl were with them. Israel Pemberton's Martin was also returning to Philadelphia, for he was an indentured servant and his time would be completed the following month. That left James's Richard the only servant now with the group. He rode a tall, raw-boned horse and fell discreetly behind the seven prisoners on horseback.

They got off at ten, with six new guards from the local militia commanded by Daniel Levan, Sheriff of Berks County, very much occupied with the portfolio of papers which he carried. The gentlemen of the Light Horse, having completed their responsibility in the matter, bade them farewell with genial politeness and obvious relief.

Fording the Schuylkill a few miles beyond Reading, they rode through the rich German farmland, where apples hung bright on the silver-leaved trees, barns were painted red, and the four horse teams pulling the great blue wagons piled high with yellow corn wore tinkling bells on the collars of their harness. They dined in the village of Womelsdorf and reached Lebanon before dark. There some of them were lodged at the inn and others in private houses. Caleb saw that Israel Pemberton, by going ahead, had managed to get the best room in the inn for himself and his brothers. This proved, as the days went on, to be his regular practice. He was quite open about it and seemed to feel no occasion for apology of shame; he was accustomed to having the best.

In Lebanon a well-known ironmaster, acting as the deputy of the Lieutenant of Lancaster County, met them with real kindness, going about from house to house in the evening to make sure that they had everything they needed and that no one was offering them any rudeness or hostility.

"I know your father, Mr. Middleton," he said to Caleb. "I am sorry indeed to see his son in such circumstances. You have my entire sympathy, I assure you. If the authorities in Philadelphia had not been under such stress—you knew the Council and Assembly are in the process of moving to Lancaster, the Congress to York?—I feel sure this miscarriage of justice would never have occurred."

Caleb wondered that he dared to speak so openly, but he did more. He took a number of copies of their "Address to the Inhabitants," promising to distribute them.

On the way out of Lebanon next day they passed a camp where six hundred Hessian prisoners of war taken at Trenton the previous Christmas were being held. Three hundred more had been marched to Winchester. Caleb gloomily pictured Winchester as one large prison stockade.

That night they spent at Harris's Ferry, where in a barn-like stone building they slept fitfully on makeshift beds neither clean nor comfortable. Caleb in the wakeful bouts tried to estimate how far they were from Lancaster. Perhaps twenty-five or thirty miles, he thought. If they had taken the other road from Reading, he might be sleeping tonight in the Mercers' big comfortable house in Lancaster, where his sister Sue and her baby were now staying with her husband's parents. At any rate he could have seen Sue and talked with her. He wondered if she had heard anything about what had happened to him. Now that the Council had moved to Lancaster, perhaps Sue might meet some of them and put in a good word for him. With a husband in the Continental army she should be in good standing—or, on the other hand, he thought, twisting on the bumpy pallet, having a brother exiled to Virginia might cast suspicion on her.

Next morning they crossed the Susquehanna. The river was about a mile wide, not much more than three feet deep at the ford, but swift. The four baggage wagons went first, lurching and swaying while the water swirled around them. After the wagons the sulky and the chaise went carefully into the water, followed by those who rode horseback, Ladybird picking her way daintily over the stony bottom.

It was considered safer to bring those who traveled in the wagons over the river in canoes. After they had landed, the light wagons splashed across, their floors awash. The guards on horseback came last of all. It was eleven o'clock before all were over and assembled on the other side. Even then, just as they were about to start, they were delayed by an old Quaker of the neighborhood, who came hurrying up with a present of six large rockfish.

Five hours later they were in Carlisle, where they had a friendly reception. White's Tavern was crowded, but Caleb with Edward Penington and John Hunt spent the night in a neighboring home where they were kindly entertained. The word that the British army was matching on Philadelphia came into town with the post and flew from house to house.

They stayed two days in Carlisle, for the men with the wagons refused to go any farther and more wagons had to be procured. Everywhere, people said, there was the same difficulty, in finding wagons. Supplies of food and clothing intended for Washington's army were piling up in the towns for lack of means to transport them.

When they left the little town at eight o'clock on Friday morning, a detachment of soldiers on their way to camp met them with abusive language, faces contorted with hate and anger, and some threatening display of guns. The reason for this hostility became clear when they reached Shippensburg that afternoon and found that the Epistles of the Meeting for Sufferings and the Spanktown forgery had been reprinted in a handbill and widely distributed. Dark and in some cases frightened looks followed them as they rode along the wide, grass-bordered street to the inn. This was large enough to provide comfortable quarters for all, and they had a time of silence together before supper.

They expected to get dinner next day at Chamberstown, but there was none to be had, whether through hostility or genuine lack they could not tell. The doors of the houses were shut; the inn refused them entrance. In the end they went beyond the town and fed the horses from stores in the wagons and watered them in a brook. They stayed their own stomachs with bread and cheese, which they ate sitting in a meadow looking off to the blue hills ahead.

They found no town in which to lodge that night. It was a region of forests and lonely farms. Back from the road a hospitable house, prosperous but small, received the three Pembertons. The others scattered and found what they could. Caleb with Miers Fisher and Drewet Smith slept on straw before the hearth in a log cabin, with homespun blankets spread over them. The young farmer and his wife and two children were in the loft above. In the morning the guests moved their beds, and the pale, stringy-haired little wife, whose teeth were a row of black stumps, gave them a breakfast of corn-meal mush and apple sauce sweetened with honey.

The company met at the appointed place next morning. It was Sunday again, the fourth since they had been imprisoned. Now the party spread out, for the road was rough and stony and the wagons made slow progress. It was pleasanter riding this way, and gave almost a sense of freedom. In a wild and lonely place Caleb and Miers met two Friends on their way to the Yearly Meeting scheduled to be held in Philadelphia in a week's time. They stopped to exchange names and news and the two Friends promised to see the families of the exiles and report that they were well.

It had been agreed that all should stop for dinner at Watkins' Ferry on the Potomac. The innkeeper on the north side, however, refused to take them in, and even the miserable little tavern on the south side of the river was closed against them. Seeing the dirt, the squalor, the idiot child with slavered chin peering out of a window, Caleb decided it had little to offer anyhow. But he was hungry, and there was nothing at the next house or the next. The wagons were now too far behind to dip into the stores that they carried. The afternoon was closing in, with the suddenness of late September, when at length they reached a tavern called the Red House.

Beer and bread and cheese were forthcoming immediately, in a room cool and shadowy with the last fingers of sunshine on the window sills, and a dinner of fried chicken was promised. Not long afterward the first of the light wagons came up, with the news that John Pemberton and others had made a formal protest before witnesses against crossing the state line from Pennsylvania into Maryland, and again at the Virginia line.

This, the last night on the road, Caleb slept in a bed, which he shared with Elijah Brown. Most of the party were at the Red House, with the overflow in two houses near by owned by Quaker farmers.

"There are a good many Friends in Winchester—" said Elijah, "Winchester and round about, that is. Most of them came from Chester County originally. They still belong to Philadelphia Yearly Meeting. I've no doubt that Friends will do what they can for us, but it is going to be tedious, very tedious."

In the morning a boy was found willing to ride ahead to and beyond the town to the Marlboro Iron Works, to inform Isaac Zane, junior, that the exiles were on the way. The innkeeper at the Red House told them that Mr. Zane had returned two or three days earlier from Philadelphia. He was well known throughout the countryside, he and his lively younger sister, Sally, who often visited him. His ironworks, his mill, his yellow coach, his wide acquaintance with every sort of important or conspicuous figure, his patriotism: all had a kind of flamboyance. His father and his elder sister, Hannah, who had married John Pemberton, were Philadelphians and plain Friends; young Isaac and Sarah were of the Virginia frontier.

All that day the exiles rode up the Valley of Virginia, with the Alleghenies on the right and the Blue Ridge on the left. The valley was wide at this end, and so far Caleb had not even had a glimpse of the famous Shenandoah. The rocks that scratched their way through the surface of the fields were pale limestone; the trees were oak and hickory and beech. Now and then a large fuzzy brown caterpillar hustled across the road in front of them; killdeer flew overhead crying, and in the woods acorns pattered on the ground.

The occasional houses they passed were built of squared logs or of limestone, tall and narrow at the gables. Caleb thought the proportion awkward, after the great square brick piles of eastern Pennsylvania with huge double chimneys or the older stone houses with the roof line on two levels and the hooded doorways.

The sun had set when they reached Winchester, a raw little town of new streets and vacant lots and scattered modest buildings. They met a cow being led home from pasture by a tousle-headed boy, a two-wheeled cart piled high with cornstalks, a gentleman on a handsome horse, a colored woman with a basket of laundry on her head, as they jogged slowly down the valley road, which had become the main street of the town. Lighted windows, woodsmoke in the air, the chill of evening, the voice of a mother calling her children, told of suppertime.

A man appeared out of the shadows and spoke to Mr. Levan, who rode at the head of the cavalcade. They all stopped. The horses hung their heads, blew, pawed the ground wearily. The exiles shifted in their saddles and looked around them. In the light wagons the older men were gray with fatigue and dust, their faces deeply creased and drooping in heavy lines. People passing eyed them with curiosity. After a few moments of conference among the guards they moved on again through the dusk.

A large stone building with rows of lighted windows loomed up on their right behind a screen of young willow trees. Over the door hung a sign with a crudely painted deer and the words, "The Golden Buck." A swarm of boys came running to the horses' heads and a large man with rolled-up sleeves and a big apron appeared on the front steps.

Caleb dismounted stiffly. So. This was the end of the journey.

XVIII

CALEB STOOD BY THE window of the Golden Buck, looking out at the road and an empty lot opposite, through which the Town Run took its meandering course. Between the willow trees he saw something that shot through his whole listless being with sudden vitality. Wandering alone down the road, unself-conscious and unconcerned, was the prettiest girl he had ever seen.

She was a child of the backwoods. Her slim, lissom little body was clothed in gray linsey-woolsey which clung in soft folds without any of the hoops or panniers by which city girls disguised their shape. With her white fichu, white cap, red-gold curls gleaming in the sun and her milky skin she looked as clean and fresh as if she had just been dipped in dew. He had a glimpse of a wide mouth, a short, straight nose, and gray eyes thickly fringed with black, before she stooped suddenly to pick up a walnut that had fallen to the ground from the big tree on the other side of the road. Absorbed as a child, she rubbed off the green outer shell, and looked about for another. Then, as if becoming suddenly aware of Caleb's steady gaze, she glanced up at the window, straightened her little backbone till it was as erect as a daffodil's stalk, dusted her hands together briskly, and made off down a narrow lane that passed through the field to the south of the inn. Before she disappeared Caleb had time to approve her walk, which was of a piece with the rest of her, free, graceful, and surefooted as a fawn's.

He reached for his hat on the peg by the window and was about to set off after her when John Hunt's gentle, amused voice halted him.

"There's a guard at the door, my boy,"

Feeling himself flush hotly, Caleb put his hat back and smoothed down his hair with his hand. Then he grinned. "Eheu fugaces!" he said lightly, while his mind raced on after the girl.

She was very young, not more than sixteen at the most, and as natural and innocent as a yellow chick just out of its shell. Although obviously not a young lady in the accepted sense, he reflected, she had a flower-like delicacy which suggested an innate refinement independent of her station in life. She might be an indentured servant in one of the larger houses of the town, or the daughter of an artisan. But she was like a nymph—Daphne vanishing among the forest trees—and he must somehow manage to see her again. She had passed the inn once; perhaps she had regular errands that took her this way. Or if the prisoners could get permission to take exercise in the village, which appeared to be only the minimum of humanity and decency, he could walk systematically up one street and down another until he found her.

Behind him the parlor was filling up with the exiles, who came in looking expectant and serious. Caleb remembered that a meeting of the group with the Lieutenant of the county had been set for eleven o'clock this morning. In the confusion of their arrival the evening before, of getting supper and being assigned to bedrooms, they had been visited by Isaac Zane, junior, and several local officials. All that had come out of it, however, had been the assertion that the papers of their banishment were very confused and irregular, that the Lieutenant of Frederick County was doubtful whether he had any jurisdiction over them and was in favor of sending them back to Carlisle or on to Staunton. Since it was late, decision had been postponed until the morning.

The older men filled the chairs and benches, the younger ones standing at the back. Caleb himself lounged on the wide window sill, where he could keep an eye on the road in case the girl came back.

What he saw, however, put the girl out of his mind altogether. A company of about thirty men in hunting shirts, armed with muskets, came marching up the road past Caleb's window and drew up before the front door. Behind them swarmed citizens of the town. There was something threatening about the purposeful way they approached and the angry scowls on their faces; the clamor of voices in the crowd following had a sinister sound.

"There's one of 'em!" came a hoarse shout from a man who waved his arm toward the window where Caleb sat.

A gun barked sharply.

It must have been fired into the air, for a moment later some leafy twigs drifted out of the willows, but the effect of it was to bring everyone in the inn parlor to his feet in alarm.

The front door opened and the young guard outside, who was a schoolmaster in private life, skipped in and slammed the door behind him. He stuck an agitated face into the parlor. "Where's Mr. Levan?" The next moment he vanished and they heard his feet pounding up the stairs.

Now fists began battering on the door and separate voices rose out of the angry roar.

"We don't want no Tories here!"

"Run 'em out of town!"

"Tar and feather 'em!"

The gentlemen from Philadelphia exchanged quick glances and turned pale. The threat of tar and feathers was not an idle one. Less than a year before in Philadelphia itself the respectable Dr. Kearsley had been seized by the militia at his own door, bundled into a cart, and paraded through the streets to the tune of the "Rogue's March." He had suffered a bayonet wound and barely escaped being plunged into hot tar.

Caleb sprang to close the door from the parlor into the hall and stand with his back braced against it. The others moved hastily away from the windows as grimacing faces were pressed against the panes outside.

John Hunt walked quietly across the room. "Step aside, Caleb," he said gently. "I will speak with them."

"No, John, don't!" cried John Pemberton, "It's folly! They art in no state to listen to reason."

"I am small and inoffensive," said Hunt.

Smiling a little he opened the door of the parlor and the heavy front door. Several men on the step, taken by surprise, fell back, their mouths dropping slightly.

"Friends," said John Hunt in a clear, cheerful voice, "we were no more eager to come here than you are to have us! We are peaceable people, and we—"

There was no telling what would have happened next if Lieutenant Smith had not come riding up at that moment.

"Hold on!" he shouted. He was mounted on a big handsome horse, a dark dappled gray with a white face, and he rode across the front yard of the inn and into the crowd of armed men, who moved awkwardly back out of range of the horse's heels, as men will. "What's going on here? You, Hauck, you seem to be the leader. What's all this?"

Caleb, who had come to the door behind John Hunt, was stricken with an agony of shame and self-disgust. The Lieutenant of Frederick County was a young man not much older than he was, a fiery young man on a fine horse, acting with authority and vigor, while he, Caleb Middleton, was a helpless prisoner.

"We don't want no Tories in Winchester," answered the man called Hauck. "They've got to go back where they came from."

"Send 'em on to Staunton. They've got plenty Tories there, in stockades."

"That's right"

"We don't want 'em here."

"They are here under orders from the Board of War," answered Smith in a voice that carried to the last man on the outskirts of the crowd. "We must deal with this matter in a legal, orderly way!"

"Virginia's a free state! We don't have to take the sweepings of Pennsylvania!"

"Virginia has not spoken yet. I shall write to Williamsburg and get my orders from there. Go home now and wait till we hear from Governor Henry."

"They ought to be in jail!"

"Send 'em back to Spanktown!"

"Send the fellow in the red coat to the other lobsterbacks—on a rail!"

"You know the size of our jail. It wouldn't hold a fourth of their number. This inn will be as good as a jail. No person who is not authorized will be allowed to go in or out."

"How'll you prevent it?"

"I'll put my own guards at the door. These are quiet, harmless gentlemen; they'll not make trouble. It will be only for a few days anyhow, till we hear from the Governor. You, Hauck, and you, Noakes, will you do guard duty today?"

He knew how to handle men, thought Caleb. The temper of the crowd had cooled, and Hauck and Noakes, faced with some personal effort, backed off.

"No, I can't, sir. I've got work to do."

"Get some of those fellows off the farms."

"Go back to your work now, all of you. You've made your protest, you've done all you can do for the present. I will inform the Governor of your action."

Muttering, they began to withdraw in little knots of two and three. Lieutenant Smith dismounted, turned his horse over to a boy, and came into the inn. Busch, the innkeeper, met him at the door and they went off together. A quarter of an hour later Smith came into the parlor, wearing that reminiscent look of a satisfactory interview just concluded.

"Good morning, gentlemen," he said genially. "I regret that rather unpleasant episode, but I think there is no more to fear from that quarter for the present. I shall have to require you to make no attempt to leave these premises, even for a short walk."

Thomas Wharton, as spokesman for the group, rose to his feet. "Friend Smith," he said, "we are thankful to thee for thy handling of the matter, especially if thou had nothing to do with spreading the reports of us which aroused the people." This insinuation was not lost on Smith, who stiffened and looked grim. Mr. Wharton continued, "Now, not to take any more of thy time than necessary, we have the following questions to ask of thee, and we request that thou give us the answers in writing."

"If you will give me your questions in writing, I will examine them at my leisure and make such answers as I feel free to give at some later time."

"Thou hast seen the papers delivered last night to thee by the Sheriff of Berks County," continued Wharton as if he had not heard. "We desire to know: first, are we the prisoners of Congress or of the Council of Pennsylvania, or are we prisoners of war? Second, in any case do these papers give thee the authority to take charge of us? And finally, if thou consider that thou hast such authority, wilt thou provide for our accommodation at Winchester at the public expense?"

"As I said last night, the papers are confused. I do not consider myself obliged to obey orders either of Congress or of the Council of Pennsylvania unless I have the sanction of the government of Virginia. The proper action for me to take, I believe, is to write at once both to the Congress and to the Governor of Virginia for further directions concerning you."

"Have you any objection," said Miers Fisher, abandoning as the younger Friends did the plain language when talking to people of the world, "to our also writing letters to the same authorities, to be enclosed with yours?"

"No, I think not. I should have to read your letters, of course."

"And we, in return, may see yours before they are sent?"

"I agree to that."

"In the meantime," said Thomas Wharton, "Thou wilt be in charge of us, and responsible for our accommodation at the public expense?"

"No, I cannot engage to do that. These papers give me no such authority. There is no direct order even to hold you at Winchester. There is a letter from Mr. Thomas Wharton—but surely that is a mistake. Are you not Mr. Wharton?"

"My cousin, of the same name. President of the Supreme Executive Council of Pennsylvania."

"Oh, I see. Thomas Wharton, junior. Somewhat unusual, is it not? A letter from Mr. Thomas Wharton, junior, to Mr. John Hancock, President of the Congress, says: 'Congress fixed on Staunton. They doubtless have their reasons; but if it now appears proper to stop them at Winchester, directions from your Board of War can dispose matters accordingly, for it is a matter of indifference to Council.' Then there is a note addressed to the Lieutenant of Frederick County, signed by Mr. John Adams, Chairman of the Board of War, saying that that body *consents* to the prisoners being stopped at Winchester. Now there is nothing in that which makes it mandatory on me to hold you here, and there is nothing whatsoever in any of these papers relative to your accommodation here at public expense, and I have no power to commit the government of Virginia to any such undertaking."

The exiles were silent, dismayed. Disagreeable as Winchester might be, with the populace inflamed against them, they were certain that it was much to be preferred to Staunton.

Mr. Levan, the Sheriff of Berks County, who had entered the room behind Lieutenant Smith, now spoke up.

"Someone will have to take charge of these prisoners. I have brought them here from Reading, and I must return at once to Reading and take my men with me. I can't go back without some kind of paper discharging me from my responsibility in the matter. I have delivered them to you as I was commanded to do, and now they are your charge."

Smith's voice rose in annoyance. "You can't deliver them to me because the papers are not in order. Furthermore, the inhabitants of Winchester are dangerously aroused and I can't answer for the safety of these prisoners."

"The town of Winchester has three hundred or more Hessian war prisoners. I can't see why they object to twenty quiet Quaker gentlemen."

"The town of Winchester has a record of unsullied loyalty to the patriot cause. We have some Quakers in our population but so far they have not been Tories. Put a company like this who won't guarantee to hold their tongues into the midst of them and who knows what they will stir up, not only in town but among the Quakers of Frederick and Loudon counties as well. I had three Quaker farmers at my house this morning interceding for these people, and Busch tells me he turned away a steady stream of them all last evening. The loyal people of the town don't like it. They've got sons and fathers with Morgan's division; they're making sacrifices for liberty. You saw that demonstration out there a little while ago. Those people are hungry. They're violent men. Some of them are Irish and some are Germans who left Pennsylvania just because they wanted to get away from Quaker appeasement of the Indians. They don't want a score of Quaker Tory leaders here fomenting sedition."

"Well, I can't take them back. You can't send them on to Staunton in the face of that letter from Mr. Adams. No doubt you'll hear from Congress and the Governor of Virginia in a few days. You give me some kind of a receipt saying you'll hold them till further orders come, and let me be off for home. Meanwhile they'll have to pay their own charges for food and lodging. You can post a guard to protect them from the population."

"I suppose we shall have to do something of the sort. But it must be made clear that I am accepting only a conditional charge over them."

After the lieutenant and the sheriff had gone, the innkeeper came to establish the rates for food and lodging.

Philip Busch was a German who had been twenty or thirty years in America. He was among the earliest settlers of Winchester and his word had weight on the various councils of town and county. The exiles had learned already that he was a staunch Whig and that he had consented to lodge them at his inn only at the urgent request of Mr. Zane, whom he appeared to respect highly.

"Now, chentlemen;" he began, "we must haf an understandink. You will stay in my house and I will get my pay from you. Lodgink is five shillinks a night, breakfast five shillinks, dinner five shillinks, supper three shillinks. Dot is very cheap. You must find your own cider, wines, tea, coffee, sugar, vinegar, and so on. Horses can be kept in my stables for ten shillinks a week. If I get into trouble with the townspipple for havink you here, den you will haf to go and no arguments."

"I don't call that cheap," muttered Tom Affleck beside Caleb. "I call it highway robbery. And what's more, I can't pay it. What will they do about that?"

Caleb was grateful to his father for the heavy belt about his waist. "I can let you have what you need for the present," he said. "They will surely make some provision for us later."

In the afternoon new guards, local men, appeared at front and back doors. They were unsmiling and hostile, and in comparison the men who had ridden from Reading seemed like old friends. Caleb got permission to go out to the stable to look after Ladybird, and there he found the Pennsylvania guards helping Richard and the wagoners to unload the stores and carry in the baggage.

The stables were large but badly built, with wide chinks between the logs, and they were dirty. Ladybird whinnied a welcome when Caleb appeared. He got hold of a stable boy, a skinny little fellow with big, transparent ears and pale, wary eyes, tipped him well, and stood over him while he cleaned the stall and brought fresh straw.

The schoolmaster guard came to talk to Caleb.

"We're leaving first thing in the morning," he said. "I hope you'll be all right here. Someone sent ahead a lot of those handbills about the Spanktown Yearly Meeting, and the townspeople are excited. I've been with you ten days, and I must say I've never heard anything seditious from any of you. Seems as if government's government, whichever side it's on, and the less of it the better." He hesitated, then went on with a rush. "You've got to pay for yourselves, and that's a hardship for some of the prisoners, I guess. But then so have the men that drive the wagons. They've got to turn around and go back to Carlisle and buy food along the way for themselves and their horses. Mr. Levan's just turning them loose. He says the money the Council appropriated for the journey will barely get him and us guards back."

Caleb thought of the teamsters who worked for the Phoebe Ann. They were a rough, honest, hard-working lot. They owned and maintained their wagons and their teams, lived with their families in stark little fieldstone houses pressed against the hillside, and spent most of their time lurching and heaving over the rough roads, loading and unloading their wagons, coping with broken axles and lamed horses, their only pleasure a mug of beer in one of the plainer taverns that catered to wagoners. The profit on a single trip was small, a trip that did not make expenses was disaster. The Middletons had always taken care of their wagoners at the Phoebe Ann, as they had all of their workmen, and the irresponsible attitude of the Sheriff of Berks infuriated Caleb.

He walked over to the wagon shed where he found one of the teamsters patiently mending a frayed rope harness.

"Look here," he said abruptly, "I've been told you're being sent back without any pay for your trip. Is that true?"

"It's Gawd's truth, sir. They say we may get it from the Congress some time. Huh." He spat.

"That's not fair. Here are a couple of half joes. You ought to be able to get at least thirty-six shillings apiece for them. Divide it among the four of you. It won't be much for each one, but it will help at the taverns."

"I don't like to take it, sir, not from a prisoner, like." His hand went out, nevertheless, and a slow, pleased smile spread over his knotty face. "Thank you kindly, sir. It's Gawd's truth, sir, from what I've seen lately of Whigs and Tories, I'll take Tories."

"I'm not a Tory, you donkey. I'm for a free America." The man looked so surprised that Caleb laughed and clapped him on the shoulder. "It's people like you and me that have to stand fast and make it what we want it to be."

And that, he thought, a little surprised himself as he went back into the inn, is Gawd's truth.

XIX

THE NEW GUARDS WERE farmers pressed into service, who grumbled because it was seeding-time for winter wheat and they were needed at home. Caleb talked a good deal to one of them, who, it happened, was just a little younger than he was himself, a lanky, redheaded youth as angular and tough as a young hickory tree blown and stripped by winter winds.

"I've served my time in the army," he said. "Ten months in the Fifth Virginians under General Adam Stephen, and three of them in hospital. Don't know how I come out of that alive. Tain't the guns that's so dangerous, it's the hospitals."

"What's the matter with them? Aren't the doctors any good?"

"Sure, they're good, I reckon. But they ain't got anything to work with. I wasn't so bad off when I went in, I had a flesh wound that healed up after a while, but I got a fever in the hospital that I like to died of. There was twenty of us in one room, lying on straw jammed up together, with the same shirts we was wearing God knows how long before we went in, and maybe one buggy blanket apiece, and nothing to eat but bread and stringy beef. I never want to see beef again 's long's I live. I saw twelve men carted out of that room dead—maybe more, I was out of my head part of the time."

Caleb was horrified. "But what were the surgeons doing all this time? Didn't you have any medical care?"

"Two of the surgeons got sick themselves and one died. Nurses was only men too old to fight. They couldn't even keep that room clean. I don't mean clean the way a room at home is clean, I mean decent. My time run out and I got up and come home. I was so weak I couldn't hardly stand."

"But didn't anybody stop you?"

"Oh, they didn't notice. Anybody who could move at all was in and out all the time, going to the necessary and so on. Some of them sold their guns or blankets and bought rum—there was always somebody hanging around with something to sell—and then they'd get into fights with the other men. So I walked out. Took me three weeks to get home. Rode partway in a wagon with shoes for the army, only they didn't get to the army. They went into a storehouse in Lancaster—to ripen, I reckon, till the price gets higher."

"You must have been more dead than alive when you got home."

"My mother, she took one look at me and she wouldn't let me into the house. Made me strip off all my rags in the yard and she brought buckets from the well and like to drowned me. Lucky it was spring by that time and almost warm. Then I went to bed, between sheets, and she brought me food. Lord, it tasted good. Thing I wanted more than anything else was a toasted potato, hot from the ashes, with new butter and salt."

"It's hard to believe, in this day and age. I don't mean I don't believe you, but it's incredible that conditions like that could be allowed. Were you wounded at Trenton?"

"Skirmish, afterward. My mother, she hasn't any use for officers. One day—I was still in bed in the little room off the kitchen—three captains from Nevill's company came riding up, called her out and ordered her to get dinner for them. No please or would you kindly, but just bring it out and be quick. She did, too. Then they heard a noise in the cellar and wanted to know what it was. Our dog had pups down there, and nothing would do but they must see them. So down she goes through the trap door and hands them up to the officers, one by one. 'What's his name?' says one of them when he takes the first puppy in his hand. 'Captain,' says my mother. Then the second comes up. 'What's this 'un's name?' 'Captain.' And when he asks her the same question about the third and she says that one's Captain too, he wants to know, why does she give all her pups the same name. You'd think anybody'd have more sense 'n to walk into a trap like that, wouldn't you? 'Oh,' says my mother, 'nowadays any puppy dog can get to be a captain.' I like to died laughing. I had to smother my head with the bedclothes."

"Do you know any of the girls around here?"

"Round here? Winchester? Winchester's a big town—it's got a population of eight hundred and there's a good few girls. I know some of 'em."

"I mean a girl that went walking past here on Tuesday morning and turned into the lane."

"What did she look like?"

"She was a little slim thing, young, and she had gold curls under a white cap."

"There's Katie Bason, but she's black-haired and she isn't so little. There's Miss Sally Haines, her hair's sort of light-colored, but she isn't so young. There's the McGuire twins, but they wouldn't hardly go walking by like that, they're too uppity. Their father keeps the McGuire House—twice as big as this place—and they think they're royalty. Can't tell what color their hair is, it's always powdered and dressed up like a wedding cake."

"I'd like to see this girl again. She must be in Winchester somewhere."

"You could go look for her for all of me, but the captain would kill me. I stayed home after I got well because my dad died last year and my mother needs me on the farm, but if I've got to do guard duty over Tories, I might's well be fightin'. They're most of 'em too old to need a guard anyhow, except you and the lawyer and that fellow in the red coat. Why don't you join up with Howe or Cornwallis if you're Tories?"

"I'm not a Tory," said Caleb. Flushing at the quick, incredulous look of the guard, he went on, "But even if I were I wouldn't fight. I'm a Quaker. Friends don't believe in war and violence."

"I don't like war either, and I reckon I know more about it than you do, mister, but what do you do when they march in and start shootin'?"

"You have to begin earlier, with your protests and negotiation, before the shooting starts, and I suppose you have to be willing, if necessary, to be shot at and not shoot back." But was he really, himself? And might he not have joined the Continental army, after Washington's march through Philadelphia, if he had not been taken prisoner? He saw the closed look on the hollow, freckled face of the guard, and he went on, "What I'd really like to do is be a doctor and help to relieve some of the suffering in the hospitals. Only I didn't get started in time."

Another of the guards, Caleb discovered later, was a Quaker himself. He had been gathered up from his farm five miles away and ordered to take his stand at one of the side doors of the inn. The musket that was issued to him he leaned up against the wall, refusing to touch it.

"The prisoners can leave any time they want," he said defiantly in the hearing of the other guards. "I won't stop them."

When the exiles held their meetings for worship on Sunday morning and afternoon in the inn parlor, that guard and two or three others joined them. Caleb saw his own especial friend standing outside the window looking in, along with Philip Busch and his wife and some of the townspeople, both white and colored. Lieutenant Smith came to the afternoon Meeting, probably just to make sure that they were not conspiring when they sat there in silence, but he behaved very courteously and even reverently.

The next day the exiles were permitted to take short walks about the town attended by a guard, on the condition that they speak to no one along the way. Caleb, whose restlessness indoors had got on everybody's nerves, was urged by the others to go with the first group of six that set out.

It had rained all morning, but in the afternoon it blew out blue and gold and chilly, with the sun glistening on the wet, black trunks of trees and on red and yellow leaves plastered flat on fences and doorsteps. The last rags of clouds were being blown out of the sky above the wall of the Blue Ridge, which stood up higher and nearer than they had yet seen it.

They walked to the Shawnee Spring, named for the tribe that first owned this part of the country, and drank thirstily of the clear cold water, for the well water that they got at the Golden Buck was cloudy and ill-tasting. All along the way Caleb looked for the girl in the gray dress. Each house he passed he examined carefully, hoping for a slim figure in a doorway, or crossing the yard. The little post-office, the blacksmith shop, the big stone building where, their guard told them, some of the Hessian prisoners were confined, the pond and the stony hill above it, the public well where housewives gathered: he raked each one with his eyes, inventing some reason why she might be there.

The girl whom he had so briefly seen haunted his thoughts and his dreams. While the other exiles discussed the changes in the new Essay they were writing—should not "pursued" be substituted for "manifested" in one sentence, and "just cause of" be inserted before "offense" in another?—Caleb imagined scenes in which he met the girl. She came to the inn bringing something from her mistress to Mrs. Busch. Or the inn got on fire and they all rushed out, and Caleb was brilliantly reckless and daring in fighting the flames. Out of the watching crowd stepped Daphne. She had a wet cloth in her hand, she wiped his throbbing, smoke-blackened (but not painful) face, he caught her hand and pressed it to his lips. Or he walked out with the guard—as he was doing now—they passed a little shop, and Daphne came out, having been sent upon an errand . . . .

As they crossed a rutted lane the guard nodded toward a low stone building away to the left. "Washington's headquarters," he said, "back in 1755, after Braddock's defeat. Major he was then. Lot of folks in town remember him."

Back again at the Golden Buck, after what Caleb considered so short a walk that it was only tantalizing, though Thomas Wharton commented with satisfaction that they must have gone at least two miles, the guard, a plain, middle-aged man, said to them with a burst of friendliness, "I wouldn't begrudge ten pounds out of my own pocket to have you gentlemen set at liberty. It's my belief you've been wronged."

Two or three days later this man threw up his job. He was going home, he said, to his own work. There was no sense in guarding these folks. When the harassed captain warned him that he would be fined if he left without permission, he replied calmly, "I can afford it," and off he went, to the amusement of the exiles, who made no public comment but wrote it down in their diaries.

XX

HERE, AS IN READING, Caleb shared a bed with John Hunt. The other bed in the room, a larger one with shabby curtains, was occupied by Edward Penington and Thomas Wharton. Caleb found it rather oppressive to be the young and negligible one in such a weighty group, but there was no help for it unless he shared an attic cell with Mr. Pike, a fate which he regarded with horror. Miers Fisher, the one of the exiles who was nearest his own age and whom he would have liked to know better, was always with his two brothers Thomas and Samuel, and his brother-in-law, Thomas Gilpin. Edward Penington was kind to his young cousin in an elderly, sometimes irascible sort of way, and Thomas Wharton was rather ponderously affable when he remembered to notice him at all; John Hunt, the oldest and the most religious, was by far the easiest to be with, and Caleb found himself growing very fond of his elderly bed-fellow.

One afternoon, when they had been about ten days in Winchester, Caleb was lying on his bed reading Tom Jones for the third or fourth time. His roommates were in the parlor below, conferring with visitors from the town. They were attempting, Caleb knew, to get permission for the exiles to go about freely in Winchester, to attend the meeting for worship held at the Hollingsworth house, and even, if possible, to ride beyond the town to look for places where they could board their horses for less than Busch charged. The daily walks to the spring had by now lost the first charm of novelty and were so monotonous and restricting as to be an exasperation. Even more than the others Caleb was galled by them, and as the endless slow days followed one another with no prospect of change, he sought escape by lying on his bed and reading.

One knee was racked up and the other balanced on it, his free foot jigging steadily. He was eating an apple, one of the yellow York Imperials grown on the high ground west of the town called Apple Pie Ridge. As he took an enormous bite, observing with interest the noise it made as the firm gleaming flesh parted under his strong teeth and licking up neatly with his tongue the juice that ran over the edges of the tough skin, John Hunt came into the room, a little smile on his face.

Caleb grinned and laid his book face down on the homespun bedspread. "Thee looks very pleased with thyself," he remarked with affectionate impudence. "What has thee been and gone and done, as Tacy would say?"

"I am. I have done something for thee that I think thou wilt like. Thou shouldst have been downstairs. Lieutenant Smith was there and with him the Commissary of Prisoners, Joseph Holmes, and a young lawyer of Winchester named Alexander White. They are much concerned about the sickness that has broken out among the Hessian and Brunswick prisoners who are quartered here. It seems that the only physician, Dr. Macky, is away with the militia. They had heard that Drewet Smith is an apothecary and had brought some medicine with him, and they came to ask him to attend the sick prisoners and do what he can for them."

"What kind of sickness?"

"Dysentery and colds and such-like; some inflammation of the lungs, I believe; accidents. What they are afraid of, of course, is camp fever."

"Where are all these prisoners? We've heard about them, but I haven't seen more than a handful. That stone barrack on the Valley Road wouldn't house more than fifty at the most."

"There's a stockade about four miles west of the town, and then they are hired out to farmers all around. Some are working for Isaac Zane. There will be no bounds on Drewet Smith; he will be free to ride wherever he is needed—and I have arranged for thee to go with him as his assistant."

Caleb sat up and swung his legs off the bed in a single lithe movement. "*What?*" he exclaimed.

John sat down on the room's one chair and folded his hands on his knee. "It occurred to me that Dr. Smith might well have an assistant on his rounds, and I put it to the Commissary of Prisoners, who made no objection at all."

Caleb stretched his arms wide above his head and drew a long breath. "Lord!" he said, feeling the bands about his heart already easing as he thought of Ladybird and the road and the hills under the sky. "Thee can't conceive what this means to me!"

John smiled serenely. "And to me. It is partly self-defense. Now I shall be very much obliged to thee if thou wilt refrain from contracting any unpleasant diseases thyself. It is a risk, I suppose, but less of a risk than having thee batter thy spirit to pieces in rebellion against confinement."

"Is Drewet Smith downstairs? I think I had better see him immediately. Does thee think I can really assist him—or is it just a means of getting me out? Which, heaven knows, is a worthy purpose! But I'd like to justify myself, if only to be kept on in the position. How soon do we start, does thee know?"

"I don't know what thee can do. Hold the basin, I suppose, and wrap bandages. I don't really know what Drewet Smith can do. He is not a doctor, and I hope he won't try to go beyond the little he knows about salves and purges. He is skilful in blood-letting, I believe, but whether he has solid judgment as to when to bleed and when not to is another question. But this I do know, Caleb: kindness is often a better medicine than drugs. If thee and Drewet Smith can take these poor prisoners a feeling of friendliness and true concern, you will minister to their souls and perhaps through their souls to their bodies."

Caleb looked down at him curiously. "They are soldiers," he said, "and mercenaries at that. I didn't know thee cared so much about those who engage in carnal warfare."

"They are sinners and exiles from their home—and so are we all. All exiles."

Caleb threw off his damask gown with the warm baize lining, which he had been wearing because the room was chilly, and took down his coat from a peg behind the door. John Hunt had opened his Testament. Caleb put a hand lightly on his shoulder.

"Anyhow," he said, "thank thee very much."

What he meant by that "anyhow" he could not easily have said. He had some unformulated feeling that the older man had given him a gift of obvious value on terms which were not yet clear to him.

John Hunt looked up at him with clear blue eyes in which austerity and tenderness were mingled. The little wrinkles at the corners of his eyes deepened as he answered, "Anyhow, my boy, thee is entirely welcome."

Every day after that Caleb rode out with Drewet Smith. The stable boy brought the horses, Ladybird dancing, Smith's Brownie hanging his head and heaving his gaunt hips, around to the front door. The bag with the lancets, bandages, bottles, packets, and jars, was fastened to Caleb's saddle. Smith climbed up stiffly on the mounting-block, Caleb swung himself lightly into the saddle, and they moved off.

Usually messages had been left at the inn. "Tell the doctor a man in the new stockade has a cough and a fever." "Ask the doctor to stop at Hentzel's farm on the northwest road; one of the prisoners fell out of the barn loft." At each place they visited they would hear of other cases, and sometimes it was late after noon before they returned to the inn.

The longer the ride, the better pleased Caleb was. The country was beautiful in the crisp October days, with the bright leaves flying and the bare shapes of trees emerging as from a veil. The blue of the distant mountains deepened in moving patterns as the clouds trailed shadows over them. Cedars in the folds of the hills looked greener as the fields faded and dead leaves drifted in piles in all the hollows. Water cress embroidered the edges of little runs with emerald, and the clear water gave back the blue of the sky above it.

There were more prisoners in the region than Caleb had realized. Besides the three hundred Hessians who had left Lebanon before the exiles, there were Scotch and Irish prisoners taken at Pittsburgh. Most of these were held in stockades to the west and south of the town. Some of the Germans had been hired out to farmers at seven dollars and a half a month. Many of them were skilled masons and woodworkers and they were put to quarrying stones for the mansions that were to replace the log houses as soon as possible. Often brutal in

victory, these men were docile prisoners, hardworking and phleg-
matic. Speaking little or no English, they held no communication
with the people of the Valley and no fear was felt of their poisoning the
minds of patriotic citizens, as it was thought the highly articulate exiles from Pennsylvania might do.

Those who worked on the farms suffered injuries, falling from lad-
ders, letting axes slip and lay open a foot, being gored by bulls. In the
flimsy wood and canvas huts in the crowded stockades, there were putrid sore throats, fevers, stomach disorders. There the men, suffering
the languors and despairs of imprisonment, were often dull and sul-
len, ready to be sick because they got no benefit from being well. Fed
on an allowance of seventeen cents a day, they were undernourished
and hungry.

Caleb's sleeping desire to be a doctor awoke, and in spite of his ignorance and resulting frustration, in spite of his distrust of Drewet
Smith, who, he saw the first day, had no real knowledge of the art of
healing and only a superficial acquaintance with the drugs he carried,
still Caleb felt deep within him that he was, however inadequately, engaged in the work for which he had come into the world. John Hunt's
advice stayed in his mind, and when he could do nothing else he
showed his interest and sympathy in a light pat, a smile, the tone of his
voice. After a time it came to him that this was hollow and could soon
become mechanical and meaningless, and he looked more humbly for
some actual service to perform, even though it might be a menial and
unpleasant one.

Some of the places where they went were so filthy, so degraded that
he had all he could do to fight the nausea of loathing within himself.
Some of the men whom he and Dr. Smith tried to help cursed them for
the ignorant blunderers that they were, and the hate that was palpable
in the stinking hut, together with Caleb's own feeling of guilt, made
his attempts to express good will seem clumsy and hypocritical. But to
some they did bring relief, and on a second visit they would find a response and a welcome in the haggard and suffering faces.

After the first few days Caleb began to keep a record, in a notebook
which he begged from Elijah Brown, who had a supply of little blank
books, of the cases which he saw and the treatment they received. He

studied it at night by the inn fire, absorbed and serious, not asking himself of what use it could be, thankful only to have found something to fill his mind and satisfy his need for a purpose in his days.

When they first began to go out he looked in each house for the girl whom he called Daphne and hoped at each new place to find her, but gradually he ceased to think of her, or remembered only at the end of the day to comment to himself that once more he had been disappointed.

It had begun to rain one day when they turned back toward Winchester early in the afternoon. The mountains behind them were blotted out, and a thick belt of dripping woods lay between them and the comfort of a fire and dry clothes. The horses, knowing that they were headed for the stable, became more animated, and the two men rode along in silence. Caleb wondered, as he wondered each day turning toward the inn, whether he would find there some word from home or some news from Williamsburg or York about the decisions which were presumably being made. Now that they had settled down into a fairly comfortable existence at the Golden Buck and he had his daily rides with Drewet Smith to occupy him, he was anxious that they be permitted to remain in Winchester until they should be released. Any move to Staunton now would be a great blow, and yet it was a possibility which hung over them like a dark cloud.

At the ford of the Opequon Creek a man was standing. Caleb saw first a figure under a tree, and felt a little start of surprise at meeting someone in this lonely country. As the man stepped forward obviously intending to speak to them, Caleb realized that it was an Indian, more from the swift and economical movement of the body than from any peculiarity of costume or color. He did have his hair screwed up in a sort of topknot with a feather thrust through it, and his skin was dark and ruddy, though not much more than that of a farmer who has been tanned through bouts of work in the sun; he wore a sort of leather tunic, and he was unarmed. The striking thing about him was his tall, lean, muscular body and the easy command in which he held it.

Caleb had seen Indians in Philadelphia in full regalia, come to make a protest or ask for favors or celebrate a treaty anniversary; he had employed half-breeds at the furnace; he had seen occasional little bands of men and squaws making their way along the road with something to sell; but this was the first time he had come face to face with an Indian of the forest. Though there was a long history of friendship between the Quakers and the Indians and no Indian had ever knowingly attacked a Quaker, still the massacres on the frontier and the stories of Indian raids and kidnappings reminded people that the Indians were savages still, and dangerous. Caleb felt a little thrill of excitement.

The Indian raised his hand gravely. "How," he said. "Tenskatawa "

There was no way of knowing whether the second word—if it was a word and not a whole sentence—was a name or a greeting. Dr. Smith replied with a "How!" and Caleb ventured on "Tenskatawa "

"You doctor?"

"Yes."

"Man sick. Came with me."

"I don't know whether we can come or not. It is late, and we're on our way back to town. Where is he?"

"I lead. You Follow."

Smith turned to Caleb, drew down the corners of his mouth, raised his eyebrows, shrugged his shoulders. Caleb nodded. The Indian, interpreting their expressions as consent, set off at a swift pace along a narrow trail on the west side of the creek. Caleb followed next, since his horse was livelier and he himself more interested. Smith plodded behind, sighing audibly.

It was evidently a short cut they were taking, following the loops and curves of the creek among the low growth at the water's edge. Presently they came upon a cornfield, the stalks standing dry and brown with ears of corn still hanging like flags at a masthead. At home, thought Caleb, the ears would be in yellow piles, with here and there a red ear, and the stalks stacked in tepees. Beyond was a wheat field, half plowed, and then a grove of tall forest trees and a house and outbuildings. The place was neat but bare, and in the steadily falling rain it looked meager and dreary.

They followed the Indian around the corner of the barn to what seemed to be a combination of woodshed and storehouse. There an old-looking young man with thin, stooped shoulders, evidently the farmer, met them.

"Thanks, Tenskatawa," he said. The Indian nodded and walked away without another look at Smith and Caleb. "It's good of you to come. My name's Preston—Edward Preston. You are Dr. Smith?"

"At your service, and this is my assistant, Mr. Middleton."

"We're in a lot of trouble here. I'll take care of your beasts. You go right on into the shedroom there. I've a German prisoner—name is Fritz—and he's been sick ever since I got him. He's got so bad last two-three days, I'm worried. Friend from Winchester told me about you."

There was no window in the shedroom where the sick man lay on straw on a tough wooden bed. He was breathing hoarsely and though his eyes were open he made no sign of seeing them as they went in. The odor in that dark, dank little hole was sickening.

"Ask Mr. Preston to bring a candle," said Dr. Smith, looking around for something to sit on, and finding a rough stool made of a section of a tree trunk.

Caleb was glad for an excuse to escape into the fresh air. He delivered the message to the farmer, who went hurrying off, and then lingered for a moment in the barn door, looking with idle curiosity toward the house.

It was built, like most of the houses of this region, of squared logs chinked with clay. There was a big stone chimney at each narrow end and rows of windows back and front. There were stone steps to the front door and a vine with scarlet leaves crept up the wall beside the door. It was not a large house, but it had evidently been built with hopes that had not yet materialized. As he turned to go back to the sick man in the shed Caleb caught sight of someone looking from a front window, and recognized in a flash the slim figure and piquant little face of the girl in the gray dress.

He lowered his head into the rain, spilling water out of the folds of his hat as he did so, and plunged across the yard.

She came to the front door to meet him. She was wearing the same linsey-woolsey dress with the white kerchief and a little white apron. Her golden hair fell over her shoulders in curls. Her forehead, he saw, was white and round like a child's, and her eyes under delicately arched dark brows were gray and clear, with extravagant black lashes.

"Oh, come right in out of the wet," she said with a little gasp, swinging the door wide open. Her voice was low and surprisingly rich for anyone so young and slight. "I'm so glad Mr. Preston decided to send you right over." She chuckled—a little silver bell of a laugh. "He was going to wait and see how you did with poor Fritz before he let you into the house! Mrs. Preston and the baby are sick upstairs, but it's little Ned I'm really worried about."

Mr. Preston, Mrs. Preston. Then she was not the daughter of the house, an orphan, perhaps, from some decent family, earning her way.

"Eddie's in here," she said, and led the way to a room at the left.

Caleb could hear a child whimpering and even in his bemused state of mind he knew that it was a child in pain, and weak.

The sanded floor gritted under his feet as he crossed the big square room to look down at the child in the wide bed. He saw a pale, pinched little face with dull, almost colorless eyes and parted lips, which were cracked and dry. The limp little hand which be took in his was alarmingly hot. The little boy moved his head restlessly from side to side and cried in feeble anguish.

Daphne picked up a bowl of milk from the table by the bed, dipped a little wad of linen into it, and touched it to the child's lips. He could not swallow, and only cried a little more sharply as she gently wiped away the drops that trickled down his chin.

"I'm so afraid it's putrid sore throat," she whispered, turning a troubled face to Caleb.

"I'll have to go for Dr. Smith. I'm only his assistant. I'm not a doctor—I'd give anything if I were."

She walked to the door with him, and he made the most of the moment.

"Were you in Winchester a fortnight or so ago?"

"Yes, I was. But how did you know?"

"I saw you pass the inn. I thought you were the prettiest girl I'd ever seen. I would have started out after you at once, but then I remembered I was a prisoner."

"The rain is slackening a little. I think you won't get wet if you run. But you're dreadfully wet already, aren't you?"

It seemed important to make her understand what kind of prisoner he was. "They really meant to take my father," he confided, turning back, one foot on the step, his hand on the doorjamb, "but he is old and his heart is not strong, so I am here in his place."

Her gray eyes widened, and for the first time she seemed to be really seeing him. "But that was noble of you!" she exclaimed.

She was so little that she did not even come up to his shoulder. He would have to lift her up—he could do it so easily with a hand under each of her elbows—to kiss her. Her mouth was wide and sweet, soft and delicately shaped as a flower.

"It was the only thing to do," he said, shamelessly modest. "I am young and strong. That day I saw you; I called you Daphne to myself, because you are like a nymph. I've been looking for you ever since."

"I must go back to Neddie—"

As she turned away a voice floated down from upstairs. "Loveday! Loveday! I want you a minute."

Caleb stepped out vigorously into the rain. So her name was Loveday. It was a quaint, old-fashioned name; it suited her.

He went back to the dark little room in the shed and made himself useful, finding a place to fasten the candle so that it would give light without dripping tallow on the patient, washing the man's arm and holding it still while Dr. Smith opened the vein, catching the blood in the pewter basin which they carried with them in the saddlebag.

"Congestion of the lungs?" he said to Dr. Smith, and Smith answered, "Unquestionably."

Edward Preston stood just outside the door, listening and watching. When Smith had finished with the prisoner, the farmer said hesitantly, "If you don't mind, I'd like you to look at my little boy, in the house."

"I want to get this place cleaned up a little first, and this man made more comfortable. The bed needs fresh straw, and can't you find another shirt for him? If you burned some herbs in a pan, it would sweeten the air. He's pretty ill, you know."

"Yes, I've been remiss, I realize. Perhaps Mr. Middleton would help me, while you go ahead and see the boy. Loveday—that's the girl who's taking care of him—will show you."

While Drewet Smith went off to the house, Caleb and the farmer worked together, the man apologizing with nervous volubility.

"I'm sorry to ask you to do this sort of thing. It had got worse than I realized. If my wife were well, she'd have seen that things were right. I've been short-handed. The two men I had working for me were taken for the militia. Now, that's better, isn't it? What kind of herbs, would you think? My wife has some drying up garret. I'll ask Loveday about it."

When they reached the house, Dr. Smith had already, with Loveday's assistance, finished bleeding the little boy, who lay more bleached and fragile than ever, his pitiful moan thinned to a thread. The apothecary had also visited Mrs. Preston and the baby upstairs, had decided, perhaps because he was tired, not to bleed the woman but to give her a purge instead. Mr. Preston invited Dr. Smith and Caleb into the "other room" for a glass of cider before they started back to Winchester, and Loveday went to fetch it. Caleb followed her to the kitchen in the yard, and stood beside her as she poured the cider into mugs from a big stone jug.

Teasingly he took one of her ringlets in his fingers and drew it out straight. It was warm and dry and silky, almost like something alive, and when he let it go it sprang back softly into the curl again, golden and shining.

A shade passed over the girl's face and she moved her hair out of reach of his hand. She did not toss her head, she moved it, gently, as if she wanted him not to notice and be hurt or embarrassed, yet definitely, as if she were quite sure that she did not want a repetition of the liberty he had taken.

For a moment he was vexed. She was acting miss-is, and he had no word of severer condemnation. He thought how he disliked Caroline Rutter and her trick of courting attention and then primly disdaining it, like other young ladies of her class and circle who expected a show of reverence from a man as if it were their due as creatures of a superior plane and finer clay. If you wanted warmth and reality and laughter in a girl, he thought, you had to look for it on a different social level, and for a moment Phyllis Pike's heart-shaped face and soft white bosom swam before his eyes. It was tiresome of

Daphne—Loveday—to turn miss-ish. But perhaps after all, she was only shy. There had been certainly no provocation in the gesture, which was so quiet that it might even have been unintentional after all.

A colored woman came into the kitchen with a bucket of milk. Caleb looked about for the Indian, but he had vanished.

Loveday added a plate of seed cakes to the tray with the cider and thrust it into Caleb's hands. "If you will carry that into the parlor," she said, "I'll run up garret and look for the herbs that Dr. Smith wanted."

She smiled up at him, and he saw the fine transparency of her white skin over the slender bridge of her nose, the cameo-like flare of her nostrils, the pearly shadow in the little indentation in her short upper lip, the bright color blooming in her cheeks. The next moment he saw her skirts flowing around her slender limbs and her curls bobbing against her straight little back as she skimmed across the yard. Suddenly her shadow sprang onto the wet ground, and he saw that the sun had come out, shedding a yellow glow beneath the dark clouds.

Even after they had finished their cider in the room sparsely furnished with a wooden settee, a chair or two, and a table, Loveday did not reappear, and they had to leave without Caleb's seeing her again.

It was nearly a week before he could persuade Dr. Smith to return for a second visit, and when they did come, the prisoner Fritz was up and sitting in the sunshine, though still weak, and the child had died. Loveday was nowhere to be seen. When Caleb asked about her, he was told that she had gone home.

"She doesn't live here?"

"Oh, no, she was just here to help. My wife's on her feet again now, and little Ned's gone."

"Where does she live then?"

"Over near the Shenandoah toward Williams' Gap."

"You don't say. What is her last name?"

"Parry. Loveday Parry. She's a great hand at nursing, for all she's so young. Seems as if she had magic in her touch—but even she couldn't save Neddie for us. He was such a bright, happy little fellow. I wish you could've seen him before he took sick."

Caleb thought of the small, wracked body in the big bed, so pitifully white and weak after the treatment that was to cure him, and he wondered sorrowfully if it might not have been better for Neddie after all if the Indian had not found them that day.

And what was Loveday thinking of the doctor and his assistant? The child was doomed anyhow, he tried to tell himself, but he carried a weight of remorse on his heart that he knew was irrational and yet obscurely justified. Ignorance was not innocence.

XXI

THE FIRST VISITOR TO bring the exiles news of their families at home was Elizabeth Joliffe, a widow of substance who lived near Hopewell Meeting, about four miles north of Winchester. With her friend Rachel Hollingsworth, also a widow, she had ridden all the way to Philadelphia to the Yearly Meeting. While there she had visited many of the families of the exiles, collected news of others, accepted letters for some of them, and the next day after her return to Hopewell had come riding into town to the Golden Buck to report.

She ate dinner with them in the parlor, and afterward, when the table had been cleared away, she sat in the center of the circle, her plump hands clasped in her green silk lap, her feet set firmly side by side upon the Boot, and talked, vivacious and voluble.

"I saw thy wife, John Pemberton. She was sitting on her front porch on Market Street smoking her pipe and she looked as well as I've ever seen her. She sent her dear love and a letter to thee. She has had three letters from thee."

"I have sent her seventeen," murmured John Pemberton.

"There's no doubt about it, the letters are not getting through as they might. Thy wife, Thomas Wharton, says that she has had no word at all from thee since Reading. Thy son Phineas, James Pemberton, has returned to town from Evergreen. He is as thin as a rail, but he was in good spirits and full of sound reflections upon the present commotions."

Did she know, Caleb wondered, that Phinny Pemberton was dying of ulcers on his back and knee that gave him constant and excruciating pain? Caleb thought he saw a look of pity in her bright brown eyes. Perhaps she did know. How better could she comfort James, who loved his only son almost idolatrously, and who might never see him again, than to talk of Phineas as matter-of-factly as she might speak of any other young man?

"Did thee see my wife?" asked Thomas Fisher.

"Yes, I went to thy house especially, since she is very near her time and is not going out now. These days are hard for her, but she keeps up her courage. Thy little son is a fine rascal. He is into everything and keeps that young colored girl busy just following after him. And Miers, thy little Tommy is just beginning to stagger about. He says Ma-ma and Bow for the dog."

It was no use, Caleb knew, to ask about his family, since none of them went near Yearly Meeting now, but he saw no reason why this occasion should be allowed to degenerate into ecstasies over everybody's fine two-year-olds and three-year-olds. "What about the British?" he asked, to turn the conversation. "How are they behaving?"

"Oh, as badly as possible. One might think they were deliberately trying to lose the best friends they have in this country. The commanding officers, it is true, have laid down strict rules about plundering, but the common soldiers are irresponsible and idle and they take what they want. First thing they did was to break up fences for firewood. I am sorry to tell thee, Israel Pemberton, that the Light Dragoons stationed near thy plantation broke into thy wine cellar and made off with six dozen bottles—to say nothing of thy silver spoons."

Was she indulging a private amusement at the expense of Friend Pemberton? Her face was serious and smooth, but her voice, Caleb decided, was a trace too innocent. Even concerned country Friends drank wine, but six dozen bottles and silver spoons in sufficient quantity to have some in every house one owned, even when, as Israel did, one owned four of five, must be accounted worldly. Safely out of range himself of Israel's chilly, all-seeing blue eyes, Caleb grinned openly and was rewarded by the sight of a quirk at the corner of Elizabeth Joliffe's mouth.

"That must be the 'sixty-seven Madeira,' " said Israel calmly. "Now how did they get the key? Six dozen. Humph."

"General Knyphausen is quartered at Cadwaladers' in Second

Street—the Hessian general. He speaks no English at all. They say he spreads his butter on his bread with his thumbnail."

John Hunt looked pained. "What can thee tell us of the sessions of the Yearly Meeting?" he inquired gently. "Were they fairly well attended, in spite of the difficulties?"

"Yes, Friend Hunt, actually they were. None of the New Jersey Friends could come, for the Governor of that state has ordered the river closed, but Pennsylvania Friends were there in good numbers. Nobody seemed to interfere with them on the roads. There was much expression of loving concern about the Friends in exile. A committee of six was appointed to visit the commanding generals of both armies and explain to them Friends' neutrality and our objection to war. When they went to General Washington they were instructed to intercede for you. It was easy enough to see General Howe, for he was in Germantown, but General Washington has his headquarters twenty miles out on Skippack Creek, and the committee had not returned when I left. I don't know how they made out."

"Didst thou hear anything of my wife and children in Germantown?" said Edward Penington.

"No, but I think I should have if anything had gone wrong with them. There was a big battle in Germantown the day the Yearly Meeting concluded. The Americans marched in from White Marsh to surprise the British early on Seventh Day morning. The attack was very well planned, it was said, and might have succeeded, but there was a thick fog that morning and they could hardly see in front of their faces. Some of them even fired on other Americans, thinking they were the enemy. British soldiers made a fortress of Benjamin Chew's big stone mansion, shooting cannon out the windows, and held it against attack. There was a report that General Stephen, who lives not twenty-five miles away from here, got drunk and retreated into somebody's barn. They say he'll be cashiered, if that's the word. Altogether in the end the Americans had to withdraw."

"Were there many wounded?" asked Caleb.

"Hundreds. More than two hundred, taking both sides together, were killed! It was shocking. They cared for some of the wounded in

Germantown, but the most of them were brought all the way into city in wagons. They say the Germantown Road is one of the worst in the country and the poor men suffered tortures from the jolting. The groans and cries were enough to break your heart. I saw one wagonload myself. They put the Americans in the State House and the British in the Hospital and the Presbyterian Church and the Playhouse. Thy stepson, James Pemberton, went to see an amputation and came back full of it. What the young people these days will do! He said he watched Dr. John Foulke saw through a leg bone in twenty minutes, just half the time it took the military surgeons."

She took out her handkerchief and blew her nose vigorously. Soft-hearted, Caleb thought, and interested in everything. If she wasn't at the State House watching the amputation, she certainly wasted no time in getting the details from Bob Morton afterward and crying over the poor sufferers. He could imagine her retailing it all to the Friends at each house where she stopped for the night on the long road home from Philadelphia.

"Eliza Drinker," she went on, "sent two men around to the State House and the Playhouse with coffee and wine-whey for the poor wounded men. People said that was just like her, sending something really good and comforting and plenty of it. Both sides, too. I hadn't met her before, but Catharine Greenleaf took me to call on her. Thy son Billy has been poorly, Henry Drinker, but he was much better when I left. Eliza is sorely worried lest she have officers quartered on her; she thinks it would be so bad for the children, let alone the trouble to her. That reminds me, Edward Penington, thy house at Race and Crown has been taken over by Colonel Sir Henry Johnson. And which of you is Caleb Middleton, junior? I didn't meet any of thy family, but I was told that a major has taken a room in thy house and that thy father has gone to bed."

She nodded when she identified Caleb and gave him a motherly little smile.

"The soldiers are all over the place," she went on. "Scotch Highlanders in Chestnut Street near dear Anthony Benezet's making dreadful noises with their bagpipes! They're all, Scotch and English and Hessian, well dressed and well shod and well fed. They say food will be scarce in Philadelphia this winter, but mark my words the British will have all they need."

More questions arose as each in turn inquired about his own family. Only Thomas Pike, his small eyes hard and his mouth pressed into a bitter line, had nothing to say.

"What about Mrs. Pike at Mrs. Duncannoti s boardinghouse?" said Caleb hardily.

Mrs. Joliffe shook her head. "I don't know. I haven't heard. But all the lodginghouses and inns are filled with officers or men.

"Are you fairly comfortable here?" said Elizabeth Joliffe when at length, after four hours, she gathered up her bag and cloak. "I can let you have chickens now and then, if P. Busch can't get them for you, and if you can ever get permission to move into private houses I could lodge four easily, and you would not be crowded all into one room either."

She beamed on them, benevolent, cordial, her good will fairly bursting the seams of her dress.

"Yes, Edmund, I'm coming!" she called, as her son, a wellgrown boy of fourteen or fifteen, peered somewhat disconsolately in at the window, and off she bustled, her stiff green silk skirts swishing pleasantly.

After that scarcely a day passed without visitors. The local Friends and Friends from Fairfax Meeting across the Blue Ridge in Loudon County came to bring presents of food and to discuss the situation of the country and of Quakers in the present crisis. Virginia officials called to appraise these unusual prisoners who had been inflicted upon the town.

Caleb was usually away with Dr. Smith when they came, but at the end of the day he would hear that Mr. John Harvie, the member of Congress who had his home in Winchester, had been at the inn and had expressed sympathy; that Colonel John Augustus Washington, brother of the General, had stopped to see them and had been most friendly in his conversation; and that Colonel Francis Peyton had offered to take letters for their families as far as Lancaster.

The long-awaited decisions from York and Williamsburg came at length, brought by Isaac Zane, junior. The Board of War directed that the mode of their treatment was to be regulated by their behavior and that they were to be supplied with every necessity—at their own expense. The Governor of Virginia recommended them to the care of the Lieutenant of Frederick County "until orders may be given hereafter for their removal." Inconclusive and unsatisfactory as these decrees were, they relieved the immediate fear of being transported to Staunton and resulted in the relaxation of some of the restrictions that had irked them. The guards disappeared and the prisoners were permitted to walk or ride freely in the daytime within a radius of six miles around the town.

Toward the end of the month the news came that General Burgoyne and all his army had been captured in a battle at Saratoga, and that nearly six thousand British prisoners had been sent to Connecticut. Winchester exploded with joy. Inhabitants marched up and down the streets singing, to the accompaniment of fife and drum, and a *feu-de-joie* was fired by the cannon in the public square. At night almost every window was illuminated, and a huge bonfire in the empty lot across from the Golden Buck blazed, roaring and crackling to the sky, dimming the frosty stars. No hostility was offered to the exiles, who stayed quietly within doors during the celebrations, but a local Friend had the windows which he declined to illumine smashed by patriotic stones.

The first Sunday in November Caleb rode to Meeting at Hopewell. On that clear autumn morning the Blue Ridge stood out sharp against the sky and all the gaps showed like nicks in a saw: Chester Gap and Manassas Gap, Williams' Gap, Key's Gap, Harpers Ferry Gap. To the west was Pumpkin Ridge and Apple Pie Ridge behind it; still farther west, visible now that the leaves were off the trees, the line of the Alleghenies. Hopewell Meetinghouse crouched on rising ground above a spring; built of limestone with a roof of white pine shingles, it was comely in its simplicity. It was more than forty years old now and outgrown; the members were talking about building an addition to it. Even the new stable built six years ago was too small now to shelter all the horses that brought Friends to Meeting from farms round about.

The benches inside were filled, mostly with young married people and bright-eyed, restless children, peeping at each other from behind their fingers or over the backs of benches, occasionally ruffling the silence with an audible yawn or a muffled giggle. Caleb looked for a slim, straight figure with red-gold curls, but she was not to be seen.

Elizabeth Joliffe, when he asked her after Meeting, replied vaguely that the Parry farm was near the Shenandoah and thought that the family went to Meeting, if at all, over the Blue Ridge to Crooked Run. She invited Caleb to come home to dinner and meet her young people.

The Joliffe house was a handsome stone house half a mile or so from the Meeting on the Valley Road. There were five children, ranging from Edmund to nine-year-old Elizabeth. They crowded around Caleb, who searched his mind for anecdotes about Patty and Edward and Tacy.

Caleb was happy in the atmosphere here, finding Mrs. Joliffe comfortable and jolly, like her name, and the spaciousness and dignity of the house reminiscent of his own home. They drank tea out of china cups, and stray leaves were carefully skimmed out with a silver mote-spoon with holes in the bowl. By the pride with which twelve-year-old Lydia pointed out the treasure to him Caleb realized that such appointments were rare in this new country far from the eastern cities.

He wished that Mrs. Joliffe's offer might be accepted and that four of the exiles might come to stay with her. It would not only be pleasanter and less crowded than the inn but less expensive as well. Mrs. Joliffe offered them board at a rate that was actually nominal, a fraction of what Philip Busch charged them.

Caleb was beginning to worry about money. His supply of gold was dwindling alarmingly. Prices in Winchester were high and the rate of exchange low. He had made cautious inquiries as to where he could get the most Continental bills for his half-joes and learned that the rate was nearly twice as good in York and Lancaster. He thought of his sister Sue in Lancaster and he resolved to send some money to her to change as soon as he could find a dependable messenger, but in the meantime he was looking for ways of reducing his expenses.

When he broached to his cousin Edward and John Hunt the possibility of moving to Mrs. Joliffe's, they raised the question in one of the regular house meetings of the group. It seemed that others also found the inn too expensive for them. Elijah Brown and Thomas Affleck were anxious to move into the house of Isaac and Sarah Brown, Friends who lived as far south of Winchester as Hopewell was north. The Pembertons and the Fishers, however, thought it would be unwise to separate the group, and so after a day or two of ferment, they all settled down again to the routine as it had established itself.

It was not an uncomfortable routine: a quiet, detached life spent in writing letters, reading, composing the latest Essay, correcting and copying the official diary of the group, taking long walks and visiting Friends in the neighborhood. On Sundays they held meetings for worship morning and afternoon in the parlor. So many of the townspeople, Friends and others, attended—sometimes as many as a hundred in a single meeting—that the Presbyterian minister came to John Pemberton and offered the use of his church for the afternoon Meeting. The animosity which had alarmed them when they first came to Winchester had melted away, and they enjoyed a mild sort of vogue.

John Hunt shook his head. "When everybody speaks well of Friends," he observed, "then it is time to feel uneasy. It is my settled opinion that we are in a more wholesome state, within if not without, when people are berating us."

XXII

WHEN THE BANK AT Isaac Zane's furnace caved in and two men were injured, Dr. Smith was summoned in haste and Caleb went with him. Caleb had been eager to see the Marlboro Ironworks, but as they lay two or three miles outside the six-mile limit this was his first opportunity.

One of the men had died before they got there; the other was in great pain from crushed ribs and what seemed to be a broken pelvis. He screamed if he was moved, and all that Smith could do for him was to give him laudanum to dull his agony for a time.

"I'll sit by him for a while and watch the effect of this stuff," said Dr. Smith.

Caleb was glad to escape from the sight of helpless pain and to walk about with Isaac Zane, inspecting the furnace and the other buildings of the settlement. The Marlboro Furnace was smaller than the Phoebe Ann, but it employed some new methods and its products were acquiring a reputation for toughness.

"We can cast our pots and other utensils thinner than most," explained Zane, leading the way into the casting shed, "and yet they are so tough that they can safely be thrown in and out of the wagons in which they are transported."

The brittleness of cast iron was one of the perennial problems of its manufacture. Caleb looked about him with interest at the forms for the sow and pigs, the molds for hollow ware, and noted the bulletin board on which were chalked the specifications for the latest charge and a direction about a new order. The shape of the now cold crucible swelled out and thinned again to the stack that rose above them to the smoke-stained beams high and dim overhead.

When they went outside again they saw men already at work digging away the debris of the fallen bank. When Zane appeared they worked a little harder, thrusting their shovels smartly into the mass of earth and stones, turning the laden wheelbarrows with quick mastery. The chief founder came to follow Zane, to be at his elbow in case he should want to ask a question or order something to be fetched. The ironmaster was a baron on his plantation, and when he appeared an air of excitement pervaded the place. Caleb recognized the familiar stir and felt nostalgic for the Phoebe Ann. He asked a question about the rate of production.

"We make four tons of pig iron and two tons of castings a week when we're in blast. Not much compared to the Pennsylvania furnaces, but the quality is good. I was getting ready to build another furnace down the creek a bit when the bank fell in."

For a little while they stood looking at the mess and confusion of the cave-in and the men, patient and busy as ants, chipping away the pile. Zane outlined his plan for rebuilding and reinforcing the bank and Caleb nodded.

They went on to the other buildings. Cedar Creek cut a deep gash in the hills, providing power for the bellows of the furnace and the big mill wheel. From a quarry near by stone was cut for all the buildings that clustered along the creek and climbed the steep slopes on both sides: the store, the charcoal house, the distillery, where a fiery liquor was made from Indian corn, the warehouse, and above it, overlooking all, the stone mansion house. The wagon sheds were primitive. Caleb saw three wagons standing out in the open, loaded with the long shapes of cannon under canvas covers and with cannon balls like black dumplings.

"Now let us go up to the house. I want to show thee what I am doing there."

Isaac went ahead, up the stone steps cut into the hillside. He was rather below average height, stockily built, his head, with its broad forehead and deep-set restless eyes, a little large for his body. The energy and vitality which fathered so many schemes and projects spoke in every line of his body and in the quick movements of his hands as he flung them out this way and that to point out some fresh beginning.

Everything was in process of creation, nothing finished. Piles of stones here indicated that a terrace or a wall would be built where now there was a lumpy expanse of red clay strewn with rocks and weeds, or a stack of lumber there foreshadowed a porch where now were only crude steps without even a handrail.

The Big House loomed up on a shelf in the hillside, well built but stark, with bare earth around it. Caleb thought it too near the warehouse, the roof of which obstructed the view of valley and creek.

"There will be a driveway there, so that the coach can go right to the side door," said Isaac, waving his arm. "The front entrance is here. I shall have it leveled and terraced, with rose beds edged with box on both sides of the path."

When they went inside Caleb found a solid masculine comfort. Beyond the sparsely furnished parlor was a small room with a fire on the hearth, broad-based, comfortable chairs, woolen hangings at the windows, even a red-patterned rug on the wide-planked floor. The mantel was a pleasant jumble of pipes and tobacco and spills, small ornaments and spare nails, an inkwell, a brass candlestick and snuffer. Books overflowed the shelves along the wall into piles in the comers of the room.

"Sit down," said Isaac cordially, pulling a chair forward, giving the smoldering logs on the hearth a kick. "It's a nasty, raw day, not so cold really, but the damp is penetrating."

His housekeeper, a middle-aged mulatto woman, brought a tray with two glasses, a decanter of wine, and a plate of biscuits.

"We'll need another glass. Dr. Smith will be here presently. Thee can see what I've got here. Plenty of water power—Cedar Creek is never dry, or even very low—twenty-five thousand acres of land and I'm buying more all the time. Charcoal's the problem, of course—not the wood, for I've good stands of hickory that have never been touched, but the burners. I've twenty-one slaves. I've put it in my will that they're to be gradually emancipated after my death, but as long as I live I can count on them."

He spoke apparently without embarrassment, though slaveowning was a cause for disownment in Philadelphia Yearly Meeting, and Caleb had so far met no Friends in or about Winchester who held Negroes in bondage.

"Thee's casting cannon, I see," said Caleb, wondering if the denial of one of Friends' testimonies led to an insensitiveness to all of them. "Could thee have refused the canon and balls and still have satisfied the government with pig iron and salt pans?"

"Thee means, from conscientious scruples against making munitions of war? I don't know. Possibly. I didn't try. I've no objection to making cannon. I'm a Quaker for the times, Caleb. I feel there are worse things than war, and when we win our independence and freedom, then we can look forward to living in peace with all men according to our Quaker principles." He lit his pipe and drew on it slowly. "I was a member of the convention at Williamsburg that passed the Virginia Resolutions a year ago last spring. There wouldn't have been any Declaration of Independence without that convention. I saw Patrick Henry then and had a drink with him in the *Raleigh Tavern*, and I said to him, 'Patrick, I said—' "

Isaac knew all the famous men of the day. One after another they drifted casually through the slow puffs of his pipe. Caleb listened, impressed in spite of himself.

"Friends ought not to be too other-worldly," Isaac concluded. "It was a great mistake, for instance, all of the Quakers resigning from the Pennsylvania Assembly in fifty-six because they weren't willing to go to war against the Indians. What happened? The war went on just the same and Friends lost all control of the government. They might have compromised and stayed in, and prevented or at least mitigated some of the mistakes that have been made since then. If Israel Pemberton hadn't led his flock out of government then, he mightn't be a prisoner in Winchester today."

"John Hunt says," remarked Caleb, "that while Friends may claim a divine source for their spiritual insights, their political judgments are not necessarily so inspired. But of course," he added, "William Penn thought that government and religion go together."

"I've got Penn's collected works over there on the shelf—a handsome edition I imported from London—" Isaac changed the subject abruptly. "I'm going to have a fine library here. I'm negotiating with Mary Byrd—Mary Willing that was—for William Byrd's library. I've made her an offer of fifteen hundred pounds for it, and I think likely she'll take two thousand. If I can get it for that, I will. She's having quite a time settling William's estate. It's an excellent library. The catalogue's a small folio bound in red morocco—over a hundred pages—very nice piece of work. I'm going to build a wing on to this house for it. Paneled walls. I can get a really skilled woodworker from the Hessian prisoners. Thee knows, Caleb, I see this place as another Westover, a sort of Valley Westover, a place of good books, good food, good wines, and good company—the only place of its kind west of the Blue Ridge."

Caleb took advantage of a pause in the flow to put in a word for Tom Affleck, who was desperately anxious to earn a little money.

"If thee needs some fine furniture," he suggested, "why not have Tom Affleck make it for thee while he's here? He's one of the best cabinetmakers in Philadelphia, and he's been spending his time making three-legged stools and cake paddles for Philip Busch."

"I hadn't thought of that. I've some fine walnut put away drying for three-four years now. Thee thinks he's really skillful?"

"Governor Penn thought him good enough to bring him out from Aberdeen, and he's made things for other people too. Ask the Pembertons. Classical style mostly, I believe."

"I'll talk to him. I need a highboy right now to keep linens and silver in. And other things too, of course. Chairs, a small table—"

Riding back to Winchester in the late afternoon Caleb was silent, thinking of the Marlboro Furnace, of ironmaster Zane and all his interests. He knew now that it was Isaac Zane, junior, who had intervened with the Congress to keep the exiles in Winchester instead of sending them on to Staunton, who had persuaded Philip Busch to accommodate them, who had put in a word for them in Williamsburg, and would again. He saw in Isaac what he himself might have been on the way to becoming, if things had been different. And the Phoebe

Ann was a much better furnace than the unfinished Marlboro. He wished that he had tried to find out what method they used here to achieve that toughness.

That night, sitting on the edge of the bed they shared, he told John Hunt about his day.

"A Quaker for the times?" said John dryly. "I could wish he would direct his mind more toward eternity."

"The same applies to me, I suppose?"

"Thou'rt young, Caleb; younger even than thy years. I am confident thou wilt find thy true way—when once thou really sets out to look for it."

XXIII

THE THIRD MONTH OF their imprisonment and banishment ground to its close and the fourth began, and still the exiles were no nearer to a hearing. On the contrary it seemed that the Congress and the Council, having got them out of the state, were now able to forget their existence.

In the middle of November Caleb, with Edward Penington, Thomas Wharton, and John Hunt, had moved to Elizabeth Joliffe's. At the same time Tom Affleck, Elijah Brown and two others got permission to go to the Browns' house, seven or eight miles south of the town. The extortionate charges at the inn, with the growing surliness of the landlord himself, made the move necessary. To hold the group together they decided to meet every Wednesday at the inn for a meeting for worship in the morning and, after dinner together, a meeting for business in the afternoon.

Four of them were at work on a new Essay to be called "Observations on the Charges Made Against Us in the Several Resolves of Congress" and on two succeeding Wednesdays the draft was read and discussed and corrected with what Caleb impatiently considered picayune changes in the wording. Not quite daring to express himself in the meeting, he grumbled on the way back to Hopewell, and his cousin Edward answered:

"It is essential, Caleb, that those who cannot agree with the majority make their position clear by every means open to them. People who put their faith in change by negotiation rather than violence must be prepared to spend time on discussion and persuasion. And no amount of time spent on finding and stating truth is too much."

Caleb's rides with Drewet Smith came to an end with the return of the Winchester physician, Dr. Macky, from the army and his resumption of his practice. Limited again to the six-mile radius Caleb missed the longer rides and his interest in the patients; he turned to the affairs of Hopewell Meeting.

Hopewell Friends were in the grip of a concern about the Indians who had originally owned the land upon which they lived. When they first settled there they had bought their land from the government of Virginia and no payment had been made to the Shawnees, who had moved westward out of the path of the white men. As early as 1738 an English Friend, Thomas Chalkley, had raised the question of whether they had unjustly dispossessed the Indians, and at intervals since then committees had been appointed to consider the matter, but nothing had been done. Now the Pembertons had come among them and the concern had been revived. The three brothers, founders of the Friendly Association for Helping the Indians, into which at the time of the Indian wars Quakers had poured the money they refused to pay in taxes for war, felt a proprietary interest in the Indians. It took only a few pointed questions from them to bring the whole matter to the boiling point. The winter lull had come to the farms and the local Friends had some leisure; the exiles from Philadelphia, bereft of their customary public activities, moved in with the eagerness of the starved. Meetings were held, a committee appointed, a subscription list circulated. Israel himself headed the list with thirty pounds. Caleb modestly pledged three pounds when he should get his money from Lancaster. A cousin of his sister's husband had come through Winchester and Caleb had entrusted him with letters and gold; he was daily expecting a supply of Continental money.

After several hundred pounds had been collected the question arose as to how the descendants of the original Indians were to be found and reimbursed. Though there had been rumors of scalping parties in the country to the west—a woman killed as she went to the well, a child kidnapped while picking berries on a hillside—no Indians had been seen in the Valley near Winchester.

"If it is impossible to find the direct descendants of the tribes whose land we hold," proposed a Friend, "could we not properly assign the money to the Meeting for Sufferings in Philadelphia to be used for the benefit of any Indians who are in need?"

It was late in the afternoon, and shadows were settling into the room, blanketing bodies and etching hollows under cheekbones and eyes, underscoring the lines of fatigue and patience written into the faces of men and women whose only recreation was to ride for several miles to a cold little Meetinghouse and wrestle with problems of conscience. A murmur of assent passed through the room. "I hope that will be done." "I unite with that."

Another Friend stood up and Caleb groaned inwardly. He was cold and hungry and he wanted the meeting to end.

"I don't wish to prolong this meeting unduly," said the Friend, "but before we send these funds to Philadelphia, I think we should make every effort to find the descendants ourselves. Perhaps Tenskatawa could tell us something of the Shawnees who lived hereabouts forty or fifty years ago."

At the mention of Tenskatawa Caleb sat up.

"He's gone, I believe," said another. "But he will probably return in the spring. I agree that he should be consulted when the way opens."

Under cover of the discussion that followed Caleb whispered to the man next to him, "Who it Tenskatawa?"

"He's a Shawnee, a sort of chief in a small way. Found the little Parry girl years ago when she toddled off into the woods and brought her home. He took a great fancy to her, and he still comes to see her twice a year, they say, spring and fall. His tribe has gone the other side of the Alleghenies now."

"Was that Loveday Parry-the baby, I mean?"

"Yes, it was. Thee know her?"

"I've met her. Where is the Parry farm?"

"Oh, it's fifteen-twenty miles away. Near Williams' Gap."

"Can thee tell me how to get there?"

The clerk was looking at them somewhat sternly. "Later," whispered Caleb, realizing that the meeting was settling into its closing few minutes of silence. He folded his arms across his chest to contain the pounding of his heart, and bent his gaze upon his boots as one deep in spiritual meditation.

As soon as the silence was broken and Friends turned to their neighbors for farewells and cheerfully secular talk, Caleb got specific directions for reaching the Parry farm. It was far beyond the present limit, but there might be a change in the rules or he might get special permission. Anything could happen, and in the meantime he had taken a step toward finding the girl again.

Jubilant, he came out of the Meetinghouse into the frosty dusk to find all of the sky to the north lit with a swaying curtain of color. He caught his breath. Unearthly, cold, crimson, the light shimmered and pulsed, fading, changing, swept by a wind that never blew, patting to show the stars behind it. Slowly the crimson was succeeded by the green of clear water, and a mist-white followed the green.

Caleb and John Hunt, watching in silence, turned at length toward the Joliffe house, where the light in the windows was warm and yellow.

"I have never seen the aurora more beautiful," said John. "I wonder if they are seeing it in Philadelphia now."

Caleb wondered if a girl had left the fireside in a farmhouse twenty miles away and run out into the yard to look.

At Elizabeth Joliffe's, where a fire blazed on the hearth and the children were helping to carry bowls of steaming hominy and platters of ham and eggs to the table, they found the group excited and troubled. Edward Penington had returned from Winchester with the news that Drewet Smith had not been seen for three days.

"He left on Sixth Day saying that he was going to Lewis Neale's to get some wild ducks. They expected him back at suppertime, and when he didn't come they decided he must have spent the night there. Yesterday afternoon Thomas Pike rode over to Neale's to inquire, and they said he had not been there at all. It is feared that he has eloped."

"What about his things? Did he take anything with him?"

"Evidently he took a saddlebag with necessities for the journey and his medical kit. I think it is plain that he is not intending to return."

There was a silence in the room as each thought how this might affect the group.

"Has he ever said anything to thee, Caleb, about decamping?"

"Only once that he thought the County Lieutenant didn't care whether we stayed or not."

"We have never given an actual parole, of course," said Thomas Wharton, "but it has been well understood among us that we are bound not to go beyond six miles. I think this will be regarded—and justly by our keepers as a reflection upon the honor of us all."

"Friends were discussing that aspect of it when I left," said Edward. "They notified Joseph Holmes, since Lieutenant Smith has gone to Williamsburg, and he came to dine with them today. He said he must report it to Congress but agreed to wait until tomorrow. It is most unfortunate. It seems that there has again been some murmuring about us, anyhow among the local patriots. Some of the farmers prefer to barter rather than accept money whose value is changing so rapidly. It is convenient to blame us for it"

"I wish him safe home to Philadelphia," said John Hunt with a sigh. "He has been of some service to the poor prisoners here. I have no doubt we shall be strengthened to meet whatever sufferings may come upon us. Meanwhile I think we should keep as much as possible from repeating—or even hearing—rumors, for they will be frequent and they tend to weaken us."

The color had faded out of the sky when Caleb went to bed. Late the next day snow began to fall, hissing at first against the windows and then dropping into a velvet silence that covered house and yard, barn and stable and fence and the curve of the hill beyond. When at length it ceased to fall, there was a white blanket fifteen inches deep over all the visible world. The road had disappeared, and the air was incredibly pure and light.

XXIV

BEFORE THE SNOW HAD melted away from the hollows and the shady places under the hemlocks, two visitors came from Philadelphia. Friends of the Pembertons, they had ridden by way of Baltimore, and they brought with them in their saddlebags something for almost everybody: a roll of Continental bills for Henry Drinker wrapped up in a pair of worsted stockings, woolen underwear for Israel Pemberton, reeds for John Pemberton's steel pipe, the welcome report of a little daughter to Thomas Fisher, born three weeks earlier, letters for others.

They brought news of the burning of Fairhill by the British and of the increasing arrogance of the occupation forces, the high prices in the city, the cockfights and the balls, the suffering among the poor, the sickening way that lighter elements in the population rushed to curry favor with the officers.

Caleb had two letters from home. He read Sarah Middleton's first.

My Dear Caleb,

The two letters we have received from you have been most welcome, though I doubt not you have written others that have not reached us. A whole packet of letters from Winchester was delayed ten days in Wilmington waiting for someone to bring them on to Philadelphia. It is a great relief to know you are well and that you have been able to get some exercise and change of scene.

I can report all well here, except your father of course has his ups and downs. Your letters are a great help to him for he is always troubled about you.

We have had the stove put up in the back parlor and are now

very comfortable. Food is scarce and excessively expensive, though the report that we are eating rats at five shillings apiece is not true. Candles are two and six each, so that no one reads very much of nights. Brown sugar six shillings a pound and butter twelve shillings. I tell you the worst to make it more interesting.

The British officers are holding balls every Saturday night in the City Tavern. Patty has been invited and she is wild to go, but your father and I maintain that she is too young. She is now become very grown-up in her manners. Edward with some other boys in his school got into a fight with some British drummer boys and came home with a black eye. Your Tacy is going to a dame school on Society Hill and is happy as a lark, though she still misses you and speaks of you often.

I saw Caroline Rutter yesterday and she had on the highest and most ridiculous headdress I have yet seen. She is smit, I think, with the major who stays at our house. He sleeps in thy room and uses the front parlor to entertain his guests. He has three servants and a Hessian orderly. They cook for him in our kitchen. Our stable is full of his livestock—three horses, three cows, two sheep, two turkeys and several fowls.

I hope whoever reads this along the way will not think I have written anything seditious. Our thoughts and our prayers are with you. All send love. I am

Your most affectionate,
Sarah Middleton

The other letter, written in the same hand, had been dictated by Tacy.

Dear Brother Caleb,

I am very hearty and go to school every day if it don't rain. I play with Molly Pemberton.

I was so frightened last Friday morning with the roaring of cannon. Mother and Edward and Patty and I went up on the roof to see where it was. We counted nine ships all afire by Gloucester Point.

Fairhill House was burnt down today and a great many other houses up that road.

I miss thee very much. Amos sends his love and so does Hettie.

                              Thy loving little sister,
                              Tacy

Nine ships afire! That meant that the blockade of Philadelphia that had been maintained by the Delaware forts, the chevaux-de-frise and American ships, was now being broken. The British would soon have the river as well as the city.

XXV

CALEB SKIPPED THE MEETING for worship at the inn on Wednesday morning the seventeenth of December, and was almost late for dinner besides. He had stopped at Goldsmith Chandlee's shop to order a little gold pin in the shape of a love knot. Some day he would see Loveday again and he wanted to have a gift all ready for her. He was in funds again, for forty-eight pounds Continental had come to him from his sister in Lancaster.

Goldsmith Chandlee was a Quaker and not much interested in making love knots. He was famous for his clocks and watches and surveyor's quadrants. He looked at the design that Caleb drew and pulled his mouth down disapprovingly at the corners; he had no gold for such frivolities, he said. But when Caleb gave him his last coins to melt down, he agreed, and Caleb went off to the Golden Buck in high fettle.

He found the exiles already at dinner, leaving a place empty beside Mr. Pike. Three and a half months of close association with the dancing master had brought Caleb's dislike of the man to such a pitch that he could barely give him a curt greeting. Pike, apparently unaware of his feelings, welcomed Caleb with a specious air of assuming that they two, being men of the world, had a special understanding between them.

"I've had very good news of the Congress," he said in a confidential undertone. "It happened some time ago, I believe, but I have just learned of it—we are so out of things here. Mr. Hancock has resigned from the presidency and Mr. Henry Laurens of South Carolina has been elected to the office in his place."

"Indeed," said Caleb indifferently. "I understand most of the delegates have gone home anyhow."

"Mr. Laurens is a very high-minded gentleman. I knew him well in Charleston. Indeed, I might even claim to have some influence with him. I am confident that even if he should not find it possible to release the whole group, he will see to it that I am discharged—since I am not a Quaker."

"Are you in communication with him?"

"Not at present. But a fresh Memorial to Congress has been prepared and we are all to sign it. I've no doubt that he will take note of my name there."

When dinner was over and the table cleared, the group considered the final draft of the new Memorial. Caleb moved his chair beside Tom Affleck's. Tom was now staying at a house only a short distance from the Marlboro Furnace, of which Caleb wanted the latest news.

"Isaac Zane has gone to Williamsburg," Affleck reported. "I am working on a table for him. He's got a nice piece of Pennsylvania marble he wants set into the top."

They fell silent as Miers Fisher rose to read the paper in his hand. Before he could clear his throat there was a sharp rap at the door. Elijah Brown, who was nearest, went to open it and they heard a brief murmur of voices outside. Elijah fumed, looking rather white, and said:

"Major Holmes is here. He has fresh instructions to communicate concerning us." He stood aside, holding the door wide, and Major Joseph Holmes walked in.

Holmes was a merchant of Stevens City, a few miles south of Winchester, an ordinary, ambitious, energetic man with no distinguishing features, who acquired through the war emergency the title of major and the post of commissary of prisoners for Frederick County. In the absence of Lieutenant Smith he was responsible for the Philadelphia prisoners. Usually affable, he wore now an expression of great sternness and portentousness. He bowed abstractedly in response to the greetings of the group and ignored the chair offered him.

"Gentlemen," he began, "I regret very much the necessity which brings me here today. I have received a new order from the Board of War. With your permission I will read it to you." He cleared his throat. " 'The Board of War having had sundry intercepted letters laid

before them from several of the Quakers, prisoners stationed at Winchester, in the State of Virginia, by which it appears that they have
kept up a correspondence with several others of that Society, without
previously showing their letters to the American Commissary of Prisoners, or to any other proper officer at that place. . . .' " He paused for
breath. His voice was always a little squeaky and thin.

The exiles sat tense, listening with growing indignation. On their
arrival in Winchester they had offered their letters to Lieutenant
Smith to inspect, but he had courteously declined, saying that he was
confident that they would transmit no news of interest to the enemy.

Major Holmes continued: " 'In the course of which correspondence it also appears that a certain Caleb Middleton, junior, one of the
said prisoners—' "

Caleb jumped as if he had been pricked with a pin, and the others
turned to look at him in alarm and surprise.

" '—is carrying on with sundry persons in the town of Lancaster a
traffic highly injurious to the credit of the Continental currency, by
exchanging gold at a most extravagant premium for paper money.' "

Caleb felt himself reddening to the roots of his hair. He had certainly sent his gold to Lancaster, but that it would have the slightest
effect on the credit of the Continental currency or that anyone could
possibly object to his getting the best value he could for it, had not
once occurred to him.

" 'And whereas it is represented to this Board, that since the presence of the above-mentioned prisoners at Winchester, the confidence
of the inhabitants in that quarter in the currency of these States has
been greatly diminished, especially among the persons of the same
Society with themselves—' "

But that was nonsense. Commodities were scarce, prices were high,
money bought less. The farmers preferred barter. How could that be
the fault of the exiles? The voice went on, pressing to the climax:

" 'Ordered, that Caleb Middleton, junior, be forthwith removed
under guard to Staunton, in the County of Augusta, there to be closely
confined to jail, and debarred the use of pen, ink and paper.' "

Caleb started to his feet. A hand pulled him down. Major Holmes
went on reading.

" 'That the remainder of the prisoners sent from the State of Pennsylvania be removed under the same guard to Staunton and delivered to the County Lieutenant of Augusta, who is hereby directed to require of them a parole or affirmation that they will not directly or indirectly do or say anything tending to the prejudice of these States, agreeably to the form herewith transmitted; and in case of refusal, the said County Lieutenant is hereby requested to confine the said persons in some secure building under proper guards and subject to the same restrictions with Caleb Middleton, junior, before mentioned.' "

They sat stunned, slow to grasp the fact that the blow that they had so long warded off had now fallen.

The letter continued to the bitter end. " 'That copies of these orders, together with the intercepted letters from Caleb Middleton, junior, be transmitted to Mr. Joseph Holmes and the County Lieutenant of Augusta; who are desired to carry the above measures into immediate execution.' Mr. Middleton, I have copies here of two letters from you. Will you identify them?"

Caleb looked them over. They were written in a vile hand, with misspellings, but there was no doubt that they were copies of his letters, one to his sister asking her to get her brother-in-law to change the money for him, one to Richard Mercer, thanking him for the service done.

"Yes, I wrote such letters," said Caleb. "My father gave me gold before I left home. I wanted it changed so as to pay my expenses here. I heard the rate was better in Lancaster and so I asked my sister to attend to it for me. I had no thought of doing anything illegal or wrong in any way. My money was running out pretty fast and I wanted to get as much as I could."

"I have also," said Mr. Holmes, "a deposition taken at York, which I am required to read to you. To cut short the legal verbiage, the deponent says: 'That being last week at Winchester, he heard several of the inhabitants complain heavily that since the Tories of the Quaker Society from Philadelphia had been enlarged and permitted to reside at the Quaker houses in the vicinity of the town, the inhabitants of the Society, who are numerous in that put of the country, have very generally refused to take Continental money."

Caleb boiled with sudden hot fury. The room was suffocating. If he didn't get out of there, he thought desperately, he would knock Holmes down, or drive his fist into that silly, solemn, self-important face. The calm of the other exiles, sitting there like rabbits, twitching their noses, added to his rage. Clawing at his neckcloth to loosen it, he made for the door and fresh air.

But when he reached the big front door and flung it open, he found a man standing there, who barred his way with a thrust of his arm. Caleb stared at him, incredulous. "My God," he roared, "it's you again!"

The guard, one of those whom they had come to know well during the first part of October, raised his musket to his shoulder. "Yes, it's me again," he said, and jerked his head backward to indicate that Caleb was to return to the parlor.

John Hunt appeared in the doorway behind him. "Caleb, art thou all right?"

"Stop where you are," ordered the guard. "Caleb's all right," he added in a mocking falsetto, "and he's coming right in."

John Hunt's hand, affectionate and firm, on his arm brought Caleb to his senses. Together they returned to the parlor.

"I cannot understand," Miers Fisher was saying, "why the Board of War should be concerned with our case. We were not found in arms nor charged with any measures tending to war. If we are to be removed from here, it should be done on the order of the Governor of Virginia or of the Council of Pennsylvania."

"The Board of War is the instrument of Congress," said Major Holmes in a tired voice.

Caleb, who thought that Miers tended to rely too much on narrow legal interpretations, broke in vehemently:

"If I have done something wrong and am sentenced to go to Staunton—though I consider it most unjust and unwarranted—but if that is the sentence, then send me alone under guard. It is both unjust and cruel to send the whole body of prisoners. The roads are almost impassable at best-and this is winter. We had fifteen inches of snow last week! There are no proper inns along the way. Have you no compassion, Mr. Holmes?"

"I told you I regretted this business very much, but I am acting upon orders of the Congress. I am already under censure for having permitted some of you to lodge with friends in the country."

"Thou hast done nothing seriously amiss, Caleb," said Edward Penington. "This is merely an excuse for striking at all of us. We have made too many friends in Winchester."

"I have no choice in the matter," continued Holmes, "but to act immediately. I have ordered four wagons and they will be here tomorrow. You will accordingly gather your possessions together at once."

There was an outburst of protest. "Friend Holmes, I ask thee to reflect—" "Such precipitancy is unreasonable—"

Israel Pemberton's voice, measured, authoritative, confident of being heard, dominated the rest. "When thou came in, Joseph Holmes, we were at that very moment concluding a Memorial to Congress which we hoped that one of our own members might be permitted to carry to York. Surely our departure for Staunton can appropriately be delayed until Congress has seen and considered this Memorial."

"Allow one of you to go to York with a paper of arguments? You must know, sir, even if I could have agreed to such a thing last week, it would be impossible now!"

"Well, then," suggested Samuel Pleasants, "allow us to prepare an answer to the present charges and take it thyself to Congress."

"It's out of the question."

There was no possibility of persuading Holmes to disregard the orders; delay was the most they could hope for, and they pressed the point determinedly, watching the Major's face, quick to follow up any argument which brought into the stubborn countenance even the most fleeting look of wavering. It was Thomas Fisher who in the end found an acceptable formula.

"Several of the most respected gentlemen of Winchester have shown interest in our case. If one of them should be willing to go to the Congress with our Memorial as our representative, wouldst thou not be willing to await their further determination concerning us?"

There was no doubt in anybody's mind as to whom he was referring to. Alexander White, a young lawyer and son-in-law of James Wood, the founder of the town, had found in some of the exiles interesting and stimulating companionship. There had been an exchange of courtesies; he had dined with them at the inn, and Miers and Thomas Fisher, Samuel Pleasants, and Henry Drinker had more than once dined at White's house; he had at various times openly expressed his opinion that they had been unjustly treated. He might be induced to go to the Congress on behalf of the exiles.

"I'll give you till tomorrow afternoon," said Joseph Holmes slowly. "If you can get some respectable citizen to represent you to the Congress, I will delay your departure—at least until I have further orders. The guards will remain for the present. Those who lodge in the country may go back for tonight, but they must return here tomorrow morning." He stood up. "Your servant, gentlemen," he said in conventional leave-taking, with no thought of irony.

As soon as he had gone, the exiles went to work. A note was written and despatched to Alexander White by James Pemberton's man, Richard. The older men, with the Fishers and Samuel Pleasants, withdrew into the Pembertons' big room upstairs for further consultation.

Though they all made a point of indicating kindly to Caleb by word or gesture that they did not hold him responsible for this new threat of disaster, he felt oppressed by their very forbearance, and burdened with guilt. The thought of riding back to Hopewell and pouring it all out to Elizabeth Joliffe brought some relief.

He was taking his cloak from the row of pegs in the hall when Thomas Pike came up to him.

"The Quaker gentlemen," he said disagreeably, "have been at pains to tell you they don't blame you for this new outrage. You needn't think that includes me. I have my own opinion of people who have money and don't care what harm they do if they can only get more money."

Caleb glared at him. "Never mind," he said sarcastically, "you can get your friend Laurens to let you off."

XXVI

SARAH MIDDLETON SIGHED. A little of her pent-up exasperation escaped with that breath, that faintly hissing sound as of steam, but she closed her lips quickly, pressing them firmly together. She put out a hand to impose quiet on Edward, who was scowling and squirming beside her at the breakfast table. Tacy on the other side leaned back in her chair and kicked her feet rhythmically against the legs. All three of them had stopped eating and were listening to the sounds that issued from the kitchen.

A quarrel was in progress between Hettie, the Middletons' cook, and the three servants of Major Cranborne, who now lived in the Middletons' house. The Camel, Sarah called him, because like the beast in the old story, he had first inserted his head into the tent, politely and deprecatingly, then his shoulders, then, politeness and deprecation abandoned because no longer necessary, his whole ungainly body. All he had wanted, at first, was a quiet place to sleep. He would get his meals at the tavern. He had looked at Caleb's room and found it spacious, commodious, and quiet. He would cause no trouble at all, he had assured them. The Middletons had even welcomed him, attracted by his gentlemanly manners and appearance, and by the idea that his presence in their house would save them from the necessity to billet someone more demanding, a Hessian general or a Scotch colonel. Soon he had taken the front parlor, to entertain his friends, and the study behind it, for his records and letters. His servants invaded the kitchen, first a Hessian orderly who kept his rooms and his clothes in order, then two colored men who cooked and served his meals. Since food was hard to get, the Major's servants convinced him that he should have his own supply of hens and chickens, and that there was plenty of room in the stable for a cow and horse as well. A third servant was added to take care of the livestock and he too was fed from the kitchen. Hettie and Sukie and Amos, all that remained of the Middletons' servants, resented the intrusion bitterly, and clashes like the present one, marked by the banging of pot lids, a scuffling of bodies, and voices raised in anger and taunting laughter, were becoming increasingly frequent.

Mrs. Middleton, who did her best to have the family breakfast finished and out of the way before the Major, who was a late sleeper, called for his, sighed in exasperation. "If you'd got up when I called you," she said sharply to Edward, "that wouldn't have happened. Drink your milk. You'll be late for school."

"It's sour," said Edward in a whining voice.

Sarah took a sip from his glass and had to acknowledge that it had indeed turned. The Camel had fresh milk from his cow, which ate Middleton hay in the Middleton stable, but their cow had gone dry and they had been unable to get another. They bought inferior and expensive milk from a man out Prune Street.

"Don't drink it," said Sarah, "and don't drink yours, Tacy. We'll make cottage cheese out of it. Eat your mush."

"I don't like mush."

"Don't say you don't like good food, when it is so hard to get. There are plenty of children in this city who would be overjoyed to have your nice, hot mush."

Edward took a large spoonful and sat with his cheek bulging, and did not swallow.

Sarah reminded herself that the children had been kept awake late last night while the Major and eight or ten friends, having dined well, entertained themselves by singing songs from the *Beggar's Opera* to the accompaniment of a particularly shrill flute played by the Camel himself. The children were tired this morning as well as late, and correspondingly cross and difficult.

The door from the kitchen burst open with such suddenness that it swung back against the wall, shivering. What seemed like a procession but was actually only two men with trays marched through. One of the unpleasant features of this invasion of the house was the fact that the dining room had become a passageway for the Camel's servants. From the trays came a delectable, tantalizing aroma, and both children rose in their chairs and craned their necks in indignant curiosity to see what the Major was going to have for breakfast. Sarah herself could not forbear a swift glance at the big pitcher of milk, the smaller one of cream, the pile of white bread slices that would be toasted at the parlor fire, the two fried eggs on one of her best china plates and the mound of yellow butter on another. In her nostrils was the fragrance of tea and of sizzling ham.

"Leave your mush, then," she said gently to Edward, "and eat some bread."

"Please pass the butter."

Butter was fifteen shillings a pound and hard to get at any price. Sarah measured off a small piece and Edward spread it over a thick slice of rye bread. Tacy slid down from her high chair and trotted toward the door.

"Come back, Tacy. You haven't finished your breakfast."

"I'm just going to see Major Cranborne. I haven't seen him this morning, and he's my *friend!*"

Edward uttered a howl. "She'll go in there and he'll give her buttered toast and jam and little pieces of ham *from his plate!* You aren't going to let her go?"

The little silver bell tinkled violently upstairs.

"Tacy, run up and tell Dada I'll have his breakfast there in just a minute. Make haste, dear. Don't stop to speak to Major Cranborne now. Edward, you must go or you will be late."

Rising from the table she looked down at the boy with a pang of tenderness. A dark lock of hair fell over his forehead and there were buttery crumbs on his lips. He was pale and much too thin; his brown eyes had grown too big for his face and they had an expression of strain that worried her. Patty had been sent to stay with the Chase cousins near Wilmington, to get her out of the way of the young British officers and the demoralizing effect they had on the girls. Perhaps it would have been better to have sent Edward there too, but there had been school to consider. It mattered very little if a girl's education was interrupted, but a boy was different. Edward was doing well at the Academy, even though along with his Latin he was acquiring a hatred of the British that was becoming awkward, with a major in the house.

"Go right along now, Edward. You'll have to run all the way."

She pulled Tacy's chair back from the table and set it against the wall. It was a charming chair, mahogany like the rest, with a carved back; it looked just like any other chair, except that it was a little narrower and the seat was a good deal higher. It was one that Tom Affleck had made, and she had bought it from Isabella Affleck, who was selling what she could in order to keep her little family afloat. She had been so grateful for the money which Sarah had paid her that Sarah suspected she was pretty well strapped. That had been a month ago. She must go see her again, thought Sarah.

Now she must get Tacy off to her dame school around the corner, supervise Caleb's tray and send Amos upstairs with it, soothe Hettie and confer with her about the day's meals and try to find ways of circumventing the Major's servants; but still she lingered in the cold dining room, looking out of the window at the packed gray earth of the path, mica-spangled in the glittery January sunshine, and the brown and wispy grass under the leafless branches of the apple tree.

The weight of war and anxiety lay heavy on her heart. It seemed to her that if only peace came to settle upon the land, all weariness and sorrow and irritation would cease, even though she knew quite well that in peacetime, too, beloved people fell ill, servants were unsatisfactory, children quarreled and sulked and refused to follow the straight path before them, the milk soured. She was a great gaby, she scolded herself, to stand mooning at the window when there was so much to be done.

In her philosophy, when you felt depressed, then you went out and did something for somebody else, something outside your ordinary line of duty. She would go to see Isabella Affleck this very morning, she decided, and she would begin to put in motion that idea she had had all week about young Caleb.

When she started out an hour later with a basket on her arm, her thoughts were centered about young Caleb. Here it was almost the end of January and they still did not know where he was. The word

had come just after New Year's that he was locked up in solitary confinement without pen or paper. Then that they were all to be transferred to Staunton. Then silence. But silence roiled by rumors, as the
silence of sleep is roiled by distressing dreams. The word came that
they were all set free and were coming home, but when it was investi-
gated it proved to have emanated from someone in Reading who knew
nothing whatever about it. Then it was reported that John Pemberton
had died, and the families of the prisoners were drawn together in
grief and apprehension, for if John Pemberton died, who else might
not die too? This rumor had been canceled out by a report from a
Wilmington Friend that his cousin in Winchester had written of seeing John Pemberton at Hopewell Meeting early in the month. From
this it was assumed that the exiles were still in Winchester, though of
course the group might have been divided and Caleb, alone or with
others, sent on to Staunton. No one had had a letter for weeks. A
packet of mail which had been sent from Winchester to Baltimore had
been stolen from the Friend who was bringing it up from Baltimore,
at night as he lay at an inn with two strange bedfellows. The Friend
could not remember all the people to whom the letters had been addressed. There were two for Hannah Pemberton, he knew, and one
for Eliza Drinker, one for Polly Pleasants, half a dozen or more others, he could not say exactly. It made them all nervous to think what
might have been in the stolen letters, since Caleb's intercepted letters
about his money had done so much harm, but no doubt the exiles were
all doubly cautious now in what they said.

Sarah stopped at the corner of Chestnut Street to wait for a big yellow coach to lumber past. She tried to get a glimpse of the man inside,
but saw only a coat sleeve and a foam of lace. She liked to have something amusing to tell Caleb when she went home after being out, and it
would have been a nice titbit to recount that she had seen General
Howe riding in the coach which he had commandeered from Mrs. Israel Pemberton.

On an impulse she stopped at the apothecary Drewet Smith's to get
some hoarhound drops for the Affleck children. She had a jar of soup
in her basket and half a pound of butter and some corn meal, but there
was nothing in that to delight children. The hoarhound drops were

sweet and would help their throats. Poor little things, they always seemed to be snuffling and coughing.

The shop was warm and cheerful, with a little fire on the hearth, and redolent of herbs and drugs. Two red-coat officers were demanding a British preparation for toothache and accepting with disdain the bottle of Dr. Storck's Tincture which Drewet recommended. Sarah suppressed an un-Christian satisfaction that the British teeth were aching. There was, actually, nothing wrong about the behavior of those two, yet she found herself resenting them, perhaps only for their unconscious assumption of superiority. They had looked at her, found her middle-aged and homely, and forgot her. Drewet Smith might not have had any existence at all, except as a phantom conjured up to serve their immediate need. They were aware only of themselves and each other, for whom they appeared to be playing a part. They were very smart, she thought; their uniforms new, clean, well fitting, their boots gleaming, their buttons bright. Their voices were crisp and clear, their words spoken as if to an unseen audience. One was short and square and ruddy; the other tall and thin and pale; the symmetry of his face was marred by a swelling in his cheek.

"'There was never yet philosopher," said the thin one, wryly but with a kind of flourish, as if he were reciting, " 'that could endure the toothache patiently.' "

"You will find this tincture soothing, I think, sir," said Dr. Smith, screwing up his face in an expression of sympathy. He was a colorless man, with grayish skin and mouse-colored eyes; it was the way he used his face that marked him out from other people. He could not make the simplest statement without raising his eyebrows, twitching his nose, pulling his mouth down on one side. It gave an emphasis to his prescriptions that perhaps impressed the uncritical.

Sarah hoped that Caleb, associating so much with him in the care of the Hessian prisoners as he had done, had not picked up any of his facial mannerisms. Those things could be contagious, and Caleb was so good-looking it would be a pity for him to start twitching his chiseled nose or pulling his fine, molded mouth out of shape. But how absurd to worry about such trifles, when poor Caleb might be immured in some damp cell somewhere, eating out his heart in rebellion and despair.

When the officers had flung down some bills on the counter and stamped out, not troubling to shut the door behind them, Sarah turned to Dr. Smith with more cordiality than she actually felt. She disapproved strongly of his having broken his parole and come home, and she thought that his doing so might have made things more difficult for the prisoners who remained.

"Did you see the coach pass?" she asked him. "Was that General Howe in it?"

He knew General Howe. When he first arrived back from Winchester, he had been summoned before the General for an interview.

"I didn't see," he answered. "He's a very tall gentleman, very affable and at the same time dignified. You can't but admire him." He measured out the hoarhound drops. "Have you heard anything from Caleb?"

"Not a word. Have you had any news from Winchester?"

He raised his eyebrows and drew down both corners of his mouth. "They don't write to me."

"I thought you might hear something. People talk in a shop."

She left with a feeling of disappointment, which was quite unreasonable, since she had had no real expectation of hearing anything there. But there was always the chance.

She thought of Sue Mercer as she went on again, past the entrance to Orianna Court, where the popular and handsome young Major Andre occupied Dr. Franklin's sober house. They had not heard from Sue since early December. She had written with innocent satisfaction that she had been able to get her brother's money changed for him advantageously, but that was before the money made so much trouble for Caleb. Sarah had wanted to try to get a letter to Sue, asking whether anything was known in Lancaster about Caleb's fate, but father Caleb had refused to allow it, declaring that Sue might be in difficulties just as Caleb was and that any communication with Philadelphia, if it became known, would only make matters worse.

As soon as she entered the front room of the Afflecks' little house on Second Street, Sarah knew that trouble had moved in since she had last been there. The little room was bare, except for a plain chair or two and the green-painted paneling which gave it a certain cheerful charm, empty as it was. Sarah noticed at once that the beautiful tallboy which she had coveted was gone, and so was the table and the comb-back Windsor chair that used to stand beside the fireplace. The hearth was empty even of ashes, and the room was icy. Most ominous of all, there was the dank, thin, sour odor of sickness and poverty.

"Come away into the kitchen," said Isabella Affleck quickly. "It's warmer there."

Thomas Affleck's wife was a young Scottish girl still in her early twenties. She was not pretty, with her unruly sandy hair escaping from under her clean mobcap, her rather small, pale eyes, her long nose which rose aspiringly at the tip, her wide mouth; but her teeth were white and even, her skin had the color and texture of apple blossoms, and even though she looked this morning thin and tired and anxious, there was about her an air of unquenchable buoyancy that brought the words, "blithe" and "bonny," which were not in Sarah's daily vocabulary, into her mind.

The kitchen was a large, cheerful room and a good fire burned in the big fireplace. A hooded cradle rocked slightly by the hearth and two small children with runny noses, very much bundled up, sat on a braided rug pulling a cornstalk doll apart.

"Whisht!" said Mrs. Affleck, wiping their noses, hoisting them to their feet, and whisking away their employment with a single long sweeping motion like a breeze in a pile of leaves. The younger one promptly sat down again with an angry bellow, while the older stood sucking his thumb and scowling at Mrs. Middleton.

Sarah, taking the chair her hostess drew up for her, noticed that the younger child had a bad fever sore on his lip, that the older one had a croupy cough, and that a wail which was much too feeble was issuing from the cradle. She said nothing, but opened up her little poke of hoarhound drops, and as the children crept forward, shy but irresistibly drawn, she sent a swift glance around the room and saw the bare shelves, the empty rafters from which hung no more than some bunches of herbs and a few ears of popcorn.

"Isabella," she said, "what's happened?"

Isabella, sitting on a stool with her foot on the rocker of the cradle, gushed to the roots of her hair.

"I've sold the tallboy, and we've eaten it up." Her Scottish inflections changed the vowels slightly and made what she said even more poignant. "I've sold the Marlboro table and paid the rent and bought medicine. And now I've nothing more to sell but the beds and with all the bairns sick most of the time I can't sell them!"

"But isn't there anybody to help you? What about the Meeting?"

"I could never go to the Meeting. Tammas was disowned when he married me. Governor Penn would help if he was here. He brought Tammas out from England to make his furniture and he was always kind. But he's been banished himself, poor man, he's got troubles of his own, no doubt. I'm a Presbyterian and all the bairns were christened in the Second Church, but that has been taken by the British army for a hospital, and most of the members are gone to the country or to Reading. We've no family here, and there's nobody that has a duty to help us. I'm too proud to beg but I'm not too proud to work—only I can't leave the bairns."

She poured it all out, as if she had said it many times over to herself.

"It's Jeanie I'm anxious about," she went on, and Sarah saw that her blue eyes were swimming in tears. "Would ye juist come upstairs and look at her, Mistress Middleton?"

They went out into the cold again and up the narrow, boxed-in staircase to the second floor. Jeanie, who at five was the eldest, lay in the big walnut bed in the front room. She was asleep. Sarah, looking down at her, saw the limp hair spread out over the pillow, the thin little body that scarcely made any thickness under the covers, the open lips, parched and colorless, the shadow of the lashes on the hollow cheeks. Her breath came noisily with a wheeze.

"She looks sick to me. Have you had the doctor?"

Isabella shook her head. "I haven't liked to leave the house to go after him—and I don't know who to go for anyhow."

"Dr. Bond is practicing again. The Council put him in prison, but they left him behind when they went and the British let him out. He's kind and very able, and he wouldn't expect to be paid now. I'll see that he comes."

They tiptoed out of the room and down the stairs again.

"Now, Isabella," said Sarah firmly, "I've left a basket of little things in the kitchen, but it doesn't amount to anything. It won't do more than help you with one meal. What you need is money. You take this now, and I'll see you get more later. It isn't charity, it's a loan. When Thomas comes home—and he shall come home—he can make me a tallboy like the one you sold. Don't cry, child. You've been a brave girl, but you can't do everything by yourself."

It was time to go home, but as the front door closed behind her Sarah turned resolutely in the opposite direction and set out again. A half-formed purpose which she had been turning over in her mind for a week or more had now crystallized. When she said, Thomas *shall* come home, she meant all that was implied by the use of "shall" instead of "will." She was going to do something about it herself. They should all come home, not only Thomas, but Caleb and the rest.

She could not act alone, of course, she would have to have help. Men had tried and failed. This was a business for women. She would go to Mrs. Drinker first and enlist her support, because she knew Mrs. Drinker a little better than the other wives and mothers. Mrs. Drinker also seemed to her a stronger and more positive sort of character than some of the others.

As she marched along the sidewalk with so much vigor that her cheeks shook, she rehearsed the arguments that they would use, she and Mrs. Drinker and whoever else, not more than two or three, should go with them. The injustice and illegality she put aside as undeniable but irrelevant. Men could always talk you down with abstractions, but when it came to young wives left without means of support and little children sick and hungry, then men were helpless before really roused and determined women.

Fifteen minutes later Mrs. Middleton sat in Mrs. Drinker's well-furnished parlor where a Pennsylvania iron stove with polished brass knobs gave out a delicious pervading warmth.

"I'm sorry to entertain thee in the back parlor," said Eliza Drinker, "but our British guest has taken the front parlor."

With some difficulty Sarah resisted the temptation to compare notes on British guests, but she knew that if they got off on that subject there would be no time left for the thing that had brought her here.

"My idea is this," she said, "for four or five of us wives and mothers—four would fit into a coach better—to go directly to General Washington himself at his headquarters at the Valley Forge and lay the whole thing before him. He is humane, everyone says so, and he has the power to act."

She watched Eliza Drinker's face eagerly for her reaction. It was a strong, sweet, serene face, framed in the Quaker cap, but it was not an immediately revealing one. There was a long pause. Finally Mrs. Drinker spoke.

"My own heart has been full of some such thing," she said, "but I don't see the way clear yet. It has not occurred to me to go to George Washington. He is, after all, though a general, in the employment of the Congress. I had thought that a delegation of women might go to York directly, to the Congress itself."

"And to Lancaster, too, to the Council," cried Sarah, catching fire. This was a much larger undertaking. It was three or four times as long a journey as it would be to go to the Valley Forge. But she could see Sue in Lancaster, stay with her at the Mercers' house, no doubt. And Mrs. Drinker was right, it was a matter for ultimate authority. "We shall probably have to see the General too," said Sarah, "to get permission to go through the lines."

But she was progressing too fast for Mrs. Drinker.

"It was only a thought. I have not discussed it with anyone. We should have to consult the Monthly Meeting. And there is another thing. Isaac Zane—the old one, not the son—has gone with some Friends from Pipe Creek Meeting to appeal to Congress. If they are successful, our trip would not be necessary. In any case, we should have to wait till they returned."

Though she was eight or ten years older than Eliza, Sarah felt oddly young and impulsive as she listened to Mrs. Drinker's calm, unhurried voice. Sarah was ready to start off for Winchester itself, if necessary, before the week was out. She had no faith in the success of any committee headed by old Mr. Zane. To wait till those old men tottered off and said their say and tottered back again seemed to her an appalling and possibly a fatal waste of time. Quakers! she thought impatiently.

She felt a gentle touch on her hand.

"Let us keep an open mind," said Eliza Drinker, "and proceed as the way opens."

XXVII

CALEB WAS CHOPPING WOOD, splitting logs for Elizabeth Joliffe's fireplaces to work off his energy and the fret in his mind. Six weeks had passed since the decree that they were to be moved to Staunton, and the exiles were still in Winchester, still uncertain of their fate.

The pleasant popularity which they had enjoyed for a short time in the autumn had vanished utterly. The townspeople had objected to their use of the Presbyterian Church on Sunday afternoons, and now no visitors came to their meetings for worship in the inn. Because of the storm of disapproval resulting from Drewet Smith's departure, they rode abroad no more than was necessary for their regular gatherings on Wednesday at the Golden Buck. Rumors circulated about them, blaming them for high prices, for the scarcity of food, and the refusal of some Quaker millers to grind grain for distilling spirits. Twice the Commissary for Prisoners had come, displaying letters from the Governor of Virginia ordering them to pack up for immediate departure to Staunton, and twice they had wrested a reluctant reprieve from him on the ground that Congressional action was pending.

Alexander White had consented to go to Congress on their behalf, and had actually spent three weeks in York and Lancaster, where he presented their Memorials and delivered a strong plea for them in his own words, urging that they be set free on grounds of humanity, justice, and expediency. All that he had achieved, however, had been a statement from the Council that it considered the exiles the prisoners of Congress. From individual members of Congress he got so many expressions of personal opinion to the effect that no good purpose was served by continuing to hold the prisoners that he believed if it came to a vote they would be released. Some members, however, indelibly prejudiced against Quakers, were strong enough to postpone action on the question. Mr. White had returned to Winchester the second week in January empty-handed but expressing the belief that he had set forces in motion which would yet bring results. At least Caleb's letter explaining his financial transactions in detail had been accepted and though he received no answer there had been no further complaints against him as distinct from the rest of the group.

After White's return Thomas Gilpin's brother George, a colonel in the Fairfax Militia who lived in Alexandria and was a personal friend of several members of Congress, had made a visit to York for the exiles. He was still there. A delegation of concerned Friends from Pipe Creek Meeting in Maryland, joined by Isaac Zane, senior, had also gone to plead for them.

They were not forgotten, there were men working for them, there was hope. Meanwhile the winter was cold, their supplies of tea and coffee and chocolate and wine, those comfortable beverages that lift the spirits as they warm the body, were exhausted. Some of the exiles had no warm clothes and none could be bought at any price. One after another they were falling ill, and they had no medicines. Even vinegar, so essential for health and hygiene, was not to be had.

It was cold this Monday morning, with a blustery wind out of the northwest whipping the bare trees, blowing chips along the ground, flinging gritty dust into Caleb's eyes. As he worked his thoughts moved jerkily, weaving together bits he had heard from here and there, from letters, from talks at the inn, where an occasional traveler brought news, from the *Pennsylvania Packet*, which John Dunlop was printing now in Lancaster, an occasional copy of which reached Winchester, to be passed around until it was as soft as a rag and the print was worn off on the creases.

In the cities, in spite of the war, there were balls. In Philadelphia, in York, in Lancaster, fiddlers played gay music, cold collations of wine and sweet cakes were set out on polished tables in the candlelight, and girls in their high silly headdresses danced with officers in smart uniforms. It made no difference, seemingly, whether the soldiers wore scarlet coats or blue and buff—Caleb tossed a chip of wood at a hen that came jerking her neck and spreading her toes, and the creature fled squawking—but soldiers they must have to dance with and no others would do.

There was no dancing for the men in winter quarters on the hills above the Valley Forge. George Gilpin had told them about that, when he stopped on his way to York. The men in Washington's army were in need of everything, breeches, shoes, stockings, blankets, flour—though barrels of flour were spoiling on the banks of the Susquehanna for lack of boats and wagons. On Christmas night the soldiers in their tents shouted to each other across the snow till the cry echoed back and forth from hill to hill, "No meat! No meat!" Isaac Potts had come on Washington praying. They were using Isaac's big house to bake bread for the soldiers, when they could find the flour.

The forge itself had been burned earlier by the British. What was happening to the Phoebe Ann? Caleb straightened up to rest his back, and leaned the axe against the chopping block. The Phoebe Ann was no farther from the Valley Forge than he was now from Isaac Zane's ironworks.

The charcoal had given out at Zane's, and the furnace was out of blast again. The Phoebe Ann had never had to shut down for lack of charcoal, even though they had less than half the acres of woodland that Zane had. But they had cut wisely, they had replanted, they had hired good men as cutters and colliers and treated them well. They had stayed on the job—until last August. I. Zane, junior, was off again, gone to Westover no doubt to dicker for his books.

Caleb spat on his hands and took up the axe again. For all his big ideas, Isaac, junior, was not half the man his father was. Caleb thought of old Isaac as he had seen him in Reading that day in September, with the blood running down his cheek where the stone had hit him, and the hurt, astonished look in his hooded eyes.

He would like to go to York himself, he, Caleb Middleton, junior. Ride off without telling anybody, not to Philadelphia to escape, as Drewet Smith had done, but to York, to face the men who would not grant him a hearing. His axe hit a knot and the blow shivered up his arm to his shoulder. He would like to stride into the inn where they met, pound on the door of the room where they sat deliberating, the few of them who were still there. Some had gone home. Mr. Adams was in France. Mr. Hattie in Winchester and some others had gone to the camp to investigate Washington, to find out if he was a suitable Commander-in-Chief. Some snake had whispered that no man was more a gentleman than Washington or appeared to more advantage at his dinner table, but that his military talents were despicable. A new Board of War had been appointed with General Gates, fresh from his victory at Saratoga, at its head, and an investigating committee had gone to the Valley Forge.

Or perhaps Caleb would go to Lancaster and confront the Council, because this was a matter for the state after all. He would say to them—a piece of wood split suddenly and the halves bounced away—"You would not be in Pennsylvania today if Quakers a hundred years ago had not refused to take oaths of allegiance to the King. Those early Friends could have freed themselves from the charge of being secret Catholics, when a Catholic was considered as dangerous as a Tory is today, but they had a bone-deep knowledge that taking an oath of allegiance at the command of an official, to avoid trouble for themselves, was an offense against liberty as well as against God. They refused and went to jail, and then they founded a colony where there would be no test oaths because there would be civil and religious liberty for everyone. Now what are you doing to their colony? We can't take your test oath," he would tell them, "but we're serving liberty just the same, if you could only see it."

The dinner bell rang and he hung his axe on the wall of the shed. He was in Winchester, not in Lancaster.

That afternoon, as the Monthly Meeting at Hopewell was about to conclude, John Hunt rose to speak. His face was white and still, his blue eyes had a look of exaltation. His voice when it came was harsh and rhythmic. Caleb felt alarmed. Was he going to have a seizure?

"I have heard with my inward ear and have seen with my inward eye," he intoned, "and now I am free to express to you. The night is far spent; the day is at hand. All about me in this sorrowful time I see people indulging themselves in pleasures, pride and dissipation, notwithstanding the calamities prevailing in the land."

It was not a seizure. He was saying again what he said so often sitting before the fire in the evening, the Friends had gone far from their original simplicity and their vision of a life based on the Sermon on the Mount, that they lived instead in conformity with the world, seeking wealth, luxuriating in fine furniture, rich food, expensive clothes and equipages; but he was speaking, not quietly, calmly, half-humorously, but prophetically, as if he were in the grip of some force outside himself.

"Desolation from the east, desolation from the west, desolation from the north and from the south, even the sword . . . except the inhabitants of America repent and mend their ways . . . I have spoken," he finished, suddenly reverting to his normal gentle tone but with a solemnity that deepened the silence in the room almost to breathlessness, "under a weighty concern and exercise of mind, apprehending that I shall not have a public opportunity again."

He sat down. For an endless time, it seemed to Caleb, there was no slightest sound in the Meetinghouse. Then gradually there came a breath, a cough, a rustle.

The final word from Congress was brought three days later by old Isaac Zane. The rest of the committee from Pipe Creek had returned to their homes, but he made the long detour around by Winchester to take the word to the exiles and to visit his son. He rode into town on Thursday and asked that all the group be called to the inn that evening, so that he could speak to them together.

He would spend that night at the Golden Buck and go on next morning to Marlboro. Isaac, junior, had come back the day before.

Thomas Wharton was well enough after his illness to ride to town, but John Hunt was down now with pain and fever. Only two were able to come from the Browns' and at the inn three were confined to bed. February, everyone said, was always a sickly month, but this was worse than usual.

Isaac Zane sat in the big chair by the fire, and the firelight falling on his thin face and ragged features made him look like some ancient bird of prey. His voice, though it had a quality of sadness, was strong and clear and he showed no great fatigue after his long ride.

He told his story in his own way, not willing to be hurried by questions or persuaded to reveal the end before he had gone through all the preliminary stages. He and the five Friends from Pipe Creek, whom

he named, had had many conferences with the delegates, both together and separately. They had corrected many false reports. At
length the Congress had appointed a committee of three to confer
with them.

"They admitted to us," he said, "that they had no other accusation
against you than the several Epistles of Advice which had been published by the Meeting for Sufferings in Philadelphia, exciting the
members of our religious society to maintain conduct consistent with
our religious principles."

In that case, thought Caleb, surely they must see the injustice of im-
prisoning and banishing seventeen members at random out of a membership of thousands.

"The committee reported back to Congress, recommending that
you be either set free or that Congress hear you in your own defense."

"And what action did the Congress take?" demanded Miers Fisher
impatiently.

But Caleb knew with a sharp foreboding that had it been one or the
other they would have been told before now. Good news bursts out in
the first few minutes.

"They debated several days more, and then they passed a Resolution, of which they gave our committee a copy. I have it here and you
may keep it for your records. You will be discharged from your confinement and banishment—upon taking the oath or affirmation of allegiance."

There was a bitter silence in the room. No one spoke. No comment
was necessary.

XXVIII

SPRING SPOKE THROUGH A crack in the wall of February. It was in the shadows that lay along the brown earth, delicate and precise; in the sudden chuckling sound of the brook where ice was melting; in the innocent blue of the sky; in the long, sad call of the white-throated sparrow in the cedars.

Caleb said nothing of his intentions in the house where John Hunt was still in bed racked with fever and the ache in his head, and Edward Penington sat with a book in his hand, the pages unturned, refusing to admit the pain that crept on him. He passed the axe hanging on the wall in the woodshed without a glance.

He saddled Ladybird and rode into Winchester and out again, on the road that led east to the Opequon and the Shenandoah, the Blue Ridge and ultimately Baltimore. He would go, he told himself, to the Opequon and no farther. He would go to the end of the six-mile chain that tethered him like a dog to its kennel.

He rode without joy and without thought, a body driven by inner compulsions, a spirit held in desperate suspense, seeking a release the terms of which were not spelled out even in the secret recesses of his heart. Though the chain that bound him was not of his own forging, he had accepted it. Whether it would snap when he pulled it taut or jerk him to the ground upon his back, he did not try to know; he only rode blindly, pursued by malevolent phantoms of his own being, driven to lose himself through escape or exhaustion.

He came to the ford of the Opequon where he and Drewet Smith had found Tenskatawa waiting for them that day. The leaves were off the bushes now; there was a rim of white ice at the edge of the stream; but he recognized the trail and the great buttonwood tree in the field, spreading its white limbs against the sky, patterning the clouds with its dancing brown balls. Beyond the creek the muddy rutted wagon tracks that were the main road to Baltimore stretched east toward the mountains, where a series of gaps nicked the clear blue line.

He let Ladybird drink, shifting in his saddle as she lowered her head to the water.

It came to him that he might turn and follow the trail along the creek to the house where Loveday had been that day. He might go and see how that family was getting along, the bent-shouldered, young-old man, the young wife with the baby and the gaping hole in her heart where the little boy had been, that little wisp of child they had tried to cure and perhaps had killed. The Prestons would welcome him. People who lived so far away and alone welcomed anyone, and he had news of the world: of the changes in the Board of War, the murmurings against Washington, the extravagances of the British army in Philadelphia, the suffering of the poor there, the conditions in the Walnut Street prison where a brute named Cunningham mistreated American prisoners of war. He had no hope that Loveday would be there. She would be in her home, where the hidden Shenandoah moved near Williams' Gap.

Ladybird raised her head and shook it, water flying in drops from her mouth. Caleb sat irresolute, half wanting to turn to the safe distraction of the farm on the creek, yet resisting a solution so tame and futile, so inadequate an outlet for the pressure within him.

He heard hooves on the road behind him and turned to catch a glimpse over the little rise in the ground of a familiar red coat. He pulled Ladybird around and waited for Pike to come near.

The red coat was dingy now but the ruffles on the shirt beneath it, though badly frayed, had been starched and ironed. Pike's greatcoat lay folded across his saddle bow and his worn valise was fastened on behind. More than these, his expression of dismay and anger on seeing Caleb betrayed the fact that he was riding away from Winchester with no intention of returning.

The mounting dislike which Caleb had held in uneasy control for the last five months rose now to an angry flood.

"Where are you going?" he demanded peremptorily.

"I resent both your question and the manner in which it is put."

"You don't need to answer. I know where you're going. You're decamping." His righteous indignation was all the hotter for the impulses that lay unacknowledged at the bottom of his own mind.

Mr. Pike's small, pale, too close-set eyes narrowed to slits; he answered in venomous fury: "I am not a Quaker. I had nothing to do with the Advices of the Meeting."

Caleb silently admitted that there was justice in this. He tried to be more conciliatory. "You are aware of the damage to the reputation of the group caused by Drewet Smith's sneaking off as he did. You have suffered from it yourself. Can you elope now without a thought for the fate of those you leave behind?"

"The rich and important Pembertons and Fishers and Pleasants—and Mr. Middleton, of course—will be able to take care of themselves."

"Do you imagine that they will believe you when you take the oath of allegiance?"

"I have no idea of taking the oath of allegiance. I have no faith in the rebel government. I am going to Philadelphia. My wife is there without support or protection. There are opportunities for a dancing and fencing master in Philadelphia today such as there have never been before—and I am not bound by pious hypocrisy."

"Nor, apparently, by any vestiges of honor."

"If I had my sword I would defend my honor now—though it would be small satisfaction to run through a Quaker and a coward."

"Get down off your horse and I'll fight you with bare fists!"

For answer Pike plunged his horse into the ford. A moment later, splashing, he was out on the other side and off at a gallop down the rough road ahead.

Caleb wheeled and urged Ladybird after him, but even while the cold water of the creek swirled around him he knew that it was no use to follow. Overtake him he might, pull him off his horse and tie him up with his own reins and drag him back to Winchester, but what then? Such a violent and possibly bloody act would only bring scandal and ridicule upon them all.

Even as Ladybird scrambled up out of the creek Caleb knew he was defeated. He watched the red coat grow smaller in the distance. At a curve in the road Pike turned and waved mockingly before he disappeared.

Barring mishaps he would be in Baltimore in three days, in Philadelphia before the week was out. He would be with his Phyllis.

Primitive jealousy seized Caleb, hot and suffocating, and shook him fiercely. When the moment passed he squared his shoulders, tucked in his elbows, and spurred Ladybird forward, faster, recklessly, and faster, burying the thoughts that stung and goaded him under the clatter of hooves.

As he rode his mind slowly cleared. When the road forked he turned unhesitatingly to the right into a wood beside a holly thicket. He knew now where he was going, where he had intended to go all along. This was the way to the Parry farm.

He reached the place he had been told about, where the road forked again at a big rock, and took the narrower lane, pressing deeper into the woods. Once he passed a cabin in a clearing and asked the way of a woman there. It was past dinnertime now, but he had no thought of hunger.

A wide field of winter wheat with stubborn stumps still standing in the vivid green told him that he was approaching the farm. Presently the road he followed came to an end in a pair of whitewashed gates and a long lane lined with cedar trees on both sides. The formality of the dark green, cone-shaped trees marching toward a hidden house surprised him. He rode slowly along, accompanied by the crisp chip-chip of a redbird flying from one tree to another beside him.

The house, which was built of stone, stood at the end of the lane, framed by the cedars. Mounds of English box, shining and fragrant in the sun, flanked the doorway. The lane curved to the left around the house.

Caleb might have been expected, so promptly did a servant appear to take his horse, a neat, respectful colored boy such as Caleb had not encountered in many a long day. As Ladybird was led off, Caleb turned to mount the white painted steps to the front door, where gleamed the kind of brass knocker common enough at home but rare in this frontier country. As he lifted it and let it fall, he was suddenly conscious of his dusty boots, his shabby leather breeches and old green broadcloth coat. A little nervously he adjusted his neck cloth, which had been clean that morning.

The door was opened by a colored man-servant. Behind him a middle-aged, moon-faced woman came hurrying forward with outstretched hand.

"Oh," she said, her expression of smiling welcome fuming swiftly and rather comically to uncertainty, "it isn't—I was expecting someone else."

"I am Caleb Middleton, junior. I came to see—" he stumbled, "is this where—" he decided to use the Quaker form— "Loveday—Parry lives?"

"Yes. Come in. I am Loveday's aunt, Mary Freame."

She led the way to a parlor, where a fire burned brightly. It was not what he had expected at all. He must look strange and wild, he thought, and tried to adjust his countenance to a polite, conventional look, to hide all the confusion and frenzy of the day's emotions.

"Thou art one of the exiled Friends from Philadelphia? Pray sit down. I will call Loveday and my brother. We have very few visitors here—and now today, two. Good things come in bunches, don't they?"

Too restless to sit down, he went to one of the windows and looked out between the brown and white hangings, which had a French-like pattern. There was a garden, the beds marked out with box hardly larger than sprigs and neatly tucked in with a covering of dead leaves. The redbird hopped about on the path, crested and elegant.

Caleb heard the click of the door-latch and a light step, and turned quickly. Loveday was there.

He had been expecting the gray linsey-woolsey dress, but she was all in blue. It made her eyes, which had been gray, as blue as the sea. Her hair was done up on top of her head, so that the line of her neck showed in all its young purity, and the exquisite modeling of her little jaw and chin. It was like meeting a stranger, a stranger who reminded him almost too poignantly of the girl he loved.

For three months she had dwelt in his thoughts, young and slim, gray-eyed, gray-gowned, pliant to his will; now he found her looking altogether different, ensconced in a house with a door knocker and

French hangings and guarded by an aunt and a father. His little nymph of the wilderness, product of two glimpses and his romantic dreams, had turned out to be the daughter of a country squire, set about with a palisade of conventions of thought and behavior, of which he had already broken several.

He bowed. "I am afraid I intrude," he apologized. "You were expecting someone?"

"We are expecting my—he's my second cousin, actually Griffith Parry. But I knew he couldn't get here so soon."

Even in silk, with her hair up, she had that enchanting look of freshness and cleanliness, that young gentleness and innocence that had held his imagination captive these long months. The expression of concern which she had worn when she was with the sick child was gone, and in its place was a glow that delighted Caleb even while it removed her indefinably but perceptibly from his reach.

The aunt came bustling back and competently got them seated, Caleb in an armchair across the room from the stiff little sofa where she placed herself and Loveday.

"Richard Parry will be here directly," she said. "Thou must be thirsty after thy ride—hungry too. I am having a little refreshment brought to thee."

"This is the Caleb Middleton I told thee about, Aunt Mary, who came with Dr. Smith to the Prestons when little Ned was so sick. He died," she turned to Caleb, "did thee know?—in spite of everything."

What was it the farmer had said of her? Caleb searched his memory. "She's a great hand at nursing, for all she's so young . . . . Seems as if she had magic in her fingers . . . ." They looked like capable little hands, folded and quiet against the little flowered apron that she wore with her silk dress. This was pioneer country, and anyone with the gift of nursing would be called upon to help in cases of illness far and wide.

"Yes, I was so sorry," said Caleb slowly. "We went back later, but the little boy had died, and thee was gone. The Hessian prisoner, at least, recovered."

The scene in the Prestons' kitchen flashed into his mind, the familiar way he had played with her curl and the tenor of his thoughts and impulses as he stood so close to her and fingered her hair. His face gushed hot. The sudden shame he felt was not so much because he had thought her then a serving maid, though there was a little of that, for he should have known from looking at her what she was; it came rather from the insight into himself which the shock of this knowledge gave him. He had met innocence that day and he would have taken advantage of it if he could, forgetting that it was his duty—any decent man's duty—to protect innocence wherever he met it.

The door opened again, and Richard Parry entered. Even without Mrs. Freame's introduction, Caleb would have recognized him as Loveday's father. A man of medium height, both benign and shrewd, he had something of her look of cleanliness. His eyes under a box-like brow were gray and keen, his nose short and straight, his mouth wide, his chin square. There was little of the farmer about his dark gray broadcloth suit and buckled shoes, but the weatherbeaten neck beneath his neat wig and the sinewy scrubbed hands told of hours in the open air.

"I remember hearing thou was of service to poor Edward Preston," he said cordially, fitting himself into a chair. "Dr. Smith later took French leave, I hear?"

"Yes. He—and Mr. Pike too—did not consider themselves bound in the same way as the rest of us. Dr. Macky has returned to Winchester now and resumed his practice."

They must be wondering why he had come, Caleb thought uncomfortably, for all they sat there so polite and friendly. He looked from Richard Parry to Loveday.

There she sat on the sofa in her blue dress, with her eyes shining, beautiful, capable of compassionate and humble and loving service, more desirable than ever and more difficult to attain. Difficult, but not impossible. He would have to ask this father's permission to address his daughter, and before that put himself into a favorable light with the father. But no doubt he knew all about the exiles from Philadelphia; as a Quaker he would feel respect and sympathy for them. A feeling of extraordinary happiness swept through Caleb. That he should have come all this distance, through such anguish of mind, such discouragement and futility, such weight of injustice, and then find, in this unfamiliar wilderness, the girl of all girls in the world, whom he could love and protect and cherish all his life! It made him feel that there was something in the idea of destiny after all and in the mysterious workings of God's purposes.

"I thought when I heard thy horse in the lane," Richard Parry was saying, "that it was Griffith Parry. He's riding up from Alexandria. Where my great-grandfather settled. Where I grew up. We are one of the few families to come to Frederick County over the Blue Ridge. Most of the people hereabouts came up the Valley from Pennsylvania. Griffith and my daughter Loveday will be married this summer—perhaps she told thee?"

"No," said Caleb, while the earth fell away beneath his feet and the sky crashed on his head. "No, I didn't know."

Fool. Imbecile. Idiot. Triple-dyed fool that he was. How was he to get himself out of this before he betrayed his folly?

"Mr. Griffith is to be vastly congratulated," he said between stiff lips, and realized at once that he had got the name wrong and made himself more ridiculous than ever.

The aunt spoke, idly, garrulously, to fill a pause, as women will, and put the cap upon his humiliation.

"How did thee find thy way here?" she asked. "Isn't thee a good bit beyond the six miles, or whatever it is they allow you?"

Caleb ran his finger inside his neckcloth and pulled at it to prevent himself from suffocating and stood up abruptly.

"It is," he said wildly. "Far beyond. I am out of bounds—in every way. I must bid you good day. Servant, sir, madam."

He did not look at Loveday again, or speak to her, but strode from the room, all but knocking down at the door the butler, who was bringing a tray of light refreshment for him. Outside he found his way around the house to the stable, shouted for the boy to bring his horse, tossed him a five shilling note, and galloped off down the lane between the cedar trees.

XXIX

HOT-EYED AND TORMENTED, CALEB lay flat on his back in a dark-
ened room. His head was a hollow vessel made of some heated metal,
on which blows were struck that reverberated down his spine. His
joints ached with an intensity that left him panting. Fever mounted
hour by hour, as the locust's shrill rasp in July days screws upward to
the breaking point.

It was the same pain, the same fever, that had assailed Thomas
Wharton and John Hunt, the same for which Drewet Smith had
treated the German prisoners in the stockades. Dr. Macky came from
Winchester with his lancet and his doses. He was a thin, dark, sallow
young man with coffee-colored eyes. He said he had never known
Winchester to be as sickly as it was this winter. He would not agree
that Caleb had camp fever. It was quite different from what he had
seen in the army, he insisted. Mrs. Joliffe was a good nurse, he said.
Caleb would be well in no time.

The hours stretched endless and confused, broken by voices and
faces, by bitter draughts held to his mouth and trickling down his
neck, by hands on his forehead, cool and heavy or cool and light. He
slept fitfully during the daytime, woke with a start to see the sunshine
on the floor or to hear rain spattering against the window, slept again
and woke at night in the dark, lonely and stricken with irrational fears.

Sleeping or waking, he dreamed. He thought he was the guard at
the Golden Buck, sick in an army hospital, and he struggled to get
away, to walk out of the hospital and leave it all behind. Hands held
him down, fastened the bedclothes tight over him, like a shroud. He
was not dead, he tried to tell them, but the words would not issue from
his throat, and when he fought against the restricting hands, they
turned into Thomas Pike and he shouted aloud at him to prevent him

from leaving. Once the hand on his forehead was so light and gentle that he thought it must be Loveday's, but when he spoke to her it was John Hunt's voice that answered, "Lie still, Caleb," and he was quiet, dreadfully tired but clearheaded for a time.

People came into the room. He could not talk to them, but they talked to each other and he heard them, sometimes through a mist, from a long distance, sometimes clearly and sharply, as they said things not intended for him, which he remembered and thought about afterward.

"A sum of five hundred pounds has been subscribed at Hopewell for the Indians."

But the Indians were all gone. Tenskatawa had found a little girl lost in the woods and carried her home. What had Loveday been like as a baby? Curly-haired and confiding, with no fear of the tall savage who picked her up in his arms. The thought of Loveday was a stab at his heart and a heaviness afterward and he could not think why, until he remembered the last time he had seen her and all the mortification of that day came back. The faces of Loveday and her aunt and her father floated before him, and they were all smiling—smiling at him and the way he had behaved. He groaned.

Two letters came for him. He took them in his hand, but he could not read them.

Later John Hunt read them to him and Thomas Wharton came to listen. Edward Penington was sick in the next room and out of his head. They could hear him crying out and Elizabeth Joliffe soothing him.

They all wanted to know what was in Caleb's letters. Everybody's letters were pressed and squeezed for news, like lemons for juice, but they were all dry. No one dared write anything but moral sentiments lest the letters be intercepted and they be accused of giving intelligence to the enemy.

Caleb's father kept his room and fretted much about his son. Tacy had been inoculated for the smallpox and her little arm was a mass of sores, but it was better than having them later on her face perhaps. Edward was well and sent his love. Patty was still with the Chase cousins. The Center Woods had all been cut down for firewood.

The Center Woods cut down. The ringing of the axe sounded in Caleb's ears and mingled with the pain in his head. That would be the British. They had burned all the fences and some of the great houses like Fairhill and Peel Hall. Caleb's father would not like that. "Caleb can learn something about liberty at first hand," he had mocked. Well now, thought Caleb, moving in the bed to ease his blazing, aching body, his father could learn something about tyranny.

Someone brought him milk to drink, and he slept.

When he woke, he discovered that though he was weak he was without pain.

The relief was a joy in itself, so fresh, so light, so keen that he wondered if life could hold any greater bliss than this. With an effort he turned his head and smiled.

Dr. Macky was there again, and John Hunt, looking angelic with the sun behind his fluff of white hair, and Elizabeth Joliffe, substantial and motherly.

"Feeling better, aren't you?" said the doctor.

"Yes." Caleb heard his own voice, distant and faint. He made a further effort. "Hungry," he said, pleased with his achievement.

The broth which Mrs. Joliffe brought and fed to him as if he had been a baby was good. The room was big and peaceful, and so bright that it seemed to glisten and dance. He saw a rim of white on the muntins of the windowpane, and beyond were the balls of the buttonwood tree, topped each one with a little white hat. Snow, that's what it was. That was why the house was wrapped in a velvet silence and the sun sparkled and the air that seeped through the cracks around the windows had a different smell.

Reaction came later when he tested his returning strength trying to get up, and found himself much weaker than he expected. Half dressed, he lay down on the bed again, his feet trailing over the side, and pulled the covers over him. Discouragement sifted like blowing sand into all the crevices of his spirit.

Not only his own humiliations and failures lay like a weight on his chest, but the woes of his country, torn by civil war, by suspicion and fear, overrun by foreign troops and ruled by bunglers who betrayed the very principles of liberty and justice for which their ragged Continentals were starving and dying of sickness, not of wounds. "No meat! No meat!" those poor devils shouted across the hills at Valley Forge. They might as well cry, all of them, himself included, "No hope! No hope!" for where would it all end?

As if in answer to his need John Hunt came in and sat down in the tall-backed chair by Caleb's bed.

"Thou'rt looking better," he said. "Thomas Wharton is himself again, and I am well. Edward Penington is still bad. He is light-headed, as thou was, only his talk is all of oppressed Indians and thieving clerks, not lovely girls like thine."

"Did I say anything about Loveday Parry?"

"Thou did mention her."

"I suppose I made myself more ridiculous than ever," said Caleb bitterly. "I broke my parole," he went on with a rush, "for that's what it amounted to, even if we have given no formal promises. I went to see Loveday and I made a complete fool of myself. She is engaged to somebody from Alexandria." It was a relief to say it. He swung his feet up on the bed and doubled his pillow under his head so that he could see John Hunt more comfortably. There was a great deal that he would like to say about himself to an understanding and interested listener.

"If we repented our sins," remarked John, "as heartily as we repent our ineptitudes, we should all be considerably farther along the road to perfection than we are."

"Perfection! What do I care about perfection? I want just two things—not to make a fool of myself in front of Loveday Parry and to get out of here and go home." He saw John Hunt's face, which wore an expression of patience, and he felt ashamed of his vehemence and the crude simplicity of his desires. "Or not home," he qualified, "to the Congress. To face them and make them hear us." He paused. The moment for talking about himself and his private troubles was lost. "Where do we stand now?" he asked.

"The Congress has postponed action again, but we are evidently not to be sent to Staunton, at least not at present. Some of us thought Friend Pike's departure might have an adverse effect upon our situation, but apparently it has made little if any difference. Major Holmes sent an express to the Board of War about it. I don't know what he said, but they are apparently not going to take any action because of that."

"But is nothing being done? Are we to molder here indefinitely?"

"George Gilpin was in Winchester day before yesterday on his way home from York. He reported that some of the members of Congress told him privately that if the Council of Pennsylvania asked for our discharge they thought the Congress would acquiesce."

"Did he go to the Council then?"

"No, he thought that would not be prudent. He is, after all, a Virginian. But he reported that a committee from Western Quarterly Meeting is in Lancaster applying to the Council for our release. They are not there for us alone, but also for four Friends imprisoned in Lancaster for refusing to bear arms, and I believe they are bringing up the whole question of test oaths as well."

"Another committee!" Western Quarterly Meeting. That would be Friends from the country Meetings of New Garden, Kennett, West Grove, London Grove. The delegation from Pike Creek headed by old Isaac Zane had failed; Alexander White had failed; Colonel Gilpin had failed; why should these do any better? Especially if they were scattering their efforts on several issues instead of concentrating upon the exiled Friends.

"But Colonel Gilpin did say that some members spoke to him privately?" pursued Caleb as hope squeezed up again through the one crack left open. "Did he say who they were?"

"Not to me. They spoke in confidence."

"But what are we going to do now?"

"Do?" said John. "The only thing we can. Wait."

XXX

WHEN CALEB WAS UP and about again, James Pemberton rode out from Winchester to see the little group at Hopewell. He ate dinner with them and afterward the five exiles sat around the fire and talked. Edward Penington was downstairs for the first time, looking so thin and old that everyone was shocked.

The talk was hardly cheering, composed as it was of anxiety for their families in Philadelphia, illness in Winchester, and uncertainty about their own future. Samuel Pleasants was down sick, and fretting about his wife and children at home, all of whom, he heard, had been stricken with fever. Henry Drinker had succumbed to fever and Thomas Gilpin had been ill two weeks or more with a heavy cold upon his chest.

"Thomas is a little better," added James. "At least, his brother George felt easy to leave him on Second Day. But this morning he had Miers making some changes in his will."

"My wife," said Thomas Wharton with a chuckle, "says that I believe myself on the point of death if I have so much as a sore toe, but even I have not as yet called in my lawyer to alter my last will and testament."

"Perhaps thy lawyer was not so readily available as Miers. Dear me, we are become a poor weak set of people," said James with an attempt at lightness that missed fire. He sat hunched in the big wing chair; his large, kindly, ragged face drooped in folds, and at the tip of his bulbous nose a drop hung but did not fall. "Israel is very low. John seems to be the only one of the Pembertons who retains his spirits, and his physical strength has actually increased." He sighed. "John has inner resources that Israel and I lack."

"Also he is childless, and his wife is with her father. He hasn't your worries," Edward Penington pointed out. "Hast thou heard anything of thy son Phineas?"

"Very little. He suffers constantly. His handwriting shows a loss of vigor. I wonder sometimes if I shall see him again in this life."

"Has there been any word from Lancaster?" said Thomas Wharton.

James made a wry face. "Only that they have had a very fine ball at the inn, with a Hessian band and cards at a hundred dollars a game for those who did not dance. Thy cousin Thomas was present, it seems."

"The British have a ball every Saturday night in Philadelphia," said Caleb quickly.

"It is not necessary for the Americans to follow the bad example of the British in everything," commented John Hunt mildly.

"Congress like Pilate has washed its hands of us," said Edward, bringing out a handkerchief from his pocket with a tremulous hand and touching the tip of his own nose as an example to James. "They have thrown us back upon the Council and the Council is too occupied with dancing and gambling to consider our case."

"A letter came from my son-in-law, Tom Parke, a day or so ago via Baltimore. He writes rather more freely than the rest."

"What did he say about the Hospital?"

Thomas Parke was one of Philadelphia's most promising younger doctors, and four of the managers of the Hospital were there in Winchester, James and Israel Pemberton, Thomas Wharton and Edward Penington. Caleb looked up, his attention caught as always by any mention of the world of doctors and medicine.

"The British have a firm grasp on it. A few of our sick are still in the new house and garret, but the big wards are filled with their sick and wounded. They have emptied the lunatic wards completely, and no one seems to know where the poor creatures have gone. The managers have lost most of their authority."

When the fresh news from Dr. Parke's letter was exhausted, less recent items of intelligence from the city were retold, reexamined and deplored. General Howe had commandeered Mary Pemberton's coach and rode out in it daily. A certain Lord Murray who was occupying James Pemberton's plantation near Gray's Ferry had been so destructive and had behaved so outrageously to the people in the tenant house that Phoebe Pemberton, a worrying, timid woman accustomed to let her husband stand between her and the world, had screwed herself up to the point of going to General Howe to protest.

"The sorrowful Howe says such things are unavoidable," said James with a touch of sarcasm.

After the American vessels blockading the Delaware had been destroyed by the British, ships had come in freely from Virginia loaded with Tory shopkeepers and Scots from North Carolina, who had swarmed into the shops left empty by those who had fled the city. They had taken over the stock already there and added merchandise from the West Indies, so that though food was scarce and expensive, all kinds of imported luxuries were plentiful. William Smith, "broker," who had felt comparatively easy about his wife, believing that she could carry on his store on Third Street for some time without adding to the stock that he had, now was anxious lest she had not been able to hold on to the store at all. She had no other resources, and there was a boy of six and a younger girl to provide for. He had had no word from her for over a month.

"There's another thing," said James. "We at the inn are likely to be turned out of our lodging. Our landlord has been openly tiring of us for some time, in spite of the exorbitant board we pay. But lately he has become actually abusive and he has said that we must look for another place to live. I don't know just what we shall do. There isn't another inn in the town that would take us."

"I suppose some of the townspeople are getting after Busch," said Thomas Wharton morosely, "impugning his patriotism, no doubt."

"In the first part of our banishment," said John Hunt, "we were aware of the gracious dealings of the Lord and tasted of the cup of consolation, but lately we have experienced a season of drought and poverty. I hope we may learn from this and not grow slack, but rather more attentive and watchful, humbly waiting till the Lord is pleased to knock again at our hearts."

A silence followed his words, deepening perceptibly into the living silence of the meeting for worship. When, half an hour or so later,

someone stirred and the stillness was broken, the older men looked
less troubled, as if some measure of comfort had been given them, but
to Caleb, caught in the grip of a black depression, the cup was bitter
and tasted only of failure.

"I wonder just what good we are doing," he said to John Hunt that
night as they were undressing, "rotting out in this back country."

"We have taken a public stand against injustice and oppression, and
I assume that is a useful thing to do. Yet we are a mixed company and
we may have acted from a variety of motives. I think it is important
that we inquire, each one of us, into the true ground and spring of our
action."

"Does that matter, if the act itself is good?"

"I think it is of primary importance. Do, for instance, human con-
siderations chiefly concern us—the prospect of reputation and honor
among men?"

Caleb flung himself into a chair, his neckcloth dangling from his
hand. "We may possibly win reputation and honor among Friends,
but among men at large, no. They consider us not merely Tories but
shrewd and devious as well."

"With some of us, only the opinion of Friends counts. But while
such approbation may fortify us to endure suffering for a time, if that
is all, if there is not some firmer basis, we may shrink and fail if severer
hardships should come."

Self-examination and the analysis of motives were disagreeable to
Caleb. He was a stranger to himself, except as he met himself in the
mirror of other men's minds, where he appeared some times young
and strong and lovable, as in John Hunt's clear soul, sometimes dis-
torted and willful, as in his father's mind, sometimes—and the memory of that day at the Parry's flooded him with a hot bitterness that
made him wince—absurd and ridiculous. He kicked off his shoe with
unnecessary vigor.

"What motive ought we to have, then? I came because it seemed to
be the only thing to do. I was like a boy sliding down a haymow. After
he gets started there isn't any way to stop."

"Thou dost thyself an injustice. There is a deeper strength and purpose in thee than that. But of this I feel sure, Caleb: when a man undertakes to stand out against the massed convictions of his fellow men—in our case against two governments, for neutralism is an affront to both sides—he must be sure his motives are pure. A true love of liberty and justice, or true devotion to the testimonies of the Society of Friends may be enough, but we are really supported, I think, only if we know ourselves to be carrying out the will of God."

Walking across the room to get his night cap from the peg, he stumbled suddenly, as if his leg had given way. He bent down and ran his hand over his left foot and ankle.

"Curious," he said. "It's numb. I can't feel a thing."

Caleb jumped up and helped him into the chair. Dropping down on one knee before the older man, he removed his slipper and chafed the foot and ankle with his hands.

"Thee still doesn't feel anything?"

"No." John pressed his fingers into the flesh and pinched it. "It's as if it weren't there. Most peculiar."

Later the pain came, sharp and agonizing. Caleb woke in the night to find John sitting up in bed, breathing hard, like a man who had been running. "Don't disturb anyone," he said. "I am sorry to have roused thee. It's inflammatory rheumatism, I think. I have had it before."

"Can't I get something for thee? A hot fomentation?"

"No, let it alone. I don't want to drive it upward. I'll just wait, and no doubt it will pass over."

But in the morning it was no better. The pain was acute, he admitted, and he felt an intense heat in his foot. Caleb, examining it, saw on the instep and the ankle ominous spots.

"I'll call Elizabeth Joliffe," he said, stuffing his shirt into his breeches.

Before he went downstairs he placed a pillow so as to take the weight of the bedclothes off the foot. John's face, drained of color and etched with deep lines around his firmly compressed lips, was eloquent of suffering.

The big kitchen was warm and crowded. Lydia, the

twelve-year-old, sat on a stool in front of the fire with a stocking around her throat and her little red nose dripping. There was a fine smell of sizzling ham as the colored woman held a long grill over the coals. Hoecakes browned in a row at the edge of the hearth. Elizabeth Joliffe with her sleeves rolled up to her elbows, revealing arms surprisingly round and white and young, was stirring a big pan of fried potatoes with a long spoon.

"Dear me," she said, when Caleb had finished, "that sounds bad. What next!"

Caleb backed up to the fire between the two women and patting his coattails enjoyed the warmth on his rear.

"Thee's had a good deal of trouble with us and our illnesses," he said sympathetically.

"No, no, I didn't mean that. But I'd hate to have anything happen to dear John Hunt. Here, Lyddy, blow thy nose and take this spoon for a few minutes while I go see about Friend Hunt"

When Mrs. Joliffe had taken a quick look at John Hunt's face and a longer one at his foot, she said, "I think we'll just send into town and ask Dr. Macky to stop by and see thee. Shall I send Edmond, Caleb, or does thee feel equal to the ride?"

Downstairs she turned an anxious face to Caleb and whispered, "Make sure he comes, and as quickly as possible. I don't know I've only seen it once before—but those spots look like gangrene."

"Gangrene! But he hasn't had an injury—"

"I know. But it comes sometimes with older people. Thee sure thee feels able to go? Wrap thyself up well, it's cold. I shouldn't be surprised if we had more snow."

In spite of his concern for John, Caleb's spirits lifted as he went out of the house into the clean, raw air, which had in it a tang of the stable, a dampness from the patches of snow in the shady spots, and an acrid curl of wood smoke. Ladybird was fresh and frisky. He rode off under the gray featherbed of the low-hung sky, thankful to have horseflesh between his knees again and the wide valley before him, stretching gray and dun and black to the purple hills on both sides. It was the first of March. They had been here, thought Caleb, for five months, imprisoned for six months.

He went first to Dr. Macky's house on Piccadilly Street, but the doctor was not there. His wife told Caleb to go on to Busch's inn.

"He was sent for, two hours ago," she said, "for Mr. Gilpin. They say he's dying."

XXXI

THOMAS GILPIN'S DEATH WAS a shock to them all. Caleb, who had liked him without ever having known him well, was surprised now to learn how distinguished a man the others considered him. Though he had been an able partner in the firm of Joshua Fisher and Sons, his real interests had been scientific, and the Transactions of the American Philosophical Society were full of his studies and surveys.

"It was largely owing to Thomas's work on the silkworm and mulberry tree," said Edward Penington, "that we formed the Silk Society. I grant thee, that was rather an abortive effort, but it was one of several attempts to stimulate domestic manufactures and so to free ourselves from English domination. I wonder sometimes at the ignorance of these new men who are so angry with the merchants and so certain that they themselves are the only true patriots. They seem to have no understanding of the groundwork done by those who signed the non-importation agreement—it was Joshua Fisher who drafted that, by the way—and advanced the economic independence of the American colonies. A political accommodation redressing the wrongs done us by Britain—and none of us denies there were wrongs—could have been built peacefully upon the economic foundations we were laying, and all this internecine strife could have been avoided."

"It was too slow, Cousin Edward," said Caleb. "Life goes by quickly and people can't wait forever."

"Growth is always slow, but it is steady and safe."

"But, on the other hand, the pains of labor are swift and birth is sudden and bloody."

Edward shrugged away Caleb's metaphor with an expression of distaste and returned to the subject of Thomas Gilpin. "His studies of the wheat-fly, the seventeen-year locust, the coal deposits of Pennsyl-

vania and the like are the best that have been done and of very practical
worth in the development of this country. Three or four years ago he
designed a chain suspension bridge for the Schuylkill. The powers
that be pronounced it too expensive, but in the long run I think it
would have proved cheap and we shall someday have it. And then he
made plans for a canal to connect the Chesapeake Bay with the Delaware River and so prevent Baltimore from getting all Philadelphia's
back-country trade, and someday we shall have that. This man," said
Edward bitterly, "who was not quite fifty, had in him years of service
to his country intrinsically more valuable than any mere general's and
what has the new government done? They have tossed him aside and
killed him."

"His spirit was singularly gentle and pure," said John Hunt, shifting his position in bed to ease his leg. "What was it thou told me about
his will, Caleb? The doctor was busy with me and I was not entirely attentive."

"When he realized he was dying he asked Miers to draft a codicil to
his will. Miers had put in it something about his being unjustly banished with a number of others and he told him to take that out. He said
it might cast a reflection upon persons who had caused it. They say,"
Caleb added, "that he never expressed any complaint during his illness."

"I have known him many years," said Thomas Wharton thoughtfully, "in the affairs of the Hospital—he was a manager at one time in
the Philosophical Society and on Meeting committees, and I found
him always steady in maintaining his own opinions but with care not
to give offense to others. He was liberal and I think as free from big-
otry as a man can be. It is a great loss. He will be missed in many quarters and especially at home. He has a young family."

Caleb remembered Josh Gilpin in the crowd at Lodge Alley so
many months ago. "How many children are there?"

"Three living, I think. Two died. The youngest is a mere babe. Ma-
terially they will be well provided for, but nothing can take a father's
place."

Thomas Gilpin was buried at Hopewell on the third of March.
Snow fell all the day before and continued throughout the night. By

Tuesday morning it had stopped, but the blanket was three feet deep and the roads had not been broken. The friends who accompanied the wagon with the coffin from Winchester were three hours on the way.

Caleb thought it unwise for his cousin Edward to venture out so soon after his illness and tried to dissuade him, but Edward, testily declaring that Caleb for all his airs and pretensions was no doctor, put on most of the clothes he possessed and labored through the snow-drifts to stand in the wind at the grave and sit for two hours in the chilly Meetinghouse afterward.

He leaned heavily on Caleb's arm on the way back. "Now our original twenty is reduced to seventeen," he said. "I think it will be sixteen before long. Dr. Macky is careful not to commit himself, but our friend John Hunt does not look right to me."

Caleb saw a redbird fly out of a cedar by the buried fence, skim across the snow in a bright flash, and disappear into another ever-green. It brought back the redbird that had followed him up the lane to the Parrys' house that day, and he closed his mind hastily upon the memory of Loveday. He tried to shut out as well the idea of losing John Hunt, but Edward's somber words stuck in his heart like a barb.

Dr. Macky, though he came regularly, could do nothing for John's leg. The mortification crept steadily upward and with it came fever, pain, and great weakness. After he had made five deep scarifications in the calf with his knife and John had felt nothing, the doctor shook his head. Later, away from the sickroom, he said to those gathering anxiously around him, "I see no hope of recovery. The gangrene will rise higher in his body and he will die. It is only a question of time and of making him as comfortable as possible."

"But in such cases is not an amputation in order?" said Thomas Wharton.

"An amputation might save a younger man. Mr. Hunt is old and very weak. It is a most painful operation. I should be sorry to inflict such agony upon him and then see it unavailing anyhow. Besides," the young man paused, flushing, "I would not hesitate in an emergency involving a healthy young person, but in such a case as this I do not feel competent. I have assisted in more than one amputation, but I have never actually performed the operation myself."

"Isn't there anyone else we could call in?" said Caleb. "Surely there must be an experienced surgeon somewhere in this part of the country."

"There's Dr. General Stephen. He's a good twenty-five miles away near the Packhorse Ford of the Potomac. He's out of the army now, and he's a good surgeon, whatever else you may think of him."

From the look that passed between Mrs. Joliffe and Dr. Macky Caleb understood that both knew something further about Dr. Stephen and that it was not to his credit.

"Would not his advice be useful?" said Thomas Wharton. "A consultation can do no harm, surely, and might bring forth something valuable."

"He got his training at Edinburgh," Dr. Macky conceded. "I would trust him to operate, if in his judgment it was the right measure. Suppose we wait and see how Mr. Hunt is tomorrow. Now I had better visit our other patient."

Edward Penington was ill again and his life too hung in the balance. Elizabeth Joliffe, exhausted by more than a month of nursing and with ailing children of her own upon her hands, had pressed Sidney Wright, a member of Hopewell Meeting, into service. A strong, plain, hearty young woman, Sidney was a capable if somewhat brusque nurse. She divided her time during the day between Edward and John, and at night she slept on a trundle bed in Edward's room, ready to jump up and attend to him when necessary. Caleb, whose touch was lighter and surer, cared for John Hunt during the night.

After Dr. Macky's cuts upon his leg he slept little and his mind was restless. He complained of strange imaginations and unsettled fancies.

"They have not let me know," he said once, "how ill they think me. I am aware that my situation is critical."

The morning after the first mention of Dr. Stephen, John Pemberton came to sit with John Hunt. He had come a long way, now that he, with his brothers and Samuel Pleasants, had moved from Philip Busch's to a house south of Winchester. A young Quaker couple with five children under ten years old and a sixth on the way had hospitably offered a home to them when the landlord of the Golden Buck refused to harbor them any longer. The three Fishers were moving to another Quaker home on the Opequon as soon as Miers, who was ill with fever, should be well enough.

Caleb, leaving the two old friends together, sitting in silence or talking reminiscently about John Woolman, whom both had loved, sought out Elizabeth Joliffe to ask her point-blank what was wrong with Dr. Stephen.

"He's that Adam Stephen," she said, as if that explained everything. When Caleb still looked inquiring, she went on, pushing her cap into place with the back of her hand, "They say he's a good surgeon, but he's really more of a soldier than a doctor. He fought with Braddock and they gave him five thousand acres of land near the Potomac for that. He built himself a big house and he was Sheriff for a while. That's all right and nothing to criticize. But there've been things that haven't sounded just right. He was elected to the convention three years ago and then they wouldn't let him take his seat because there was some scandal about the election. He took his old soldiers to the polls to see that people voted the way he wanted or something of the kind. But he was made a general anyhow in the Continental army and he fought well at Trenton—or said he did, he seems to have got most of his praise from himself—and then after the engagement at Germantown last Tenth Month—thee must have heard people talking about it, it made a great stir here—he was tried for unofficer-like conduct and dismissed. Drunkenness, some say it was, though I never heard that that was particularly unofficer-like."

"I remember now. That one. But is he really a surgeon?"

"He was trained at Edinburgh, and I suppose there isn't anything better. He operated on a member of our Meeting about fifteen years ago and he's been as well as most people ever since."

"I can't see that it could do any harm to call him in for consultation."

The odor of gangrene was now a problem to everyone. It pervaded the house and added to the misery of John Hunt himself. On his evening visit Dr. Macky decided abruptly that if Dr. Stephen was ever to be summoned, it must be done immediately.

"If someone were to ride tonight," he said, "we could get Dr. Stephen here by midday tomorrow."

"I'll go," said Caleb promptly, thankful for action at last. "Tell me where to find him."

The directions were simple: to ride north on the Valley Road almost to the Packhorse Ford. Before he reached the river there would be a road to the left, and on that road, on the right, would be the gate to Stephen's farm, marked by stone pillars and a long lane under an avenue of maples.

"You can inquire when you get near. Anyone can tell you."

"What about the six-mile limit?" said Caleb, suddenly remembering that he was a prisoner.

"I'll take responsibility for that. In a case of life and death nobody could object."

It was after midnight when Caleb mounted Ladybird and rode off. The weather was mild and the gibbous moon was high in the sky. In spite of the seriousness of his errand, he could not help feeling a certain elation at being set free to ride so far. The darkness of the woods and fields, the sound of Ladybird's hooves in the night, the sudden sight of a pair of green animal eyes shining out of the blackness of the roadside bushes, the possibility of meeting Indians or highwaymen or militia on the way, combined to give him a feeling of excitement that was pleasant after the long doldrums of illness and confinement.

As the time went past without incident he had to fight against sleepiness, and he sang, to keep himself awake, the "Liberty Song," snatches from the popular "World Turned Upside Down," and bits from hymns which he had heard Sarah Middleton sing.

The moon was halfway down the western sky when Caleb saw a dim light from the open door of a stable and found a tired farmer tending a cow in labor. The man told him how to reach General Stephen's house, but would not let him go till he had the outlines of the emergency that brought Caleb in search of the surgeon at this time in the morning. He shook his head and clicked his tongue in sympathy, but was obviously cheered by the drama of it.

Half an hour later Caleb was pounding on the door of a big stone house.

The General, who came to the door himself, was a big man in his late forties, rugged of feature, with the swollen and pitted red nose of the habitual drinker. In gown and nightcap, with an untidy pigtail down his back and a candle in his hand, he looked more like a Dutch farmer than either a surgeon or a general, but his response to the challenge of need was quick and decisive.

"I'll just get into some clothes and we'll have a bite to eat and I'll be off at once."

He shouted for "Jed" to come and take Caleb's horse and for "Marthy" to get up and make breakfast, and within minutes there was a stir through the house and a light moving in the stable. A tiny, toothless, colored woman drove a boy to rake the ashes from the kitchen hearth and build up the sleeping fire, and soon the copper pots hanging from the ceiling winked back at the flames. Someone showed Caleb where to wash. When he returned to the kitchen a rich fragrance of coffee filled the air. It was weeks since Caleb had tasted coffee and he sniffed the aroma eagerly.

"You'd better snatch a bit of sleep before you start back," said the surgeon, pulling on his coat as he came in, "and give your mount a rest. I'll go ahead. But first we'll eat."

Caleb had seen paneled doors closed upon the wide hallway by which he had entered, but evidently the kitchen was the room that was used. They sat at a well-scrubbed pine table before the fire and ate the bacon and scrambled eggs that the woman named Marthy brought steaming from the iron frying pan. While he ate, Dr. Stephen asked questions about John Hunt's condition and Caleb answered them briefly and as exactly as he could.

"You talk like a physician yourself," said Dr. Stephen, offering him bread on the point of a knife.

"I'd like to be one," said Caleb, "but it's too late now."

"Too late? It's never too late to do something you want to do. Who are you, anyhow? One of that crowd of seditious prisoners they've got down there in Winchester?"

For a moment Caleb wondered if he would refuse to attend anyone whom he considered a Tory.

"We are members of the Society of Friends, which has been opposed to warfare and fighting for a century and a quarter, and we can't

take part in the present commotions on either side. But we are not seditious, sir."

"The rebels don't know who are their enemies and who aren't. If it
hadn't been for me and my Fifth Virginians at Trenton the war would
be over now and certain high and mighty patriots would be in British
prisons—if they weren't hanging from British gibbets. But did that
keep them from making a scapegoat of me when my division and
Greene's got tangled in the fog at Germantown? Now that Frenchman, Lafayette, has got my division, and Greene's been made Commissary General, but here I am, a country doctor, getting up before
daylight to ride across the country to try and save the life of some poor
old Quaker that the Congress decides is seditious. It's a crazy quilt of
a world, and anyone who looks for gratitude, or even justice, is defeated before he starts. Jed, fetch my bag of instruments out of the surgery and be sure the saw is in it, the big one. I'll be off. You finish your
breakfast, Mr. Middleton, and then take a nap on the sofa over there.
It's comfortable and it's warm. I've had many a snooze there."

He drank the last of his coffee and set the cup on the table with a
thud, wiped his mouth with a damask napkin, and tramped down the
hall, shouting directions to Jed.

Caleb followed him to the front steps. Dawn had come, and in the
gray light from an overcast sky Caleb saw mist rising from the fields
beyond the line of maples. A tall, powerful bay horse pawed the
ground beside a mounting block made of a mammoth tree stump.

The surgeon checked the contents of his bag before it was fastened
to the saddle and sent Jed scurrying back for a pot of ointment and a
roll of bandages. Another Negro held the horse's head, and while he
waited for Jed Stephen tested the saddle girth. Dressed and seen by
daylight he was rather an impressive figure of a man, with his height,
his broad shoulders, and straight back. His massive red nose and
three-day growth of beard detracted from the elegance of his appearance but took nothing from his look of power.

"Get yourself a nap," he called to Caleb as Jed came running with
the last things for the bag. "Good for your horse too."

He mounted, wheeled, and was off down the lane, mud splattering
up behind the bay's hooves.

Caleb went back to the kitchen and sat down on the edge of the old and battered sofa. Marthy came to pull off his boots.

"You're asleep on your feet," she said. "Now you jus' rest you'se'f."

"I mustn't sleep more than a couple of hours," said Caleb, finding a hollow that fitted his body.

"No, sir. I'll call you. Lift your foot so's I can free this blanket and spread it over you. Miss Ann knitted it herse'f before she ma'ied Captain Alexander Spottswood Dandridge. Master sure do miss her."

When Caleb got back to Mrs. Joliffe's early that afternoon, the conference between Dr. Macky and General Stephen was over. The General advised an amputation in spite of the risk, and John Hunt, facing all the possibilities, felt, he said, "Free to it." It would be done the following morning.

The night was restless and disturbed for everyone, with the shadow of that great trial hanging over all. Edward Penington, who was on the mend but still very low, felt the unease in the house and demanded to know what had happened. His distress for his friend put an end to sleep for both himself and his nurse Sidney. John Pemberton had stayed over to be with John Hunt and slept in Caleb's bed. Since the doctors were in the spare room, Caleb crawled into bed with Edmund, who kicked, and ten-year-old Amos Joliffe, who ground his teeth, and he thought with longing of the bumpy sofa in the General's kitchen.

When morning came and Dr. Stephen looked again at John Hunt's leg, he said nothing, but stood tapping his lower lip with blunt forefinger. Then he nodded to Dr. Macky and they left room, followed closely by Caleb.

"The mortification has increased during the night. I am afraid that the blood vessels will be so relapsed that we should not be to stop the bleeding. For him to bleed to death that way would be very affecting and the pain of the operation wasted. Under the circumstances I am not willing to amputate. But I don't want to be the one to tell him, after raising his hopes. You do it, Macky, you know him better."

"Let's ask Mr. Pemberton to open the subject, and then we can continue. Would you be so good, sir? He would take it easier from an old friend like you."

A few minutes later John Pemberton came out of the room. "He said at once that from your withdrawing he understood that you were discouraged."

They all went back again into the sickroom, Caleb silently scornful of their estimate of John Hunt. He would meet death—death by torture, if necessary—with all the courage and manliness that any soldier could show, and with good will as well.

In spite of the odor, which was almost overwhelming, there was a look of freshness and sweetness about the man who lay propped up in bed under the sentence of death. His fine fluffy white hair, his white skin with the flush of fever on his sunken cheeks, his deep-set blue eyes with their unquenchably youthful expression, even the sharp bony structure of brow and nose and chin, seemed translucent, revealing the strong and loving spirit within.

Dr. Stephen, making his harsh voice unaccustomedly gentle, repeated what he had said outside.

"I understand," said John. "But I would like to ask, how long dost thou think I am likely to be continued? I am afraid I may be too heavy a burden upon my friends."

"It is impossible to say exactly, sir. There are several factors, the natural strength of your constitution, and so forth."

"Shall I continue the use of the bark?"

"I recommend it, sir. It will protract the time."

"That's hardly what I desire. But I should like to be a little sweeter—"

"The bark will help. I hope—" the General cleared his throat and said in the stiff, determined tone of one who feels obliged to attempt a foreign language to a person whose native tongue it is—"I hope, sir, you will be resigned to the Lord's will."

"I hope I am," said John meekly.

Dr. Stephen took John Hunt's thin hand in his and held it, patting it affectionately. "It's a fine thing to be in such a state of mind," he said warmly and naturally, and a little enviously.

When he got out of the room and before he departed, "I wish I could do something for that fine old gentleman," he said. "Call me again if you need me. You don't need to send a messenger. The post comes twice a week."

Less than a week later he was back again. John Hunt had been sleeping better; the fever was less; the gangrene had ceased to move upward. There seemed to be a very good chance that an operation might be successful and his life might be saved. Once more the doctors met and conferred.

This time they were united in the decision to proceed with the amputation.

"I'll need two assistants," said Dr. Stephen, and turned to Caleb. "Would you be willing to lend a hand, sir?"

XXXII

IT WAS SUNDAY MORNING, the twenty-second of March. A spring rain lashed against the windows and a robin sang over and over his amiable, insensitive refrain. Thomas Wharton plodded off down the muddy lane to Meeting, taking with him the five Joliffe children, while their mother sat with Edward Penington to keep him company and to be within call in case she was needed by the doctors. Sidney Wright had been taken sick with the fever and had gone home the day before.

In John Hunt's room everything was in readiness. A big table had been brought up from the kitchen and placed between the windows where there was most light. On a round table beside it, spread out on a towel, were the implements which the surgeon would use. Caleb picked them up one after another and looked at them curiously: two knives, a larger and a smaller, a saw, so much like an ordinary carpenter's saw that it made him shudder, a slender, sharp-pointed hook attached to a handle, called a tenaculum; a pair of nippers, a pair of shears, a pot of a stiff kind of ointment, a strip of thin leather, a reel of coarse black thread, an assortment of bandages, and a wad of lint. There was also a china dish with a sponge on it, and a pitcher of warm water. Underneath the table, unobtrusive but sinister, stood a bucket.

Dr. Stephen, wearing the same purple broadcloth coat in which he had ridden from his home the day before, looked over the array.

"Everything there but the tourniquet," he said. "We wouldn't get far without that."

Dr. Macky hurriedly dived into the satchel behind the door.

Caleb turned to the fireplace in the corner of the room and poked up the apple logs to a brighter flame. His own hands were clammy with

249

nervousness. What silent torment must John Hunt be enduring now, as he lay there so quietly in bed, his eyes fixed on what far vision?

"It won't be long now, sir," said Caleb in a low voice. "Half an hour, perhaps, and it will be over."

"Well, gentlemen," said Dr. Stephen heartily. "We're ready to begin. We'll all have a dram, to stiffen our hearts and steady our hands."

He poured whiskey liberally from a bottle on the chest of drawers into four glasses and offered the first to John Hunt, who smiled faintly and shook his head.

"My best advice to you, sir, as your physician, is to take it. You'll find it helps you."

John continued firm in declining, and after a moment's hesitation Caleb too refused. The two doctors tossed off their glasses in a matter-of-fact way and swallowed a small chaser of water. Dr. Stephen took off his coat and rolled up his shirt sleeves. Then, as if a curtain fell, or a door opened, or a clock struck, the very climate of the room changed; time stopped as the serious business of the day began. Caleb forgot his clammy palms, his beating heart; his whole being flowed into a listening ear, a watchful eye, an obedient hand.

With Dr. Macky he lifted John, who proved to be unexpectedly heavy, and placed him gently on the bare table, uncovered the diseased leg.

"Do you wish me to apply a tape first, sir, as a guide?" said Dr. Macky.

"No, I don't use a guide. It isn't necessary. The tourniquet, as near the groin as you can get it. Some operators who don't wish to take the time to fasten a tape will draw a line on the skin or use a thread dipped in ink," said Dr. Stephen, addressing himself to Caleb as if he were lecturing to a class of students, "but I think that merely causes a delay when speed is of the essence."

He took his stand on the left side of the table—"If it were the right leg, d'you see, I'd stand on the other side, in order to give my left hand more command of the upper thigh"—and motioned Caleb to the end of the table. "Your task, Mr. Middleton, is to hold the leg steady and firm—wrap that towel around it—until I tell you otherwise."

He tested the tourniquet and picked up the larger of the knives. "Now, Dr. Macky—"

Dr. Macky grasped John Hunt's thigh below the tourniquet with both hands and pulled the skin upward as tensely as possible. Caleb, feeling the motion in the lower leg, tightened his hold, concentrating on keeping the leg motionless a little above the surface of the table.

The surgeon laid the sharp edge of the knife against the outside of the leg, paused for a fraction of a second, estimating with his eye the course of the incision, then made a swift cut directed obliquely upward, carrying the knife carefully around the limb in the same direction. There was a muffled cry from John Hunt, and the muscles of his leg retracted sharply.

"The first incision goes through the integuments only. Watch carefully. Give me the other knife."

Avoiding, after one brief glance, the sight of the bitten lips, the clenched fist, the drops of sweat on the victim's forehead, Caleb fixed his eyes on Dr. Stephen's left thumb and forefinger, turning back the skin, while his right hand with the smaller knife carefully freed skin and membranes from the muscles beneath. Dr. Macky drew up the flap thus formed and held it out of the way. A short, sharp groan forced itself between John Hunt's white lips.

"The other knife. No, no, boy, the *knife!*"

Again the long blade, laid close to the under edge of the turned-back skin, cut obliquely inward through the muscle to the bone in a swift circular motion.

"The retractor—that leather piece. It goes around the bone, d'you see, against the soft parts, to prevent their being injured by the saw." He handed the end of the retractor to Dr. Macky. "Careful, dammit, don't pull on it like that! No use in tearing the muscles from the bone. The last thing we want is exfoliation. Some authorities recommend scraping the periosteum from the bone, but I don't hold with that at all. The saw. Now, gentlemen, you can't be too steady."

Caleb braced himself. This part would be less painful, he knew, than the first cutting of the skin, but it seemed nevertheless the most dreadful stage.

The saw met the bone squarely; the strokes were light, careful, short. The hideous, unforgettable, grinding noise of saw on living bone went on as if it would never cease. John Hunt moaned and moved his hands convulsively, the bloody muscles shivered.

The sound of the saw changed, then stopped, and in the same instant the living leg in Caleb's hands became a dead and severed weight. Fighting down a wave of nausea, he dropped it, towel and all, into the bucket under the table.

"The bone nippers. The sponge. Squeeze it out in warm water."

The rough points at the edge of the bone were pinched off, the bone gently wiped with the sponge to clear away the small particles that followed the saw. Caleb's part was finished. He watched the other two at their work of tying the arteries, absorbed and silent. Dr. Stephen forgot to lecture now. His fingers, which appeared so big and blunt, moved with unexpected delicacy and precision, gently drawing out the end of the femoral artery with the tenaculum, tying it with the well-waxed strands of shoemaker's thread.

"The tourniquet. Only a little."

Dr. Macky slackened the pressure of the screw. The big artery pulsed but the ligature held.

"All right. Let it go."

With all pressure removed, the blood spurted from several smaller arteries, and oozed from the whole surface of the stump, even from the bone.

"Put your finger on it, wherever you see an artery spurting, and press—not hard, moderately, regularly. Your finger, sir—"

"Do you mean me, sir?"

"Yes, you. Who else? We need three pairs of hands. Only a little, just enough to restrain the blood. Some of them will stop of themselves. The others we'll tie."

Dr. Stephen and Dr. Macky, working together, tied four more of the smaller arteries and stopped. Caleb's finger was no longer needed. He wiped the blood away on the sponge, which he washed and squeezed out again with warm water just in time to put it into Dr. Stephen's hand for the final cleansing of the stump.

Now Dr. Macky, encircling the thigh again with both his hands, pressed the collar of integuments and muscles down to cover the end of the bone. The bandaging was begun, with a strip of cotton starting at the top of the thigh wound spirally downward close to the lip of the wound.

"We've almost finished now, sir," said Dr. Stephen, speaking for the first time to the patient. "We've only a little more to do. We're going to move you back to bed for the last part. It will be easier so."

Caleb hastily prepared the bed, pulling the sheet taut and placing across it a pad of old linen four layers thick, before they laid John gently on it, on his side as Dr. Stephen directed, with the stump underneath and the good leg bent and resting on a pillow.

"The most important thing is to keep the body relaxed and easy. You'll suffer less and the stump will be a better one. Now, Dr. Macky, if you'll raise that stump a little I'll slide this bandage underneath. It's a many-tailed bandage, sit, a modern invention that saves the patient considerable discomfort."

The blood that flowed again because of the moving from table to bed was washed away, the ends of the ligatures were carefully drawn to one side or the other and cut to an even length with the shears. Dr. Stephen sat on a chair facing the bed and swiftly, skillfully, drew the lips of the skin over the muscles, pressing the upper edge over the lower in a straight line, covering it with thick pledgets of lint spread with an ointment made of wax and oil. Over the whole he spread lint compresses, which he held in place with the tails of the bandage deftly woven and fastened.

It was finished. John lay in bed, white, exhausted, but able to manage the ghost of a smile. Already Dr. Macky had wiped the instruments and stowed them away in the bag. Caleb had summoned the servants to carry away the table and the bloody cloths and the thing in the bucket. He heard the rain again on the windowpane and the robin still singing. Answering a tap on the door, he found Elizabeth Joliffe anxious on the other side and told her that everything was all right. The amputation was a success.

"I won't come in now," she whispered. "Just let me know when I can do something for him."

Caleb took out his watch and looked at it. A century had been encompassed in less than fifty minutes for everything. He went to sit beside the bed. John's eyes lifted to him affectionately.

"It has been—" Caleb bent over to hear the faint voice which was scarcely more than a breath—"a very practical lesson—in surgery—for a prospective doctor."

Dr. Stephen grasped his hand. "Sir, you have borne it like a hero!" he exclaimed.

"I hope—I have borne it—like a Christian," said John, and he closed his eyes as his muscles twitched and a whip of pain lashed at him.

"I'll give you an opiate now and leave another for tonight, if needed. Dr. Macky will be in to see you early tomorrow, sir, and I shall be back again on Tuesday or Wednesday for the first dressing. I hope you will endeavor to lie as still as possible. Keep the muscles relaxed and the mind serene and we shall avoid spasms and hemorrhage."

Both doctors left after dinner, having given Caleb careful instructions as to what symptoms to watch for, what to do to make the patient comfortable. Thomas Wharton, returning from Meeting, reported that he had mentioned their need of a nurse to Friends there and that one of those present had promised to go immediately and put the situation before a young person whose competence and tender devotion he praised very highly. It would be late in the day before this person could be there, if she consented to come at all. Everyone was deeply concerned about dear John Hunt, and even before dinner was over the stream of friends bringing dishes of calf's-foot jelly, custard, and chicken broth had already begun.

Caleb sat in the room all afternoon while John slept under the influence of the opiate. Rain fell steadily; the fire sank to embers. Caleb dozed.

A little commotion outside the closed door and a murmur of voices roused him at length. The next moment the door was opened and Elizabeth Joliffe was saying, "Mercy! it's dark and chilly in here! I declare, if they're not both asleep!"

Caleb rose to his feet, automatically running his hand over his hair. The nurse had come, at last.

Mrs. Joliffe crossed to the hearth, laid a log on the coals, and applied the small bellows briskly. In the flare of firelight Caleb saw the little figure that had followed her into the room: the gray dress, white-aproned, the lissom body, the nimbus of shining hair, the little flower face.

"Loveday!" he exclaimed incredulously.

"Sh-h!" she whispered. "Thee'll wake my patient!"

XXXIII

THE DAYS THAT FOLLOWED were for Caleb days of intense yet airy happiness, a sequestered time filled with bright, insubstantial beauty, like the golden light that brings to vivid color the undersides of leaves and the shadows of flowers while the unwatched clouds gather silently overhead. All his life Caleb was to remember the strange, enchanted quality of those days and the way his unreasoning heart soared.

John Hunt was better. Almost free of fever, he slept well; his appetite was good; though he spoke little, he was cheerful and even lively in his gentle way. There was a persistent rumor that the Pennsylvania Council had asked the Congress to return the exiles to its jurisdiction, which could only mean that it had determined to take action at last. And Loveday was there.

Caleb slept in the room with John and cared for him at night. He performed during the daytime the offices that were too heavy or unsuitable for a young girl. But Loveday had taken command. She knew a dozen ways to make the sick man comfortable, to ease the weariness and ache of the long lying in one position, to soothe and refresh and encourage. Under her hand the room took on new order and serenity. The clutter disappeared from the mantelpiece, the curtains hung straight and kept the light from the patient's eyes, there was a little vase of fragrant arbutus on the table by the bed, the pillow slips were smooth and cool, and the rag rugs lay straight on the floor. Loveday moved softly about the room, her step light, her voice low; she had no fussy ways.

Working closely with her, both young people held in the bond of their reverent affection for John Hunt, Caleb fell more deeply in love with her with every hour. It was not a blind, bemused infatuation that he felt. Like one surprised by a stroke of good fortune he counted the

257

separate items of his treasure, or as a lapidarist holds his gems to the light to enjoy their color, the perfection of their shape, and their flawless purity, he was soberly aware of every facet of her character that made her different from all the other girls in the world.

Her beauty satisfied him completely, and he found fresh loveliness each hour as, unobserved, he watched her moving with slender grace about her tasks, wearing the simple gray dress in which he had first seen her. But almost more than her beauty he valued her attitude toward it, one that had not been part of his experience so far: an acceptance of it without either underestimating it or putting a false value upon it. He liked girls to know they were pretty and to expect the deference that was beauty's due—he felt it took some edge from it if they were wholly unconscious—but it bored him when they were constantly aware of it, estimating its effect or using it to provoke attentions.

But Loveday's beauty, he told himself, was only the beginning, and he must have loved her without it, if it were possible to imagine her plain and awkward. He considered that question for a time, while his voice went on reading at John Hunt's request from John Woolman's *Journal*, pronouncing the words without the slightest impression of their meaning. She could never be plain or awkward, because the greatness of her heart must widen and deepen even the smallest and most pig-like eyes, and her tenderness express itself in the curve of even a small and thin-lipped mouth. Inward grace such as hers must inform the movements of even stiff and angular limbs.

It had been her freshness and innocence, her look of dewy cleanliness that had first attracted him so that he remembered so vividly his first sight of her walking lightly down the road in front of Philip Busch's. Even that, he saw now, was more lovable because with it went a womanliness that gave it depth and meaning, and in conjunction with her youth added a piquancy that made his heart overflow with tenderness at the thought of her. His imagination ran away, picturing her presiding at a breakfast table or holding a baby in her arms.

She had intelligence enough for a woman, he thought, and in its best form—a robust common sense combined with sensitive awareness of other people's ideas. Experience of life, and a husband's kindly tutelage, would expand it into wisdom. He thought he detected spirit and fire in the angle at which she carried her head and the willow-wand straightness of her back, but he had not yet seen her under circumstances that brought it out. He would like to put her to the test, and he busied himself happily picturing appropriate occasions.

There was humor there too, but buried. Her fault—if she had a fault—was that she took herself so seriously. She was young, she was an only child, she lived with an adoring father and aunt, and she was known and valued throughout this part of the Valley as a skillful nurse who would come to the rescue in time of need. No doubt, too, that second cousin of hers was a solemn, pompous owl who would quench any budding impulses toward humor that might venture to expose themselves. What she needed, Caleb decided, was to be teased a little, and how delighted he would be to do it.

He had a serene and unblemished confidence that her engagement to the pompous cousin would wither away and drop off like a useless and premature twig on a tree, and that he, Caleb Middleton, was the man for whom she was destined. Why else had fate brought her here to Elizabeth Joliffe's at this time?

He tried to put a curb on his voice, on his hands, on his thoughts, to remember always that John Hunt's care and comfort during these critical days were his first duty and commanded all his energy and loyalty. He succeeded in being discreet, sober, tirelessly helpful, but he could not control, because he was not aware of it, the light in his brown eyes, which danced and gleamed and followed Loveday's every motion when she was in the room, accompanied her to the door when she left, and watched eagerly its every opening, looking for her return. He could not subdue the elation in his heart.

He saw her one morning from the window, coming across the corner of the meadow with sprays of pussywillow in her hands. She was wearing a blue cape with the hood thrown back, and the morning sun played with all the lights in her red-gold curls. Behind her, her shadow moved on the awakening green of the grass, sharp and delicate as shadows are in spring. Just before she disappeared from Caleb's sight she gave a little skip and broke into a run, as if the life and joy in her could not be contained in a walk.

"I saw thee," he told her later, when they met in the wide hallway downstairs, "capering out under the trees like a spring lamb."

"Capering? I wasn't capering. I was walking with dignity."

"Dignity? Who's he? Some suitor of thine I don't know about?" He exploded into laughter at sight of her reproving face and proceeded to elaborate on the theme. "I must look out for this fellow Dignity."

"Don't be so simple, Caleb. Thee isn't funny."

She was so enchanting when she was ruffled that he revived the feeble jest in the scattered moments when they were alone, for the pleasure of seeing the color mount in her cheeks and her eyes darken with severity.

"The one I'm jealous of is that Mr. Dignity," he would say, or, politely, "How is thy friend Dignity this afternoon?" Until at length she broke down and laughed, and he had to fold his arms across his chest to keep them from going round her.

Dr. Macky came every day and on the fourth day Dr. Stephen arrived at the same time to change the dressing of the wound. It was a painful business for John Hunt, but he endured it without complaint. The wound had suppurated, though not excessively, and the bandages were hard and dry and stuck fast to the stump. When it was all over and the fresh bandages were in place, both doctors declared themselves satisfied that the patient was doing well

They moved him into the other bed, which had been made up with clean sheets, and then sat for a time talking and watching him covertly to see how he was taking the shock of the dressing. Caleb lounged against the fireplace, resting his elbow on the mantel, and Loveday stood quiet and attentive at the foot of the bed.

"I think our young friend here has the makings of a physician," said Dr. Stephen. "He seems to think it is too late, but I tell him that it is never too late to do what you want to do. I'd be glad to have him as an apprentice—though my practice these days is not very extensive."

"That's very good of you, sir. But I am a prisoner in Winchester, and it is doubtful if the Congress would permit me to move twenty-five miles away from the rest of the company."

"If you ever get back to Philadelphia—or I might better say, when you get back to Philadelphia," Dr. Macky corrected himself hastily, "you might combine apprenticeship with lectures at the Medical College there."

"I have thought of that," said Caleb. "Even with some of the best lecturers, such as Dr. Rush, away, the courses continue, I hear, with Dr. Shippen and Dr. Parke and others."

He was grateful for Dr. Stephen's interest and encouragement, but had no desire to be apprenticed to him. James Pemberton's son-in-law, Dr. Parke, would be his choice, with the hope of an ultimate year or two in Edinburgh, when the war should be over. The rumor that the Council was again taking an interest in them had set him to speculating on what he would do if freedom should come at last.

John Hunt spoke from his bed. "Would thy father still oppose thy wish to become a doctor?"

"I don't know, sir. I rather think not, now. Sometimes I think he might not have continued firm even then, if I had persisted, that perhaps I yielded a little too soon. But even if he should—" he looked at John Hunt but he was speaking now to Loveday—"it would not be insuperable. This fall I shall have my twenty-fourth birthday and then I come into the property that my mother's father willed to me. I shall be financially independent, and I can set up my own home any time I am ready."

"Ho, ho," said Dr. Stephen jovially, "under those circumstances, why work at all?"

"Unless," said Dr. Macky sourly, "the Congress decides to confiscate all Loyalist property. Revolutions are expensive, and the money must come from somewhere."

"Their prisoners don't cost them anything at any rate," said Caleb shortly.

"Keep an open mind," said John Hunt, "and proceed as the way opens."

His voice sounded weary, and the two doctors, prescribing rest, prepared to leave. Caleb went off to see about their horses.

The next afternoon John felt so much better that he urged his nurses to go out for a breath of air.

"I'll just lie here quietly and rest," he assured them. "I promise you I'll not get up and dance a jig or commit any other rash and unseemly act. Youth needs light and sunshine, and you are both beginning to look too pale for my taste."

The air off the mountains was keen and pure. Plowing had begun and the newly turned earth had a clean, hopeful smell.

"Let's walk over to the woodlot and see what wildflowers we can find," said Loveday.

"My mother always watched for the first wildflowers. The woods around the Phoebe Ann were full of them. The white lady's-slippers were her favorite."

They broke twigs of flowering spice bush and chewed the ends, which held the whole tangy taste of spring. They mocked a squirrel that scolded them from the branch of a hickory, counted nine cedar waxwings perched on a bare bough, and stood long listening to a mockingbird which sang so near them that they could see its throat pulsing and swelling.

Inevitably he kissed her there in the woods, out of sight of the house. He took her by surprise, but she ceased to struggle when he pressed his mouth firmly down on hers. Her lips were even sweeter than he had thought they would be.

He was not prepared for her anger when he released her. Her little hand, swift as a kittens paw but surprisingly hard, flew out and delivered a stinging slap upon his cheek.

"Caleb, thee had no right to do that! I trusted thee and thee took advantage of me. Thee knows very well I am engaged to Griffith."

He stood looking down at her, half aba   ed, half inclined to laugh. He had wanted to test her spirit, he thou   ht exultantly. Now he had done it. He knew better than to apologi   . In a solicitous, gingerly way he felt his cheek and allowed a hurt, r   oachful look to appear on his face.

"Oh," she said uncertainly. "I've   er done such a thing. Did—did I hurt thee?"

"No. No, not seriously. Just knocked   oth out, I think."

He had gone too far. She knew he was   ghing at her and her eyes flashed fury.

"This was a nice walk but it has been c   letely spoiled. I'm going back now, but I don't want thee to come   h me."

"May I walk behind thee? Very respectfully?"

She deigned no reply to that, but turned on her heel and marched off. Caleb followed after, loving every line of her erect, indignant little person. He was not troubled by her displeasure, though he had no doubt that it was genuine. He had shocked and startled her—but she had kissed him back.

That night there came a change in John Hunt. He had been so much better that Caleb had ceased to sit up in the chair watching him, but had gone to sleep in his own bed, with his mind set as a mother's is for the least sound of distress from the other side of the room. He awoke suddenly, aware that his name had been spoken.

"Yes? I'm right here. Can I get something for thee?"

"Is there any water? I am—very—thirsty."

Caleb lit the candle and saw even as he held the cup to the dry lips that the tide which they had thought was coming in had now started to ebb.

"Is thee in pain?"

"No, very little." He spoke with an obvious effort. "Weak."

Fear mounted to Caleb's throat as he stood holding the candle and looking down upon his friend. He saw a sharper line about the nose, a transparency at the temple.

"Dear John," he said, "don't talk. Just hold on to all thy strength. I'm going to put some clothes on. Don't pay any attention to me."

Making as little stir as possible, as one might move who feared by some unregarded motion to jar the petals of a rose, Caleb pulled on shirt and breeches, stepped into his shoes, and took his jacket off the peg.

"Caleb." The voice was so low that he had to bend over the bed to hear it. "I have never had—a son—but if I had—he could not be any dearer to me—than thou—hast become."

Unable to speak, Caleb kissed John Hunt's cheek and tiptoed out of the room.

He knocked softly and steadily on Loveday's door until a sleepy voice within said, "Umm. What is it?"

He opened the door and stuck his head in. "He's worse," he whispered. "Can thee go to him right away? I'm going for Dr. Macky."

He feared as he galloped toward Winchester that John Hunt would be gone before he got back; but after all he lingered nearly two days longer.

He made no dying speeches. His eyes rested affectionately on those who tended him or came to sit with him. He was, he said once, quite composed. For several hours before his spirit finally slipped its moorings, he was unconscious. On Tuesday evening a week and two days after his operation, he died.

"The amputation was successful," Dr. Macky said. "It was his heart that failed."

Caleb helped Mrs. Joliffe to perform the last services for the body, and then he went into the empty silent parlor and cried.

Loveday, stealing into the room without a candle, found him. He felt her light hand on his shoulder before he knew she was there and turned as if she had struck him. Ashamed of his tears he was thankful for the dark.

"I am so sorry, Caleb. I can imagine what this means to thee. Even as little as I knew him, I loved him."

"I've never known anyone else like him. He was so human and understanding, and yet he was so good. I think he was the only person I've ever known—except perhaps my mother and I was too young to realize what it meant then—who actually experienced God. Other people say they believe and have faith and so on, but it was real to him."

"He loved thee very much. And thee was very good to him. I should think that might comfort thee."

"Yes. Perhaps. Thank thee, Loveday."

She slipped away as quietly as she had come. He went to the window and looked out at the shadowy garden. A weight of depression settled down upon him. It was the thirty-first of March. Seven full months had passed since he had been taken prisoner. Here they were, still in Winchester, still with no definite charges against them and only a rumored prospect of a chance to defend themselves. Two of the group had died, one of them the man who had been closer to Caleb than his own father, who had given him as no one else had ever done an inkling of the reality of the unseen, a sense of the abiding power of love. If John Hunt had only lived longer, or if only, Caleb thought with the remorse that accompanies the fresh wound of death, he had paid more attention to his words, had asked him more, he might have grasped firmly the understanding which already was receding from him.

John would be buried on Thursday at Hopewell, and after that Loveday would vanish. She would go back to her home near the Shenandoah and to the plans for her marriage, and because Caleb was tethered to Winchester by his six-mile chain he could not go after her, could not see her again until, most likely, it would be too late.

It was Loveday that he thought of that night during the hours when he could not sleep. He knew now that he loved her with heart and mind and body; that there had come to him the single opportunity of a lifetime—one given to but few people, for most make do with what chance or propinquity or interest sends them—of a marriage in which there could be such complete union that one would not know where flesh stopped and spirit began, or even what was man and what was woman. It was almost within his reach, such happiness, and yet about to recede from him merely because of obstacles imposed by his imprisonment. He composed long pleading speeches to Loveday, to her father, to Major Holmes of Winchester, to the Congress and the Council, until at length, exhausted, he flung himself without undressing upon his bed and slept.

All the next day, which was clear, cold, and windy, the house was filled with people coming and going, with messengers and arrangements. John Pemberton was the first to arrive. He had ridden out to see John Hunt, expecting to find the improvement of the previous days continuing smoothly.

Haggard with shock and grief, he sat beside the body for a time in the parlor where they had laid it. "Dear me," he kept repeating, "dear me. Poor Rachel, this will be a bitter blow to her." He turned to Caleb. "It is hard for thee too, my boy. I know how it is, because when I was young I enjoyed—under different circumstances—a somewhat similar friendship with an older Friend whom I revered. I was just thy age when I traveled in England and Scotland with John Churchman. Perhaps the name means little to young Friends now. He was an English Friend, a great spiritual leader, and his influence changed the whole direction of my life. After his death I felt for a time almost rudderless.

It is men like John Churchman—John Woolman—John Hunt, who light the brand and pass it along to those who come after. Or perhaps they *are* the brand." Silent for a moment, he added, almost as an afterthought, "The spirit of man is a candle of the Lord."

The news which John Pemberton had brought with him, expecting to cheer John Hunt with it, he forgot to mention to anyone else. Miers Fisher told it a little later, riding over from Lewis Neale's in a state of excitement.

"A gentleman in Winchester had word direct from Mr. Harvie, the Winchester Congressman, that the Congress have ordered the Board of War to deliver us to the State of Pennsylvania, who will send for us shortly and bring us to trial."

John Pemberton, restored to the present, admitted that he and his brothers had had the word the day before, from the same source, and had spent the evening discussing its implications. No one had any further information than just what was contained in the bare statement from Mr. Harvie's letter.

Caleb carried the news to his cousin Edward, who still kept his bed in the mornings. Thomas Wharton joined them.

"So we shall be brought to trial," said Edward dryly. "On what charges?"

"Whatever the charge, we can clear ourselves easily enough," cried Caleb. "It is something clear and definite at last!"

"What assurance have we that they will not merely put the test oath to us once more?"

"They know that would be useless. At the worst we shall be in Pennsylvania again, facing our accusers—not in this twilight imprisonment here, away from all touch with the people who claim jurisdiction over us."

To Penington, who under the long strain had lost his ironic imperturbability and had sunk into pessimism and bitterness, the news represented only a mirage and a quagmire. To Caleb it was the first step to vindication and freedom. It removed one great barrier between himself and his love. He went in search of Loveday.

She was in the kitchen, helping Mrs. Joliffe to organize her preparations for the next day.

"With the funeral in the morning, we are certain to have a large party here for dinner afterward. Ham at one end of the table and fried chicken at the other. Dilly can make the biscuits in the morning, but we should get the ham boiled this afternoon and the chickens plucked. We'll need at least two big cakes, and custards of jellies of some sort as well."

"I can make a syllabub."

Caleb left them. It was not the time to pour out his heart to Loveday. That afternoon he got her alone in the small parlor.

"Loveday, I know this is not a suitable time to say what I am going to say to thee, but it's the only chance I shall have. Tomorrow will be even worse and then thee will be gone."

"Then don't say it, Caleb, whatever it is. Don't. Some things are better unsaid."

"But I must. I can't let thee go without a word. Thee needn't answer now, if thee doesn't want to. But thee must know—I love thee with all my heart and soul. I want to marry thee as soon as I am free, and I shall be free before very long now. There will never be anybody else for me but thee. Thee needn't say yes now if thee isn't ready. Only say that thee won't marry that cousin of thine. Just promise me that, my darling, and I won't ask thee anything more now. As soon as I'm free I'll go and ask thy father properly, and then I'll claim thy love."

She drew back, the color draining from her cheeks. "I asked thee not to say it. Thee only gives pain to thyself and me. Thee is so determined, Caleb, and so headstrong and so handsome thee confuses me. But I do love Griffith."

Caleb's vanity gave a leap when she conceded that he was handsome, but his mind suppressed it quickly, divining that to her, the innocent, serious, stubborn little angel that she was, any physical attraction he might have for her would be only a disadvantage to him, a stimulus to her loyalty to Griffith.

"And besides, the date for our wedding is all set."

"When?"

"The twenty-first of Sixth Month."

"Is thee sure thee does love him?"

"I know I do. I always have, since I was a little child and he used to come to visit—seeming very grown up and important to me—and bring me sweetmeats. And I've promised."

The note of finality in her soft voice was unmistakable. Caleb searched her face for some sign of yielding but found none. Her eyes met his, clear and unfaltering; the sudden tears that blurred their gray-blue depths he was obliged to put down to compassion.

"So thee'll go back to the Shenandoah and I'll go to Lancaster and on to Philadelphia, and thee'll be married before I ever have a chance to try to confuse thee further. Thee couldn't postpone the wedding, just till fall?"

She shook her head.

He took her unresisting hand in his, looked at it, turned it over, and kissed the palm.

"If thee should ever change thy mind," he said, "let me know."

He went out into the yard and for as long as it was light enough to see he chopped wood for tomorrow's kitchen fire. He heard voices now and then from the house. From time to time Bob, the colored boy, brought a visitor's horse to the stable or led one back to the front steps. Lydia wandered out to look at the growing pile of split logs and the scattering of chips and demanded shrilly, "Do we need all that wood?" but in a moment her mother called, "Lyddy, I want thee," and she ran off. No one else came to interrupt him. When at length he hung the axe on the wall of the dim shed and turned toward the house, the realization swept over him afresh that the only person to whom he might have talked about his pain and who could have found some ease if not an answer for it had passed beyond the final and irrevocable door.

It was raining early on the morning of the funeral, but by the time that the lines of people on foot and on horseback, the wagons and the scattering of sulkies converged upon the little stone Meetinghouse, the sun was shining on the puddles, glistening in every drop that lingered on blades of grass or rolled down twigs. Trunks of trees were black with wet, but the sky was a deep clear blue and the only clouds that remained were puffs of white moving toward the faint blue of the eastern hills.

All of the Quaker community was there, from Hopewell and Center Meetings, from Crooked Run and even from distant Fairfax, as well as many people who were not Friends. In accordance with custom the interment took place in the graveyard before everybody gathered in the Meetinghouse for an hour or more of silence broken by messages. There was not room for all to sit down, and some stood at the back.

Caleb sat on the men's side of the house between his cousin Edward and Miers Fisher. Out of the corner of his eye he could see Loveday across the aisle, motionless and remote. Her hair was hidden under a bonnet and she was wearing a sober brown stuff dress and cloak which her aunt had brought her when she and Richard Parry arrived that morning, to attend the funeral and to take Loveday home afterward.

From the facing-benches, from the body of the Meeting, and even from the back where James Pemberton's man, Richard, and some of the other servants stood in the doorway, came an outpouring of expressions of love and respect for John Hunt. Even Caleb, who had been so close to him, was amazed by the number and variety of people who had been affected by the quality of his life. Many referred to the last time he had come to Monthly Meeting and his prophetic outburst then.

When dinner at Elizabeth Joliffe's was over, Caleb with a crowd of others saw the Parrys into their chariot. Except for Isaac Zane's it was the only four-wheeled carriage in the countryside and many of the gaping children had never seen such a marvel before. The roads were so bad that the occupants would probably have been far more comfortable on horseback, but it was generally felt to be a mark of respect both to the dead and to himself that Friend Parry had brought out his coach for this occasion.

If either Loveday's father or her aunt remembered Caleb's ridiculous behavior that humiliating day that now seemed so long ago, they gave no sign of it. They greeted him with impersonal kindliness and said a brief good-by. Loveday, who had avoided his eyes throughout the day, gave him at parting her full gaze and put a cold and tremulous little hand in his.

"Farewell, Caleb," she said. "I—I won't forget thee."

XXXIV

ON THE FOURTH DAY after leaving Winchester the cavalcade of the exiles approached York. Edward Penington, whom the months of banishment and his severe illness had turned into a broken old man, yellow and haggard of face and tremulous of hand, rode with Charles Eddy in his sulky; Israel and John Pemberton rode in Israel's chaise. The rest were all on horseback, their own or borrowed mounts. The baggage, which had filled four wagons on the way from Philadelphia, required only one wagon for the return. Much of it had been used up and worn out, much left behind to be sold or given away.

Caleb rode in silence beside one of the two officers sent by the Council to escort the group. The young man, who happened to be a cousin of his sister Sue's husband, had manifested from the beginning an attitude of reserve and disapproval, which had not been dispelled by the turn-out of Quakers all along the way to greet and congratulate the returning exiles, to welcome them into their houses and entertain them with a tender and admiring respect that might suitably be offered to a cross between sainted martyrs and victorious generals. The young officers, who detested neutrals even more than Tories and who regarded Quakers as tight-fisted and Jesuitical relics from former dark ages, were outraged. Lieutenant Lang had chosen to ride by Caleb, evidently regarding him, because of his respectable relations by marriage, as less sunk in darkness than the others, but even with Caleb he was stiff and silent. For his part Caleb, though he knew he could have won the young man over with the expenditure of a little effort, did not feel like taking the trouble. His heart was heavy and his thoughts were somber.

Except for a perfunctory question or two he did not even talk about

271

Sue and the Mercers. He knew that he would be seeing his sister in Lancaster and probably spending two of three days with her. He would find his stepmother there too. With Mrs. James Pemberton, Mrs. Pleasants, and Mrs. Drinker, Sarah Middleton had driven from Philadelphia with an "Address to the Congress and Council" and supplies of food, medicine and clothing for the exiles. They had intended to demand permission to go all the way to Winchester but when they had reached Lancaster, finding that the prisoners were already on the point of starting home, they settled down there to wait for them, applying themselves meanwhile to working for better terms of release for them. Caleb had had a triumphant letter from his stepmother and he was looking forward to seeing her with all the enthusiasm of which his sore heart was at the moment capable and much more than he would have thought possible a year ago.

They rode through the wide rich country with the blue bulk of the South Mountain behind them and all the glory of spring at its height spread out around them. The apple trees were in full bloom and dogwoods were greenish white with promise at the edge of the woods. Birds sang on fence posts or swooped across the road under the horses' noses in all the busy purpose of the mating season.

Every step of the way through the bridal world was taking Caleb farther from Loveday. During the final week in Winchester, when they were packing up and waiting for their escort to arrive, riding about to say their farewells to friends in town, to Isaac Zane, junior, to the Meeting families, the restrictions of the six mile limit had been forgotten. Caleb had ridden to the Parrys' house in an attempt to see Loveday once more, only to find that all the family had gone to Alexandria for a visit. The butler, recognizing Caleb, had invited him in to rest himself and had brought him a dish of tea. He sat in the room where he had sat before, looked out of the window on to the box-bordered garden where yellow cowslips and tall white narcissi were in bloom, and squirmed at the memory of that ludicrous and painful previous visit.

He had left with the butler a small package for Loveday, containing the gold love knot which he had had Goldsmith Chandlee make for him out of two of his unfortunate half-joes. He had put the pretty bauble away in his portmanteau and forgotten it until he took everything out to repack. It had been intended for Loveday from the beginning, and though he had not planned to give it to her as a gift upon her marriage to someone else, he certainly was not going to give it to any other girl. So he left the little box with the butler, wondering if Loveday would ever see it and what she would think if she did. It was a last gesture and, he had thought, riding away, it had fizzled out as flatly as every other effort in his relationship with Loveday. As flatly, in fact, he thought now, riding through the rich Pennsylvania farmland, as every other effort in all of his life. He looked back upon his twenty-three years and saw them as a futile groping in the dark, a series of failures and lost turnings. "We are all exiles," John Hunt had said once, "trying to get back to our true home."

He missed John Hunt and thought it an added turn of the screw that he should have died just before their release came—like Moses barred from the Promised Land. Although, Caleb reminded himself, they had no idea, really, what lay ahead of them: a trial and the opportunity to clear themselves, or only the test oath and renewed imprisonment, or perhaps a nominal release and the confiscation of their property.

The first report, in the letter from Mr. Harvie, had said they were to be brought to trial. The next, a Resolution of the Council dated April eighth, ordered that they be brought to Shippensburg "and there enlarged," at the same time being informed of a law recently passed by which persons going into British-held Philadelphia "on any pretense whatsoever" without obtaining written permission from General Washington, the Congress, or the Council, were liable to fine and imprisonment. Furthermore, the Council ordered that the whole expense of arresting and confining the prisoners, the expenses of their journey to Virginia and all other incidental charges were to be paid by the said prisoners. This blast was followed several days later by a letter from Timothy Matlack, the Secretary of the Council, friendly in tone, saying that at the request of Phoebe Pemberton, Sarah Middleton, Mary Pleasants, and Eliza Drinker, the place of their release had been changed from Shippensburg to Lancaster, which, he pointed out, was greatly in their favor.

The fact that the four women had had a chance to present their Address and that it had had some result was a good omen, and Caleb, turning away from the past as he saw the spire of a church pricking into the sky above the trees ahead, began to look forward to the future with some feeling of pleasure.

York, which had been a pleasant and flourishing village a few years earlier, had grown overnight into a hobbledehoy of a town, with the influx of Congressmen, their wives, and all the men who follow a Congress in search of favors or the hope of a good stroke of business. As they crossed the bridge over Codorus Creek, Lieutenant Lang pointed out the house where Tom Paine lived and a little later, at the corner of Market and Beaver Streets, the building where Mr. Franklin's press printed the Continental bills. Caleb looked with some interest at the source of the money the value of which he had been accused of attempting to depreciate by having his half-joes changed in Lancaster instead of Winchester. He would have been grateful if they had printed an extra roll for him now. When he had paid Elizabeth Joliffe's almost painfully moderate charges for himself and his mare during all the months of warm and generous hospitality, small as the sum was it left almost nothing in his pocket. He hoped that his stepmother had come well provided.

They reached George Updegraff's ordinary and rode into the yard. Caleb dismounted and led Ladybird into the stable, where he unsaddled, fed, and watered her himself, since there were not enough stableboys to take care of so many horses at once. He went into the house, which was large and cool, dim after the bright light outside, and hunted up a place to wash his hands and brush his coat. When he came downstairs again he found the rest of his party receiving a caller in the parlor. From the stir in the room he knew that their guest was a man of some consequence, but even when the group parted and he saw a tall genial man in a Continental uniform with a general's epaulets he had no idea who it was.

"Friend Gates," said Edward Penington, obstinately Quaker to the last ditch, "I should like to present my cousin, Caleb Middleton, junior."

Caleb met the hero of Saratoga and the President of the Board of

War with interest. There had been much talk and rumor about him during the winter, which had drifted even as far as Quaker circles in Winchester. He was known to have criticized Washington bitterly for slackness and inaction and it was widely inferred that he considered himself a suitable person to take over Washington's job. The committee sent to Valley Forge to investigate the Commander-in-Chief had, however, brought back a favorable report. But Gates's position as President of the Board of War with permission to serve in the field, so that he was Washington's superior and yet at the same time under his command, must have been a severe trial to Washington. Caleb, who had been deeply impressed by the nobility of General Washington's person and bearing that day of the march-through last August, regarded Horatio Gates with reserve and wondered just why he was going out of his way now to conciliate the Quaker exiles from Philadelphia.

"If I had been in Philadelphia at the time of your being arrested and sent into exile," he said suavely, "I should have prevented it."

Then why, Caleb asked silently, didn't you exert your influence this winter to bring us to trial? That was all we asked.

"We have just had intelligence from London," the General continued, "that will no doubt be pleasing to you who have the peace as well as the prosperity of this country so much at heart. The Parliament of Great Britain has passed Resolutions, by which they will repeal several of the Acts oppressive to America. They have appointed commissioners to come to this country to treat with us and settle the unhappy contest." He stopped, as if waiting for a burst of joy and approval.

"This is indeed good news," said Israel Pemberton cautiously, "if all is as favorable as it appears to be. I should like to know more—what Acts the Parliament is ready to repeal, how much power to negotiate will be given to the commissioners, and with what disposition the Congress is prepared to receive them."

"I think that this time Great Britain has agreed to all that the Americans have hitherto asked or contended for, but of course we have had only a preliminary report. We shall have to await further intelligence from the commissioners themselves. But I thought you would find it heartening. I hope that the conditions of your exile have not been too severe."

"We have had much to be thankful for," said John Pemberton, "especially when I think of the sufferings of the primitive Friends, who were beaten and branded and imprisoned in foul dungeons with not even straw to lie upon. We have indeed been favored by divine support and on the whole preserved from murmuring."

"My dear sir," the General waved his hand deprecatingly, "those persecutions you mention were more than a century ago. Even in England such things are unheard of today, and this is America. Was your journey hither made without mishap or inconvenience?"

"It was very comfortable, thank thee." Samuel Pleasants now took up the thread of the conversation. "We have come to York on our way to Lancaster, and most of us intend to spend tonight here, to rest our horses. But some would like to press on today without waiting for the guard to accompany them, if thou approves of it. I do not know if we require a pass for that purpose?"

"It might perhaps be just as well to have one, in case you encounter some overzealous militia." The General turned to the desk, where he found a sheet of paper and a quill of which he complained humorously. He scratched a line or two, sanded it, and gave it to Sammy. "That will get you past any scouting parties or the like. There is another matter. The wind has been very high at the Susquehanna ferry. I'll have my aide give you an order to Major Eyre, who is commanding officer there, to assist you over, if that should be necessary." With a further cheerful assurance of good will, he departed, and a little later a messenger came from his headquarters next door with a note for Major Eyre at Wright's Ferry.

Since the day was already half spent and Lancaster was twenty-four miles away with a wind-blown river to cross, most of the group decided to remain where they were for the night. Caleb with Sammy Pleasants and James Pemberton, whose wives were waiting for them in Lancaster, decided to go on immediately after dinner.

They were grateful for General Gates's letter when they reached the ferry, for the wind was high and the public boats all hugged the opposite shore. Four ship carpenters, who were building boats for the

American service, put them across, and Major Eyre, on the far side, sent the ferryboat back for their horses. The whole process took close to two hours, and it was after suppertime when at length the three reached the town which had been the Pennsylvania capital for the last six months. Caleb's companions parted from him at the main street. Their wives were lodging with a Quaker family on the Sadsbury Road beyond the town and they rode on eagerly.

The sun had set and candles were lit when Caleb reached the house under the big oaks where Sarah Middleton was staying with Sue and her parents-in-law. The sound of horses' hooves brought all the family to the door, and Caleb, seeing their joy and feeling the genuine warmth of their affection, was happy for the first time since he started on his homeward trip.

Sue with her lusty son on her arm and another baby already expected was the embodiment of happy and fruitful young womanhood. She was tall, with flashing brown eyes, more nose than chin, and a loud, cheerful voice.

Caleb kissed her and kissed the soft fluff on the top of the baby's head, and turned to his stepmother, who embraced him, crying, "Caleb, I can hardly believe we've really got you at last! It seems too good to be true!"

Square, squat, hairy, almost bursting out of her fashionable silk gown, she beamed at him in self-forgetting delight. For the first time he saw beyond her homely exterior to the robust beauty within.

"It was good of thee to come, Mother. How's Father?"

"Better. Very eager to see you. He can hardly wait. This winter has been a great trial to him, but he has been remarkably patient—all things considered. Let me look at you, Caleb. You're thinner—more mature—but I do believe that you're taller and handsomer than ever. How far have you ridden today? You must be tired and hungry and I keep you standing here. Come in, come in."

Sue's husband was with Washington at Valley Forge. His father was a prosperous lawyer, his mother the daughter of a New York merchant. Their house in Lancaster had all the comforts and elegancies of city living. There were plenty of well-trained servants. A neat nurse-maid came to take the baby after his uncle had admired him sufficiently, a man in dark livery brought Caleb supper in the big dining room where candlelight winked on glass prisms and on china with small prim flowers and gold borders, and the paneled walls were painted a cool green.

After Caleb had eaten his fill, he and Sarah and Sue sat in what was called the Blue Parlor talking till late.

Sarah was jubilant over the success of the ladies' mission. "If it hadn't been for us," she pointed out, "you'd have been turned loose in Shippensburg to find your way home without passes, liable to be taken up and imprisoned and fined at any time. You still haven't got passes, but you're in Lancaster where you can attend to that."

"What we want is to hear the charges and speak in our own defense."

"You'll have to arrange that for yourselves! We've done all we could!"

"You've done a great deal and we're all thankful to you. How did it come about?"

"It was my idea in the first place. I thought of it way back in January when we didn't know where you were. I thought we would just go to General Washington and plead with him for your freedom. I went to Mrs. Drinker about it and she thought we ought to go to Congress, but that we'd better wait. So we waited—*and* waited—till we got word that you were sick and Edward and others and that your stores of tea and medicines were all used up and then we thought we'd go all the way to Winchester. We had a number of meetings with other wives in various houses. Then we heard that Mr. Gilpin died—wasn't that too bad, such a good man, and three young children! The weighty Friends had to sit on it—you know how it is—and in the end the four of us came in Polly Pleasants' coach. Mrs. Israel Pemberton would have liked to come, but she is seventy-four—did you know that? Twelve years older than her husband! She doesn't look it. Where was I? Oh, Mr. Israel Morris accompanied us on horseback. We felt rather doubtful about him, especially Eliza. She was determined that he was not to do our talking for us with the Council. But he has really been very helpful."

"But how did you get through the American lines?"

"Oh, we went straight to headquarters at Valley Forge and asked General Washington for permission."

"Did you see the General himself?"

"We certainly did. He invited us to dinner, and we had an elegant dinner with him and General Lee and General Greene and fifteen other officers. Mrs. Washington was there too. She's a pretty, sociable kind of woman. General Washington gave us a pass to go through the lines and a letter to President Wharton saying we wanted permission to go to Winchester and protection for the coach, and then he wrote, *'Humanity itself pleads in their behalf.'* He couldn't have written much more strongly than that, could he?"

"It takes a big man to take time for the troubles of people who aren't of any importance to him," said Caleb thoughtfully.

"It took us four days to get here. We spent the nights with Quaker families along the way. How you Friends do rally round each other! It is like belonging to an enormous family with a very strong sense of family duty and unity. I don't think other churches are like that. I shouldn't expect strangers to lodge and feed me just because I am an Episcopalian. The roads were unspeakable. The armies marching over them have cut them up and then the rains added to the mess. We didn't see the sun for a week. We were out of the coach almost as much as we were in it. In one place we climbed three fences to get around the mud. And when we forded Conestoga Creek the water came right into the coach and wet our feet. I thought we should be caught in the coach and drowned like rats."

"I think they were very brave," said Sue. "I should have been terrified."

"They *were* brave. The whole thing was brave. Did you have any trouble seeing the Council when you got here?"

"Wait till you hear about that! We went straight to Mr. Wharton's door. We were admitted right away, but there were a number of others present, so we asked to see him alone, but he said he was just going out to coffee. He was wearing his sword. They say he wears it all the time, morning, noon, and night, isn't that ridiculous? So we had to wait till the next day. Timothy Matlack came to see us and advise us. He appears very obliging, but I fear it is from the teeth outward. He has that brick house you passed before you turned the corner to come here. We had a dish of tea with his wife, who seemed very glad to see us. She and Polly Pleasants are old friends. One of the members of the Council lives with the Matlacks and we talked to him and two others. Mr. Matlack took our Address to the Council meeting and said he would come back for us. We waited an hour and then he came and said our presence was not necessary. Not necessary! Just putting us off. I was real cross because I thought we should do better if we talked to them ourselves. But they did change the orders from Shippensburg to Lancaster. We knew by that time, of course, that you were going to be released and there was no need for us to go to Winchester."

"What was in your Address? Did you keep a copy of it?"

"Yes. Sue, what did I do with it? We wrote it in Philadelphia before we left. Everybody had a hand in it. Such a to-do you can't imagine. All the ministers and elders or whatever you call them had to look at it and the time they spent haggling over a word here and a word there! But we stuck to our own ideas and said what we wanted to say ourselves. We all signed it, all the wives of the prisoners and three mothers and the Fishers' sister Esther. Thank you, dear. Here, Caleb, read it for yourself."

"It's shorter than the ones we wrote," commented Caleb, running his eye down the page. " 'The melancholy account we have lately received of the indisposition of our beloved husbands and children, and that the awful messenger—death—has made an inroad on one of their number—' That was Thomas Gilpin, I suppose. Haven't you heard about John Hunt?"

"Not till after we got here. That was very sad. You liked him especially, didn't you?"

"He was the best of us all. This is a good point. 'This application to you is entirely an act of our own. We have not consulted our absent friends.' " He read it to the end, folded it, and returned it to Sarah. "It's a very strong appeal, better than most of ours. Have you heard anything about peace Resolutions in the British Parliament and the commissioners who are to come over to treat with America? General Gates was full of it when we saw him today in York."

"Oh, that's been all over the town these two days. There's nothing to it. The British will grant everything—they say—except independence, and the Congress will not yield on that, especially now that the French have made an alliance with us and recognized Mr. Franklin as the ambassador from a free country. Hadn't you heard that? It has been common property for a week or more. They are waiting for some final official word before it is to be publicly celebrated throughout the land."

Caleb heard this with excitement. Recognition, and a promise of help from a powerful ally! It marked a point from which there could be no going back, no possibility of accommodation with Great Britain now. The struggle for independence would be carried through to its conclusion and to—it must be—ultimate victory. The feeble, scattered little army, the discredited Congress, the divided people were committed before the world to make a reality of the nationhood which they had assumed. They could no longer return like a child to its father's tyrannical but protective care; they must win their way through to independent life, however bitter the suffering.

The rest of the exiles came to Lancaster the following morning, which was Saturday, and the group found a central and convenient meeting place in the Mercers' parlor. They appointed a committee consisting of Israel Pemberton, Henry Drinker, and, to his own surprise, Caleb Middleton, junior, to go to President Thomas Wharton. Thomas Wharton, senior, was at first named but he declined saying that his relations with his cousin would in no way be conducive to the success of the mission.

The three waited on Thomas Wharton, junior, after dinner. They found him alone, wearing, Caleb noted with amusement, his sword. He did not look well; his eyes were dull and his complexion had a gray cast; he seemed to be hearing and seeing them from a long distance. Though he had known Israel Pemberton and Henry Drinker well over long years of association, he greeted them impersonally.

Israel Pemberton spoke first. "We have come to acquaint thee with the fact of our being come to Lancaster, agreeably to the appointment of Council."

"So I have been informed by Mr. Matlack. Pray be seated."

"We should like to have an interview with the Council," said Henry

Drinker. "We are ready to answer any charges that they have against us—and presumably they have some reason why they felt justified in depriving us of our liberty and keeping us in exile for so long."

"The Council has adjourned until Monday morning. I will deliver your message to them when they meet, but I recommend to you that you put in writing whatever you think necessary to say to them. I know that they will not grant you a personal interview."

He spoke civilly enough, but there was nothing further to be said. Heavily they made their farewells and went down the street under a shower of tassels falling from oak trees in blossom.

After Meeting for worship the next morning in the Meetinghouse, they got a word with Timothy Matlack, who, to the surprise of local Friends, had attended Meeting for the first time in years.

"The Council won't see you," he said. "It's no use expecting it. But I'll see that your Memorial is read, if it's short."

They composed their final appeal to the Council that afternoon, the last of a long line of Remonstrances, Addresses, and Memorials. This one at least was short, whittled down to the bare minimum. For the last time Caleb made a fair copy and they all signed it, sixteen now instead of twenty.

To the President and Council of Pennsylvania:

We, the subscribers, inhabitants of the city of Philadelphia, having been there arrested and banished to Winchester in Virginia by your authority, upon groundless suspicions, without any offense being laid to our charge; and being now brought to this place by your messenger after a captivity of near eight months, think it our duty to apply to you to be reinstated in the full enjoyment of the liberty of which we have been so long deprived. We are your real friends, Thomas Fisher, etc.

The committee took the Memorial to the inn where the Council met and having delivered it to the secretary sat down in an anteroom to wait, on the chance that they might even yet be admitted to face their accusers. At the end of two hours Colonel Matlack appeared.

"The subject matter of your Memorial has been debated," he reported, "and the Council has ordered that you be sent to Pottsgrove and there discharged from confinement. You will be furnished with a copy of the Resolution, which will be deemed a discharge, and also with a pass for each one of you permitting you to pass unmolested into the County of Philadelphia. This will complete the matter. I must add emphatically that any further application on the subject is unnecessary. The Council will not hear you."

A moment of incredulous silence followed.

"But this," exclaimed Israel Pemberton indignantly, "is manifestly unjust and unreasonable. This order is to be *deemed* a discharge. It contains no acknowledgment of our innocence, no statement restoring us to full liberty. You have violently separated us from our families, unjustly detained us in exile, and now at the end, as in the beginning, you refuse to hear us in our own defense!"

"I can only repeat, sir, any further application will be useless. I beg of you not to attempt it. It would only take your time to no purpose and that of the Council, who have affairs of public importance to attend to."

"There is nothing we can say that will move you?"

"Nothing. The passes will be delivered to you at your lodgings. The escort is ready to accompany you to Pottsgrove."

It was freedom at last, thought Caleb, but what a shabby freedom.

"Colonel Matlack," he said, detaining him as he prepared to return to the Council room, "the government of Pennsylvania and of the United States is based upon principles of freedom and resistance to tyranny and oppression, is it not?"

"I think it is not necessary for me to answer that, Mr. Middleton."

They looked at one another squarely. It crossed Caleb's mind that Timothy Matlack eight months earlier had done him the favor of substituting his name for his father's and perhaps now expected some acknowledgment. He let the thought slip past, intent on what he had in his mind to say. Long ago he had ceased to think of himself as his father's substitute, so completely had he identified himself with the others and with the fundamental truths on which they had taken their stand.

"How do you reconcile these principles of liberty and justice with the treatment that has been accorded us?"

"Mr. Middleton, in an internecine struggle for existence there can be no neutrals."

"You should know—and Thomas Wharton, junior, and others who are or have been Friends—that since Quakers cannot conscientiously fight for you they are equally debarred from fighting against you. But there is a principle at stake more important than what happens to a handful of Quakers, and that is whether a government based upon freedom can live if it does not guarantee to its citizens freedom of conscience and protection against imprisonment without the chance of defending themselves."

Timothy Matlack, who was known for the violence of his temper, made a quick gesture with his hand indicating that he had heard all this before and that his patience was nearing an end.

"No, please, let me finish. This is of the utmost importance to me because I have vital decisions to make. We have been standing out for eight months for a principle, the basic principle of civil and religious liberty. Two of our group have died. I have thought that the government of the United States was based upon the same principle, but if the Congress and the Council do not recognize that it even enters into our case, what am I to think of the future of our country?"

The look of anger on Matlack's long, heavy face softened to one of understanding and even sympathy for Caleb's passionate earnestness.

"I understand what you are driving at. You are young, Mr. Middleton, and idealistic, but you must not expect perfection of men and politicians under great stress. An open and free statement of error in a private person is becoming. It is otherwise when governments make mistakes; you must not expect an apology. Governments, though they must appear infallible, are made up after all of ordinary, faulty, harassed men who are in the main striving to do their best for their country. If the result is a little more than half good, that is perhaps as much as we can expect. The only way to increase the proportion is for more men of vision and devotion to offer their services to their country. But this I will tell you for your enlightenment and comfort: when the Council decided to ask the Congress to return the Virginia exiles to our jurisdiction in order to release them, it did so because—and this is spread upon the records of the Congress— 'the dangerous example which their longer continuance in banishment may afford on future occasions has already given uneasiness to some good friends to the independency of these States.' Does that remove any of your doubts?"

"I see," said Caleb soberly. "Thank you."

It was not very much, not what he had expected. But as he turned over in his mind this inadequate, elliptical, almost casual expression of the reason for the Council's decision, upon which the Congress had acted, he came to feel that it was of value, that it was perhaps all that he ought to have expected, and enough to go on with. It represented an action taken for a particular occasion, to avoid a bad precedent, rather than a statement of an enduring principle. Yet perhaps it was only by particular acts that general principles could ever be established, and then not once but over and over again. And in the building and preserving of a nation's freedom both kinds of citizens had their essential part: individuals determined to follow their consciences at cost to themselves and against the drift of public opinion, without expecting exoneration and praise at the end; and faulty, harassed men in government striving in the main to serve their country's interests, correcting mistakes as best they could as they went along.

XXXV

LOVEDAY CLOSED HER BEDROOM door carefully and pressed against it until the latch caught with a little click. She was home again. She had said good-night to her father and Aunt Mary; she had thanked Nannie for unpacking her portmanteau and shooed her out of the room. She was alone for the first time in more than two weeks.

Visiting, you are never alone. In Alexandria, at Cousin Anna and Cousin John's, she had shared a room with Aunt Mary, and in the daytime Griffith was always with her. He had so much to show here and to tell her and to teach here, for he was twelve years older than she, that he filled every minute with a flow of talk. "If thee's got a minute, Loveday," he said over and over, like a refrain, "I want thee to see the secretary that Father had made for me when I was fourteen. I wrote my first brief at that desk." Or, "Don't run away. Thee has plenty of time to dress for Meeting. We have a minute now, and I want to explain to thee how a lawyer's wife can help him—"

The only time she was alone in that house, thought Loveday with a little gulp of laughter, was when she was in the necessary. It was a very splendid one, of brick, with a little fan doorway, but one couldn't stay there forever.

Her room looked simple and country-like after the house in Alexandria, the mantel unadorned, the floor bare, with only a little braided mat by the bed, the bed-curtains of white muslin, hemmed, without fringe, the chest of drawers made of cherry wood from their own trees by an itinerant cabinetmaker, gleaming softly in the candlelight but with none of the carvings or the shiny brass handles of the chest-on-chest in Cousin Anna's spare bedroom. But Nannie had put a spray of apple blossom in the blue vase on the table and its delicate fragrance mingled with the faint spicy odor of the pomander hanging on the bedpost; the bed had been turned down and her nightgown and slippers laid out; the room was welcoming and spacious and suddenly so dear that she did not want to leave it, ever.

The three days in the coach, bumped and jolted and tossed over rough roads, fell away, and the two weeks of visiting, of company manners and endless appreciation, of paying attention to everything Griffith said, fell away too. Griffith was a great talker, much more than she had realized. Or perhaps it was only because he felt he had to make her understand everything about him before they were married, and there was so little time. He talked so much and so fast—she took off her dress, the brown one she had worn to dear John Hunt's funeral, and laid it thoughtfully over a chair—and he seemed to get so excited over it, that he was just a little bit exhausting.

She had wanted to tell him about dear John Hunt, for though she was young and there was very little in her life that was interesting, she had known—had nursed—had loved a rare and beautiful character, and had sat beside him when he died. She had, being close to him, undergone some change, some enlargement of her own spirit, and all her life something of John Hunt would shape her words and thoughts. Perhaps it was because of him and the sorrow that she felt for him that she carried a heaviness of heart like a stone inside her, and not all the plans for the wedding or for the home they would build could lift its weight from her. She had tried several times to tell Griffith about John Hunt, but always he had interrupted her, intent on expressing some thought of his own.

"Griffith, if thee has a minute," she had said at last, playfully but with determination adopting his own favorite phrase, "I want to tell thee about John Hunt. Oh, I *wish* thee could have known him. He was so gentle but so—so penetrating—"

"Thee mustn't be morbid," he had said, kissing her. "When we are married thee is not to nurse anybody but me—and of course our children."

He was always kissing her. She poured water from the flowered pitcher into the basin and washed her face, which was suddenly heated by the memory of Griffith's kisses. She felt ashamed. His lips were so soft and so wet—squashy. (Caleb's lips were hard and searching and piercingly sweet. But she must not think of that.)

She scrubbed her face dry with the towel. Yes, she thought with a rebellious rush, and Caleb was lean and lithe, while Griffith already had a settled look. Oh, he was a fine, tall, well-favored man, of course, but he spent too much of his time sitting, and when he walked his coattails bulged rhythmically.

But she was going to marry Griffith. They were going to have the whole second floor of the ell in Cousin Anna and Cousin John's house, with Griffith's secretary in the sitting room and Griffith's wing chair and his books and his diploma from William and Mary and his maps and his charts and the instruments that he explained to her over and over and she still couldn't understand. He knew a great deal about ships and navigation and he was going to specialize in maritime law. In the fall they would begin to build their own house on a lot which his father had given him, which had a fine view of the Potomac River.

The ponderous wheels of a Quaker marriage had already begun to turn. They had "passed Meeting" once. They had written to the Monthly Meeting at Crooked Run declaring their intention to marry. Griffith's parents and Loveday's father had written letters conveying their consent. A committee had been appointed to visit both and ascertain their "clearness." At the next Monthly Meeting the committee would make its report, and overseers would be appointed to have charge over the wedding itself. The date was tentatively set for Sixth Month twenty-first.

The soft cambric folds of her nightgown descended over her head and fell around her slim body. She pulled her blue wool dressing gown around her, for the spring evening was chilly. She was not ready to go to bed yet. She would brush her hair a hundred times and she would say her prayers properly. How could anyone say her prayers right with Aunt Mary in the room, reading a chapter of the Bible and shutting the book with a slap, plumping down on her knees, and beginning to talk about closing the window and blowing out the candle almost before she opened her eyes and heaved herself, gasping, to her feet again?

What was "clearness," exactly? To the committee it meant, evidently, that they had not given promises to anyone else. So that she was "clear" as to Griffith but obviously not clear for Caleb. And she had told him so and he was to forget her and she was to forget him. She was not to think of his deep-set brown eyes gleaming with laughter or clouded with pain, or of his thin, skillful, long-fingered hands (Griffith's fingers were short and stubby) or of his tenderness and strength as he lifted John Hunt, or—She was not to think of Caleb.

But she did think of Caleb. If it were not for her constant, vigilant control of her thoughts she would be thinking of him all the time, and wasn't that also a sin against clearness, the more deadly because it was secret and hidden?

There was a tap at the door and before Loveday could say, "Come in," Aunt Mary in her gray dressing gown with her night-cap tied under her chin, had swept into the room. She had a cup in one hand and a teaspoon in the other.

"Loveday, isn't thee in bed yet?"

"No, I'm brushing my hair."

"I've brought thee a dose of sulphur and molasses. Thy father and I both think thee looks peaked, and there's nothing like sulphur and molasses for clearing the blood in the spring. Now don't make a fuss, dear, just take it right down, and thee'll feel better tomorrow."

The gritty stuff, sweet in a nasty way, stuck to Loveday's lips and tongue as she obediently spooned it from the cup and swallowed it. She got some water from the washstand to take the taste away and handed the cup and spoon back to Aunt Mary, smiling at her affectionately—and pityingly. Poor Aunt Mary, she thought, forty at least. Once she had married and loved, or thought she had, and had a little baby that never lived, and lost her husband, all so long ago that she had forgotten it and now thought there was nothing like sulphur and molasses.

"Hop into bed, Loveday, and I'll tuck thee in."

Loveday wielded her hairbrush. "Sixty-seven, sixty-eight, sixty-nine," she counted, choosing numbers large enough to suggest that she had brushed enough already to make it worth while to con-

tinue to the hundred mark, yet small enough to make it desirable for
her to get on with the job if it was not to take all night.

"Thy hair's very well as it is, it's thy face that needs help. Thee has
dark shadows under thy eyes and thee's had no color in thy cheeks for
days. Thee needs a good night's sleep now. Is anything worrying
thee?"

"Seventy, seventy-one, seventy-two," continued Loveday, sweetly
obstinate, as she could be.

"Well, if thee's going to be like that, there's nothing more for me to
say."

Loveday flung the brush on the bed and ran to hug her aunt, fairly
strangling her in a fiercely affectionate, silent embrace.

"Mercy!" said Mary Freame, returning it was well as she could, impeded by the cup and spoon. "Girls!" she muttered helplessly, finding
herself on the other side of the door. "I'm certainly thankful I don't
have to go through being young again."

Gathering her robe around her and abandoning the brush and the
prayers, Loveday swung herself up onto the broad sill of the west window and clasped her arms around her knees. It was raining outside, a
gentle spring rain falling on the leaves of the ivy, splashing a little now
and then on the sill. She could see the wet splashing a little now and
then on the sill. She could see the wet gleam of the branches of the big
oak, still bare, though there was a softening pattern of tassels and
swelling leaves against the cloudy sky.

There were none of the town sounds that she had grown accustomed to: the footsteps on the sidewalk, the creak of a wheel, the
sound of voices. She heard only the patter of the rain and a familiar,
half-forgotten, almost mechanical noise, as of a saw cutting through
wood or a clock being wound in the distance, over and over, with
pauses in between. The monkey-faced owls were bringing up their
young in the big oak again.

If only, thought Loveday, drawing her knees up close under her
chin, she could recapture the feeling she had had when she and Griffith were first engaged, go back over the months to that time which
had seemed so magical and which now appeared remote and unreal.

They had gone to Grandfather's plantation near Alexandria at Christmastime, she and Father and Aunt Mary, and Griffith had been there, part of a big family gathering. Friends did not pay very much attention to Christmas as a general rule, but last Twelfth Month twenty-sixth was Grandfather's seventieth birthday, and all the relatives had rallied round. There were swarms of children always on the run, from the hay barn to the attic, the big ones ahead, the little ones puffing behind, but for the first time Loveday had not been with them. Everyone had had something to say about Loveday's having grown up. She moved sedately in a whole new world, suddenly on the same level with Cousin Griffith, who had always seemed to her a superior being.

He was tall and fair-haired and substantial, not only in his person but in his mind and in his position in the world. He had been to the college at Williamsburg, he had traveled for a year in England and France, he had read law in Alexandria, and he had won his first case. But still he was a plain Friend, sober in his dress and speech, beginning to take a part in the Monthly Meeting. On First Day at Meeting for worship, he had risen to give a message and he had spoken modestly, as became a young man, yet with the assurance of one who spoke not in his own voice but as a channel for the Spirit.

Thinking of him now, recalling him as she saw him then, Loveday could remember her feeling of awe and excitement when he spoke to her after Meeting, gravely yet urgently, and asked her if she would take a walk with him after dinner.

It had been a mild winter day, with a little color lingering in the leaves that still clung to the oaks and a few sweet limp roses still in the garden. They had taken the favorite First Day afternoon walk of courting couples, down to the creek and across the bridge, and back through the woods and over the west field to the end of the garden. There were a few chestnuts in brown burrs on the ground, and blue jays and redbirds flashed their brilliant way among the bushes in the garden.

Speaking slowly and in a hushed sort of voice that made the occasion very solemn, Griffith told her that he had loved her ever since she was a little girl of ten with her golden curls flying as he pushed her in the swing that used to hang from the big maple tree—did she remember? He had known then that she was the only girl for him and he had vowed to wait for her to grow up. Now she was sixteen and old enough to be married. Did she think she could care for him?

The wonder of it! Cousin Griffith, so important, so respected, so wise and good, noticing little Loveday Parry from the other side of the Blue Ridge, waiting six long years for her, asking her so tenderly and so humbly if she could care for him!

He had kissed her, reverently, gently, lightly as if a kitten's paw had touched her lips—not at all as he kissed her now—and they had gone at once to talk to Father.

Father had not been surprised. He had long thought something of the kind might happen. He was fond of Griffith, he thought it eminently suitable. True, Griffith was twelve years older than Loveday, but he himself had been ten years older than Loveday's mother, and no marriage could have been happier than theirs. His only objection was that Loveday was too young. "I counted on having my little girl a few years more."

At the thought of leaving Father lonely and deserted, Loveday was ready to abjure marriage altogether, but Griffith began to speak, in his persuasive, reasoning voice. He had waited six years already, he was twenty-eight, it was time he established himself in life.

Father had promised to reconsider after Loveday had had a little more time to think it over, but somehow before the day was out everybody knew that Loveday and Griffith were to be married in Sixth Month, and the joyful interest in their engagement had almost put Grandfather's seventieth birthday in the shade.

She could remember how it felt, every minute of it, her happiness, her admiring love for Griffith, her humble and wondering gratefulness because he had chosen her and had waited all those years when she was so unconscious and careless—but she could not feel it again. She could only feel that odd heaviness inside, as if she had eaten some sad pastry. It was as if a veil hung between those happy, innocent days and now, a veil made of her sense of guilt because she had begun to pick flaws in Griffith, who was just as splendid as he had been before, and because she could not forget Caleb, who had laughed at her and

teased her, who for a week had been almost a part of herself as they together loved and served dear John Hunt.

Feeling cramped and chilly and a little drowsy, she thought that
now she might be able to go to sleep. But as soon as she got into bed
she was wide awake again, and her thoughts were racing.

Marriage, she knew, was not all new house and kisses and passing
Meeting. It was also bed, where something happened which was in-
delicate if thought about beforehand but sacred when the right time
came. She would die of embarrassment, getting into bed with Griffith!

She rolled over and the happy realization came to her that for the
first time in over two weeks she had her bed to herself, without Aunt
Mary. The thought was so exhilarating that she stretched herself
crosswise in the wide bed and let her head hang over the side, her hair
falling down to the floor behind her. The rain kept dripping outside
and the monkey-faced owls continued to grind out their peculiar, sad,
mysterious noises.

What she must do, she thought with sudden energy, resuming her
normal position in bed, was to see Caleb again. Today was Fifth Day.
They must go to Meeting at Hopewell on First Day. There had been
some talk, she remembered of the prisoners' being released, or promised a chance to defend themselves, but it had been quite vague; it
would take time before they could really get away.

She would see him again, and then she would know.

So now she could go to sleep.

She straightened her nightgown, thumped the pillows, pulled the
covers up to her chin, and closed her eyes. Downstairs the big clock
struck twelve.

The first time she had seen Caleb, the very first, was that day at Edward Preston's, before little Neddie died. It was raining then too. She
had gone to the door to let the doctor in, and Caleb had been standing
there. That picture of Caleb was quite different from all the others in
her mind, because it was the first, and so a little separate, and very distinct. She had seen someone young and tall, with broad shoulders,
brown eyes intent and shining but not glittery as some brown eyes

were, soft, with depth, and a straight nose and smiling mouth, a square-cut chin, very clean and firm.

"I'm not a doctor," he had said, "I'd give anything if I were."

She had felt his sorrow.

Out in the kitchen, when she fetched the cider, he had taken liberties with her curls, and so she had not come down again after Catherine Preston had called up upstairs. But that was his way, teasing, admiring. No one had teased her before. She had to learn how to take it. Even when John Hunt was so ill, Caleb had teased her.

John Hunt loved Caleb. It was in his eyes and his voice, in his veined, transparent, trembling hand as he lifted it to touch Caleb's arm.

But she was going too fast. That was much later. She had seen Caleb at the Prestons', and then that day he had come here to see her, that *funny* time—

The clock struck again, but whether it was twelve-thirty or one or one-thirty, she did not know. She heard it strike two and three and four. She was afloat now on a broad stream and she had no wish to pull herself to land. When she had recalled every time she had seen Caleb and everything he said, every look and gesture, then she began to dream other times of seeing him, imagining what he said and what she said, up to the moment when his arms went around her. Some of the scenes she went over twice, they were so lovely. Some she improved on the second run. Once she pictured a beautiful scene of renunciation and sacrifice, when she told Caleb farewell and returned to Griffith, but that was too painful and she revised it, with Griffith simply non-existent, in the comfortable way of fantasy.

All the time, as the hours and the half-hours ticked away, her body was light and taut and vibrant, like a violin string. She was not in the least tired and had no need of sleep.

Sleep she did, though, just as the night turned gray, and when she awoke the sunlight was brilliant in squares on the dark honey-colored floor and Aunt Mary was calling her to breakfast.

She was tired now, she thought, as she hurried into her clothes, so tired that she ached and felt cross. She could tell by their quick looks of surprise and concern as she slipped into her place a few minutes later, that Father and Aunt Mary were quite aware of the turmoil within her. They had waited "silence" for her, and as she bowed her head her prayer was not one of gratitude for the home food, plentiful and fragrant, on the table, but a plea that they would stop noticing her.

Her prayer was answered. Neither Father not Aunt Mary seemed to see her at all, and the talk at the table ran cheerfully on the subject of the garden and the wood robins, which had returned and were whistling sweetly on every side.

When breakfast was over they pushed back their chairs a little from the table and Joseph brought the Bible and placed it before Father. Joseph and Nannie and Hess and little Elijah filed in and sat down in a row against the wall. Father opened the Bible and began to read from the Book of Ruth, where they had left off when they went to Alexandria. The names rolled over Loveday's head, Elimelech, Mahlon and Chilion, Orpah and Ruth and Naomi.

" 'And Ruth said, Intreat me not to leave thee, or to return from following after thee; for whither thou goest, I will go; and where thou lodgest, I will lodge; thy people shall be my people, and thy God my God; where thou diest, will I die, and there will I be buried: the Lord do so to me, and more also, if ought but death part thee and me.' "

She knew the words were said by a widow to her mother-in-law, but they struck at her heart as the inevitable promise of a girl to the man she loved, words which she herself could never say to Griffith but would offer to Caleb with her whole being.

The reading was finished, the Bible laid aside, the family settled into the customary few minutes of silence before starting the affairs of the day. Loveday closed her eyes tight, but still the hot tears squeezed under her lids and rolled down her cheeks. She put up a finger hastily to wipe them away, hoping desperately that no one had seen.

The servants rose and went out. Richard Parry nodded to his sister and she too slipped away without a word. He turned to Loveday, who gave him a bright, determined smile.

"Lovey," he said gently, "what's the matter? What is troubling thee?"

She blinked rapidly and swallowed, unable to speak.

"If thee doesn't want to marry Griffith, either now or later, thee doesn't have to, thee knows. I've thought all along thee was too young."

She shook her head violently. She was not too young. That wasn't it, at all.

"What we want above all, thy Aunt Mary and I, is for thee to be happy. But I can't help unless I know what is wrong. Here, take my handkerchief and dry thy eyes and blow thy nose and look at me, Loveday, and tell me—is there anyone, else?"

Loveday accepted that most reliable of comforts to a woman, a loving man's big, clean, linen handkerchief, and dabbed at her eyes and gulped. Before she could command her voice, Joseph came back into the room with a little package in his hand and laid it on the table before her.

"Mist' Middleton left this," he explained, "after you all went to Alexandria. He expected to see thee, and when thee wasn't here he asked for paper and a pen and he wrote something inside. It altogether slip' my mind to give it to thee last night."

Wondering, Loveday opened the little box and lifted the bit of paper inside. There on a bed of cotton wool she saw a bit of gleaming gold, a pin in the shape of a bow knot. Her heart beating and her hands trembling, she unfolded the paper and read,

"I am sorry to miss thee. This must say farewell for me. We leave for York and Lancaster in a day or two, and Philadelphia after that. C.M. Jr."

She raised a stricken face to her father.

"He's gone!" she cried.

XXXVI

CALEB AND HIS FATHER sat together in Mr. Middleton's bedroom. Through the open window came a warm breeze and sunshine filtered through the new green leaves of the buttonwoods outside.

"This is the only room we have left to sit in," complained Mr. Middleton. "That puppy has absorbed most of the house, like the camel that got into the tent. Thy mother calls him the Camel."

Caleb had been home two days. He was already weary of the subject of the British occupation of Philadelphia. He had seen for himself the devastated outskirts of the city, the fields despoiled of their fences, open to wandering cattle, the charred ruins of houses and barns, the general look of desolation. He had been shocked by the filth in the streets of the city itself and the shabbiness of buildings that had been neat and well-kept, the broken windows mended with paper, scarred doors where a stick or the butt of a gun had been used instead of the knocker, the front-door settles defaced with carved initials, all the evidence of the senseless and idle abuse of property by irresponsible men. He had met the British soldiers everywhere, arrogant and careless, with the "frail women" who used to ply their trade on Water Street at night, walking openly beside them in full daylight.

He had heard over and over about the sins of the Major who was ensconced in his own room, so that he had to share a bed with Edward. Not only had Major Cranborne spread out over most of the house, but he gave dinners almost every night for eight, ten, or twelve officers, or else he was out till all hours, coming in at three or four o'clock, drunk and noisy, waking everybody up.

Caleb felt some amusement over Patty, exiled to Wilmington after she and Caroline Rutter had engaged in an unusual contest for the attention of the Major.

"She always managed to be on the porch or the stairway when be went in or out," complained Patty's father, "and she was bent and determined that he should invite her to a dance at the coffee house!"

Edward had tagged after a band of town-boys who made their headquarters at Morris's brew-house and fought with the British drummer boys, until one of the drummer boys was killed. Edward had come home once with a broken head and another time with a black eye. Tacy fortunately was too young to be much affected by any of it, though she was a great favorite with the Major and his friends and they encouraged her to be forward.

"I got the coach out of the way," said Mr. Middleton with satisfaction, "before any of the red-coated gentry realized I had one. That monster of rapine, Howe, is riding about in Israel Pemberton's coach, and several others have been taken, but mine is well hidden in the Water Street warehouse and the horses are in Wilmington."

At first secretly amused by the change in his father's attitude toward the British on better acquaintance, Caleb rapidly grew weary of the repeated accounts of their depredations.

"They assume such extraordinarily superior airs, Caleb, walking about the streets of Philadelphia—which is after all a metropolis second only to London—scornful and arrogant, forcing respectable citizens off the sidewalks. Their social affairs are all-important; they stuff themselves with food and drink, no matter what prices are or how many go without. And they have a trail of sycophants following after them, obsequious and eager to please—and to make a profit. Anyone who maintains his self-respect they condemn as a rebel. But it's the wanton destruction that is the worst. They burned the house where Colonel Reid lived, they destroyed Thompson's tavern, they went into Colonel Bayard's and cut his books to pieces with their bayonets, emptied the featherbeds, mixed up a mess of paint and linseed oil and dumped the feathers into it!"

Tacy came and climbed onto Caleb's knee and leaned back contentedly against his chest, her thumb in her mouth. He took it out gently, but as soon as he released it she popped it back in again and tipped her head back to smile up at him challengingly.

"I suppose I've said enough about all this," said Mr. Middleton. "Sarah tells me I harp on it too much, that this is war, and what can we expect. It isn't what I intended to talk to thee about."

"Yes, Father?" He put Tacy down, suggesting that perhaps she could find a four-leaf clover for him in the garden. The child trotted out and Caleb turned his full attention to his father.

In spite of all the annoyances and anxieties of the winter, the older Caleb was looking well. The folds of flesh in chin and neck were a little fuller and softer, the pouches under his eyes deeper, his shoulders rounder, the veins in his hands knottier, but he was vigorous as he had not been in the autumn, and his voice was round and full.

"The Phoebe Ann, as I told thee, has been confiscated by the Americans. Thee said it would be, I remember. Thee was right. But they've kept Jacob to run it"

"Jacob! But I thought he was going home to his father's farm!"

"Well, he didn't. I expected him to, but it seems he thought differently. He's lost his wife, by the way. Very sad. They've built an army hospital at Yellow Springs, and Gertrude took milk and eggs and such-like to the patients every week, till she caught a malignant fever and died of it. Perhaps the same kind of fever thee and Edward Penington had. It's a miracle to me that you both escaped."

"Poor Jacob, he must be lost without his Trüdchen. I suppose the oldest girl is able to cook for him and care for the younger children."

"All of the furnaces and forges in the region have been making munitions for Washington's army," Mr. Middleton lowered his voice. "Jacob sent me word through some spy or other coming into the city. A colored man sold us some country eggs and there was a note in one of them. There's a good deal more communication than might be supposed. Jacob's done his best, but he's had trouble keeping colliers and one thing and another, and he hasn't produced nearly as much as they want and expect—an average of only eight or ten tons a week. But it isn't only difficulties with colliers, he's had some failures. Jacob's a good man but his judgment is not all it might be. In spite of thy youth thee had a surer sense of mixing and timing. Now. All that by way of preliminary."

Mr. Middleton pulled himself erect in his chair, rolling a little, stretching the corners of his mouth till the cords stood out in his neck, and leaning forward toward Caleb, went on in a voice so low that it was almost a whisper, "Thou wanted last August to go on with the furnace and make iron for the use of the Americans and I overrode thee. I don't like to eat crow any better than anyone else, but I believe thou was right." He leaned back in his chair, expansively, as one who has made a world-shaking statement and awaits recognition of his courage, candor, and generosity.

Caleb looked down at the palms of his hands as if he expected to read something there. "It's very good of thee to say that. I don't know. One can only do what one thinks best at the time."

"Yes, yes, of course. The point is this. They need more iron than they are getting from Jacob. They are using him to run the furnace but so far as I can tell they haven't sold it or transferred the title to anyone else yet. I believe if thou went to them and offered to increase production, thou could get the furnace back and go on with the work thou wanted to do."

Caleb, in his turn, leaned back in his chair, clasping his hands behind his head and looking out of the window. In all his plans for the future, the conversations which he had imagined with his father, he had not foreseen that they would take this turn. He had his own plans. Why could his father not have asked what they were, instead of laying before him a ready-made outline?

"Well, why don't thou say something? What's the matter?"

"Thee's changed during the winter, Father. So have I."

His father directed at him a long, keen, shrewd look, and then burst out laughing. The sound was shocking in that already tense room and Caleb winced. Mr. Middleton, sober the next instant, spoke with an undertone of bitterness. "I've seen too much of the British and thou's had too much of the Americans. Armies are much the same, no matter which side they are on, and so too, no doubt, are governments. But this is our country, Caleb, the hills and fields and creeks and the iron in the ground. We live here. The English don't."

"It's not that. Thee doesn't understand. I've become more of an

American this winter, not less, in spite of the Congress and Council. I think our army under Washington is different from the British army and certainly different from the Hessians. I think our people are set on freedom as well as independence. But I've become more of a Friend as well. I thought once I could make munitions. I even thought I could fight. But now I cannot."

"I am not suggesting that thou fight. I am offering thee an opportunity to do just what thou proposed last August—to make pig iron and salt pans."

"I should have to make cannon and cannon balls if I undertook to run the furnace now, and I can't see that there is any essential difference between making munitions to kill people and killing them with one's own gun. In fact it's worse because there's no personal risk in it. A soldier may be killed himself, but the munition-maker is safe—and he is making a good profit too."

Seeing his father's troubled and bewildered expression, he tried to explain further. "I used to talk to Isaac Zane, junior, sometimes in Winchester. I'll tell thee all about it sometime." He hurried on, wishing to avoid having to give all the technical details of the Marlboro Ironworks. "He is making cannon. He says he's a Quaker for the times. He's very prosperous, buying books and furniture and building a big house, and his plantation will be a fine one when it is finished." For a moment the memory of the Phoebe Ann swept over Caleb, the big, elegant house, the wide acres of meadow and woodland, the fires against the sky at night, the village where the workmen lived, and the excitement when the ironmaster walked abroad. He felt a pang of homesickness.

"Well? What's the matter with that?"

"I don't want to be a Quaker for the times."

"Caleb, sometimes I think thou opposes me just for the sake of opposing me. I thought that surely in this at least we would be in agreement."

Caleb looked at his exasperated parent with a sinking heart and the familiar feeling which he thought he had conquered or outgrown, the emotional paralysis which so often had made him unable to express his thoughts fully or defend his desires, and he felt the tide of inarticulate resentment slowly rise and with it the undertow of self-contempt and futility.

"No," he said slowly, trying to think how he would put it if John Hunt were there before him instead of his father. "I don't mean to do that. But I have another plan, which I have thought of a great deal, riding from Winchester."

"Well, what is it?"

"Medicine is my real vocation. I have come to realize that more fully than ever. At first I thought I should apply to Dr. Parke to be his apprentice as soon as I should return to Philadelphia, and then enroll for the courses in the Medical College in the fall. I thought I could combine the medical courses with the apprenticeship and then later, when travel becomes possible again, finish with a year or two of study in Edinburgh. But more recently, after being in Lancaster and coming to a clearer understanding of the nature of the struggle for independence, I realized that I could not after all embark on a selfish enterprise of my own, but that I must throw in my lot with my country—"

"Then why not take up my suggestion about the Phoebe Ann for the present, and go to Edinburgh later, if thou still wishes to?"

"I want to save life rather than destroy it. So I have decided," continued Caleb hastily before his father could speak again, "to go to Dr. Hutchinson. He is Israel Pemberton's nephew. He was very helpful to us in September, and since then he has gone into the army as a surgeon—

"I heard all about that. At twenty-two shillings a day."

"He is at Valley Forge now. I have decided to seek him out and offer him my services as an assistant or an apprentice or any way at all that I can be useful. One of our guards in Winchester—a good-hearted young lad from the country—had been in an army hospital and from what he told me I understand that they can use almost any kind of help. I have had a little experience this winter, and I know that I could be useful. I should be doing something that would harmonize with both my inclination and my conscience and yet—" he hesitated, feeling himself flush, "not be too easy."

"I don't like it, Caleb. It seems to me a waste of thy talents and resources. Those army hospitals are full of fevers—look at Jacob's wife, just visiting one. If thou got sick thou'd only be an additional burden instead of a help. It postpones thy establishing thyself in life. And though it seems not to mean anything to thee, it would in all probability result in our losing the Phoebe Ann entirely."

"Yes, it might. I should be sorry for that."

"It doesn't alter thy decision?"

"No"

They looked into each other's eyes. The father's gaze shifted first.

"If that is what thou hast made up thy mind to do, I have nothing more to say. It is thy life and thy decision. I can point out the hazards in the road, but I cannot stop thee from flinging thyself upon them. When dost thou think of going?"

"In a very few days, as soon as I can collect the things I need, talk to some people, and so on. I wanted to see thee and the children first."

"Yes. Umm. Well." His father made a series of noises in his throat indicative of a philosophic acceptance of the inevitable. "Don't hurry away now. Tell me more about thy experiences. I went into Dr. Smith's shop for some elixir one day last winter, and he told me how thou had been his assistant, attending the Hessian prisoners. I told him," he chuckled, "that that might increase the hazards of imprisonment for some of those poor devils. He got quite huffy. He's no sense of humor at all."

"He is at Valley Forge now. I have decided to seek him out."

"Speaking of Smith makes me think of Pike. Has thee heard anything of him?"

"He's gone to England, he and his wife. He came to see us after he got back from Winchester to bring us word about thee. Very obliging of him. Thy letters were coming very irregularly and very few of them. He was quite unabashed about taking French leave the way he did. He was worried about his wife, alone in the city without resources. I had some sympathy with him."

"It was decent of him to visit you. We parted not very amicably."

"Thy mother had had Mrs. Pike make some things for Patty. She's a good little soul, and a very able seamstress, Sarah says. But it seems Pike heard from his father in Bristol and a ship was going, so they packed up and left. Isabella Affleck has had a very hard time. Sarah was able to help her and so did Polly Pleasants as soon as she heard about it. I think of all the cases that was perhaps the most unjust, that and John Hunt—and thee, of course. Well, they all were."

They were still sitting there, exchanging news with a surface interest while each was busy with his own thoughts and a reappraisal of their relationship, when Sarah came bustling into the room.

"There's a colored man downstairs who wants to see you, Caleb," she said. "He says he's come from Winchester with a letter for you, which he must deliver directly into your hands and no other's."

His father chuckled. "A man of affairs!" he said.

Caleb smiled perfunctorily as he rose and left the room. Running down the stairs he tried to think who in Winchester could have anything to write him of so much importance that it required a special messenger. Had anything happened to one of Elizabeth Joliffe's children—or Philip Busch discovered some long-overlooked item for which he could charge him—did Dr. Stephen wish to press his offer of taking Caleb as an apprentice? Could Loveday—but that was impossible.

He did not recognize the man standing in the front hall, silhouetted against the open door, until he turned and spoke. Then Caleb knew him as the Parrys' houseman—wasn't his name Joseph?

"You have a letter for me?"

The man was gray with dust and fatigue. Through the door Caleb could see a horse hitched to the post outside, his head drooping, his flanks lathered.

"You've ridden hard," he observed, while Joseph fumbled in an inner pocket of his coat. "When did you leave the Shenandoah?"

"Las' Friday, Mist' Middleton. I had to go round about a piece, near Wilmington, so's not to meet the militia." He brought out a letter covered with a blue cotton handkerchief. Caleb waited for him to unfold the wrappings, barely able to restrain himself from snatching at it.

When he had it in his hand, breaking the seal with fingers clumsy with eagerness, he thought how strange it was that he had never seen her writing—yet he would have known anywhere that this clear, open, delicate hand was hers.

"Dear Caleb," he read. It was short. It did not cover one side of the sheet. He read it once and scarcely understood its meaning, read it again, and felt happiness and delight pour through him and lift him up on a great surging wave.

He looked up and saw Joseph standing there, tired, patient, but smiling, as if he caught some reflection of joy from Caleb.

"You must rest," said Caleb, "and have something to eat. Amos!" he shouted. And while Amos was coming, Caleb's mind raced among his plans, overturning them and setting them up afresh. He could ride to Wilmington at once and spend the night with the Chases, go as far as he could on the Baltimore Road tomorrow, borrowing a fresh horse at some Friend's farm along the way. He could reach the Shenandoah in four days, or, with luck, a little less.

"Amos, this is Joseph Parry. Take him to the kitchen and see that he gets a good meal. Then make up a bed for him in your room. And take care of his horse. He's tied outside. And Amos—wait a minute—saddle Ladybird."

He unfolded the letter and read it again.

Dear Caleb:

Thank thee very much for the pin, which was waiting for me here when I came home. It is beautiful and I shall wear it always.

I love it especially because it gives me courage to write thee now. Thee said to tell thee if I should change my mind. I am not going to marry Griffith after all.

Thy true friend,
Loveday Parry

He could reach the Shenandoah in four days, and after that, after he had seen Loveday and talked with her father, who must be willing or she could never have sent Joseph with the letter, after that he would go to Valley Forge without returning to Philadelphia. Joseph, apparently reluctant to go off with Amos, was saying something. With difficulty Caleb broke away from his thoughts to listen.

"Miss Loveday, she say for me to come back quick's I can with an answer."

Caleb clapped him on the shoulder. "I'll take the answer myself," he cried exultantly. "I'll be there before you are."